DILIGENCE

The Guild Book Two

Nichole M. Willden

-For Amber-
11/14/18

All these years, I thought I knew about love.
I wrote about it with Diligence, with Confidence, with naivety:
I "loved" certain colors, certain places, certain foods,
certain sentence structures. I "loved" many movies,
many shows, and many, many songs.

And then you loved me.

And I realized I never knew love before at all.
And now that I do, I don't ever want to let it go.
I want to spend my life getting to know it better.

Will you marry me so I can love you forever?

A Note Before Entering The Guild

Diligence, The Guild Book Two by Nichole M. Willden deals with topics that may be triggering to some readers. This book delves into the experiences and psyche of an underage girl trapped in a dangerous secular cult. It attempts to capture an experience of being in the world but separate from it. Additionally, it has content including emotional and physical abuse, bullying, indoctrination, murder, martial arts, mild homophobia, weapons (including handguns), threats, teen identity crisis, adult language, and physical and psychological violence. If any of these topics could be triggering for you, this may not be the best book for you to read at this time.

The author and publisher do not condone violence or abuse to anyone, especially minors.

Chapter One

Emma's head jerked around as a door slammed downstairs in the House. She paused in step on the landing, listening intently. When she heard nothing more, she crept up the hall to Scott's bedroom door. Late afternoon light streamed in through the high windows in the hall, a bright glow that reminded Emma how quickly evening approached. She needed to talk to Scott before dinner. Before Leader came home.

Scott had been allowed to join the varsity football team this year. Emma did not know why. No one in her family was ever allowed to join in sports or extracurriculars. For some reason, Leader had made an exception for Scott this year. It meant that Scott often stayed late at school. Usually, Emma didn't care, but today it was an inconvenience.

She turned the doorknob slowly, glancing again up and down the hall to be sure no one was watching her. She felt the knob catch and looked down at it in shock. Scott had locked his door. She knew it meant he was in the shower but still she was furious. Locking a door in the Guild House was ridiculous. There was no privacy even behind locked doors. Emma wanted to punch Scott for being so modest.

Another sound from downstairs made her stomach plummet. She could not be sure, but she thought she heard the murmur of Leader's voice. She shook Scott's door handle again, livid with him. Anyone who saw Emma waiting outside Scott's door like a lapdog would know something was wrong. She certainly never danced attendance on Scott if she could help it. Despite his position as her direct superior, everyone knew Emma refused to be ruled. In the past two years, her rebellion had gotten her into a lot of trouble with her superiors, including Leader. She dreaded trouble with

Leader and had managed to avoid it for the past few months. The sound of her brusque voice downstairs made her realize how much she feared the end of their stalemate.

A click alerted Emma to Scott's door unlocking. Her breath exploded from her in relief. Tall, broad, and glistening with fresh cleanness, Scott emerged. His dark blonde hair was damp, and his shirt looked skewed, as if he had pulled it on over a chest and shoulders not quite dry enough. When he tried to step out, Emma blocked his way, both hands splayed on his chest.

"I need to talk to you."

He raised a brow at her, almost reproachful. Emma clenched her fists in his shirt, her eyes pleading with him. Scowling, he stepped back to invite her into his room. She scurried in, relieved to be out of the hall where anyone might see her and question her odd behavior. When Scott closed the door, Emma reached past him and locked it. He narrowed his eyes at the tiny defiant gesture. It was defiant, because Emma knew they were not supposed to be locked in a room together, but if Scott could lock himself in for a shower, there was no reason for Emma not to lock it for a private conversation.

Despite his apparent dismay at her frantic appearance, Scott was Emma's best friend in the world. Over the past couple years, she had spent more and more time with him. His desire for peace between them had overcome his original animosity. Meanwhile, her need for a friend made her forgive him for the years of being bullied. Unfortunately, as her confidante, Scott knew her well enough to know that she would never have locked the door unless there was real trouble.

"What's wrong?"

The doubtful tone made Emma pull a face. He read her very well.

Now that Emma knew he had a heart, she could admit to herself that Scott was an attractive young man. His hair was a darker blonde than hers and curled around his ears and at his neck. If Leader allowed him to grow it out a little, like he wanted, it would probably prove to be even curlier. Scott had always been in good shape but due to a rigorous weight training regime, he'd bulked up well. She loved to tease him about his driver's license picture from two years ago, before he started weight training. He took it in good spirits, because she gave him so many more opportunities to tease her in return.

These days, Scott stood nearly a foot taller than her. Last time Scott had been measured, he'd been six foot four, but Emma did not think his growth spurt had ended. She expected him to be six foot six before he was done. Maybe taller. Meanwhile, Emma's growth seemed to have slowed. She hoped to be at least as tall as Leader one day but started to feel it was a childish hope that would not pay out.

Looking up into Scott's stern eyes did not make her feel better about what she had to say. She paced away from him and the doubt on his face. He followed her, a movement that only made her feel like she was being stalked across the room to his desk. She pulled herself up onto it, faced him, and dragged her feet under her to sit cross-legged next to his haphazard pile of textbooks.

"What's wrong, Emma?"

The depth of his tone was another change over the past couple years. His voice had strengthened and deepened as he matured and was now as powerful as any man in the House. Without taking his eyes off her, he pulled his desk chair out, turned it around, and straddled it backward. Emma watched numbly and drew her thumb up to her mouth. She tended to chew on the end of her thumbnail when she was anxious. Scott ran out of patience, his blue eyes losing warmth while she kept him waiting.

"I failed Chemistry." Emma never could beat around the bush. The unfortunate side-effect of that was Scott was never completely prepared for what she said even when he was literally waiting for a confession.

"What?" His shock reverberated off the walls as he jumped to his feet, knocking his chair over. Emma desperately tried to shush him, glancing hurriedly toward the door. The lock was no privacy if Scott's yells brought all their superiors down on their heads. "You're supposed to be the brains around here! How did this happen?"

Emma opened her palms, grasping at the universe for an acceptable answer. There was no way she could come up with a good enough excuse for failing to make top marks in a class. She was too smart not to ace every test, and too well-organized not to stay on top of her homework. Above all, though, Emma was too good a memorizer not to recall the Guild Book edict: *The Juniors have a responsibility to get an education. Their education shall be the first mission in their mind—their primary responsibility.*

As Scott reached toward her, preparing to shake out a confession, Emma snapped, "Mitchell's a clod!"

That was as far as she got before Scott's finger pointed firmly in her face. "Oh no, Emma! Don't you blame the teacher for this. Leader will never let you blame the teacher. What are you going to do?"

Her hands closed in desperate fists on her knees. "I don't know, Scott, that's why I came to *you*." Her heart beat painfully in her chest. Scott had been her only hope. If he had shown some compassion or had some idea of how to present this to Leader, she might not feel hopeless.

The desperation in her tone worked. Scott righted his chair and resituated himself, studying her thoughtfully. She saw his mechanical mind churning. Scott was a problem-solver; he could usually find reasonable solutions. Resting his chin on top of his hands on the chairback, he asked, "What was your final score?"

"Seventy-three."

"That's not a failing grade," he insisted, but his defense was weakened by his involuntary wince.

"Right, Scott! I can see me now," Emma's scoffing voice became sweet and mocking. "'Leader, here is my newest grade report. Aren't you proud? I got a C-minus in Chemistry. But at least it's not an F.'" She pantomimed handing over a report. Then her fake smile dropped away, and she widened her eyes at him. "What am I going to do?"

Scott sat up straight again and drummed his finger on the back of his chair as he considered the problem. "When do grades release? Isn't it next week?"

Emma nodded.

"Well, I think you need to tell Leader before they post," his tone suggested that he was agreeing with her. "Is there possibility of extra credit?"

"No," she said through clenched teeth. "The teacher's a wanker, remember?"

Scott rose slowly and pushed the chair out of his path. He closed the distance between them in two strides. He leaned on the desk until his face was right in front of hers. His eyes held subdued amusement, but his voice was all seriousness.

"*How* exactly did you manage to get such a poor score, Little Em?" He knew she was too smart to have failed on her own merits.

Even though he was uncomfortably close to her face—close enough she could smell the fresh mint of his toothpaste on his breath—she did not back away. She met his eye and gave an innocent shrug. "I didn't understand the concepts?"

It came out more like a question than a statement and Scott shook his head ruefully. They both knew Emma never had problems understanding academic concepts.

She shoved him back, two hands pushing at his shoulders. "All right! Before he passed out our test today, that sorry excuse for a teacher said science was wasted on girls. I called him a misogynistic moron who wouldn't know an amino acid from a bowl of soup."

Scott shook his head, amusement and exhaustion warring for attention. "Emma, you promised this school would be different."

What he meant was: she had promised *she* would be different at this school. It was true. She had made many promises when she enrolled at Sacred Heart. Leader's cold threats had chilled her. *"I will tolerate no further misbehavior from you, Emmalyn Stone. If you get yourself into trouble at this school, I will homeschool you, and damn the expense."* Emma did not know why homeschooling could be more expensive for Leader than a fancy private school education, but she did not want to find out. She knew that the emotional expense of being home all the time with Leader and the Senior Guild was a price Emma was not equipped to pay.

"Help me," Emma demanded, grasping Scott's t-shirt again with desperate fingers.

He swatted down her demand and her hands in one gesture, then pointed toward the door and the idea of Leader. "Not even God could help you now, Emma. What do you want me to do?" His gaze clouded. Amusement leeched away from his tone and his face. "Wait. Did he fail you because of what you said? Because he can't do that."

Emma winced and scooted away from him on the desk until her back contacted the wall behind it. "Not exactly. I was dismissed from class for disrespect, and the dean informed me I forfeited the opportunity to take the final test." When Scott tried to react to that, she interrupted. "It's in the student handbook that if you are not present when the administrator begins the test, you lose the opportunity to take the test."

Scott grasped her shoulders. "I know *that*! I'm not shocked that the dean enforced the school policies. I'm shocked that you brushed past the part where you were *sent to the dean's office*!"

She blinked at him guiltily and muttered, "It was implied."

Scott's hands slipped off her shoulders and he shook his head. "Oh no, it's not. What did he say to you? Was it just a warning?" Scott backed away, raising his hands as if in surrender while his voice dropped to a harsh whisper. "Oh my God, Emma! Leader's going to kill you."

Emma leaned forward and snapped, "Help me!"

Scott scoffed. "With what? You dug yourself a grave and jumped in voluntarily!" He gestured helplessly toward the floor, where Emma could imagine the deep, dark, abysmal grave. "I can't believe you were sent to the dean. And for disrespect? Really?" He rubbed his face with his hands, as if trying to clean himself of the filth of her broken promises. When he came back to her again, his eyes looked worried. "Is this test really so important that not completing it will lower your score to a C-minus?"

Emma tried not to show her guilt on her face, but he caught it.

"What?" he asked darkly. She gave an uncomfortable shrug.

"I had a load of homework that was due today, but I didn't get it in before Mitchell turned into a colossal asshat. When I tried to deliver it later, he said 'You missed the deadline, Miss Cole. That work was due by the end of the period.'" She rolled her eyes on the memory. "It's not like he had started grading already!"

Scott cocked his head to one side and narrowed his eyes. "Yeah, that's rude," he agreed absentmindedly before saying, "Question, though: Why is it you had a 'load' of homework due today? Have you not been turning in your work in a timely fashion?" When she grimaced, he clicked his tongue at her. "That does not sound very Diligent to me."

It wasn't. That was the trouble. Her current Guild responsibility was Diligence. Leader was very strict about homework completion. It was the duty of everyone in the Guild to get a good education. Emma had been schooled in that from her first day in kindergarten. The issue was that her homework was finished, but if Leader knew she had waited to do it until the night before it was due, there would be pain and trouble. Procrastination was the opposite of Diligence.

She climbed off the desk and grabbed Scott's shirt again in pleading hands. "Help me, Scott! What can I do?"

He slashed his hand down to again break her grip on him. "I'm sorry, but you don't have a prayer. Em, the only people who can intercede with the school on your behalf are Leader or Amos. But that means you have to tell them. Today."

Emma retreated from his solution and into her thoughts. She searched for a way out. Earlier in the day when she realized what this would mean for her official grade report, she tried to smooth things over with Mr. Mitchell. She tried to convince him that she deserved to turn in her homework. She reminded him that it was his fault she hadn't been in class. She argued until he threatened her with another trip to the dean. Twice in one day would have led to a suspension. There would have been no way to avoid Leader's wrath then. If only Emma could solve the problem before speaking to Leader then at least she could come forward with a solution. It might not save her from punishment, but it would certainly look Diligent.

"You can't think your way out of this, Emma," Scott toned in that slightly condescending way that reminded her he was her superior.

She glared up at him. "I'm not trying to think my way out of it! I'm hoping for a brilliant idea of how I can present this to Leader as a good thing."

He held up a finger, his blue eyes flashing in warning. "Careful of that tone." Then he smiled. "And good luck. But I officially withdraw my assistance on this one." He backed away from her and moved toward the door. Almost nonchalantly, he looked over his shoulder and added, "I'll tell Leader tomorrow if you don't do it before then." When her expression turned violent, he explained, "My Guild Skill is Confidence, Emma. I won't be implicated in this by failing to have the Confidence required to rat you out." His smile seemed to suggest he reveled in her discomfort.

He didn't really. Emma knew him better than that now. He did not want her to get into trouble, but he took his Guild duties very seriously. Not just the expectations of Obedience, Diligence, and Confidence, but also his responsibility to Emma as his subordinate.

Emma would never make him tattle to Leader about her. She knew there was no way for this to stay hidden. Even if she had decided to try and hide it, everything would come out when the grade report posted. The thought of Leader's eyes seeing a seventy-three percent chilled Emma from head to toe. Again, Emma heard Leader's voice in her mind, hissed threats from the last time she had been suspended for disrespect and misbehavior: *"I hope for your sake you can overcome this bout of teen rebellion, Little Girl. I will not suffer you to fall out of Obedience and Diligence."*

Emma had hoped to have viable excuses and strong solutions when she faced Leader's sternness today.

Chapter Two

A knock on the door got Emma's heart racing again.

"Come in," Scott called. The person tried to comply, but the door was locked. Shooting Emma a glare, he strode across the room and opened it.

Victoria looked in cautiously, saw them both, and said, "Dinner is ready. Amos says come now."

Victoria turned seven a few weeks ago. Most kids her age were full of bouncing curiosity and long-winded stories about all the things in life that they were just discovering. Victoria could not be more different. She was speculative, serious, and deliberate. She used as few words as possible to get her ideas across.

Scott responded sternly. "Go and tell him we're coming."

Victoria nodded once, looking up at him past her thick lashes. Over the past two years since Victoria's arrival, Emma had gone out of her way to make the child feel safe and included. Since Victoria would be her subordinate for life, Emma thought she might as well build a good rapport with her. Scott had not even tried, and now the child was frightened of him.

She was a beautiful little girl and her almond-shaped dark brown eyes had the weight of the whole world in them. Her hair curled exuberantly, defying gravity beyond the butterfly clips that kept it off her tiny face.

"Wait!" Emma ordered and shot a glare at Scott for his brusque handling of the child. She always tried to take an interest in Victoria's life so the child would feel connected to them instead of isolated. Emma's own lonely introduction to the Guild had been something she refused to allow Victoria to experience. "How did you do on your spelling test today?"

The angelic little face pulled into a fierce frown. "Missed one."

"Which word?" Emma led the child out of the room with a guiding hand on her shoulder. They moved together toward the stairs.

"Picture," Victoria answered, but she looked nervously over her shoulder at Scott who followed them like a menacing bodyguard.

"Did you forget the 'c?'" Emma had drilled the spelling words with her last night.

"No. Put an 'h' in."

Emma stroked the child's face once, gently, to take the sting out of her orders, "You'll have to study it well and correctly so you do better when you review."

The child nodded in agreement. "Already wrote it five times."

"That's a good start. What did the teacher say?"

"Smiley face sticker." Victoria's tiny shoulders lifted in a confused shrug. Her teacher was constantly rewarding mediocre work with stickers and encouraging words written on the top of the papers. If she was trying to soften the blow that Victoria had not done as well as she should, she wasted her stickers. Mistakes were not rewarded or softened in the Guild. Victoria had no need to be coddled.

"Did you ask her not to reward your failures?"

Victoria pulled a frightened face and shook her head. Emma wasn't surprised. The child was shy. She probably did not want to make a spectacle of herself at school. Indeed, she shouldn't. Emma's behavior at school set a bad example. She was relieved Victoria did not know anything about it.

"Well, don't get into the habit of being babied," Scott added sharply. Victoria stiffened slightly under Emma's hand. Emma shot Scott a furious glare, but he ignored her. "You need to study harder next week so you don't make stupid mistakes. And tell that teacher to stop giving away her stickers when they're not deserved."

"Yes, sir," Victoria whispered. She was the perfect example of submission and Obedience. She would probably go to her teacher on Monday and repeat Scott's words exactly, despite her shyness. Emma winced to think of how she behaved when she was studying Obedience. She would never have obeyed Scott's orders then. She rarely did now.

Emma shooed Victoria ahead of her down the stairs. Once the curly head was out of sight around the corner, Emma turned a glare on Scott. "Why are you so mean to her?"

He scowled in confusion. "I'm not *mean* to her. I just refuse to baby her the way you do."

"I don't baby her. But she's just a little girl, Scott. You have to be nicer."

He scoffed as his foot hit the bottom step. "Being nice is not helpful. It's a lie you're feeding her that will eventually lead to disappointment and frustration. If you want to help her succeed in the Guild, *nice* is the last thing you should be doing." Then he shot her a malicious grin. "Not being nice worked on you, didn't it?"

Emma scoffed. She had hated Scott passionately all through her elementary and middle-school years. "You're a bastard."

Scott's retort was cut off by a reprimand from the kitchen, "Hey! Watch that language."

Emma came around the corner, waving an apologetic hand toward Amos. The man's scowl of displeasure smoothed away into his customary smile at her obeisance. He nodded toward the stacks of dishes and serving platters arranged on the black and silver marble countertops. Immediately, Emma and Victoria grasped dishes to set the table.

Amos tossed Scott a drying rag and began rinsing previously washed prep dishes and passing them to the young man. The two could have been brothers; they looked so similar. Amos' hair was a little lighter but still blonde. They had a similar strong nose. Their eyes were the same shape, though Amos' were brown, deep, and warm. His build was slightly stockier than Scott's and his smile more affectionate.

Amos's voice was deep as he greeted them with kind interest, "Evening. How was school?"

Emma did not want to talk about school, so she only smiled. Scott answered with some complaints about his football coach. Once they started talking about football, all thoughts of schoolwork and teachers fled from Amos's mind. Emma and Victoria were able to set the table in silence while Scott regaled Amos with elaborate play-by-plays of his football misadventures. Victoria filled glasses with water and set them carefully beside each of the twelve plates Emma placed around the table. The twelve members of the Guild often ate together at the dining table. They were required to eat at least one meal a day with everyone. Two years ago, when Leader had begun the practice, it was annoying but now Emma enjoyed it. She felt a stronger association to these people with whom she was destined to spend her life.

While she was setting the table, others arrived and took their designated seats. The Guild always sat in order down the table, with Leader at the head, odd numbers to the left and even numbers to the right, finishing with number twelve at the foot end. When Emma finished setting the table, she sat in her chair at the end of the left side. Since Victoria's arrival, Emma had moved up from the end and across from Scott. He always sat at the perfect kicking distance and utilized this commodity any time she spoke without thinking.

Adam slunk in, banging against Emma's chair unnecessarily as he shoved past her to sit in the Number Nine spot to her left. *Too beautiful for his own good*, Emma thought resentfully as he shot her a malicious smile that showed rows of perfect, white teeth. He had dark hair and eyes. If he was less sarcastic or taunting, she might have dealt with his beauty better. As it was, she always felt his personal attractiveness was a mask covering up his inner demon.

The others trickled in as the long hand on the dining room clock climbed steadily toward the top of the hour. Scott helped Amos put the last serving dishes on the table then took his place across from Emma.

Leader stepped into the room right as the clock chimed on the hour. The woman entered with a stately, dangerous grace earned from hours of daily martial arts training. She was fit, muscular, and slim. Her jet-black hair fell midway down her back. She had large, slanted dark eyes that seemed to see everything. Emma's gaze drew to her immediately, hungry for the sight of her, desperate for her approval.

As Leader approached the table, silence fell in the room. Her long fingers folded themselves over the back of her chair, red painted fingernails glinting in the light of the dining room chandelier. There was grace even in her slightest movement. Grace was the best word for her overall. Her every move looked like a step in a deadly dance.

"Good evening," she greeted the room. Her eyes swept down the length of the table and back up the other side. Though she made eye contact with Emma only briefly, it was electric: measuring, considering, approving. Emma felt intense relief at the approval, and a knot of fear in her belly when she remembered she did not deserve it.

Leader pulled out her chair and sat. She crossed her legs and leaned forward to take hold of the cracker sitting alone on her plate. She paused with the cracker an inch above the plate, then lowered it back down to rest in the center. The energy in the room tightened. Delay in breaking bread meant she had something to say to the entire Guild.

"We're moving," she announced without preamble, her voice a crack of lightning.

The Guild reacted quietly with stunned expressions and exhalations. Amos' slight recoil shocked Emma more than the news. Amos was Leader's right hand. He usually knew about everything that happened and was often part of the decision-making process. Moving was a big decision to have come to without Amos' input. While his emotions quickly vanished behind a mask of indifference, Emma could have sworn this news had caught him by surprise.

Across from him, Julianne did not try to hide her relief. Since they had moved to Virginia in the summer, Julianne had been working as a surgeon at the Reston Hospital Center. Julianne served the Guild well in her capacity as a doctor, but she did not like to work as a professional. The stress and long hours of any medical job wearied her. Moving away meant starting over somewhere new, with a new identity for each of them. Chances were good that Julianne's new identity would not include a medical degree.

Mostly, though, the news was not earth-shattering for the Guild. This would be their third move in two years and did not signify any major life changes. For them, their real life was in the Guild itself, not in the house or town where they lived. They would be given a new name, a new school, a new story to tell, but otherwise life would continue much the same.

"When?" Amos asked. Emma could see his mind working behind his blue eyes, probably figuring out how to securely remove surveillance from their schools and offices. Amos' primary responsibility as an engineer was to oversee the tech that went into Guild operations. He was really good at it, as Emma knew all too well. His surveillance had caught her in several compromising situations a couple years ago.

"Next week," Leader answered with her same sharp brusqueness. "I hate to move the children midyear again, but I can't wait until June. I will, however, wait until I receive a grade report. These schools are supposed to be top-notch."

"So, next Friday?" Amos asked, his tone betraying disapproval.

"We'll talk about it later." What she meant was the Senior Guild—the top six members of their little family—would discuss it in Summit: their covert morning meetings to which the Junior Guild was not invited.

Emma tried to hide her apprehension at the mention of the term end. Grade cut-off was today but the term did not officially end until next Friday when grades were released. Scott's expression communicated compassion but also insistence. He nudged her shin under the table. Emma drew a long breath while looking desperately into his eyes. He was the only one who could sympathize with her discomfort.

Leader broke the cracker in two, finally allowing the Guild to serve the food. Emma was glad to have an excuse to shift her gaze away from Scott's concerned, insistent eyes. She dished the food to herself and Victoria as it was passed around the table. She hoped the discussion would change to a new topic, but it didn't.

"So, does this mean I have to drop out in the middle of the semester?" Adam grumbled. "I doubt the University will approve a transfer for no good reason."

"I'll take care of it," Ilene promised. She was Number Five and dealt with public relations more than anything else. Despite her taciturnity with her Guild-fellows, she was excellent with the public. Her beauty—as icy as her attitude—had an astonishing effect on outsiders.

"Two weeks doesn't seem like enough time to get everything organized," Julianne added in her thoughtful way.

"It's only a week, actually," added Thomas, the punctilious businessman.

"Next Saturday," Leader agreed before placing a forkful of pasta into her mouth. Amos had outdone himself tonight; the food was delicious. Emma wished she could have enjoyed it more, but her fear had overcome her tastebuds. Everything tasted like ash with her grade report looming. How could she fix her grade if she only had one week to negotiate with Mitchell?

Scott tried to catch her eye again, but she ignored him until he kicked her under the table. "What are you going to do, Em?" he whispered across to her. "You don't have a lot of time."

"I have no time," she hissed back. She was only glad Adam was preoccupied in the discussion at the far end of the table. Victoria's eyes skipped back and forth between Scott and Emma. She might not have heard their whispers, but Emma couldn't be certain. The child missed little.

"If Leader talks to the dean tomorrow, they may make an exception," Scott went on. "God knows they should with all the money she dumps into the place."

Lara's gaze flashed their way now, too, and narrowed. She didn't pry because it wasn't her nature, but she did raise an eyebrow at the pair of them.

Scott smirked at Emma's glare. "You might not even have to say anything, really. You can let the report card speak for itself. Hand it to her and let it do the talking."

"Shut up," Emma ordered, kicking Scott in return to get him to realize they were drawing attention to themselves. The action backfired because Scott started at the pain and knocked over his water glass.

"What is going on down there?" Leader asked sternly, silencing all other conversations. Scott used his napkin to clean up the spill. Lara handed hers over when one napkin appeared to be insufficient. Scott's preoccupation left the explanation to Emma.

"Nothing, Leader," she said in her most convincing tone.

Leader put her fork down. That was not a good sign.

"Are you really going to sit there looking me in the eye and lie to my face?" she asked coolly. Scott ducked his head and filled his mouth full of pasta to avoid having to come to Emma's aid. Emma glared at him for the evasion then lifted her face to meet Leader's stern, demanding gaze.

"No, of course not, Leader. Can I talk to you about this later?"

Leader lifted a brow.

"Privately?" Emma clasped the edges of her chair, desperately hopeful.

Leader shifted in her chair and somehow seemed even more menacing than before. "Talk about what?"

Emma cringed. Privacy had been denied. Though the idea of saying anything in front of the entire Guild was horrifying, she could not disobey Leader's indirect command to disclose. Following the woman's example, she put her fork down and attempted to ignore the furtive glances of the other Guild members. "I am getting a C in Chemistry."

Scott winced. This was the worst possible scenario either of them could have imagined for telling Leader. The effect was exactly what they could have expected in this scenario. Amos's head dropped into one hand, which he used to pinch the bridge of his nose. Julianne shook her head and continued eating. Ilene's icy indifference, Thomas' scoff of disdain, even Piper's silent smirk were to be expected. Adam gave a snort that suggested he reveled in her pain. Lara's eyes took on a haunted look of concern; Victoria studied Emma with wide eyes; and Scott stuffed in another mouthful of pasta.

"What?!" was Leader's ferocious exclamation, followed quickly by Amos' exhausted, "How?"

Emma spread her hands, trying to find the best words to explain. "I wasn't altogether diligent . . ." She winced when she said it, already wishing she had selected another word. ". . . with regards to my homework."

Leader's intense stare had a dangerous flavor of contempt. "You haven't completed your homework?" Her fierce glare shot to Ilene, who was responsible for checking homework daily.

Emma's hands bounced up to ward off the accusation and bring it back on herself. Ilene could become vicious if blamed for the failings of her subordinates. "No, Leader! I have *done* my homework!" Then, when she realized what she was about to say was just as bad, she slipped back into hesitance. "It's just that it's . . . still in my backpack."

Leader only blinked. Probably because it made no sense to complete work and not turn it in. She got over her perplexity quickly and her tone became grim. "We need to talk about this privately."

Emma growled an exasperated expletive too quietly to be heard. She had wanted to talk privately and had even *asked* for privacy! "Yes, Leader."

She retrieved her fork with a tiny exhale of relief and loaded it with pasta.

"Right now," Leader ordered sharply, startling Emma into looking up again into her grim, angry eyes.

"Oh."

Leader backed away from the table and climbed swiftly her feet.

"Yes, ma'am," Emma answered and dropped her fork on her plate at once. She placed her napkin in her chair and hurried after Leader's retreating back. The woman's graceful stride seemed determined. Emma's heart sank. She had at least wanted to have a last meal.

Chapter Three

Leader's office was an extremely modern black and white, with occasional red accents. She had a white sofa with black cushions in one area of the room. It might as well not have been there since Emma was convinced no one ever sat on it. Her desk, the prominent feature in the center of the room, was made of glass. Leader walked to the black leather desk chair and sat, leaving Emma to stand opposite her. Emma remembered her days as Number Twelve, when she had always been invited to sit as soon as she entered Leader's office. But their Leader had been a different person then, a dark and cruel man who showed his dominance in towering over victims trembling in chairs below him. The current Leader did not need such devices. She had chairs, of course, but they were pushed an uncomfortable distance away. They were never offered to the Junior Guild.

Leader's hands folded on top of her desk and she examined Emma with dark, unreadable eyes. She was just as terrifying as Emma's previous Leader, with her ferocious affection and exacting expectations. Her presence was overpowering. People in the streets sometimes gazed at her as if she was a passing celebrity, and not just because of her unparalleled beauty. Emma thought it was mostly due to the authority in her posture, the grace in her movements. Or perhaps it was the threat in her eyes. She handled Leadership as if she had never been anything but Leader.

"Tell me in which ways you failed to be Diligent," Leader commanded in her normal brusque tone. Emma's courage shriveled up, and she found she could not meet Leader's eye. She folded her hands in front of her and dropped her gaze to the glass-top desk.

The truth taunted her from its hiding place, chattering like monkeys in a cage while she tried to find a way to explain the situation that did not end up with her on the wrong side of the woman's wrath. Leader's approval was intoxicating. Emma sought it like a drug.

"Mr. Mitchell, my chemistry teacher, assigns homework each period but his due date is always test day. Of course, he accepts the completed work at any time, and for the first month or so I was meticulous about daily completion of the homework. I turned it in on time each day."

Emma paused to take a breath and to figure out the safest route to proceed with what was an incriminating series of events. Leader waited, watching her with unrelenting expectation.

Emma plunged on. "Our new unit began three weeks ago and instead of completing my homework daily, as I ought to have done, I put it off. I completed most of it over the last two nights in preparation for being turned in today."

Emma winced when Leader lifted a single finger, even though the gesture was not violent. She stopped speaking at once. "You did all of your homework from three weeks' worth of lessons in just two evenings?"

Emma cringed. Her throat felt parched when she answered, "Yes, Leader."

Leader raised a single brow, but her eyes still betrayed nothing of her thoughts. She prompted quietly, "Go on. You completed your assignments and then . . . ?"

A wave of confusion doused Emma. How did Leader not already know about this? Emma knew the Guild surveillance recorded her school days. Surely the entire episode between Emma and Mitchell had been flagged as priority and forwarded immediately. Nothing in Leader's expression suggested ignorance, but Emma had the feeling the woman was hearing about this for the first time. It made her choose her words carefully.

"Shortly after I arrived in class, Mr. Mitchell made a few derogatory comments. When he specifically said something about girls in science, he looked directly into my eyes for a reaction." Emma was pleased with her explanation. It was clear, utterly truthful, and placed the blame on the inept teacher—where it belonged.

The fingers of Leader's right hand drummed with rhythmic clicking on the glass. It was a soft sound, but Emma felt a wave of panic as if an alarm sounded in the room.

"And you gave him the reaction he was looking for." This was not a question. Emma heard it in the tone: it was an accusation. She shifted uncomfortably.

"What was the reaction you gave him, Number Eleven?" Leader's crisp voice could have sent ice crystals skittering across the glass beneath her clicking fingernails.

Emma looked up into Leader's steady brown gaze and answered truthfully, "I insulted his intelligence."

When Leader's only reaction to that was a judgmental sound in her throat, Emma clenched her fists. "It's not like it's that hard to do, Leader. Mitchell is completely inept. Did you know he only has a *basic* teaching degree? He never even went out for his Masters. And now he thinks he gets to have an opinion about me becoming a scientist? No. No way! Don't sit there looking at me like I did not do what needed to be done! Mitchell needed to be put in his place and—" Leader's fingers stopped tapping. It was the only warning Emma needed. She bit back the rest of her angry words and dropped her eyes.

"And he sent you to the dean," Leader supplied in a knowing voice.

"Yes," Emma muttered down at her feet. It seemed Leader had received the surveillance footage after all.

"What did the dean say about your wildly disrespectful behavior?"

Emma cleared her throat to bury her arguments about Leader's choice of phrasing. *Wildly disrespectful* seemed to imply that she alone was at fault when Mitchell's disrespect had started the whole thing.

"It was proverbial slap on the wrist. I received a mild rebuke and an exhortation that my conflicts with my teachers should be handled in respectful, preplanned meetings away from the classroom atmosphere and audience. A lot of rhetorical questions followed. Then he informed me that I could see myself to Skills since I had missed the beginning of the term test and had forfeited the right to take it."

"Skills?"

"Skill-building. It's similar to detention, I guess, but it's in a computer lab where we work on various skills, or we can opt to complete our homework."

"And this is your first visit to Skills?"

Emma cringed. "No, ma'am, I went several weeks ago after I made a chemical concoction that caused a fire in the lab. Mr. Mitchell was bubbling mad when his lab coat caught fire and he had to be extinguished. I slipped out to Skills when the lab tech ordered it. By the next day, Mitchell and I silently agreed never to speak of it again."

Emma's stomach plummeted at Leader's words, "Do you think that gets you off the hook for keeping it from me?" They seemed to have dark consequences attached.

"I guess not," she muttered. Then she took a step closer to the desk, lifting a beseeching hand. "I'm not a menace, Leader. I swear I'm not! Mitchell just . . . I hate him! He's in a constant state of superiority with no justified reason to be so. He loves to belittle the students who have a hard time understanding the concepts he teaches. And, as a bonus, every time I ask him a question, he rolls his eyes like what I said was idiocy when what he really means is he doesn't have an answer."

Leader looked up at her with pursed lips and for a moment Emma thought she might emerge from this unscathed.

"Since when did you become a student who asks questions in class?"

Emma squirmed and backed away from the desk. Leader knew her too well. This woman had raised Emma. She had been her legal guardian since she was four years old. She knew Emma did not ask questions in class. Emma was the type of student who read the chapters ahead of time and only half-listened to the class discussion, and still aced the class. She did not participate. She did not ask questions when she could get answers easier and faster online.

"So, you ask questions deliberately to trip up this teacher," Leader went on before Emma could manage to collect another argument. "And you have the nerve to say he rolls his eyes instead of answering. Why are you determined to undermine this teacher in front of his students?"

Emma's first response would have included profanity, but she did not need to provoke Leader unnecessarily. She answered slowly.

"He is an insufferable narcissist, unqualified for his job, and out to shame me at any opportunity because he can see that—even if I had brain trauma—I could teach his class better than he does."

Leader's expression never changed, but she murmured, "Hm." After a couple quiet moments in which Emma squirmed under Leader's gaze, she followed up with, "What else have you done to upset this man?"

She could not stop the exasperated sound from escaping. Leader was determined to turn this all around on her as if she was determined to ignore the teacher's ineptness entirely.

"Besides asking basic questions he should be able to answer but can't?"

"And lighting his lab coat on fire and challenging his authority in front of his own class," Leader added. Emma winced. She enunciated her next question, probably annoyed at having to repeat herself: "*What else*?"

"I sometimes speak in French because he is supposedly fluent but isn't," Emma admitted on a sigh. There was no reason to keep any of it from Leader. The woman would only search through the surveillance, if she did not already know it all. This could simply be a test of Obedience, to see if Emma would tell her everything when she already knew the mischief she had made. "Another time, I got the entire class to agree to answer a multiple choice quiz in a pattern as a protest against pop quizzes." Emma was careful not to smile because she knew Leader would not be amused by her success. But, really, Emma had been amazed! Every single student in every Chemistry class of the day—even the brainy ones who were trying to get into Ivy League schools—had answered in the pattern she had dictated. It was a rare feat to get that many kids to join a silent protest, and Emma was delighted with her success.

"Another time, I organized a stand-in where we removed all the chairs from the classroom, including his desk chair, and hid them. Every period of the day, his students had to stand, although he did allow us to sit on top of our desks." That had been another wildly successful plan.

"What were you protesting that time?"

She gave a slight shrug, wishing she had a better answer. "Nothing. It was funny to see him racing around between classes searching for chairs. For some reason, the door to the storage room with the extra chairs had been fused shut by a chemical reaction he ought to have known how to counteract, being a chemist and all. And if that failed, he was given a note at lunch that gave clear instructions that the chairs were in the ladies' room under construction on the third floor." When Leader arched a questioning brow, Emma admitted, "Of course, the note was in French."

Emma thought she saw a glimmer of amusement in Leader's eyes, but her voice was as hard as ever. "Anything else?"

Emma could not keep from smiling this time as she said, "The shop kids disassembled his car and reassembled it in an unused classroom. That was really gold-star-worthy execution, but I can't take the credit since I didn't even lift a power tool."

"What *did* you do?" Leader knew her too well. Emma swallowed her amusement.

"I paid them. One morning, Amos accidentally gave me a couple hundreds when he meant to give me tens for book fees. Four guys divided the money equally; they thought it was worth it."

Leader's head shook ever so slightly. "I hope you at least used your wiles to seal the deal." It was impossible to tell by her tone if she was being sarcastic, so Emma chose not to answer. "How is that you have not spent half the year in the dean's office?"

Emma slipped her hands behind her back and clasped them to keep herself calm and controlled.

"I have creative methods of keeping myself undetectable. Like the time I switched out all the water samples the class had collected with urine and destroyed his lesson on the differences between water samples from various sources. He tested the urine to see whose it was, in the hope he could capture the culprit, but when it turned out to be his own, he had no recourse. He *knew* I was the only person who could have achieved such a spectacularly invasive switch, but he had no concept of how I could have done it. Going to the dean would have been absurd."

"I'm not even going to ask you how you managed to get vials of his urine, Emma," Leader said. Disapproval finally tinged her tone. "But it seems to me that not getting your homework turned in on time was just the cherry on top of the well-iced cake of your idleness."

Emma opened her mouth to argue but thought better of it.

"What?" Leader snapped. "What can you possibly have to say?"

Emma's brows pulled together, and she frowned. "Just that, technically, I haven't spent even a single idle moment in regards to his class. And Mitchell refused to accept my homework after Skills only because he claimed it had been due during the period and I hadn't gotten it in."

"*Mr.* Mitchell is well within his rights to refuse to allow you to turn in the work after he had justifiably sent you to the dean," Leader answered, and now she was on her feet. "And furthermore, don't you stand there and pretend that everything you did this term constitutes Diligence simply because you were busy. Diligence is the opposite of frivolous activity, and you spent your term completely engaged in frivolity. If all you had done was insult this man today, he might have relented. But he *knew* you were the ringleader of the coup against him all term, so he was sure to take this opportunity to set you in your place. I wholeheartedly support his decision."

Emma argued. It was never a good idea and today was no exception, but what choice did she have? "Leader, the work is *done*. He kicked me out of the test and then refused to accept my work based on a grudge. Not even the dean would allow that. How can you possibly support it? I'll get a C-minus!"

"A C-minus you deserve," Leader replied, and now she sounded angry. "You deserve a C simply on the merits of your complete lack of Diligence all term. As if it wasn't enough that you used your intellect to annihilate your teacher's reputation and authority, you idly squandered your learning opportunities. If you don't understand the difference between being busy and being Diligent, I will be happy to teach you." When Emma opened her mouth to argue, Leader sentenced her, "*Busy* is how you'll spend your weekend weeding the back five."

Emma's eyes slid shut at the pronouncement and she stifled a groan. The back five acres of the Guild property was away from any roads, completely overgrown, and not used for anything. Leader could not have selected a more mundane, pointless, waste-of-time chore. It was doubly insulting because she was supposed to practice for her driving test this weekend.

"Thomas is supposed to teach me to drive this weekend," she muttered, hoping Leader had forgotten and would now reconsider the punishment. But Leader never forgot anything.

Leader's smile, like her tone, was polite and acidic. "Even the Department of Motor Vehicles claims driving is only a privilege." She walked around the desk and toward the door, preparing to exit and close discussions. Emma remained where she was, searching for a way to rework this conversation so she came out a victor. "I allow only the *Diligent* members of my Guild the privilege of obtaining a driving license." Leader stopped at the door and turned back, brows raised. Emma had not followed her toward the exit.

"If I get a C, it will irreparably damage my GPA. I'll have to go to a state college, like Adam and Lara."

Leader made a facial shrug in response to Emma's whispered fears. "Hindsight."

Emma reached out a beseeching hand. "Please, Leader, don't let him give me a C simply to teach me a lesson. Just tell me what I need to do to get you to pounce on the school with claws unsheathed." The notion that she was some kind of dangerous feline appeared to amuse Leader, but she shook her head.

"Let's just see what you can do, Emma, when you know your harmonious home-life is on the line." The idea that her current existence constituted harmony made Emma wince at what Leader might have planned when her grade card arrived.

"C *is* a passing grade," Emma said, but more to console herself than to convince her superior. She tried to imagine how she could apply to an Ivy League school with a less than perfect GPA.

Leader snapped her fingers. It was a sound no one in the Guild could have ignored, as it reverberated somehow down into the ear canal. It did what it was intended to do, pulling Emma's gaze up.

"What constitutes a *passing* grade in my Guild?" she asked in the dangerous tone Emma secretly called *Leader Condescension*.

"A ninety-six."

When Leader continued to stare expectantly, Emma went on, quoting Leader's own words. "But even a ninety-six is not acceptable from me, as my intelligence suggests I would only receive a ninety-six out of a lack of Diligence. For this reason, anything below one hundred percent is unacceptable and will not be tolerated." Emma drew a long breath. She never really had to work to receive one hundred percent. It was true that everything came easily to her. If Leader would have let her take the classes, Emma could have graduated this year. As it was, she might have been able to complete her generals before she ever started college. That had been her plan all along. This C was an unexpected hiccup in her plans. Despite her aptitudes, she hated studying science in any form. This C came not from a lack of Diligence as much as from a lack of interest. She could have passed Mitchell's class in the first week of school and never gotten wrapped up in the mischief that now deprived her the right to drive.

Leader nodded. "It seems you are well-versed in my expectations."

Instead of walking out, Leader turned and leaned back against the door. "I have another question."

Emma barely contained her frustration at being further detained. With anger pushing against her heart, all Emma wanted to do was escape and go upstairs to vent her frustrations.

"When were you planning to disclose this information? When were you planning to tell me about your constant pranks on your Chemistry professor?"

Emma unthinkingly snapped, "He's not a professor. He's barely a teacher!" Leader's only response was to shift her feet and pull away from the door, but Emma recognized it as a coiled stance. Leader often used it when she was about to physically discipline someone. Emma immediately backed away from tones and words that could trigger Leader to uncoil.

"I wasn't going to tell you if I could avoid it." The mischief Emma had made at her last school, or rather Leader's punishment for it, had made Emma more secretive this time around.

Leader nodded, and Emma saw the stance relax somewhat. "That's what I thought. You forgot who you are. You forgot your purpose and your obligations. Allow me to correct you." She opened a palm toward Emma. "You are here in my hand, and you belong to me. Everything you do reflects on me and my Guild. When you do as I ask or as I instruct, you live here." She tapped a finger into the palm of her open hand. "When you do not live up to your potential, you live here." She closed her fingers in a crushing grip. "But you are always here in my hand, Emma." Her hands fell only far enough to be folded under her chest. "When I say to you, 'How was school?' and you refuse to tell me that you stole my money and used it to pay shop boys to assemble your teacher's car inside a small classroom, you lied to me. How do I respond to liars?"

"Exactingly," Emma said through gritted teeth. Her anger was building under Leader's insistence of condescending tones. Nothing bothered her more than someone talking down to her.

"I require full disclosure."

Emma drew a long, furious breath. "Then you should know that before school today I concocted a brilliantly strong adhesive in the lab and glued the contents of Mitchell's entire desk to the ceiling. And that *that* was his justification for hinting I should never be a scientist; girls don't have the discipline. Apparently, our femininity, including menstruation, renders us unable to control our impulses. He said that we never could expect to make any true contributions to science because everything we do is based on an underlying penis-envy we cannot control. And then he finished that speech with a 'There, there! Women have a very noble place in the world of childbearing and housekeeping.' And 'What would the world be like if no one went to school to be a flight attendant?'" She spread her arms wide. "Full disclosure!"

Emma did not need to examine Leader's stance to know she was seething. "And then you said . . . ?"

"A lot of things I shouldn't have," Emma snapped back, her fury making her truthful in a way nothing else could. "Not the least of which was the use of the F-word, which was the only ammunition he had for sending me to the dean. But my parting shot was that I used my phone to send an order to the printer beside his desk. It printed an application to a flight attendant training school and when he figured out what it was, I told him to use the essay section to write explicitly about his latest menstruation."

Leader's eyes snapped shut as she gave a single involuntary chuckle. "Emma," she breathed out, trying to stay mad. "You should have demonstrated some self-control."

Emma scoffed back. "Why? He did not deserve it!"

Leader's eyes opened, and she studied Emma narrowly. "You write me a good, strong, convincing essay about everything you ought to have learned in Chemistry this term and I will *consider* going to your dean on Monday to dispute unfair treatment."

Emma's anger deflated. "Thank you," she sighed, and she was really grateful. Then, feeling bold, she asked, "Can I still learn to drive?"

Leader seemed almost surprised by her boldness. "Drive? You won't have the time this weekend, Little Girl. You'll be *busy* weeding the back five."

Emma felt a wave of defeat roll over her. She slipped down on her knees onto the black and white floral rug on the office floor. Leader watched her with an amused expression and said dryly, "Dramatic."

Chapter Four

Leader walked out the office door, leaving it ajar. Emma collapsed on her back on the rug with a sigh, really living up to Leader's comment. She knew she was being dramatic, but she felt justified. This had started out as a bad day and had only gotten worse. And now the weekend she had been looking forward to with so much hope would be ruined with a pointless task.

Leader popped her head back through the open doorway, cocked a brow at Emma's sprawled position, and said, "Incidentally, what have you been doing during your allotted homework time each day?"

Emma shot up to a sitting position, her expression pained. She had not even thought about this, but of course Leader had. The Guild schedules were a big deal to her. No one was permitted to tamper with them. Emma swallowed and pulled her gaze inward. She felt Leader's intense gaze, but she needed to collect herself. When she felt sufficiently ready to accept any penalty for her forthcoming explanation, she looked up.

"I was writing."

There was no way to actually startle Leader—the woman was ready for anything. But Emma's words came close. Leader leaned back against the doorframe, studying Emma as if she had never seen her before.

"Writing?" Leader's tone did not betray any surprise, but Emma thought it was a little more intense than normal.

"Yes, Leader. Not for any assignments or anything like that. Just . . . creating original work. I used my homework time because it was the only scheduled time I had during the day where I was by myself."

Leader nodded. "Because your privileges have been consistently revoked for disrespect to your superiors, Em." When Emma tried to argue that Ilene hated her and took every opportunity to make her life miserable, Leader cut her off with another question, "What do you write?"

Emma looked away again, afraid to share the only part of herself that was completely her own. She knew she could not refuse to answer, though. Obedience had been her ten-year study in the Guild. The last thing she wanted was for Leader to give her a refresher course. Hesitantly, she met Leader's studying gaze.

"Poetry."

Leader's tone was devoid of emotion when she repeated, "Poetry," as if she had never heard the word before. "Where is this poetry you've been writing?"

Emma had a flash of reservation. Why did Leader want to know where she kept her poetry? If she found out, would she confiscate the work in the name of Guild priorities? Would she burn it? Emma did not think she could handle watching her heartfelt words disappear into ashes.

"Emma," Leader repeated, voice crackling with impatience for having to repeat herself. "Where is it?"

"I have a notebook," she explained hesitantly. "I bought it at school at a book fair a few months ago. Before that, I had been writing mostly in the margins of my notepaper . . ." She glanced at Leader's hand on the door, at her long legs against the doorframe. ". . . and in my daily diary."

That startling tidbit made Leader's grip on the door tighten, whitening her knuckles. "Your diary? You have written something other than daily experiences in your diary? I have been extremely clear about how I expect your diary to be completed. It's not a journal for wandering thoughts and emotional expression. It is for the factual daily goings-on in your life, with a brief personal interpretation of how you were affected."

Emma nodded. "I know," she explained hurriedly. "But the words just flow from me, Leader. As I would type my dailies, the words would just come, and I would write them. I knew you would never approve of that use of my diary, and the words kept coming, so I spent part of my emergency cash on a notebook. And when I filled it up, I purchased a second."

Leader's lips pressed into a line and for a moment they were locked in a silent gaze until Emma's discomfort made her shift her shoulders and look away.

"Go and get them," Leader ordered. "These secret notebooks; go get them and bring them to me."

Emma pushed herself up and jumped to her feet. "Yes, Leader." She had no other choice; she could not possibly disobey her. Additionally, Emma felt a spark of hope and excitement that someone else would read her work. From necessity, she had kept her work to herself. But the idea that Leader would see her work, would read it, would possibly understand the anger and anguish she had been experiencing the past few years . . . it filled Emma with hope.

Leader opened the door just enough for Emma to squeeze past her. She did not dare look up, but she felt her gaze. Leader swatted her—not gently—on the backside to hurry her along. Emma jogged to the back stairs. She avoided the front stairs because she would have had to pass through the dining room and the judgmental eyes of her superiors. She heard Amos and Scott arguing and she certainly did not want to walk into more contention, especially since she was relatively certain her name was being batted around between them.

The notebooks were in the backpack beside the desk in her room. She extricated them with some effort, shoving aside textbooks and school notebooks. She had been careful to get ones that looked like her regular notebooks. She had avoided the beautiful covers and book-bindings that made her sigh. Function was what mattered when hiding her writing. However, Emma never mistook them for her school notebooks, with their pristine covers and perfectly organized notes. Her love for these two writing notebooks was in their tattered covers and crinkled pages. Her heart had been poured into these. She smoothed the cover of one with a gentle hand before hurrying out of her room.

She made it back down the stairs in time to hear Amos commanding silence at the dining table with a crack of his hand on the wooden surface. The sound caused Emma chills; ferocity was not in Amos' nature.

Leader stood where she had waited against the doorframe to her office. Emma offered the books to her, but Leader refused. She instead nodded toward the desk and Emma had to squeeze past her again. She placed the notebooks reverently in the center of Leader's desk, taking a moment to straighten them. Leaving them behind was almost physically painful. Would she ever get them back? Would the words be lost forever? Words that had saved her sanity and brought her rage under control?

When Emma turned to leave, she found Leader standing directly behind her. Giving an involuntary gasp, she tried to step back, but was trapped against Leader's desk.

"Why do you imagine you have to hide from me?" Leader said in a voice soft enough it could have been called a whisper if the words were not so hard. There was nowhere to get away. Emma was forced to stare deeply into the condemning dark eyes. A chill ran down her spine, spreading goosebumps up her arms. She felt real worry for the first time since this conversation began.

"I'm not trying to hide." She was trying to survive.

"Your secretive manner would suggest otherwise," Leader argued in a wintry voice. She lifted an admonitory finger. "If you came to me about your troubles with Mr. Mitchell instead of starting a campaign of mischief against him, I might have been able to help you. Did you think of that?" Emma did not have a chance to consider the question before Leader pointed her stern finger at the notebooks. "If you needed time to work on something heartfelt and deeply personal, you could have come to me and asked. Do you think risking my wrath is better than asking my permission?"

Emma had not considered Leader's wrath when she wrote the words that bubbled up inside her. Perhaps because the poetry was not about her. Or perhaps because she had always been tough with Emma, even before she had become Leader. She had always been exacting. She had always known Emma better than their previous Leader, and Emma had known her, too. Emma assumed she would not anger as quickly or as deeply as the previous Leader—the one who had been responsible for teaching Emma to be Obedient. Yet, it was the dark-eyed woman standing in front of her who had made the lessons in Obedience effective. It had been her cool condemnation two years ago that had proved Emma could never escape Leader's wrath. Emma could see the scene with perfect clarity, despite two years attempting to dispel it from her memory. In Emma's ears, she could still hear the sound of screaming, of two gunshots going off almost simultaneously. Try as she might, the image of a man dead on the paved street would not leave her mind. He died saving her life after she had disobeyed him. Emma was the reason he never rose from the street that day. Leader had solidified the brutality of that lesson by labeling the event "The price of disobedience." The price of Emma's disobedience had been a profound and heartbreaking loss. Her notebooks were full of the losses of that day.

"I would not wish to excite your wrath, Leader," Emma whispered, breaking from the woman's gaze. It was a true enough statement. None of the country's laws against brutality, cruelty, abuse, and neglect could save her from Leader's wrath. Those laws had been created to protect citizens, and Emma's first allegiance was to the Guild.

"It will be interesting to see if you do," Leader murmured, and as if that was not enough of a threat, she added, "Pawn on e4." Chills crawled up Emma's spine. The chess reference was a cry to arms. It was an acknowledgement that she and Emma had joined a battle of skills. Emma did not want to be in that kind of battle with Leader. She met the woman's eyes and saw the glittering danger that was Leader's trademark.

Chapter Five

Emma leaned against a tree. She brushed sweat from her eyes with the back of her long sleeve. Using her teeth, she opened her water bottle and poured the now warm water into her parched throat, and then over her sweaty, dirt-smeared face. Despite the warm staleness of the water, Emma drank it thirstily. It had been several hours since the last time she had halted her work to drink. When Leader asked her about her day, Emma wanted to be able to truthfully tell her she had completed the onerous chore with appropriate Diligence.

She looked over the land. She had managed to mow only three complete acres with a push-mower, and for the last hour or so she had been using a trimmer to clear weeds from around trees and large boulders of about one acre. It was the most pointless work Emma had ever done. Well, *almost* the most pointless; she had once spent several hours setting and unsetting a table. At least the yard work resulted in a beautiful landscape. The pointless part was that no one would ever see it. No one ever came out this far, even members of the Guild. And since the Guild was moving out of state in the next few days, this plot of land would be overgrown again in a matter of weeks, and no one would ever know she had been there.

Emma collapsed onto the freshly mown grass beside the tree. Her muscles complained as she stretched. She was never idle, but her muscles were not used to this kind of ongoing regime. As usual, she had endured her daily time on the mats practicing self-defense, sparring, and weaponry. She was accustomed to that type of workout and subsequent pain. But after that, she had spent nearly nine hours pushing mowers, toting trimmers, and carrying trash bags full of grass. And she wasn't remotely close to finished with the job. She still had to mow the two acres along the fence line, and then clean up four of the five. She would be lucky if she could finish the job tomorrow.

The walkie-talkie she wore at her hip gave a loud chirp. *"What are you doing?"* Amos' voice came in loud and clear.

Emma groaned as she came up to a sitting position. She grabbed the walkie and put it up to her mouth. Pressing the button, she answered, "Dying."

"You know perfectly well that if you die in that position, Leader will revive you long enough to beat you for your lack of Diligence." Amos teased her. Emma glared around at the surrounding trees, looking for any camera paraphernalia that could explain his creepy knowledge of what she was doing. He laughed through the walkie-talkie. *"It's time to come back to the House."*

Emma pulled a face. On the one side, she was grateful at her deliverance. On the other, leaving before dark meant she would probably be here all day tomorrow, too. "If I stay another couple hours, I won't have as much to do tomorrow," she told him, still looking around for a camera she could not find.

"Nevertheless: Come in now."

That was a command, and Emma would not disobey him. She gathered her equipment, loaded it onto the trailer, and took one last look around at the cleared land. She supposed it did not matter if she finished the job. Leader could always find other busy-making, pointless tasks. She started the ATV to which the trailer was hitched and drove back the way she had come. This was the first vehicle she had learned to drive. She was comfortable with it by now and knew she would have no problem with the Family cars if she was ever permitted to drive them.

Emma drove as fast as she dared with the heavy load she was pulling. The wind tugged at hair that had fallen from her braids, cooling her sweat-streaked face and neck. It was less than a mile to the house, but she enjoyed the ride, dreaming of a hot dinner waiting on the table. Her lunch had been deli sandwiches and carrot sticks wrapped and packed by Victoria under Amos' direction. It had satisfied her hunger at noon, but she was hungry for hot food now.

She made a stop to drop off her equipment in the tool shed and the bags of grass in the dumpster. The ATV and its trailer were parked at the end of the long garage, next to three identical vehicles. Since she knew what was good for her, she removed her filthy boots in the garage rather than tracking dirt and grass into the house. Ilene was responsible for the cleanliness of the house and Emma would not for the world upset someone as unpredictable as her. She was already mad because it was her job to check up on homework completion and Emma's looming C demonstrated to Leader that Ilene was not doing her job. Emma was certainly glad she had not been invited to attend the meeting this morning where Leader surely read Ilene the riot act. She was also glad her work had removed her to the edge of the property this morning just as Ilene emerged to take out her anger on subordinates stuck in the house.

Fortunately, Ilene was nowhere to be seen when Emma came through the door. Amos was in the cloak room emptying the trash when she came in to put her boots in her locker. He grinned after one good look at her.

"Well, I guess you were *busy*," he said with a chuckle.

Emma rolled her eyes. "Yes, I was busy. I can now explain with meticulous detail the difference between being busy and being Diligent."

Amos laughed again. "It's a shame you can't just convince Leader of your Diligence with footage of your pranks. You spent a lot of time and effort on those pranks. I viewed them today and emailed them all to Leader. I'm convinced we have enough to make a respectable slideshow of your achievements."

Emma dropped her boots in her locker and glared over her shoulder at him. "Can I expect this mockery to go on for some time, Amos? Or am I free to go shower for dinner?"

Amos seemed surprised. "If you're going to shower, you had better go fast. We need to leave."

"We're not eating dinner in tonight?" Emma's disappointment dripped from her tone and her crumpling posture.

"We already ate, darling. I made you a plate and left it warming in the oven, but if you have to shower you may be drinking protein meal-replacement instead. Scott's game is tonight, and we leave in fifteen minutes."

"Why do *I* have to go?"

Amos' cheerfulness began to dissipate. "Everyone is going tonight."

Emma made a noise of dismay, but she did not stay to argue. She would only lose and possibly turn Amos' mood against her in the process. She jogged away up the stairs, stripping as she went. She showered in record time but had to forego blow drying her hair. She wrapped it in a towel as she went to select her clothing. Uniforms were required during school hours, so she rarely got to enjoy the trove of clothing treasures in her closet. She forced herself to be decisive as her hot meal was dependent on dressing quickly. She slipped into black-and-gray patterned tight pants and a gray t-shirt with the word "Primal" printed across the bust in swirling black, white, red, and silver lettering. She pulled on a tight-fitting red jacket with three-quarter length sleeves. She snatched a black fedora from her hat shelf in the closet. She wouldn't wear it until her hair dried a little more, but she carried it as she hurried from her room. She only paused long enough to grab her phone from the charging tray on her desk, and the house keys she was never supposed to leave the property without. She tucked them into the pocket of her red jacket.

She dropped the towel into the laundry chute on her way down the steps. When she got to the kitchen, she snatched the plate out of Amos' hands as he moved toward the trash with it.

"I'll be fast!" she promised and sat up to the bar.

Next to her plate, he put a glass bottle that clearly had her protein meal-replacement in it. "Two minutes," he said with an admonishing tap to the side of the plate. "If you make me miss kickoff, not even your brilliant pranks will save you."

She was good at banter with Amos, but today eating was more important than winning a spat. She smiled and shoved a forkful of food into her mouth. It was not the delectable meal she had hoped for, but she was lucky to be getting it at all since she had missed dinnertime with the Guild group.

Two minutes later exactly, Amos pulled the plate away and dumped it into the trash. He hardly rinsed it at all before depositing it into the dishwasher and saying, "Let's go." She had not even made it through half the meal, so she unhappily grabbed the bottle on her way out the door.

"Let's go!" Amos shouted up the stairs. It was quiet in the house, so Emma assumed everyone else had left already. Victoria, eyes swollen from crying, came at a run, pulling on her jacket.

Emma, alarmed at the evidence of tears, stepped forward. A warning shake of Amos' head made her step back. She groaned inwardly. If Amos did not want her to comfort the child, there was a reason. The most obvious reason was that Victoria had been punished.

"Come on, Button," Amos said when Victoria reached the main floor. He walked into the garage and toward Leader's BMW. The Volvo was gone already, so Leader was probably meeting them at the school stadium. Since it was just Amos and Victoria, Emma got to ride in the front passenger seat. That pleased her, because she was almost always stuffed in the back. For a long time, she had to be in the middle, too, which was uncomfortable. Now, Victoria's booster was in the center back in every Guild vehicle. She was really getting too big to sit in a booster, but until Leader felt comfortable letting her ride without it, she had to click herself in.

They backed out of the garage and turned in the circular driveway, taking the first road away from the garage and out toward the street. They lived in one of the nicest neighborhoods in Reston, in the Uplands. Their house was perhaps one of four that came with a substantial parcel of property, twenty-eight acres. Reston property sold well even in the plummeting economic crisis, and realtors would have loved to get their hands on Leader's unused property, but privacy was essential for Leader and her Guild. They hated close neighbors.

The property was gated, but the gates opened automatically upon their approach, allowing them onto Gatesmeadow Way. Shortly, they were out of the neighborhood.

"Are you buckled?" Amos asked belatedly as they pulled onto the heavy traffic of Baron Cameron Avenue.

"Yes, sir," Victoria said quietly from the backseat. Amos always asked, but Emma did not even bother to answer anymore. Of course, she had fastened her seatbelt; it was strictly against Guild regulation to go without it.

"Why are we all going to this game?" Emma was disappointed she was being forced to go. She went to Scott's first game of the season a couple weeks ago, privately delighted that Leader agreed to let any of them engage in a contact sport. Emma's bitter disappointment still made her want to clench her fists when she found out that her school team was not very good. They suffered a humiliating defeat that night. Emma did not even understand the game, but she still hated the idea of Scott playing on a team that was unworthy of his talents.

"We support Scott," Amos answered blithely.

When Victoria snorted from the backseat and Emma shot Amos an eyeroll, he grinned. "And because Leader ordered us all to go tonight." That was the only reason they needed: Leader said so. "It will be good for us to go and cheer Scott on since Leader probably won't let him join another team. This could be his last game." He adjusted his mirror to look back at Victoria's pretty little face. "Don't you want to cheer Scott on?"

Victoria's eyes widened at being expected to answer but she told the truth, "Not really."

"That's okay," Emma jumped to her rescue. "None of us really want to go. But Leader's in charge, so we do what she says." Victoria accepted that information with a solemn nod. Emma felt a tiny bit of pain on the child's behalf. Being on the bottom of the Guild power chain was the worst place to be. Obedience was required of Victoria no matter who the order came from. It was difficult always to be subjected to the whims of every other person in the House. But Leader was the final topmost authority. If she had a reason for insisting they all come to Scott's game, no one could dispute her.

"Is Scott the quarterback?"

Amos scoffed at Victoria's question, then smiled kindly at her when he answered. "No. He's just one of the big boys who stands on the line and knocks over the guys who try to pass him. His job is to stop the other team from moving the ball downfield."

Victoria shrugged, losing interest about as quickly as Emma had when watching the first game. The child's attention turned to watch the buildings and road signs as they passed.

"You better drink up," Amos encouraged Emma. "Leader's probably not going to buy us any snacks or popcorn."

Emma pulled a face at him and took a long drink from her bottle. Leader did not often allow them to ingest food with low nutritional content. Even their most delicious meals were made of the most wholesome, heart-healthy ingredients available. Leader would never be tempted to purchase popcorn. She believed too many events surrounded food. She was of the opinion that food was for nourishment purposes only.

The mocking retort on the tip of her tongue, a response to Amos' teasing, disappeared as she tasted the protein drink. He had given her a chocolate flavor. She smiled fondly at the drink before turning the smile on him in thanks. He could very well have given her the standard issue tasteless sludge, but he had chosen to give her the tasty kind. It was one of the small comforts he often gave to his subordinates. In no way could anyone construe that he did this behind Leader's back or because he did not agree with her handling; He supported Leader in everything. But he did make Guild life less arduous on days when it could have been the most trying.

"What do you think, Button?" Amos asked Victoria as he merged onto Reston Parkway. "Do you think we can sweet-talk Leader into getting us some popcorn?"

Victoria blinked and in a sudden, surprising moment, she smiled. It was gone again right away. "Maybe if *you* ask."

Amos nodded and snapped his fingers, as if he had never thought of asking. "So, that's the trick, is it? *I* must ask, and then Leader will let us have the evil, artery-clogging, buttery delight."

"I wouldn't call it that," Victoria cautioned in a breathless rush, and Amos and Emma both laughed at her pragmatic warning.

"Noted," Amos answered as he turned the car onto the road to the school.

Chapter Six

Sacred Covenant's campus had several buildings. The first section was the elementary school, with its fields and playgrounds. That's where Victoria attended school. The middle school was next. It was fenced with chain link and was the least attractive and least inviting of the three schools. The high school was last, taking up the largest space as it was made up of three education buildings, a large stadium, and a pool.

They drove to the stadium parking lot and Amos took an empty spot at the back with several other Guild vehicles. It was obvious to Emma that they were Guild vehicles despite their blending in with all the other private-school-parent cars in the lot. Whereas most Americans drove around looking for the spots closest to the front of a parking lot, Guild members were just as likely to select ones closest to lot exits. They did not mind walking longer distances, especially when it was not freezing outside. Leader's Volvo wasn't here yet.

Amos took Victoria's hand and walked toward the stadium, urging Emma to hurry after them. She finished her drink before she followed and left the bottle in the car. She caught up to them before they reached the crowded section of the parking lot, and they entered the stadium together.

The stadium bleachers were crowded, but anyone looking could have identified the Guild. It amused Emma to see them sitting together in an unwelcoming clump in the direct center of the Home-Team bleachers. If they were trying to blend in, they failed. Anyone who saw them would have been able to recognize that there was something different. It was the aloofness, the dangerous grace, the cold-eyed stares that made others avoid sitting near them.

Emma pointed them out to Amos, and he led the way. There was nothing particularly scary about Amos in comparison with others in the Guild, such as Leader and Thomas, but Emma still noted the distance others gave him as he walked through the crowd. They stepped out of his way and pulled children out of his path. He did not seem to notice.

Julianne greeted them. "I'm glad you're here. Leader called and said she's running late but asks if you'll record it for her."

Amos' response was to roll his eyes. "It's recording already."

Julianne passed over a handheld video camera Emma might expect other real families to have out at a football game. "She wants it recorded on this."

Amos scowled and muttered, "Why?" He opened the recording device and studied it as if it might give him a contagious disease. He settled down on the seat between Julianne and Ilene.

"She didn't say." Julianne smiled at Victoria and patted the seat next to her. Ilene scooted down to accommodate her. The child obeyed the gesture, took a seat and crisscrossed her legs. She very rarely got to sit like a real kid because her daily uniform was a pleated black and white plaid jumper. Skirts did not lend themselves to crisscross, as Emma well remembered from her elementary school days. Tonight, the little girl wore jeans and a pink blouse. Her hair had been styled into two pigtail puffs and tied with pink ribbons. All evidence of crying was gone with a swipe of a wet wipe from Julianne's purse.

"There you go," the doctor said with an affectionate pat on the girl's back.

Emma sat on the bleacher above them, at the end of the row next to Lara. Beside Lara, Adam sat leaning forward, forearms on knees. Piper and Waylon sat beyond him. Lara shot her a brief smile before returning her attention to Adam and whispering words in his ear. Emma was only glad she couldn't hear what was said, since it was obviously more arguing. That's all the two of them seemed to do these days.

"Did you get the back five done?" Ilene asked, turning icy-blue eyes on Emma.

"Not yet. Amos said I had to come to the game."

"Be careful of your tone," Ilene replied tersely.

Before Emma could answer, Amos interjected without looking up from the camera in his hands, "That's enough, Ilene. She'll finish it tomorrow. She had to come to the game, you know that."

Emma folded her arms on her chest and patted her hat onto her head. "I think it's less about work getting done than a lesson being learned, anyway. It's about being busy, not being Diligent," Emma muttered.

Julianne turned a pointed look at her at the same time she held up a stalling hand at Ilene. "Stop it," she told Emma pointedly. The look she then shot at Ilene carried the order over. Emma thought it would be best to obey Julianne. It would be humiliating to be reprimanded in front of people who knew her from school and already thought she was bizarre.

Thomas joined them and took the seat next to Ilene directly in front of Emma. "I asked the cheer coach if she could move the cheerleaders downfield a little way so we aren't forced to stare at their mediocre acrobatics the whole game."

"What did she say?" Ilene asked hopefully.

He answered sarcastically. "She was really classy. She flipped me off and said I could sit with the rivals if I didn't want to see their mediocre acrobatics up close and personal. Then I'm pretty sure she called me a fag as she stomped away."

Waylon chuckled but Emma failed to see what amused him about the story. His curly brown hair was styled perfectly and with his preppy-dress business-casual, he was one of the more attractive men in the Guild. She wondered why he especially thought the derogatory use of the word "fag" was humorous. She was pretty certain he was gay.

Emma thought Thomas' annoyance with the cheerleaders well-placed. They were distracting already, and the game hadn't even started, so they were really just practicing. Emma knew the girls in the squad unofficially since she was in classes with most of them. Before coming to this school, Emma had always believed the stereotype that "cheerleaders are spoiled and bratty" must be exaggerated. It wasn't. These girls were the epitome of mean and nasty. They used words to bully others and thought they were the cream of the crop. Emma idly dreamed that they would drop a flyer

and have to rush to the hospital. At least they would be out of Thomas'
sight then.

She shook herself. It was never a good idea to dream up harm.

Lara jumped to her feet and commanded Emma, "Switch me!"

Waylon put up a hand before Emma could make the move. "No,"
he ordered in his quiet way. His dark eyes were stern, and he pointed a
firm finger at Lara. "If you have Emma jumping between you every three
minutes, she won't get to see the game. She came here to support Scott. We
all came to support Scott, so stop your petty bickering right now."

Emma rarely saw Waylon exercise his authority over his subordinates,
but she was pleased. It was true Adam and Lara could fight and make up
a dozen times in a few hours. Moving around every few minutes would
fatigue her more than her predawn wake-up call followed by hours of
menial labor. She mouthed "Thank you" at Waylon. He stood higher than
Lara, so Emma had to obey his order over hers.

"I second that sentiment," Piper said without even looking at them. Her
red hair was, as usual, plaited back out of the way since Leader wouldn't let
her cut it short like she wanted. She was dressed like a confused college boy
in a black suit-vest over a rock t-shirt and too-tight slacks, skater shoes, and
half-a-dozen leather bracelets. The only makeup she wore was heavy black
eyeliner. Fortunately, she looked young enough that she could pull off the
look without being ridiculous. If anyone knew she was in her thirties, they
would probably encourage her to settle down and dress like an adult.

Amos set the camera on a tripod and adjusted it several times until he
seemed resigned that it was not as sophisticated as he wanted. He pressed
the record button and then looked over his shoulder at Adam and Lara.

"Me, too."

Waylon shot Amos a glare, and then turned it on Piper. "Forgive
me for saying so, but I was very clear about my expectations. I don't
need you to second me for others to take me seriously." Amos shrugged,
almost apologetically, but Piper's response was a long, drawn-out look of
superiority.

She snorted. "A couple years in Loyalty, and you think you know what
it means to be a leader?"

She returned her attention to the pregame activities with another snort, not watching Waylon's shoulders and face tense up. He did not respond. Like Piper, he turned to watch the field. The band played and the teams ran out.

Emma tapped Victoria's shoulder. "We're the green team. The Giants."

Victoria's answer came after a thoughtful frown. "If we're the Giants, why is the mascot a beaver?"

Emma wondered that many times herself. The Beaver costume wore a green Giants shirt and waved a Giants flag, but it made no sense to her, either.

"Maybe giants are scarier than beavers, so they changed the name," Emma offered her own theory.

"Maybe they couldn't afford a Giant costume, and they already had the beaver," Adam put in with a sly grin.

"Spring for a new mascot," Victoria answered doubtfully.

Emma and Adam chuckled at the child's sophisticated take on the situation. Amos leaned across Julianne to tweak Victoria's nose and said, "Maybe it's a giant beaver. Did you think of that?"

"There's Scott," Emma announced, pointing at the incoming green-clad Giants. Scott had the number twenty-three emblazoned in white across the back and front of his green jersey. The back also had the last name Cole printed in white letters. Cole was their assumed last name in Virginia.

Fans on the bleachers all around them cheered for the team as they broke out onto the field. This made the Guild even more conspicuous, since they did not know how to be good fans. They sat and watched in silence while the rest of the fans shrieked their support. Emma had tried cheering last time but had felt ridiculous and given it up. Amos liked football, though. Once he had checked the recording device again to be sure it was doing its job, he stood up and hollered like the rest of the crowd.

"Get up," he commanded his silent subordinates. "This is why we came."

"To look absurd?" Thomas asked, but he obediently climbed to his feet and offered some ill-tempered applause. They all stood up at Amos' order, though standing only made it marginally less obvious that they did not belong in this setting.

After kickoff, Amos sat back down and waved at them all to be seated as well. And promptly Emma got bored. The most entertaining moment of the first five minutes of the game was when some exuberant fan accidentally tossed his drink down on the cheerleaders. Thomas cheered well enough at that, and they got to see the cheer coach flip him off again.

After half an hour, Lara whipped some nail polish out of her purse and asked Emma if she would paint her fingernails. Emma shrugged and complied. Scott's team was not doing well enough that she would miss anything special by spending a few minutes looking at Lara's hands. In the chilly night air, the polish didn't dry very quickly, but Emma persevered.

"Well, if it isn't General Emma Cole," said a gallant voice. Emma looked up at her Chemistry lab partner and gave him a grin. He dropped onto the empty space in the bleacher next to her. "I don't suppose you convinced Mitchell to let you take the test?"

Joel Berkowitz was one of her coconspirators when it came to harassing the Chemistry teacher. He called her "General" because he said such brilliant planning and execution deserved to be given a rank. Several of his friends called her General, too.

"No," Emma answered. She screwed the cap on the polish jar and placed it in Lara's purse. Lara was back to whispering with Adam again. "Nor is he likely to, since he finally got his chance to make an example out of me."

"Example?" the dark-eyed boy asked with a laugh. "All he did was make you into a martyr. Practically everyone in the class refused to answer questions on the test. He threatened to make us take an incomplete, but I'm willing to bet we have a test retake Monday. He can't turn out grades like that and stay on at a private school. You're in the clear."

Emma smiled in smug satisfaction until she saw Ilene's stern look. She cleared her throat. "I certainly don't want to be responsible for people getting bad grades if Mitchell retaliates."

Joel shrugged. "Ah, who cares? The sooner we drive him out the sooner we can get a respectable replacement." He motioned toward the field. "Your brother playing?"

Emma nodded. "Yeah, he's the only guy on the line that doesn't get clobbered by the other team during each play."

"Maybe giant beavers aren't as intimidating as one might think," Amos said, suddenly standing and turning to face them. He held out a hand to the newcomer. "Hello. I'm Emma's father. Who are you?"

Emma scowled at the abruptness, but she introduced them. "Joel Berkowitz, meet my father, Amos Cole. Father, this is my Chemistry lab partner, Joel."

"How do you do?" Amos said and, although his tone was polite enough, his gaze was vastly unwelcoming. He did not trust any of the Junior Guild's acquaintances. He had good reason for that. Emma knew from personal experience. But there was nothing to fear from Joel. He was not an attractive young man and, even if he was, Emma was not interested in dating. Her one and only boyfriend had only befriended her for a chance to get to Guild information, and then had tried to kill her when she failed to supply anything. Amos had shot him in the streets to protect Emma. It was a collection of events that was not easy to forget.

Joel seemed oblivious to Amos' inhospitable demeanor. "I'm doing well, sir. Your daughter is somewhat of a legend at our school. My compliments." Joel slid a companionable arm across Emma's shoulders. When that caused Amos' eyes to darken, Emma shrugged it off.

"Daddy's proud," Amos said sarcastically, cutting his eyes at Emma. "All I ever wanted was a daughter who could make herself a celebrity for sloth and trickery." He flicked his wrist. "Get out of here," he told the young man. "My daughter is not a toy. She's a brilliant girl."

Emma wished she could take that compliment to heart, but his tone was dark enough that she couldn't. She pushed slightly at Joel to get him moving but he resisted.

"She *is* brilliant. She's practically carried me all semester."

Amos' eyes widened and he looked at Emma in disbelief.

"How is he still here and still talking?" Amos asked, switching to Mandarin so only Emma understood.

Julianne came to the rescue, rising to her feet beside Amos. "Okay, Em. Time to say goodbye to your friend." She offered the young man a consoling smile. "It was nice meeting you, Mr. Berkowitz."

Joel shrugged at Emma and jumped to his feet. "Go, Giants," he said at them as he walked away down the bleachers.

Amos opened a palm as if in presentation of the boy. "That slacker loser, Emma? Really?"

Emma raised her hands as if in surrender. "Really *what*, Amos? We don't get to choose our lab partners. They're assigned by the teacher. If you have a problem, I welcome you to take it up with Mitchell."

"*Mr.* Mitchell," Julianne corrected.

"God! It's just a common honorific, Julianne. It's not like I'm supposed to be saying *President* or *His Majesty the King* and I'm slighting him. He is a *high school teacher* with a *basic* teaching degree."

Julianne raised stern brows but before she could say anything, Amos ordered, "Come sit over here!" He motioned to the space on the bleachers beside him. Emma got up immediately and moved. He pushed her down onto the hard bleacher seat, then flicked her ear just for good measure.

"Don't argue with Julianne."

Emma scoffed and rolled her eyes.

Amos went back to watching the game. For a wonder, he seemed to actually understand what was happening out there. Emma did not. All she saw was a bunch of boys squatting in the grass facing one another, then for some reason tackling each other, and then starting over again in a new place. The student announcer narrated the game for them but since Emma did not understand the terms, his commentary made no sense to her.

She sighed in complete boredom and looked across the stands to where Joel had parked himself with a group of his dedicated buddies. They waved at her when they saw her looking. One of them even shouted out "General!" and tried to beckon her over. She smiled at them but shook her head. There was no way she could leave the seat next to Amos to go sit with her friends.

Chapter Seven

People stood up to move aside for Leader when she walked into the stands. Maybe because she was beautiful but probably more because their deepest soul sensed that she could kill them with her pinky if provoked. She wore her business suit, including her high heels, and carried a laptop case. Under her arm, she held a brown grocery sack that, when he saw her burdened, Waylon went to retrieve.

"They're shirts," she informed them when she got to their place on the bleachers. "Pass them around. If we're here to be a sports family, we may as well do a good job."

Waylon removed a green t-shirt from the bag as if afraid it might bite him then passed the bag to Piper. Without any hesitation and hardly taking her eyes off the game, Piper grabbed a shirt and hauled it over her head. It was the school t-shirt with the word "Giants!" across the front and a cartoon picture of a beaver wearing boxing gloves. Emma thought it really solidified Victoria's claim that Giants and Beavers had nothing to do with each other. Emma added to that thought: Why was it wearing boxing gloves given the primary job in football was to move the ball down the field?

Emma twirled her shirt up into a thin, tight length of cloth and tied it around her middle to act as a belt. That was as close to wearing the thing as she would come without a direct order.

"Are these the best seats you could acquire?" Leader asked Amos with a pinched expression. She motioned with one hand for Emma to scoot over and give her room next to Amos and the camera.

Amos looked confused. "We're at the fifty-yard line. Where would you rather be?"

She did not answer. Instead, she looked at Emma. "You're sunburned. Didn't you wear sunscreen today?"

"No," Emma answered defensively. "It's fall. I thought the rule was that we don't have to wear sunscreen in the fall."

Julianne leaned over. "*Any* time the sun is shining, it's a good idea to put on sunscreen."

"And watch that tone," Leader added, shooting Emma a stern glance. Then she leaned around to look at Victoria. "Are you enjoying the game?"

Victoria seemed unsure what to say and, in the end, as always, opted for honesty. "No."

Leader grabbed a t-shirt from the bag and tossed it into Victoria's lap. "Maybe that will help." She took a look at Emma's shirt being used as belt and scowled. But she didn't put on a shirt, either, so Emma relaxed a little.

"Popcorn might help," Amos suggested innocently. Hope blossomed in Victoria's eyes at his words.

Leader scowled again but this time at Amos. "Popcorn? And give in to the common cultural norm that seems to suggest food must accompany every activity in which we choose to engage? Why would I encourage that?"

"Because it is yummy," Amos answered with a grin. "And because maybe it's part of the way football is celebrated in this country. Without it, we might be missing out on an important element of fandom-hood." He gestured around at the game and the spectators on the bleachers. "How will we know if we're doing this right without blending in a little better with the football culture?" Emma smirked because she knew popcorn would not make them blend in any better.

Leader settled into her seat with a sigh. "Very well, Amos. But not very much. We're not here to eat a million calories."

Amos jumped to his feet and called to Victoria, "Come on, Button! Let's go get us some popcorn." She followed him quickly, and though her face did not display much excitement, she seemed energized by the idea of a treat.

Leader slid an arm around Emma in a way a normal mother might greet her daughter. But when she got Emma close, she whispered, "I hope your tone and your belligerent expressions are not indicative of how you spent your day." When Emma shook her head in denial, Leader gave her a hard squeeze and sat back. "Good."

A few minutes later, Leader said, "I read your work."

Emma stiffened. The activities on the field became a blur as her mind tried to cope with the idea that someone in this world had read her deepest heart.

"It was quite good, Little Girl. It's clear you have a talent for it."

Emma could not look at Leader. Her eyes slid briefly closed and her heart beat painfully in her chest. The compliments seemed weighted, as if there was a "but" about to follow. Leader only continued to watch the game, though.

"Does that mean you're okay with it?" Emma asked finally, breathlessly, looking aside at the older woman.

Leader pursed her red lips thoughtfully while watching the game. She folded her hands on her knee and then turned to Emma with raised brows. "I think you know that depends on you, Emma. Knight to Queen's bishop Three: Writing is not a career. It's a good, uplifting hobby that is probably helping you deal with some of your . . ." She shook her head. Emma knew that she was referencing the past couple of years' worth of mischief and rebellion. Ilene had different ideas.

"Grief."

Chills shot down Emma's spine and she sat as still as if she had been frozen by the woman's icy words. Her mind flashed to a beautiful, dark, cruel man dead in a gutter. Her throat constricted and for a moment Emma thought she was going to cry. She shoved the tears away when Leader shot Ilene a quelling glare and continued her quiet conversation with Emma.

"I do not generally discourage these kinds of hobbies. But, Emma, if your hobby interferes with your good judgment, or your homework completion, it's a problem and I will squash it like a bug."

Emma sat up straighter and nodded. The teams were squatting on a line again, just like they seemed to be every time she looked.

Of course, Leader *had* to say writing was not a career. In the Guild, arts were generally considered a waste of precious training or studying time. Emma was nearing a black belt. She was on a scholarly path toward a prestigious science degree at a fancy college. If writing interfered with Leader's goals for her, Emma had no doubt it would be effectively squashed.

"I will find a more appropriate time for it," Emma promised but she did not dare meet Leader's eye when she said it. The woman's subtle reference to chess again made Emma cringe. She did not ever like to think of Leader as her opponent, even in a simple game of strategy.

"You will use your privileges time from now on," Leader shot back. "And you will not deviate from my schedules for you ever again."

"Yes, Leader."

Emma's heart shifted to a more normal rhythm. She breathed in and out, pleased with the overall outcome of the conversation. Sometimes these bouts with Leader did not end so well for Emma. Images of her last school—her expulsion from her last school—clouded her mind. *It will be different here*, she promised Leader only a couple months ago when enrolling at Sacred Covenant. *I'll do better.* And Leader answered threateningly, *You* must *do better here Emma. We can't keep doing this little chess match from Hell.*

Leader broke Emma from her miserable reminiscences. "I left you notes on some of your less well-structured pieces. See to it that if you're going to spend your time writing, you're doing a proper good job of it, Emma. I wouldn't have you wasting your time in mediocrity."

Emma's shoulders slumped and her heart sank to somewhere near her stomach, but she answered the only way she could, "Yes, Leader."

Thomas stood up suddenly and motioned toward the teams conferring on the field in two separate huddles. "All right, we're completely lost," he announced to Leader, although he carefully omitted her title. "What are we supposed to be doing here?"

"Watching the game." Leader lifted a hand and gestured toward the field. When Thomas continued to look doubtfully at her, she gave him an amused chuckle. "I'm trying to decide if I should overrule the Guild Book edict that states we should not engage in contact sports. Scott is my trial player. This is my decision-making game."

Leader stood up in sudden alarm as some late fans tried to sit down in one of the two empty bleachers in front of them. "Oh, no! Not here. Move along." She got dirty looks, but they obeyed. They probably couldn't help it. People frequently obeyed her without knowing why. They were like sheep, Emma thought. Emma could get people to obey her, too, just like the kids in her Chemistry class all joining the pranks. The true testament of her power was their deliberate failing of a test she was thrown out of, just to force Mitchell to retest the lot of them. It was a dangerous power the Guild members tossed around like candy.

Amos returned and passed small cups of popcorn around. Emma refused hers. She had never felt the need for popcorn in her life before; she didn't intend to start now.

Emma was glad her eyes were on the field when, in the next play, a rival player grabbed Scott's facemask and tried to drag him to the ground. It was a spectacularly illegal move and the referees had already blown the whistle when Scott retaliated. He shoved the kid away hard enough that he tripped several others in the process.

"Ah, Leader?" Emma said, pointing at the action. But Leader was already watching.

Three other players attacked Scott. His teammates came to the rescue, but Scott was a man on fire. He tossed aside the smaller of the three boys and the kid crumpled into a heap. The other two were bigger and came in swinging fists. But they were no match for a boy who had spent literally hours every day learning to kill. Their padding was the only thing saving them from serious injury.

Leader moved faster than Emma would have thought possible in those six-inch heels. She stepped directly on the bleachers and worked her way down quickly. Now both teams were in the fray and referees shouted and blew whistles all around them. Leader ignored the shouts for her to get off the field and plowed right to the center of the fight. It was dying down by the time she reached Scott. She grabbed his facemask and pulled him several feet away from the others. Emma would have given a kidney to know what she was saying.

"I guess the edict stands," Thomas said with a slight smirk at Amos. Amos scowled and looked back at the field.

"He's going to get thrown out of the game," Piper muttered unhappily. Like Amos, she seemed to be enjoying this event.

Julianne spoke up with concern tingeing her tone. "I think the greater possibility is that he will be *pulled* out of the game. She can't possibly let him continue to play if he's a danger to others."

Emma scoffed and, when they all looked at her, was forced to explain her derision. "We're a danger to people just by being on the same street with them. If we wanted to avoid being dangerous to others, we would move to the Bunker and set up shop for good." The Bunker was their safe house. There was no phone service, no internet, no television . . . really, no way to access the outside world. It was the safest place Emma could imagine. Not for the Guild—they could harm and humiliate each other anywhere—but for the rest of the world. Again, images of death filled her mind. This time, it was a young man—her first boyfriend—staring vacantly at the sky with the remnants of startlement on his face.

Amos flicked Emma's ear again and she winced out of her terror daydream. He did not explain this action, but she knew it was probably for the disrespectful tone.

Leader still had her fingers coiled around Scott's facemask and, though Emma could not see Scott, she thought he seemed humbled. The referee shouted out penalties when Leader pushed Scott away and strode back into the bleachers like she owned them. He watched her go before returning to his team and his furious coach.

"I guess the edict is still up for debate," Thomas complained, resettling himself uncomfortably on the bench.

Leader glanced around at them all as she returned.

"What did he say?" Amos asked quietly. The only reason Emma heard him was that she was sitting right next to them.

"Nothing," Leader replied as if that should be obvious. "*I* did the talking. He'll be careful if he knows what's good for him."

"The other boys *did* attack him."

Leader turned her body to give Amos a hard-eyed stare. "What is it about me today that makes my subordinates think I'm up for an argument?"

He looked away. "I apologize. It won't happen again."

She nodded in acceptance. Emma dreamed of the day when all it would take was an apology to get Leader off her back.

"Why were they fighting?" Victoria wanted to know, her giant liquid eyes raising to find Emma, her little hand poised over her popcorn cup.

Emma shrugged. Leader answered, "They aren't well-disciplined. And when undisciplined children fight, they often turn into an unmanageable horde. Scott is well-disciplined, so it only took a few words to remind him of my expectations."

Victoria accepted that explanation with a nod. She turned a wide-eyed look on Emma. "I'm cold," she admitted in a whisper. Emma smiled softly and offered her the red jacket. If she had to sit here in complete boredom, the child at least should not be cold.

"Did you make a decision about the move?" Amos whispered to Leader. Clearly, Emma was not meant to hear, but of necessity in the Guild she had developed a keen sense of hearing.

"Yes. We'll split the Guild. It won't be comfortable, and it won't be fun, but it will serve my purposes. I had planned to keep all the children together with Ilene, but considering how thoroughly Emma trumped her, and Lara's and Adam's arguing, I don't completely trust her with them."

Amos agreed. "Julianne's the better choice by a landslide."

"I need too much of her time," Leader replied on a sigh. She looked over her shoulder at Adam and Lara, whose argument was no longer simply whispers.

"I told you two to stop arguing," Waylon suddenly snapped, rounding on the pair. "Adam, move to the bleacher below Leader. This has gotten out of hand."

Leader looked back at Amos as Adam obediently moved to the empty bleacher in front of her. "We'll separate them." Amos nodded his agreement.

"I call dibs on Lara," Amos murmured, causing Leader to scowl in teasing. Then she leaned forward and kneaded Adam's shoulders in an affectionate way.

"You will have to learn to maintain your temper sometime, Adam," she cautioned in his ear. "It's part of a healthy Self-Control."

"Yes, Leader," Adam answered emotionlessly without looking at her.

Emma wondered what it meant to split the Guild. She had spent a healthy dose of time with the Guild and to her certain knowledge they had always worked and lived as a single unit. What would a change mean? Emma looked out at the field and Scott. What exactly did "split" mean?

When Leader sat back to watch the game, Amos asked, "Are you planning to send a forward party?"

Leader considered his words for a few moments while she watched the game. "Yes. I suppose I could send you in the jet to get set up, and the others could be on the road as early as tomorrow. You would have a few days to secure some dwellings for us and scout the surroundings."

Amos nodded in agreement. "If I leave tomorrow, you could send Ilene and Thomas with the children right away, since term is essentially over. I could be ready for them in a couple days, no problem. If you keep Piper and Waylon, they can close down. And Adam."

Leader glanced at Emma, who tried to appear like she wasn't eavesdropping. Leader wasn't fooled. "I have to keep Emma in school at least through next week so she can sweet-talk her teacher into giving her an acceptable score."

"Her tool of a lab partner came over a while ago and told her he thought the teacher would be retesting them all. She has a shot."

Leader placed a firm hand on Emma's knee, squeezing slightly. "Well, whether or not that works out, I would never deprive her of the opportunity to finish the back five and demonstrate her willingness to be Diligent."

Emma gave her a pained look. "Leader, I learned my lesson. You wanted me to alter my behavior and I have. I spent an entire day doing the most pointless work in the world to show that I know my pranks were busywork and did not constitute Diligence. I will abide by your schedules religiously.

Is it really necessary for me to go back out and weed the property edge tomorrow?"

Leader patted her face hard. "Little Girl, I would not deprive you one second of your opportunity to prove yourself to me." She shot a glance at Amos. "She's definitely staying with me."

He chuckled. "Agreed. And I think you should also consider her staying with you once we split. It would not be fair to saddle Ilene with her clever machinations."

Leader leaned to look at Ilene sitting down the bleacher. "I think you're probably right." She squeezed Emma's leg again. Then, abruptly, she was on her feet whistling with two fingers so it carried to the field. It did carry well, and Scott looked up from what could possibly be another fight in time to see Leader motioning to him. She picked up her laptop bag.

"The edict stands," she told them all. "Let's go." And she led them out of the bleachers. Scott, ignoring his coach's shouts, removed his helmet and ran off the field to join them as they reached the stadium entrance.

Chapter Eight

Emma stood in the garage clutching her breakfast shake in her hands. She blinked into the morning light streaming through the open garage doors. Yesterday, she spent her day making the back five look like a state park. Then, when she thought she was done working for the night, she worked another few hours helping to pack and load supplies in the three vehicles headed out of state this morning. Amos had left yesterday with a hug and a whispered admonition to "be good for Leader." Today, Julianne planned to lead the rest of the forward party on a road trip across the country.

Emma sagged against Leader's Volvo. After all the work yesterday, she had managed only a couple hours on the paper she turned in to Leader this morning. It was neither well-written nor very informative due to the lack of time Emma spent on it. She figured that meant Leader would not assist her today in convincing the dean to examine her case against Mitchell. The thought that she would be on her own for that fight at school today made her want to crawl back between the sheets.

Nothing was as tiring, though, as Scott leaving her behind. His sudden walk off the field Saturday night would probably be all anyone could talk about at school. He was relieved at his deliverance. Emma was relieved for him but sad for her own loss. Besides Amos, Scott was the only person she ever wanted to talk to in the Guild. Emma was pretty sure "split the Guild" meant "live in different houses." She had no idea when she would see him again.

She rubbed her eyes with the back of her hand and reminded herself that she could not cry. She needed to be an example for Victoria. The child walked into the garage looking a little lost while carrying a backpack and her raggedy teddy bear. She sidled up to Emma and slipped her little hand into Emma's. They stood there, side by side, leaning against the car, waiting for the miserable moment of parting.

Three Guild vehicles were parked in the circular driveway, all to be driven across the states by Julianne. They were filled with luggage and the few irreplaceable items the Guild owned. Each person had been allotted one suitcase for clothing and personal supplies to tie them until all their things were replaced. Everything that could be replaced would be, including clothing, furniture, and appliances. That was the way it always was when the Guild moved. In fact, they even left their cars behind a few times, stored in the garage of the abandoned houses.

Julianne walked through the garage door carrying her purse and a manila envelope. She gave an exasperated sigh when Emma and Victoria were the only people waiting. Touching the intercom app on her phone, she spoke sharply, "I am leaving in two minutes. However, I will stop at the first rest stop I find so I can beat anyone who made me wait." Then she grinned at Emma and Victoria. The little girl, who took these threats seriously, widened her eyes. Emma squeezed the child's hand reassuringly. Julianne was probably mostly joking but even if she wasn't, Victoria had no need to fear. It would hurry the stragglers, which was what it was meant to do.

Thomas, who was renowned for taking his time getting ready each day, came striding through the door about thirty seconds later. In jeans and a plaid button-down shirt, he looked strange to Emma, who was used to seeing him only in his business suits.

He was closely followed by Ilene and Lara. Julianne gave out papers and cards from her manila envelope as people came through the door. When they started loading into vehicles, Emma disengaged her hold on Victoria's hand and leaned to kiss her temple.

"Be good, okay?" she cautioned unnecessarily. The child was exceptionally well-behaved, especially in comparison to Emma. Emma glanced around at the drivers getting into the cars. Ilene cast her a long, icy stare before gliding gracefully behind the wheel of one. Lara climbed into another. Thomas got into the passenger seat of the third—the one

Julianne would be driving. "Ride with Lara," she hinted at Victoria. Lara was the one most likely to be kind and sweet to the little girl.

"Can't," Victoria whispered back. "Leader told me I have to ride with Ilene. She's the safest driver."

Emma was disappointed but decided not to say anything. She just gave the child one last hug and then pushed her softly toward Ilene's car.

When Scott ran through the door, eyes bleary and hair still wet from the shower, Julianne glanced at her own watch and shot him an arched look. He shook his own watch at her, where it was grasped tightly against his belt and his phone in one hand. His backpack was in the other.

"I made it with three seconds to spare," he argued playfully.

Julianne lowered a brow at his technicality, but she did not refute him. She merely pulled a paper and a card from her envelope and slipped them into his back pocket. "You'll be riding with Lara to start with, since Thomas and I need to ride together for a while. The card is the driver's license you'll need for the first leg of our trip. I'll give you others as we need them. The paper is to be tucked above the visor in case we go through a checkpoint, or you get pulled over while driving. Give it to the officer and drive away. They should leave you alone."

After giving those terse instructions, Julianne turned to meet Leader, who emerged from the house. Leader snapped her fingers at Emma, who stood up straight instead of leaning against the car. Then Leader slid a hand on Julianne's shoulder and guided her away down the driveway to give them some privacy.

Scott shoved his phone, keys, and watch into Emma's hands in greeting. She took them without complaint and followed him as he walked out of the garage, threading his belt through the loops on his jeans. He asked her, "When are you guys going to follow?"

"I don't know." She opted not to tell him what she had overheard about splitting the Guild. "Next weekend, maybe. I hate that I can't just go with you today."

Scott shrugged. "You have a test to take, Em. You need to pass that class."

"Maybe." Emma had serious doubts about Mitchell relenting. "Take care of Victoria, okay? And don't be mean to her. She's scared of you enough already."

Scott pulled a face. "She is not scared of me. I just don't baby her like you do. She'll be fine." He removed the wristwatch from her hand and slapped it on, securing it into place. He put his phone in his back pocket with his license and Julianne's creepy clemency paper. Last, he swung his backpack onto his shoulder. "And you'll be fine, too, Em. Just don't do anything stupid and piss Leader off while Amos isn't here to serve as her buffer."

Emma rolled her eyes. "It isn't Leader I'm worried about."

"Who?" Scott asked in surprise. When she raised her brows at him in challenge, he glared. "Adam? He's as tame as a lapdog, Emma, if you stay out of his way. Don't do anything to piss him off, either."

"Despite what you may think, I don't deliberately try to annoy people."

Scott grabbed her face, covering her mouth with one of his massive hands. He was much stronger than he used to be, not always aware of how easily he could hurt her. She did not fight his grip, because that was the easiest way to avoid his unintentional bruises. He smiled at her. "I'll miss you, too." She glared over his hand at him for being able to read her so well. She would miss him. The ache in her heart as he stepped back and removed his hand was more painful than his grip had been. He patted her cheek once, not gently. "Be good."

Her retort was cut off by Leader calling for her. She shot Scott a glare as he grinned and jumped into the passenger seat of Lara's car. Emma lifted a hand to wave at Victoria in the backseat of Ilene's vehicle. Then, when Leader called again, Emma ran back into the garage. Leader stood in the open door of her Volvo, holding Emma's backpack.

"Get in," she ordered brusquely. "You're going to be late for school."

Since no one else was riding with them, Emma took the front passenger seat. Leader dropped the backpack on the floorboard between Emma's legs and put the car in reverse. She worked her way through the three cars parked in the driveway and managed to get into the lead position. As a result, the three vehicles followed her until they reached Reston Parkway. Leader turned north while Julianne and the others turned south. Emma turned in her seat to watch the cars until they were out of sight. Her chest hurt with an almost physical pain at this separation from Scott.

Leader's announcement pulled Emma back around in her seat, "I read your paper."

Emma studied the woman's profile intently, waiting for her to pronounce that it was not good enough and she was on her own.

"It was not your best work."

"I know. I was too tired to do a proper job of it, Leader. I'm happy to redo it tonight during my homework time, if you want that."

Leader studied her with a quick glance, and then shook her head. "No. I got the gist. You should never have been in this class to begin with, if your half-hearted effort on that paper turned out explanations and procedures with such clarity. If it only took you two nights to complete several weeks' worth of homework, you were never being challenged. That's partly my fault. Your education is my personal responsibility."

Emma sat up straighter, hearing a hint of possibility in Leader's words.

"Does that mean you will be speaking to the dean on my behalf today?"

Leader considered her for a moment, glancing at her several times while driving.

Emma doubled down, feeling hopeful for the first time since her trip to the dean on Friday. "Leader, please! I will be in your debt forever if you do this!"

Leader snorted around a smile. "Is that supposed to induce me to come to your aid? You're in my debt already, Little Girl. I *shouldn't* help you. I *should* let this lesson stand on its own." She clicked through her teeth and shook her head. "But that chauvinistic bastard Mr. Mitchell needs to know he can't make judgments about a person's aptitudes based on their gender. I figured a conversation with a female scientist might change his mind."

Emma was puzzled. "You? Are you a scientist?"

Leader glanced askance at her and shook her head in amusement. "As much as I was ever a lawyer or a broker." She had worked in both professions since Emma had known her. "I'm enough of one that I can outtalk a mediocre high school teacher." She turned the car onto Sacred Lane. "But even though I do talk to him about this, Emma, you will not gloat. If at any moment I think you're taking pleasure from his pain, I will set you down right in front of him. Is that clear?"

Emma nodded eagerly. She was elated not to have to fight this on her own. The dean already did not like her and would never agree to help her if she went by herself. Mitchell would not even pay her the courtesy of listening. Emma had always known Leader was her only chance of getting that grade turned around before Friday.

"I mean it, Emma," Leader snapped, her tone darkening into dangerous territory. "One little glimmer of satisfaction from you and I'll turn you over the dean's desk."

Emma flushed at the idea of Leader paddling her like a child in front of Mitchell and the dean. "I understand, Leader."

Leader pulled into the only available parking space in the visitor lot, the handicapped spot directly outside the front doors of the office. She retrieved a handicapped hanger from the glove compartment and slipped it over the rearview mirror. The campus rent-a-cop monitored parking religiously, and Leader had been ticketed before. When Emma reached for the handle to climb out of the car, Leader made a negating sound to stop her exit. Emma slid back against the car seat and let out a sharp breath.

"Look at me," Leader ordered.

Emma folded her hands together on her knees and turned to look at the woman's face. There were creases in her skin that had not been there two years ago; Crinkles around the corners of her eyes and between her brows. The weight of being Leader seemed to make a physical impression in a way time did not seem to affect members of the Guild. She was still the most intimidating person Emma knew. Her eyes crackled with a deep fire that reminded Emma of the last person she had known with the title "Leader."

"We need to have the real talk before we go in there."

Emma swallowed down a panic that tried to grip her throat with bile-tipped fingers. She nodded even though she didn't understand what Leader meant.

"I'm really disappointed in you, Emmalyn. You knew this class was not challenging you and you never said a word to anyone. You let yourself get wrapped up in mischief and idleness, and you simply wasted your entire term. That is precious time you can never get back. It's time that did not belong to you. It belonged to me. You know better than a lot of people in this Guild how very precious my time is."

The screaming began in Emma's mind. Screaming. Running. Gunshots. She could see the blood as vividly as if it had been shed yesterday. Scarlet against a white shirt. Emma's disobedience had killed the previous Leader. She knew exactly how precious time was. There was only ever one second between life and death. One second was all it took to turn the world upside-down. One second had made the difference between her life and his. She lived and he died because of one second. Emma drew a guilty breath and looked away through the windshield.

"Look at me!" Leader demanded in a harsh tone. Emma obeyed immediately but did not try to shield the anger in her gaze. She did not want to talk about this. She did not want to deal with the moment that had shoved this woman into the position she was now in. Avoiding that memory was Emma's full-time job.

She expected to see fire in Leader's eyes, but there was none. There was no condemnation where she expected to find it, but neither was there any compassion. "God knows you're smart, Emma. Your IQ is over 160. It's frankly surprising you're able to exist as well as you do in normal society. I know academics come to you easily. I also know that if I allowed it, you could easily graduate in the spring with Scott. But there is a reason I won't let you move any faster. The experience of high school is too important to pass up simply because you're smart enough to run a marathon of it.

"Do you think I don't know that you read your textbooks in the first three days of a class and can quote from them word-for-word the rest of the year? On your first day of kindergarten, you picked up the teacher's manual and skimmed it when her back was turned, and then for the rest of the year corrected her teaching." Emma did not smile at the idea because she was still burning with the pain of avoiding her guilt. But she was amused at the reminiscence of her younger self. It sounded like the kind of thing Emma would do today with any teacher who tried to bully her. "And she was a *good* teacher, Emma. I can imagine the havoc you would have made of her year if she had been a bad once."

Leader shook a finger in Emma's face. "I can imagine what chaos you created when you discovered that Mr. Mitchell was not a good teacher. If given the opportunity, you could have taught his class with better precision and mastery than he has in his ten years as a Chemistry teacher. But you weren't given that opportunity. You *stole* his authority. You robbed him of his influence over his students. Furthermore, you deprived the less intelligent students of learning anything from him. *You* did that, not Mr. Mitchell."

Emma let out a frustrated breath and sat back hard against the seat. She was frustrated at how much Leader's disapproval pained her. She wished she could not care about her approval. If she simply did not care, she could do whatever she wanted and not blink an eye at the consequences. But she felt a gnawing need to earn Leader's good opinion, to deserve her praise. She searched for a way out, a way to turn this around, back on Mitchell's incompetence. She looked away out the window again.

"Hey!" Leader barked and slapped her. "Look at me!"

Emma's hand jumped to her face, protectively covering the place where Leader's hand had contacted with mild force. It hadn't been real force, or Emma would have cowered and wept.

"You are responsible for your education, Emma," Leader went on as if she had not just hit Emma in broad view of anyone who happened to be watching. "If you are not being challenged, it is your responsibility to change that. If you can't figure out how, that's what the Guild is for. Ilene could have helped you, or Julianne or Amos. Or me. Always me, Little Girl!

"Diligence is more than just industrious completion of tasks. It's taking responsibility for your actions. It's living up to your potential. You failed to live up to your potential this term and if there was any real justice in the Guild, I would make you stay here and live with the consequences until spring. It would serve you right to have to toady to Mr. Mitchell all year after you destroyed his semester."

Emma opened her mouth with a rebuttal, but Leader put up a warning hand.

"However, we are moving out of state next week and that means you get a lucky break and a new start at a new school." She leaned closer, grasping Emma's gaze in an intense, almost fevered ferocity. "When we get there, I am going to push you. You are too smart to be left to your own devices anymore. I will push you like you have never been pushed before. And mark my words, Emmalyn Stone: you had better live up to my expectations."

The rage that had been bubbling in the pit of her stomach started to claw its way out. Assisted by two days of hard, menial labor, of hopelessness and sadness over Scott leaving, and now with an ultimatum thrown down on her, the rage grew wild on pain from disappointing Leader. But it erupted in cattiness. "What if I don't?"

This time, Emma saw the slap coming and let it land, jarring all the way to her tailbone. Real force; tears sprang to her eyes.

"You will live up to my expectations." There was a crisp, vicious certainty in Leader's tone. She exited the car with her usual ferocious grace.

Chapter Nine

Emma lifted a trembling hand and pulled down the visor. Glaring back at her was a discernible pink handprint across the side of her face. It would probably bruise, and then she would have to try and explain it away all day. Handprints were so much harder to excuse than other bruises that could be from falls. For something like this, her best bet was to say it was from a failure to block in martial arts. She closed the visor with a frustrated snap. She had brought this upon herself, she knew, goading Leader with sass and disrespect. She had hoped somehow that angering her would make the rebuke less painful. It didn't. Now, Emma had a mark on her face matching the ache in her heart.

Leader did not rush her. Emma was grateful for the time to collect herself. She fought the urge to cry from pain and disappointment. It was all true, what Leader had said. In her very first class with Mitchell, she had known he was incompetent. At that point, she could have reported him to Leader or Amos. Certainly, she should have reported him after the first test, three weeks into the term. Emma knew he could offer her nothing when his test was a ludicrous multiple-choice far beneath her ability. She wrote essay-style answers all over it with a series of footnotes telling him exactly why his questions were mediocre, watered-down reflections of real questions. Mitchell was forced to give her a full score for the test. Anyone who glanced at it knew she fully understood the content. He had not been happy about it, though. His reaction told her exactly how unsuited he was to be her teacher. Instead of going to her superiors, though, she kept it to herself. She enjoyed the flavor of his dismay. She wanted more of it. But if Leader had even gotten one look at that test, she would have hauled her out of the class so fast that Mitchell would have been knocked over in the slipstream.

Emma grabbed her backpack from the floor. She initially felt relief when Leader announced she was coming to the school this morning, but now she was hollow. She knew all of this preventable trouble was her own fault. If she was Diligent, as Leader expected, she would be sitting next to Scott today on a road trip. Instead of barely scraping by with a below-average grade, Emma might have been able to complete the entire class in the first quarter. If she went to Mitchell with a concern that the content was too easy for her, he might have become her champion instead of her enemy. She could have transferred to Studies for Gifted Students and worked at her own pace, instead of sitting through a useless class all term. That would have been an appropriate venue for exploring her poetry, too. Leader might have encouraged her interest in writing, all if Emma did it at the right place and time.

Leader was right. She was always right. In this, Emma behaved badly. Looking back, she knew what happened. Complaining with Joel and the other students about Mitchell's lack of competence was fun. Instead of doing something about it, Emma was sucked into the pit of gossip, elated by the peer attention she attracted by fighting Mitchell. Her subsequent popularity was also an alluring charm. In the previous three schools, Emma was "that weird girl with no friends." She could not exist in normal society, no matter what Leader said. Emma liked being part of the group, laughing with the crowd instead of being the object of ridicule. She was intoxicated with her power to influence others. Looking back now, Emma could see that most of her pranks were designed more to gratify her need for power than to anger her teacher. Every time she suggested deliberately failing a quiz or requesting a lavatory pass, and the students agreed, she felt a satisfactory sense of power over them. She was a puppeteer, pulling strings and laughing when the obtuse puppets danced.

Shame came in a cascade, overpowering her anger, which slipped away quietly. She swallowed back her tears, fighting them hard. Leader's approval was intoxicating, too. More satisfying than all the dancing puppets in the world.

When Emma sufficiently stifled her regrets and repressed her tears, she exited the car. Leader waited on the curb, purse looped over her shoulder. She was the epitome of graceful patience in her six-inch heels and form-fitting skirt suit. Emma might be as smart as Leader claimed, but she always felt clumsy and stupid around Leader's superior elegance. She trudged up beside her.

"I'm sorry," Emma said icily, just managing to keep emotion from betraying how truly sorry she felt.

Leader nodded her acceptance of those words and their heavy implications. "Let's go."

She strode toward the entrance to the school. Emma followed a step behind, head down to keep other kids from seeing any evidence of Leader's handprint on her cheek.

Leader was not the only concerned parent waiting to see the dean. There were six others, at least three of who were accompanied by students in Emma's Chemistry class. Leader did not wait for much in her position, but for this she decided to be patient. She motioned Emma into a chair and went to speak to the secretary.

"Hey, General," said Max, one of Joel's friends. He walked away from his angry parents and dropped into the available seat beside her. "Your mom here to complain, too? Mine is furious about Friday's test. She thinks Mitchell should be suspended."

Emma almost winced when the words caught Leader's attention. She arched a reproachful eyebrow at Emma.

Emma answered Max once Leader's attention returned to the secretary behind the counter, "It's not his fault no one passed the test."

Max scoffed, "Yes, it is. We told him we would all fail if he didn't let you come back and take the test. The choice was his. He wanted to swing his dick around. Now look what he got in return." He nodded around at the waiting room full of people.

Emma felt a sliver of guilt. These were the kinds of sentiments she tried to attract all year. They made her feel important and alive. She felt no satisfaction at her success now, especially not with Leader in earshot.

"It was a stupid prank, and it's not his fault," Emma answered coldly, shooting Max a belittling stare. "You chose to fail that test. He should not have to suffer for your incompetence."

That silenced Max. He made a disgusted sound under his breath, then got up and returned to his mother's side. Leader took his vacated seat, saying, "That's not going to win you any friends."

Emma expelled a frustrated breath, "He's an idiot to blame Mitchell when he failed the test of his volition."

Leader gave a snort of laughter and patted her knee. "Em, he probably can't even spell 'volition.' You don't need friends like that."

"I know," Emma agreed, but she felt a pang of loss. These meaningless friendships were all she had to show for her time at this school.

They did not end up waiting long. When the dean walked out, escorting Joel and his father, he took one look at Emma and called her name. He ignored his secretary's attempts to show him a clipboard listing all the people ahead of her, people who had been waiting longer. He beckoned to Emma with a summoning wave of his hand and then turned and walked back down the hall to his office.

Leader rose with that deadly, seductive grace that defined her every movement. She crossed the office, attracting every eye in the place. Emma clunked along after her. She heard a lot of whispers and wondered if they were all about her. Some undoubtedly were. These parents could not harbor any love for a girl who ignited rebellion in their children.

"Dean Parish," Leader greeted when she found him waiting outside his office door. She offered him her hand and they shook. "Thank you for agreeing to see us. I see I chose the right day to initiate a meeting."

He answered sternly, "I would have called if you hadn't come, Mrs. Cole." He nodded at Emma. "Miss Cole."

Emma returned his salutation with a respectful nod and a quiet, "Dean Parish." She saw the look of surprise in his eyes at her subdued manner. She was usually sarcastic and boisterous when she crossed the threshold of his office. She had never taken any of his reprimands without at least a little pushback.

The dean's office was not empty when they entered. Mitchell sat in a chair beside the desk. His eyes glittered hatred when they landed on Emma. For a moment, they stared at one another in mutual loathing.

"Take a seat," the dean invited, cutting through the tension with his no-nonsense attitude. Emma went to her normal seat in front of his desk. Leader settled herself in the chair beside her.

"I understand there have been some disturbing developments in Chemistry this term," Leader began as the dean lowered himself into his own chair. "According to my daughter, she seems to have spearheaded a coup that resulted in bad rapport between Mr. Mitchell and his first period class."

The dean seemed relieved by Leader's accurate account. Emma was mortified and felt her face burn.

"The results run a bit deeper than bad rapport, I'm afraid. Apparently, after Miss Cole's office referral Friday for disruptive behavior and violent language, Mr. Mitchell's class refused to take his test unless she be permitted to return. As you may know, school attendance polices state that in order to take a test, a student must be in her seat at the time the test begins. Since Miss Cole's outburst in class prevented her from being present when the test began, she forfeited her privilege. Miss Cole and I already discussed this when I sent her to Skills after our conversation Friday."

Leader gave a slow consenting nod. "Yes. Emma explained the situation in . . ." She glanced at Mitchell significantly, ". . . great detail. Emma signed the school code of conduct when she enrolled. She knew her inappropriate behavior in class led to a disqualification from her Chemistry test. Emma's behavior has been appalling. I doubt anyone is here to argue that point."

"I am glad to hear you say that, Mrs. Cole," the dean replied with a sigh. "We all know how bright and talented your daughter is but rewarding her for her disruptions will never be beneficial."

"Forgive my saying so, Dean Parish, but my daughter is not *just* bright and talented. Emma is gifted. Mr. Mitchell's Chemistry class was never a challenge for her, and she unfortunately chose to waste her time in destructive ways." She shot an arched glance at Emma, who sat a little smaller in her chair. "What I would like to know is why her genius has been overlooked. Emma seems to think it has something to do with her gender. After her first test in this class, couldn't Mr. Mitchell see that Emma had been incorrectly placed?"

The dean seemed confused, so Mitchell jumped in, "It was very difficult to see her intelligence through her mischief and disruptions. For all I knew, she was using misbehavior to mask *incompetence.*"

Emma started forward in her chair, gasping out, "Incompetence? You had to have a Chemistry professor from the university score my first test, you duplicitous jackass."

"Emma!" Leader snapped, and when Emma looked at her, she saw the promised threat in her eyes. If provoked, Leader would discipline her right there in front of the dean and her teacher, and child services be damned. Emma dropped her gaze to her hands folded in her lap. She let out a frustrated breath and then forced herself to focus on maintaining a humble state of mind.

"Is this true?" the dean demanded of Mitchell.

He squirmed slightly. "Emma did not answer any of the questions with my multiple-choice options, Dean Parish. Instead, she wrote complicated formulas all over the test and, for a few of them, I did check the answers with my friend, Dr. Weinstein, at the university."

His admission gave Emma a smug sense of satisfaction, which she carefully hid behind her humility when she sensed Leader's gaze. The only reason Emma knew about the help from the university was because Joel overheard his conversation on the phone one morning while waiting in the hall for first bell.

"If she did not answer the questions as you intended, why did you not give Miss Cole a failing grade?" The dean was clearly embarrassed that his faculty had to go to the university to get help.

Mitchell did not respond to the dean's question because he did not want to have to admit that Emma's first test was the thrown gauntlet that started this pissing contest. It was a direct challenge to his intelligence—a challenge he lost, whether he admitted it to her or not. He scored her test like the others because he wanted her to believe he was smart enough to be her teacher when he absolutely wasn't.

The dean turned on Emma, "Miss Cole, when the test is multiple choice, you select A, B, C, or D and that is all. Do you understand me?"

Emma might have responded hotly if Leader did not place a firm hand on her knee right then.

"Yes, sir."

Leader nodded significantly toward Emma's backpack. Obediently, Emma removed her three weeks' worth of homework, bound appropriately, and handed them to her outstretched palm. Leader placed the homework on the desk in front of the dean.

"I was given to understand that Mr. Mitchell assigns homework on a regular basis but his due date is on test day. Emma said she attempted to turn in her homework, but Mr. Mitchell refused to accept it because she had been justifiably dismissed from class for disrespect. I can understand Mr. Mitchell's refusal to allow her to take the test, Dean Parish, but I simply cannot understand why he would refuse to accept her homework."

Mr. Mitchell, probably feeling the weight of his idiocy falling down around him, had the nerve to pretend confusion, "I never refused to accept Emma's homework."

Emma's hands clenched on her knees. Leader patted them firmly, encouraging her to keep her cool.

"Is that so?" Leader asked, pretending surprise right back at him. "Emma told me all about the words she said in class and her office referral. I find it strange to believe she would lie about that when she was very forthcoming about why she was sent to the dean." She shot Dean Parish a doubtful glance before returning her attention to the teacher. "Emma told me she went to you after class and tried to turn in her work, but you refused. Don't get me wrong, Mr. Mitchell, I can understand the desire to refuse Emma. I have raised this child. I know how trying she can be. I'm sure if I was in your position, nothing would give me greater satisfaction than flunking her, but I do not think by your school standards that Emma deserves to fail."

Mitchell looked at the dean, "Emma is in no danger of failing. She's very bright." Then, trying to save face, Mitchell said to Leader, "It was just a misunderstanding, Mrs. Cole. I thought she was talking about the test when she came to speak to me, not her homework."

Leader nodded, accepting his lies. She proffered the stack of homework. "I see. Then, I trust you will still accept the homework now, considering this misunderstanding."

"Of course," Mitchell said, taking the homework from her hands with a forced smile.

The dean leaned forward, folding his arms on his desk. "Miss Cole," he addressed Emma firmly, drawing her eyes. "I hope you know that your tomfoolery in Chemistry this term has been the source of a great amount of contention between the students, their parents, and the faculty. I am led to understand that your friends deliberately failed their test as a tribute to your absence from it. For many students, this means they *will* receive a failing grade for the term and, without a good deal of work, they may have to completely retake the class. You are a gifted student, so you do not run the same risk, but you ought to know that your influence has consequences."

Emma drew a breath to calm herself and not excite Leader's anger with her response, "With all due respect, Dean Parish, I don't think you can blame me for the actions of the other students. I was in your office with you when they staged their demonstration. I had nothing to do with it."

The dean nodded once as if he agreed, but his answer was, "I can't really be sure you didn't have anything to do with it, Miss Cole. There were a great many events this semester that seemed to revolve around you. Mr. Mitchell and other faculty members assign blame to you even though I can find no proof of your involvement. For instance, there is no definitive proof that you were part of the group of students who moved Mr. Mitchell's car into the theater classroom. The four students who could be found directly involved were suspended for their part in the prank, though none of them ever admitted you were a part of it, but you should be aware that your name seems to be batted around a lot."

Leader tucked her tongue into her cheek and sat back in her chair. When Emma looked at her, Leader's only response was to raise her brows. She may as well have scolded her out loud, but her silence was effective.

Emma let out a frustrated breath about the unfair accusation. She did not mind taking credit for things she did, but she honestly had nothing to do with the Great Test Failure of last Friday.

"So . . . what? You think I encouraged his class to mutiny on the *off chance* that I would get thrown out of the test?"

"Miss Cole," Mitchell said in his insufferable condescending tone, "I would not put it past you to deliberately violate the language code in order to be put out of the test and excite your peers to mischief."

Emma trembled from the attempt to control her anger. "What good would that have done, Mr. Mitchell? I could have aced your test after a brain aneurism. And—if your memory doesn't conveniently fail you this time—do you remember what you said that prompted my violation of the language code?"

The dean put up his hand to stop their argument, "Miss Cole, there is never a good reason to use the language you used Friday in class. I want you to understand that I have no evidence that you conspired with your classmates about this test. But whether you did or you did not, they all seem to think they have your blessing and your encouragement to flout Mr. Mitchell's authority. Their actions are their own, but you should take care when you place yourself in a leadership role. You do have some responsibility when your followers make poor choices."

Emma drew a long, furious breath, "I don't see how—"

Leader interrupted her, "You will."

The tone of her voice did not seem to indicate any threats. It was simply a promise based on Leader's superior knowledge of leadership. Mitchell and the dean, however, seemed to see Leader's promise as a threat from a mother to her child, similar to "just wait until your father gets home."

Emma dropped her gaze to her hands again. It wouldn't do to say something that actually warranted a threat from Leader.

"I am only bringing this to your attention because you still have several years at this school, and I would hate to see you wasting your intellectual capabilities in Skills," the dean went on. "Because I assure you, any other outbursts, pranks or disrespect will be handled swiftly and firmly by this office. Whatever your aversion to Mr. Mitchell, he is your teacher, and he deserves your attention and respect."

Emma pressed her lips together to keep the nasty words that threatened to tumble out at bay. She looked at Leader and widened her eyes. She did not need to ask her to intervene; the woman was already staring the two men across the desk with menace in her eyes.

"Is there some truth to my daughter's accusation that you think she is not qualified to go into a science career?"

Mitchell's eyes betrayed him, though he could pretend innocence all he wanted. When Leader saw the man blanch at her words, she turned her dangerous attention on the dean, "I do not excuse Emma's misbehavior in the slightest, Dean Parish, but I think you should know that her complaints against Mr. Mitchell have given me cause for alarm. Emma is on the road to an Ivy League school. The plan is for her to study physics. She told me that her teacher insists she ought to instead spend her time preparing for childrearing and housekeeping. Or was it flight attending, Emma?"

Emma glared up at Mitchell, "All of it. Earlier in the term, he suggested that waitress positions and acting jobs were good options for someone with my parasitical need for others' approval."

"I was joking," Mitchell shot back, holding up a hand to forestall any other accusations. "And I think you know I was joking, Miss Cole."

Leader glanced aside at Emma to see if that was true. Emma nodded, allowing it to have been a joke. It didn't matter. He insulted Emma's intellect and suggested she was a parasite; Leader was going to eat him alive.

"You *joked* that my daughter should become an actor?" Leader did not even attempt to conceal her contempt. "Were you also *joking* when you told her she could never make any contributions to science because she suffers from penis envy and menstruation?" She did not wait for him to answer, "Because I have to tell you, if you're so bound and determined to be a jokester, maybe you have selected the wrong profession. I understand there is always a need for clowns at birthday parties, but I most certainly won't have one teaching my children."

Emma felt a gigantic wave of satisfaction roll over her, but Leader grasped her hand in a crushing grip before she could enjoy it. She nearly cried out but instead dropped her gaze and attempted to be humble again.

Mitchell spluttered for an opening, but Leader pounded on, "If my daughter wishes to get career advice, she goes to the school counselor, not to her inept Chemistry teacher who cannot even grade her tests without help. And while my daughter's behavior is in no way excusable, I would think that a grown man would have more presence of mind than to engage in a battle of wits with a sixteen-year-old child. And if Emma were just an ordinary 'childbearing, housekeeping' kind of girl, she would not have come up so grossly in the lead."

The dean sat as still as fencepost while Mitchell desperately attempted to find words to defend himself. Leader turned on the dean, "I entrusted my daughter to your care. How is it that this mischief has gone on all term, and I am only finding out about it now? If her teacher could not even grade her first test, why was I not notified immediately that she was too advanced for his class? If Emma has had more than one office referral, why was I not notified?" For this, she squeezed Emma's hand again. This time, she let out a whimper. Leader was going to destroy her once they were alone.

"It is not our policy to notify parents of office referrals unless we require parental support of our decisions," the dean explained, but Leader would have none of that.

"Do not quote the book at me, Dean Parish. Were you or were you not aware that my daughter had become a menace?"

Dean Parish drew a weighted breath, "To be perfectly honest, Mrs. Cole, I was *not* aware of the full extent of this situation until just this morning."

Leader raised her brows in expectation, "Then can you explain to me why I should continue to trust your school with the care of my children? If you are not even aware of an impending disaster caused by your incompetent educators and their mischievous students, how can I be assured my children will be safe here?"

The dean rose to his full seated height in indignation, "Mrs. Cole, your daughter may well have been the ringleader of this disaster."

Leader sat forward and sneered, "Oh, I'm confident that Emmalyn is the ringleader. I'm also certain that she was responsible for the car in the theater classroom, the case of the missing chairs, and—my personal favorite—the urine in the water samples." Leader held up a hand when the dean attempted to make a furious rebuttal, "And if you think my daughter is going to slide by with her self-satisfied hide unscathed, I can readily assure you that she *will not.*"

Emma winced at the implications of that assurance.

"Boredom is such an overused excuse for misbehavior. Emma is too smart to turn to mischief just because she's bored. I promise you, she is the one I will ultimately hold responsible for not disclosing this long before now. But you, sir—*both* of you—have my phone number. Why, if she was suspected of everything but bringing the ceilings down, was I not notified?"

Emma managed to free her hand from Leader's iron grip during the silence that followed her accusatory query. Mitchell sat tall and straight as ever but sweat dripped down his face and his hands clenched and unclenched on the arms of his chair. The dean drew a heavy breath.

"I'm going to be completely honest with you, Mrs. Cole."

"I would appreciate that."

His mouth hardened, but he went on in his respectful tone, "When the pranks were first brought to my attention last month, the day the chairs went missing, there was no way I could prove Emma had anything to do with it. Even the ransom note was not in her handwriting. In fact, I could have sworn it was the French teacher's handwriting."

Emma desperately attempted to hide her smile at that brilliant stroke of genius. Leader kicked her ankle and Emma kept her eyes down.

"Mr. Mitchell was certain Emma was responsible, but without any type of proof, I could hardly accuse her. I did speak to the entire class, and then in our next assembly the entire high school, but apparently no one had any information to which they were willing to admit. Mr. Mitchell never said why he thought Emma was responsible, and without further information, I could do nothing more.

"The next I heard anything was when he called me because he was glued to his desk chair. He was certain Emma placed an adhesive on the chair so when he sat down his pants adhered and wouldn't let go. Of course, no one had seen her do it, and when directly asked, she said, 'He's a Chemistry teacher. Someone would have to be out of their mind to try a trick like this when he can so easily extract himself.'" Emma squeezed her eyes shut when she felt Leader turn to look at her with eyes on fire.

"I took that Emma would not have attempted the prank and I looked elsewhere for a culprit. Then, when his car was moved to the theatre classroom, Mr. Mitchell again suggested Miss Cole was the responsible party, but the only boys who ever came forward never admitted to her complicity." He shook his head. "You must forgive me, Mrs. Cole, for not notifying you then. I have learned from painful experience that parents do not react well when their children are accused of crimes for which no proof can be procured. Mr. Mitchell was acting under my direction with regards to contacting you. I encouraged him to have some proof ready at hand when he approached you with accusations. If Emma had been innocent, you would not have appreciated his attack of her character with no foundation."

Leader nodded as if she understood, but she said, "You are accustomed to working with parents for whom you have to walk on eggshells. These are the same sort of parents who would rather pretend their children are innocent than deal with the very real fact of life that children misbehave and must be punished. While I resent being clumped into a category with those types of parents, I can certainly understand your position. Besides, as I said before, it is Emma who must ultimately answer for keeping information from me." Emma winced again.

Leader tapped the desktop in front of Mitchell and said, "Emma will not trouble you anymore, Mr. Mitchell. However, I do expect a real and honest grade from you that illustrates your judgment of her academic achievement this term."

Mitchell nodded, apparently relieved. "She could have had an A with her eyes shut tight. But now, without the final test score, she may very well end up with a B."

The dean sat forward and in a soothing tone said, "I am sure there is a way we can find some extra credit for her to do to bring her score up. I would hate for this class to jeopardize her chance to attend an Ivy League school."

Leader waved his suggestion away with the flick of her wrist, "Not necessary. If Emma loses her chance to attend an Ivy League University because of the way she spent this term, I suppose her years at a state college will teach her not to waste my time and her education." She looked at Emma with the full frightening mantle of Leadership bearing down around her. "That would be a truly painful test in the necessity of Diligence."

Emma flushed from fear and embarrassment. But she whispered, "Yes, ma'am."

Then Leader was suddenly on her feet, "If there is nothing else, I have to be leaving. Shall I take Emma with me, or can I trust you to deal smartly with her here?"

The dean rose, "I'm not sure what she will get out of class today after everything . . ." He glanced at Emma huddling in her seat. "And if your assurances of her complicity in so many pranks can be believed, she very likely will be suspended."

Emma's eyes slid closed. Despite the fact that this was to be her very last week at the school, suspension would not be handled lightly in the Guild.

"Very well," Leader snapped. "Come along, Emma."

She stumbled to get around the chair to follow Leader from the room, but Leader stopped on the threshold. She presented the room to Emma with her hand, "Do you have anything you want to say to your dean or your teacher before we go?"

Emma didn't want to say anything, but Leader's question was as good as an order. Emma said, "I'm sorry I disrupted your class and your school."

Before either man could answer, Leader grabbed her by the elbow and pushed her out of the office. At the front office counter, she snapped, "I trust Emma's scores will be emailed to me this weekend."

The secretary assured her that she would receive an electronic copy and a physical copy would go home with her student or arrive in the mailbox, depending on the request in her enrollment papers. Leader thanked the woman then walked out. Everyone else in the office watched Emma and her mother leave the office. None of those kids could claim she was their fearless General now that she tripped along in her mother's furious vise-like grip. Humiliation and the looming threat of punishment made her timid as a field mouse.

Leader's fierce stride did not slow until they got back to the parking lot. She waved away the parking cop who stared suspiciously at the handicapped hanger in her windshield. Then she released Emma with a slight toss toward the passenger side, "Get in."

Emma tossed her backpack into the backseat, but she climbed into the passenger front and buckled. She sat small and kept her eyes forward as Leader reversed out of the parking spot. She peeled from the parking lot with what felt like reckless haste.

"Emma, I swear to God I had better never have to come see your dean ever again," Leader snarled when they were under way. Emma gave a mute nod of agreement. It seemed to be the right answer. Leader did not speak again for several miles. When she did speak at last, her tone was not as harsh.

"Regretting asking for my help?"

Emma replied truthfully, "Yes. Although, I don't think the dean would have given me the time of day without you, and Mitchell would almost certainly never have accepted my homework."

"You didn't actually glue him to his chair, Emma?" Leader asked in a skeptical tone that could not quite hide her respect for the prank.

"I did," Emma admitted.

Leader shook her head, so Emma hurried on with, "I forgot about it, Leader. I swear I would have told you otherwise." When Leader only shot her an arched look, Emma dared a smile. "He had to call the front office from his cell phone. We were all dismissed to Skills because they had to cut his pants off of him and send him home to change. From what I understand, he wore green P.E. shorts to get to his car. Someone said they got a picture and would share it, but I never saw it."

Leader shook her head, "You live in your smug satisfaction as long as you can, Emma. I have a really fancy idea in mind for your next school."

Emma did not like the sound of that. "What? Military school?"

Leader gave a derisive snort, "That cakewalk? I think not."

Emma groaned, certain she knew what Leader intended. "Not homeschooling! Please, please don't school me at home. I swear I will demonstrate appropriate Diligence in school from now on."

Leader's musing smile gave way to a head shake, "I'll hold that in reserve if I ever have to visit your school again."

Emma promised, "You won't."

"I guess your next move in this elaborate chess game will determine what happens to you." Emma's only response was a groan.

Five days later, after a week of Leader's brand of homeschooling, Emma made herself the promise that she would never again give a school any reason to suspend her. One week of this academic workload was onerous, but several years would be unbearable. The work was hard enough by itself, but it was made worse by Leader's exactingly high standards, Adam's snide comments, and Piper's constant amusement at her predicament. Emma could hardly wait to get to the new Guild House and enroll in a new school. She would have endured Mitchell all day every day over Adam's acidic words and Leader's unquenchable thirst for twenty-five-page essays.

"Emma!" Leader called from her office Friday afternoon. "Come in here."

Assuming Leader had more notes for her on her latest unsatisfactory paper, Emma rose from her corner of the library with an exhausted sigh. Around her were stacks of books, academic journals, and a laptop with several academic sites pulled up so she could toggle from page to page as needed. She was covered in highlighter ink and sure she smelled like encyclopedias.

Emma ignored Adam's derogatory snort as she passed him making dinner in the kitchen. She took the short hall to Leader's office, leaned in, and asked, "Yes, Leader?"

Leader stood beside her printer as it spat out a single sheet into her hand. She looked over shoulder at Emma, then turned and proffered the sheet to her. Emma stepped forward with a bemused frown and opened her hand to receive the page. She flipped it over and scanned it, her heart pounding. This was her term report, printed from a PDF file emailed to Leader. Her eyes scanned the scores, seeing 104 percent, 112 percent, 102 percent, 109 percent in her classes, and including her most impressive 128 percent in English. How she had managed that, she didn't know. But it was to her Chemistry grade her eyes locked on. A dousing chill ran from her head to her toes at the horrifying sight: 90.2 percent.

Her eyes shot up to look at Leader, who had moved around behind her and shut the office door. "Leader, I . . ." but there was nothing she could say. In all honesty, Mitchell was probably being very generous since her academic achievements in his class were virtually nonexistent. She had learned almost nothing and if that was the rubric for honest scoring, Emma deserved closer to a D. But this would do for her as well as any D.

"You failed to achieve a proper, Diligent grade in Chemistry," Leader announced.

Emma dropped the paper onto Leader's desk and held up a hand in her defense. She tried vainly to change the course of this conversation, "It's still an A, Leader. I passed the class."

Leader reached into the top drawer of a decorative wooden cabinet next to the door and pulled out a length of thin leather cording. Her eyes never left Emma's. "What constitutes a passing grade in my Guild, Number Eleven?"

Emma took an involuntary step back as Leader approached her, but she answered, "Ninety-six percent, Leader, but—"

Leader held up a firm hand to stall the argument and asked again, "What constitutes a passing grade for *you*?"

Emma had to tighten her knees to keep from backing away any farther. "Ninety-six percent is the acceptable passing grade in the Guild; but for me, nothing less than 100 percent will be tolerated."

"Your failure was due to your lack of Diligence," Leader agreed firmly. "A lack of Diligence is a punishable offense in my Guild." Anything could be, really, Emma thought, but the truth was that for her there was no worse crime to commit. Her entire time as Number Eleven was to learn and to demonstrate Diligence. This term was a colossal failure.

Leader's words certainly didn't bring her any comfort as she cracked the cording against itself in a menacing way, "Checkmate."

Chapter Ten

Emma tossed the last bag into the Charger, and then stepped back to look up at the Guild House. With the exception of her last twenty-four hours or so, this had been a nice place to live. She would miss it. This house was away from neighbors and on a substantial piece of property. It had allowed the Guild to be more themselves at home. That was a relief always, even when it also had painful consequences for Emma's misbehavior.

Even though she would miss this house, she was eager to get going. Their destination was far away, in Missouri. Emma had no idea what was in Missouri that generated a need for Guild presence, but it didn't matter. Leader could move them to the moon without argument from her minions.

Adam emerged from the open garage and gave her a hearty slap on the backside, "All done?"

Emma cried out, "God, Adam! You know Leader beat me yesterday! Could you possibly *not* hit me?"

He did not even have the decency to hide his satisfied smile.

"Adam," Leader called from the shadowy interior of the garage. "Do not lay a hand on her again without my express permission." There was no need to attach threats. It was never a good idea to disobey a direct order from Leader.

Adam gave a mean smile to Emma but raised his voice, "Yes, Leader!"

Piper came out through the garage carrying a laptop case and several suitcases which she deposited into Leader's Volvo. "I think that's everything, Leader. When Waylon stops putting on his makeup, we can leave."

Waylon joined them then and shot Piper a dirty look for her teasing. He wasn't wearing makeup, but as always, he looked like he was on his way to the theater.

"Do I get to drive?" he asked. He ignored Piper's scornful scoff, turning his attention to Leader.

Leader emerged from the garage and pressed the panel on the side of the doorway to close the garage and lock it.

"I don't care. You can decide. All of Adam's things are in the Charger because I assume he wants to drive. I'm taking the Porsche, so that leaves the Volvo to you or Piper."

"Dibs," Piper announced, holding her hand out for the keys. Leader tossed them to her. Waylon couldn't very well argue with her since she had a higher standing in the Guild. When Emma grabbed her bag from the front seat of the Charger and moved toward the Volvo, Waylon intercepted her.

"I'm not riding with Adam." He pointed toward the Charger imperiously, and then raised his voice, "I'm with you, Piper."

Piper, already climbing into the front seat of the car, ignored them all. Emma's shoulders slumped as she watched Adam climb into the driver front seat of the Charger. "You coming?"

Emma looked between him and Leader, trying to decide which would be worse. In her sour mood, neither of them was a preferred companion.

Leader made the decision for her, ordering "Start with him," and pointing toward Adam. "Be his copilot until the first stop. I'm sure Piper will move to the Charger as soon as Waylon complains long enough about her driving."

Settled, although unhappy about it, Emma got into the passenger seat of the Charger and sat gingerly. It did no good. Her backside and her legs throbbed ceaselessly.

Adam said nothing as they followed Leader's Porsche through the city. When they reached the interstate and the open road, he flipped the radio on. Emma could count on one hand the number of times she listened to the radio. Leader considered radio, television, and most internet sites to be a waste of time. She claimed music was distracting. It *was* distracting, Emma realized. Listening to the forbidden music took her mind off the pain from Leader's discipline the night before. She settled back to listen to the music, though she wasn't sure she understood what the song was talking about.

"Does sex have a smell?" she asked Adam after a few minutes.

Adam snorted and asked incredulously, "What?"

Emma pointed toward the radio panel. "'I smell sex and candy,'" she quoted the confusing lyrics. "What does it mean?"

He shrugged, "Hell if I know. People smell, sweat smells, human fluids have a smell. I suppose those things combined smell like sex. But I'm pretty sure he's being philosophical. The girl is pretty; he smells the idea of sex."

"And candy?"

"Don't be annoying!" He turned the music up a little louder.

After a few more minutes, she shouted, "What kind of music is this? Country?"

He turned the dial down and asked her, "Are you serious?" and for a wonder, he asked it without any kind of scorn. He corrected that straightaway when he went on, "Of course, it's not country. This is what we call alternative, and it's about as far from country as country is from opera. You seriously need to get your license, kid, so you can drive around and find out for yourself. This song is by Marcy Playground, one of the greatest bands of all time." He turned the music up again but after a second turned it down and said, "If you end up liking country, we can't be friends anymore." He turned the music up.

Emma wasn't concerned about that threat. Although, if Adam thought they were friends right now, she had to wonder how he treated his enemies.

Emma did not hear her phone ring in her pocket. She shifted at one point in her chair and happened to feel it vibrating. She did not hesitate to shut off the music when she saw the caller was Leader.

"This is Emma."

"Tell Adam I tried to call him several miles back and to shut off his infernal music," Leader snapped furiously. Emma put the phone on speaker partway through so he could hear the order for himself. "Tell him to take the next exit. We're stopping for fuel and so I can teach him what the words 'speed limit' mean in context to his driving privileges."

Adam rolled his eyes but said, "Which gas station, Leader? Right or left?"

"Left," and she disconnected the call. Adam retrieved his phone from his pocket and put it on a holding mat on the dashboard, then promptly turned his music back on. Emma reached forward to turn it off, horrified by his careless disobedience, but Adam slapped her hand away.

"If she calls, I'll see the phone light up. Get yours up here, too." He grabbed her phone and added it next to his on the mat.

"But Leader said—"

Adam slapped the music off and grabbed the front of Emma's shirt in a firm grip. "You have nothing to worry about, so stop worrying."

She tried unsuccessfully to break his hold on her shirt. "What do you mean, I have nothing to worry about?"

"She can't do anything to you for *my* disobedience. *I* am driving, Emma! And when I drive, I listen to music. So, keep your panties on." He shoved her away and turned the music back up. Pressing his foot down on the gas, he accelerated to pass seven or eight other vehicles. Emma leaned to see the speedometer, but Adam shoved her back to her seat. "Ninety-five," he supplied with snark in his tone. The posted speed limit was sixty-five. She swallowed in near panic.

The exit jumped into view and Adam swerved between cars to make it barely in time. Several cars honked their horns, but he pretended not to notice. As he pulled into the fueling station, he turned his music off and cruised up to the pump. He hopped out of the car. Emma climbed out, too, legs shaky. She was glad for a reason to be off her aching rear end, and even more glad to be out of the deathtrap. Adam leaned against the pump, not refueling. Like Emma, his only money was emergency cash, and they weren't allowed to use that unless it was a *real* emergency.

They were there several minutes before Leader's Porsche cruised in and parked in front of them. Immediately after, the Volvo blocked them in from behind. Leader leapt from her car and slammed the door behind her as she rounded on Adam. She smacked his head and then his arms when he lifted his hands to ward her off.

"What do you think Self-Control means? God! If you get arrested, I'm going to let you rot in there."

Adam backed away from the pump and Leader's furious blows, complaining, "I'm fine. The kid is fine. Relax."

Leader pursued him, pointing a finger in his face, "Don't you condescend to me, Adam Stone! Don't even try it." Without looking around, she aimed her finger at Piper. "You're driving the Charger. And if Adam even looks at you wrong, your slap him silly."

Piper passed her keys over to Waylon nonchalantly and said, "Yes, Leader." She pushed at Adam's shoulder, "Fuel up, boy."

Emma gratefully collected her belongings and moved them to the Volvo. In her estimation, Waylon was the most preferable of the three drivers. Several minutes later, they were under way again, but this time the three vehicles made a caravan down the roadway, Leader's Porsche in the lead and the Charger in the rear.

She was somewhat surprised when Waylon asked for her phone and placed it on the panel, so he could turn on his music. It was not as loud as Adam's had been, but it surprised her that even Waylon was willing to challenge Leader's authority.

"What kind of music is this?" she asked, aware right away that it was very different from Adam's.

"The greats," he answered with a beaming smile. "Big Band. Sinatra." And then he sang along for three hours.

When they reached the hotel for the night, Emma was extremely tired, pained, and cranky. Waylon had been a good enough companion, but she wanted sleep more than anything else now. When Adam approached her from behind and smacked her across the bottom again, Emma almost attacked him. Piper caught her arm to stop her from violating the

Aggression Compact—the rules that governed their daily Martial Arts training.

"Nope," Piper warned quietly. She held her in place until Adam, smirking, stalked out of range. "Let's get you a pain pill," the red-haired woman suggested in a soft tone.

When Adam walked through the doors into the hotel, Leader grabbed him and slammed him against the wall. She snarled, "What did I say to you?"

Emma swerved around them and sneaked into the restroom to avoid hearing the rest of Leader's rebuke.

The two adjoining hotel rooms were nice enough, if not as nice as she was accustomed to. Still, she ate the room service Leader ordered and went to bed after a half-hearted effort in her diary.

"I think she's sick," she heard Leader saying as she awoke. Indeed, Emma thought Leader must be right. Her head was throbbing, and her mouth was dry. She opened her eyes to see Leader seated beside her on the bed, phone up to her ear.

"I don't know what it is, Julianne. That's why I called you." Despite her harsh tones, it was a soothing hand Leader ran down Emma's face. She pulled the phone away from her mouth and said, "You okay? I sent Waylon and Piper for some real food."

Then she pulled the phone back to her mouth, "I do not know what is wrong, Julianne! I only want to know if I should take her to a doctor or if she can wait for you."

"Let's just go," Emma croaked out, but when she tried to sit up, Leader pushed her back down and pointed a firm finger at her.

"Stay there!" Leader stood up and paced away. To Julianne, she said, "I know she has a fever. I can feel it. I don't know where she would have caught anything that could infect her! She's been at home for the whole week. I think I should just fly her in. Then you can look at her in a few hours. I would feel better about that . . . Hang on." She paced back to the bedside and looked into Emma's eyes. Then she lifted Emma's shirt to look at her chest before Emma could knock her hands away in annoyance. "Yes, she has spots. What do you mean? Scott has it, too? What is it? I thought we had a vaccine for that . . . Okay. Well, if she can't fly, maybe I should keep her here until she feels better . . . A *week*? No, I can't wait that long. Fine. Fine, Julianne. I'll call you in a few hours."

She hung up the phone and sat down beside Emma. "Julianne seems to think you may have the chicken pox."

"I thought that was a kid disease. Didn't I ever have it when I was a kid?"

Leader shook her head, "No. It's very rare for Guild members to get common sicknesses. Since this struck two of you, I'm inclined to believe it was engineered specifically for the Guild. That means it might have some nasty surprises."

"Who would do that?" Emma asked, furious at the idea. She had been the center of the plot of a rival guild before. She did not relish the idea of it happening again.

"Any number of people," Leader answered unconcernedly. Then, when she seemed to see Emma was distressed, she added, "It could be a normal strain. Julianne is checking. You and Scott never had the chicken pox and you were both vaccinated, so it shouldn't be as bad as it could be."

"I just want to go," Emma complained. "Can we just go?"

Leader nodded, "After breakfast. You'll ride with me."

Chapter Eleven

When Emma awoke next, she was in a car being gently shaken by Leader. "Em, get up. Come on." When she sat up, she saw they were in an airport unloading zone. She looked bewildered at Leader, who was handling their few bags. Emma climbed out of the car and had the sudden overwhelming urge to scratch. She looked down her shirt and saw that she most certainly had some kind of disease. There were several red spots on her skin, like tiny, blistery pimples.

Leader leaned into the Porsche and spoke to Piper, who was driving. "Just stop at the hotels marked on the map, stay on the route, and you should be there tomorrow night. And I'm serious that you use whatever force is necessary to keep Adam in line. I won't have him getting into a car accident simply because he enjoys the freedom of the road." She tossed in a manila envelope, like the one Julianne had last week. "Use this to get rid of any locals. Stay out of trouble."

"Yeah. See you in a couple days." Piper cruised away before Leader had a chance to say another word.

Leader gave Emma a sympathetic look that in no way went with her snapped order, "Don't scratch!" when Emma ran her fingernails across her stomach. "Come on." She slid an arm across Emma's shoulders and led her into the airport.

Emma had never been to a commercial airport before. The airport was a place even busier than school. People of every race and class walked around everywhere toting luggage on carts or pulling it behind them by built-in handles. They were alone or in groups, laughing and crying. Among them were airport workers in uniforms, pushing people in wheelchairs, driving little motorized vehicles, or just plain walking around. The noise level was almost unbearable, but no one seemed to notice. Emma's head pounded fiercely.

"Come on," Leader urged her, walking toward a ticketing counter. Emma pulled her suitcase behind her as she saw others doing and kept up with Leader's quick pace.

"May I help you?" asked the young man behind the counter, wearing a shirt with an airline logo on the front.

Leader passed him an ID, "My daughter and I have tickets to Springfield, Missouri."

"All right. Checking any bags today?"

"No. Just carry-ons."

The man tapped at his keyboard for a moment then handed Leader a couple of boarding passes.

"Enjoy your flight, Mrs. White," he said. He nodded to Emma, "Miss White." Emma was confused by the new alias, but said nothing.

Emma groaned when Leader turned to walk away. Leader slowed her pace. "I'm sorry, Little Girl. This was the fastest way to get you to Julianne. I couldn't wait for the jet. It's parked in Pakistan at the moment." She touched Emma's face. "How are you feeling? You look peaky."

Emma did not answer. She was too busy watching the workers who strode past in various uniforms. "How do they stand working here? It is so loud, and there are so many people everywhere. That would kill me."

Leader put a hand on her shoulder and squeezed it gently, "You will never have to work in an airport. Come on."

The security checkpoint was a disaster for which Emma was not well-prepared. While waiting in line, Leader whispered instructions to her about removing shoes and placing her phone into its own tray to go through the screening, but when they finally got up to the front, Emma had a hard time remembering what to do, especially with her head cloudy from exhaustion and sickness.

"Hi," she said to the security officer. But he said nothing, just nodded his head toward the conveyor belt. Leader grabbed Emma's bag and put it on the belt. She helped Emma remove her phone from her pocket and put it into one of the dirty white bowls. She motioned Emma to remove her shoes, which she then placed into a tray and slid it onto the conveyor. The security man waved Emma through a machine that whirred around her with dizzying sounds. She closed her eyes to keep from vomiting or falling over. When Emma stepped through to the other side, the security officer waved her past him. Emma moved to the end of the conveyor belt where her belongings were just coming out of the X-ray machine. She hauled her bag off the conveyor belt, slid her phone back into her pocket, and retrieved her shoes. The sound of alarms buzzing caught her attention and turned her back around.

Leader had walked through the machines and set the alarms off.

"Are you wearing anything metal, like earrings or a belt buckle?" asked the security man

Leader looked very bored as she answered, "Yes." She handed him her ID. He scanned it once with his eyes, and then with a scanner attached to his belt. His eyes widened. He stared at the ID more closely. After blinking several times, he cleared his throat and nodded at her. He choked, "Go ahead!" He did not bother to search her person.

Leader retrieved her shoes and luggage and walked to the benches where she could put her shoes back on. Emma followed.

Emma asked quietly, "What happened? Do you have a metal plate in your leg or something? Why didn't he search you?"

Leader was bent to pull her shoe on, but she came up giving Emma a serious, studying look. "No, Emma. I am carrying my gun." Emma felt shock rock her to her core. The shoe in her hand dropped to the ground and for a moment, the world spun. As soon as everything settled, she bent to retrieve her shoe, breaking eye contact with Leader.

"Isn't that against the law?" Emma whispered at her shoes, keeping her flushed face down. She had always known that Leader carried weapons. All the members of the Senior Guild did, and some of the others, too. She had never imagined they could get away with carrying on a commercial flight. "I thought people weren't allowed as much as a sharp hairpin on commercial flights."

"That is true. But I am not like most people. Come along." She stood up, grabbed the handle on her luggage, and walked away. Emma struggled into her other shoe and hurried to follow.

She said nothing more about her discomfort.

When they arrived at the gate, there were no passengers anywhere around. The woman at the door reached for their boarding passes, which Leader handed to her with a smile.

"Mrs. White, welcome," the woman said with a significant tone of respect. "Have a great flight."

"Thank you so much," Leader answered, flashing her perfect smile. She led the way down the hallway to the plane. Emma could tell this was not a permanent hallway. It made her nervous to think about, but she attempted to copy Leader's nonchalant, dangerous grace.

Once in the plane, a flight attendant loaded their luggage into an overhead bin and showed them to their seats in front of the curtain separating first class from coach. They were seated next to one another, Emma near the window.

"You're fidgeting," Leader said.

"I'm trying not to scratch," Emma replied. And she was nervous. She had heard about commercial planes, seen pictures, talked about them at school, but she had never been on one before. She felt nervous and confined.

Leader studied Emma as if she had never seen her before. Finally, she smiled a private smile that Emma knew she could not ask about and ordered, "Buckle up." Emma immediately reached for the ends of her seatbelt and slid them together. Leader tightened the strap so the belt fit snugly across Emma's lap.

"Good afternoon, ladies and gentlemen," a voice said through the overhead speakers. "This is your captain speaking. We will be underway shortly. Thank you for your patience."

Emma looked at Leader, "What are we being patient for?"

Leader sat back against the seat, "*We* are not. The rest of the passengers are. They were holding the plane for us."

"Is that normal?" Emma whispered, already deciding it was not.

"It is for us," she answered. "I, Leader, arranged this flight, Emma; who are they to leave without us?"

Emma had no idea how to answer that, so she chose not to. She settled back against the seat and looked out the side window.

The flight attendants talked about how to fasten seatbelts and what to do in case of a water landing. Leader and everyone else in first class ignored them, but Emma could not. She retrieved the instruction booklet from the seatback pocket and followed along, identifying plane exits and learning about oxygen masks. Leader watched her from the corner of her eye.

When the plane lurched into motion, Emma clutched the armrests of her seat and watched through the window as the airport moved away. They did some taxiing which gave Emma time to get used to the movements of the plane, and then they sped up on a runway. The plane moved faster and faster, pressing Emma back against her seat. Then the nose of the plane pulled up, and they were in the air! Emma had the sensation that her stomach was dropping. She squeezed her eyes shut. Leader placed a hand on her knee, and when Emma peeked at her, Leader gave her a reassuring smile.

Emma was happy when the ascent was finished, and the plane leveled out. After only a couple of minutes, she gave in to her exhaustion and fell asleep.

Emma awoke when Leader called her name and shook her softly. She had slept through the entire flight and the landing of the plane. Now the first-class passengers were preparing to disembark. Emma looked in confusion at her hands that were now covered in white socks taped in place with electrical tape. Leader arched her brows.

"I was serious when I said no scratching."

"I was asleep," Emma argued. She held out her hands. "Take these off. I won't scratch."

Leader took out a pocketknife and cut the socks off. Emma again had the disturbing recollection of Leader passing through security armed. Some of the other passengers noticed the knife and pointed it out to a flight attendant. But the flight attendant gave Leader one brief smile and stifled the passenger's fears with a simple, "She's a federal marshal."

That was a lie, Emma knew. In order to be a marshal, she had to work for the government, and Emma was pretty sure Leader worked for herself. But the other passengers watched warily from then on.

Leader rose to her feet and waited impatiently for the cabin door to open. When she stepped into the aisle and said, "Make way," people moved to the side. She pushed Emma ahead of her.

This airport was small, for which Emma was grateful. She only had a short distance to walk before she saw Amos waving to them from behind a security gate. He took Leader's bags and said, "Hi, sicky."

"I'm fine," Emma said. When her hand lifted to scratch, Leader pulled electrical tape from her pocket in a threatening way. "I won't scratch."

"Yeah, you seem fine," Amos said sarcastically. "Come on. I'm parked right out front."

"In the fire lane?" Leader asked.

Amos shook his head, "No. You said I should try to be inconspicuous, but it's not far."

Leader put up a hand and said, "We'll wait here. Go get the car." She pulled the bags from his arms.

"I can walk to the parking lot," Emma growled. "This is a pocket-sized airport. How far can it possibly be?" And she stomped ahead of them.

She was relieved that her sickness seemed to act as a buffer, because neither Leader nor Amos mentioned disrespect to her. They followed her as far as the front doors. When she looked out and saw how far away the parking lot was, she agreed to sit with Leader on a bench and wait. Leader pulled her against her shoulder to give Emma a place to rest her head. She almost fell asleep again before Leader got her up to walk to the car.

"We'll be home soon," Amos promised as he put the car into gear.

Emma saw nothing of the city or of the house. Amos carried her in half awake and right away Julianne dosed her with something that sent her into a deep sleep.

"You'll feel better soon," Julianne promised in a reassuring voice.

Emma did feel better when she opened her eyes. She awoke disoriented and had no concept of time, but her head no longer ached, and she did not have the urge to scratch her skin off. As a bonus, the welts on her backside and legs had dulled and Emma wondered if Julianne had slathered her with something.

Daylight streamed in from a large window to one side. Through the window Emma got a glimpse of greenery and blue sky, but that was all she could see from the bed. She sat up. This was definitely her room; she could recognize it anywhere. It had been painted a light yellow and was accented with whites and darker yellows. The artwork on the walls was in black and white and there was a poster of a band she did not even know. Her room was always decorated for a pretend person Emma never could be but had to pretend to be if any outsiders were ever in her room. Which they weren't, because she would never be stupid enough to bring an outsider home.

It was a smaller room than she was used to, but it was nice enough to sleep and study in, which is all she would ever do there. Then, in confusion, she looked around for her desk. There wasn't one and she wondered if the forward party had failed to buy her one yet.

"Hi, sleepyhead," Julianne said, coming in through the white painted door with a smile. "How do you feel? Better?"

"Hungry," Emma said when her nose caught the scent of the food on the tray Julianne carried.

"Then you *are* feeling better," Julianne said. She popped up the legs from beneath the tray and set it down over Emma's lap. "Eat up. You gave Leader quite a scare, you know. I don't know if I have ever seen her so distressed."

Emma pulled a face. "I didn't mean to." She spooned the soup into her mouth. "Mm, Amos cooked." She missed his cooking.

Julianne smiled. "Yes. He made that especially for you."

Emma looked up in alarm. "How is Scott? Leader mentioned he was ill, too."

"He's fine," Julianne assured her, patting her shoulder gently. "Better than you, in fact, because I got to him right away. Not that I think either one of you should be running any marathons for the next week or so, but you'll both be fine. It was not a sophisticated attack."

Emma let out an exhausted sigh, "But it was an attack."

Julianne cocked her head to one side. "Of course, it was. A pretty simple and deliberate one."

Emma frowned. "You don't think it was Mr. Mitchell, do you? He hates me something fierce and he is supposedly a chemist."

The answer came from Leader in the doorway, "No, it's not him. I caught the culprit. A hired gun and not worth the money they paid. Don't worry about all that. You just get well. I'm only giving you the weekend to recover and get your bearings. You start school Monday."

Despite Julianne's squawk of alarm, Emma nodded. She really felt well enough that a few more days of rest was all she needed, and she could handle school again. Even whatever scary-ass school Leader had arranged to put her in.

"Are Scott and I in the same school?"

Leader nodded. "But that doesn't matter, because he enrolled under the name Scott Jameson last week and you will be enrolling next week under the name Emma Chandler."

Emma was surprised at that announcement. "Is that what you meant by 'split the Guild?'"

Julianne patted her arm and said, "Eat up and don't worry about it."

But Leader answered, "Yes. The forward party, with the exception of Amos, will live in another house across town and are going under the alias 'Jameson Family.' You, Piper, Waylon, and Adam will be here with me and Amos going by the alias 'Chandler.' And as far as you're to be concerned, Scott is just another student at your school that you have no connection to."

Emma hated the sound of that but when she tried to speak out about it, Julianne shushed her.

"Do not upset my patient," Julianne ordered, scowling Leader's direction. "She needs to rest and to sleep. She can attend a briefing Monday morning if you need to give her any more information." She pointed at the tray and commanded Emma firmly, "Eat."

Leader gave a long-suffering sigh and shrugged at Emma. She turned and left the room with a final thought, "I think you'll love your new school."

Chapter Twelve

Emma stared incredulously up at the tan brick building with school fighting flags draped down the side and graffiti-covered marquee outside. She looked back at Leader who emerged from the Volvo carrying her purse, but she seemed oblivious to Emma's scorn.

"It's a public school," Emma murmured, still shocked that *this* was the school, the school Leader thought would trouble her so much. She could do public school academics in her sleep.

"Yes, it is," Leader agreed. "Slope Oak Public High School."

"*Slowpoke* High School," Emma replied doubtfully, looking up at Leader with barely restrained contempt. "Really?"

Leader shot her an arched look, "It has great ratings."

"I'm sure," Emma shot back. In her best country drawl, she added, "Slowpoke High is probably the best darn dirt road to Ivy League we could ever hope for."

Leader spun around and looked down at Emma sternly. "Do we need to get back in the car and talk, or do you think you can get yourself under control?"

Emma scoffed, "I can't believe you think it's okay to put me and Scott in a public school."

Leader grabbed her by the upper arm and hauled her back toward the car. The danger was too big, too immediate for Emma to go tamely. She fought Leader's hold, hissing under her breath, "I'm under control, Leader. Don't!"

Leader gave her one long, drawn-out glare before unhanding her and pointing toward the front doors of the high school. Emma gave her a wary look before turning and preceding her up the sidewalk. Within a few brisk steps, Leader overtook her, and Emma had to hurry to keep up. She should have been clued into the idea of public school when, instead of giving her a uniform this morning, Leader simply instructed her to dress modestly. Emma selected black tights, a short cut-off jean skirt, and a long-sleeved white sweater with large colorful stripes. Her hair was down but was in wet braids all morning, so it had a crinkled almost-curly look that would go flat long before the day was over. She wore white boots and a simple necklace to finish the look.

Before they passed through the front doors, Emma asked, "You didn't put Victoria in public school, did you?"

Leader turned on her again with an arched look, "Who?"

Her mild tone reminded Emma that, under her current alias, she did not know Victoria. Emma let out a frustrated breath but any words she might have said were swallowed when Leader leaned over and said, "I didn't hear the tone of judgment in your voice about the way I run my Guild, did I? Did you want to start again? Your move."

Emma urgently shook her head, "No! I don't want to fight with you. I concede that you are already the winner. Checkmate. I lost."

"You sure?" Leader asked, stepping even closer.

Emma scowled at her when she saw they were attracting the attention of students passing by.

"I am sure," she hissed. "I forever concede to your authority. I retract my former tone of judgment. Your Guild, your rules."

Leader nodded in acceptance and turned to lead Emma through the doors. Emma looked skyward in a quick prayer for patience.

The office was busy, like every other school office she had ever known. It took a few minutes before anyone could help them. Leader already enrolled her last week, so the most time-consuming part was done. Emma expected to have to meet with the dean and sign the student code of conduct, but neither was required. A woman who seemed young enough to have been a student—but probably was not judging by the hideous pant suit—showed them into the counselor's office.

"Mr. Berkshire, this is Emma Chandler," the young woman said. Her voice was unreal, high pitched, and cartoon-like.

The man behind the desk was at least a hundred pounds overweight. He rose smoothly to shake Emma's hand. Leader introduced herself as "Lydia Chandler."

"It's a pleasure to meet you both," he said with a warm smile. He rolled up onto his toes momentarily when he said, "Welcome to Slope Oak, home of the Cheetahs." Emma smirked and earned Leader's elbow in her ribs.

Mr. Berkshire handed Emma a pamphlet and tapped it. "This contains the school map, your locker and combination. It's always a good idea to bring your own lock." She had one in her backpack already. "I took the liberty of marking your classes on the map. A lot of AP classes; your GPA was very impressive."

Emma blinked and then turned and looked at Leader, "Really?" This had to be a joke. AP classes? *Public* school? Leader had to drop the act soon. There was no reason Emma could imagine for her to be placed in a public school. She had always been in private schools with accelerated courses and an Ivy League track.

"You're being rude," Leader answered sharply. Then she smiled winningly at the counselor. "She's been taciturn ever since we moved back to the states. It's going to take some adjusting."

The man smiled, not seeming concerned at all. "That's right," he said, returning his gaze to Emma. "You just moved back from France. How did you like it there?"

Emma's snapped response was in French and included a few choice words. Leader pinched her beneath her handbag, and Emma jerked away. The man clearly did not understand Emma's disrespectful comments, because he smiled back and forth between his two guests while they conversed in French.

"I demand you admit this is a joke, Leader! You are not going to saddle me with some second-rate public high school! You cannot sacrifice my education this way. Tell me at once that you are putting me in a proper private school with University Preparation Program and Ivy-League Credentials!"

Leader raised a dangerous brow at Emma, but then she turned to face the counselor, forcing another smile.

"I'm sorry. Emma is usually a pleasant enough girl, but she is having trouble with the transition back into the states. She had many friends and interests in France, after seven years there. I guess she picked up some cultural snobbery. I am confident she will settle in nicely. She prefers this option to homeschooling."

The man laughed along with Leader, but it silenced Emma's complaints. Dropping her eyes to disallow Leader to catch her gaze, Emma opened the school map. She studied the cartoon campus, swallowing down her "cultural snobbery" so as not to turn Leader's wrath on her. It was a much bigger school than she expected.

"It's a big school," she whispered though she kept her eyes on the paper.

"Yes," Leader answered. She returned her attention to the counselor. "My daughter is not accustomed to schools as large as this one. The schools in France tend to be much smaller."

The Counselor rolled onto the balls of his feet once more and addressed Emma, "There's no reason to be nervous. I assigned you a student guide to help you navigate your way through the campus."

Emma looked up at him doubtfully and replied, "It's not that. I'm not nervous. And I'm not an idiot who needs some kid to hold my hand all day." She carefully avoided Leader's gaze as she added, "I'm just surprised at the size of the school, because it seems to me that there should not be this many kids whose parents want them to fail."

Leader shook her head and said, "You're such a snob," in a voice that Emma did not recognize. It was something like a cross between amusement and exasperation.

Emma frowned, frustrated not to have gotten a rise out of Leader. The counselor, though was no longer in the mood to be polite in the face of Emma's unrelenting rudeness. His tone cooled significantly as he tried to assure Emma that the school was an excellent one with high test scores, prestigious graduates, and many accomplished sports teams. Emma ignored him and continued to study the map as he spoke. Her assigned locker was upstairs, and her first class was downstairs. She had heard the bell ring while waiting in the office for this pointless meeting. Which meant, on her first day of school, she was already late for her very first class.

"It really is a good school," the man was saying when Emma tuned back into the conversation. "I think you will both be pleased." He smiled once more at Emma, as if trying to will himself not to hate her yet. "Let me show you to the Attendance Office. We have a pretty strict closed campus, so it's always good to get to know the Attendance Office well." He handed Emma another small pamphlet. "That's the student agreement. By enrolling, you agree to abide by its rules."

"That's convenient," Emma muttered. He did not hear her, but Leader did. As soon as they were in the hall, Leader held her back. She spun Emma to look into her dark, hard eyes. They seemed to promise pain in their depths. "Stop being sullen, Emmalyn! If you don't stop this, I will just take you home. Do you understand me? Stop being disrespectful about this man's school. It is one of the top schools in the state!"

Emma couldn't help herself. She pulled a face and scoffed, "In the state of *Missouri*? You're right, Leader, I *will* stop being sullen. If it's the top school in the state; excuse me, *one* of the top *public* schools in the state of *Missouri*, that probably means it's one of the best in the whole wide world." Her sarcasm attracted the attention of the counselor, who looked back in concern.

"Excuse us," Leader told the counselor sweetly as she shoved Emma back into his office and snapped the door shut. Emma backed quickly away from the fire in Leader's eyes.

"It is here or it is home, Emma. And trust me; you're safer here today because if I get you home, you're going to wish you had never pissed me off."

Emma knew she had reached the end of Leader's tether, but she was furious. She couldn't resist snarling, "It's *public* school!"

Leader snapped her fingers and ordered, "Form Twenty-Nine." The forms were part of their daily work on the mat. Emma now had over two-hundred forms memorized. Twenty-Nine was cool-down form and, like many others, assisted in meditation and relaxation.

Emma balked at the order, "You want me to do forms here? In the counselor's office while he's waiting outside the door? You have got to be kidding me."

Leader held up two fingers less than an inch apart. "This close to violence."

Emma looked away from that imminent threat, drew an appropriate breath, and stepped into the form. It didn't serve to calm her, but it silenced her complaints. If Leader put her in a public school, she probably had a good reason. It was a rare day when Leader condescended to inform anyone in the Junior Guild of the reason she did anything. And Emma was still pretty far down the Guild ladder to be risking her retribution.

"Form Twenty-One," Leader ordered when Emma returned to ready stance. Emma obeyed immediately this time. Maybe, since she corrected her behavior, Leader might be willing to forget that she failed to be Obedient before. Leader called out the names of other forms. It was several minutes later when Leader nodded in satisfaction.

"All right, let's go," she said and turned to open the door. The counselor stood waiting there with deep concern in his eyes, but he seemed relieved when they both emerged unsullied.

"I'm sorry," Leader apologized smoothly. "Emma was ill last week, and I was afraid her sour mood betrayed that she might still be unwell. She seems to think she's well enough to stay, but please call me right away if I need to pick her up." That was a threat, although the counselor took it as loving concern.

"We have good nurses. If Emma feels poorly, they can help her."

Emma held back what she might have said about a public school's idea of nursing care. She allowed herself to be led to the Attendance Office. The school was very strict about attendance. There were several procedures she would be expected to follow with regards to attendance that she had never had to bother with in private school. Perhaps that was because public school funding was based on student attendance, whereas private school tuition was due whether the child attended or not.

Leader parted from her in the commons area. "Have a good day, honey." She glanced at the counselor. "Please notify me directly if there are any problems."

"Will do," he promised with a nod.

"I'll pick you up at 3," Leader said in an undertone. "Remember who you are."

Like Emma could even possibly forget who she was for two seconds! Everything in her life reminded her she was Guild, and she belonged to Leader. Just being in a public school would serve to remind her that she was the rightful property of the scariest woman in the world. Leader had chosen this school, and so Emma was here—she could not forget that for anything.

Chapter Thirteen

"Emma, this is Chastity Monez," the counselor informed her. A young woman in pantyhose and a tweed skirt and jacket over and peasant blouse stepped up beside the counselor. She had long brown hair tied back with a ribbon. In Emma's mind she could imagine what the cheer squad at Sacred Covenant would do to this innocent girl. She, like the school, begged to be mocked. When Emma saw the girl's Mary-Jane buckle shoes, she looked away and stifled a smile.

"She'll serve as your student guide today. She'll meet you outside your door at the end each of your classes and show you around our wonderful campus," He patted Chastity on the shoulder. "She's a real good girl. I think the two of you will get along well."

Emma doubted it.

"You are going to love it here," the girl added with a student-government smile.

Emma doubted that, too.

The counselor walked away, giving them a polite nod, and saying, "Emma, I leave you in Chastity's capable hands."

"Thank you, Mr. Berkshire," Chastity replied, a sentiment that Emma seconded coolly. Chastity turned her beaming smile on Emma again. "Shall we get you into Calculus?" she asked and, without waiting for Emma to answer, glided down the hall away from the offices.

"What brings you to Slope Oak?"

At first, Emma considered not answering at all, but with Leader's order to stop being sullen still resounding in her ears, she thought she ought not to push her luck.

"Mother's business."

The girl's smile grated on Emma's nerves.

"Must have been very important to bring you here at this time of year. Where did you go before?"

Emma let out a frustrated breath and shook her head. "France," she lied.

The girl gave a stage gasp then spun to face Emma. "That's exciting! Do you speak French?"

"Probably exclusively." Emma pushed ahead of the girl toward the Math Hall.

When the girl caught up to her, she seemed confused. In frustration, Emma shook her head, and lied again, "Not much."

They took the crossing hallway and passed the trophy cases displaying several sports' worth of rewards. It was a shame Scott was not going to be permitted to be on any teams here, since they seemed to have a wide spread of choices. Chastity chattered on about the football team's successes when she saw Emma looking into the trophy cases. When Emma shot a doubtful look at her, Chastity said, "Basketball also does well. The team went to nationals last year."

"I don't care," Emma said firmly, holding up a hand to stop the girl's constant stream of useless information. "I was only looking at the case to see how securely they have the trophies locked up." Chastity seemed surprised by Emma's words, and then unsure whether or not she was joking.

Chastity gave a timid laugh as they walked on. "You're a tease," she decided. She laughed again, shaking her head as if she was finally in on the joke. "Oh, that's fun. We Cheetahs like a good laugh now and again."

Emma gave a derisive snort and stopped walking. She turned and very deliberately looked the other girl up and down.

"Are you for real? You're not just some girl the office hired to make the school seem peachy and clean?"

Chastity frowned at that idea. "No." She shook her head, adding, "I go here." Then she laughed, her entire confused expression giving way to her brilliant smile. "You were joking again. Sorry."

Emma blinked and said, "Wow," under her breath, before turning away to walk on. The girl matched her stride as they entered the hall that housed the Calculus class.

Before she reached the door, Emma had a sudden epiphany and grabbed the girl's arm to halt their progress. "Do you do this job a lot? Like, when kids enroll midyear, are you the go-to guide?"

If possible, the girl's perky smile widened. "Actually, I am president of the entire student committee, and we all get the privilege of introducing the school to new students. I was selected to help your transition. If you'd like, I can show you off to the rest of the committee at lunch."

Emma was disappointed. She had hoped the girl was the one who to perform this asinine service for Scott when he enrolled last week. She could not come straight out and ask about him, since Leader had forbidden it, and also she wasn't supposed to know who he was. But she had hoped.

Her bitter disappointment made her colder than she needed to be.

"Listen . . . Chastity, is it? Listen, Chastity, I'm not eating lunch with you. Even with all the dimensions of existence in this universe, there is not a single realm of possibility in which you and I become friends. I'm surprised the rest of the student committee agrees to eat lunch with you wearing that outfit."

The smile disappeared from the girl's face and she murmured, "We don't allow putdowns at this school."

Emma's laugh came out more like a scoff, "That's cute! Well, you know, cops don't allow people to break traffic laws but, by damn, sometimes people speed."

The girl swallowed. "Bad language," she began and Emma held up a hand to stall her.

"Save it," she ordered in a flat voice. She waved her campus map at the girl and said, "I can find my own way to my classes. You probably have to get back to your grandmother's so you can return her clothes." She strode ahead of the girl toward the door to her math class. Her phone chirped and when she pulled it out, the message displayed was from Amos: **Was that really necessary?**

Emma snarled at the message, and replied: **Don't you have anything better to do?**

His answer was: **Not particularly.**

Instead of answering, she silenced her phone and pocketed it. She did not care if it was public or private, they probably had strict rules against phone use in school. She opened the door to her first period.

The teacher, an older woman with piercing eyes that reminded her of Julianne, greeted her with an arched look and the words, "Are you lost?"

That returned Emma to herself quickly enough. She shook her head. "No, this is my class. I'm Emma Chandler."

"Do you have an Admit to Class pass, Emma Chandler?" the teacher asked, walking forward with her hand outstretched. Emma surrendered the paper she had received in the Attendance Office. The teacher looked the page over with a thoughtful frown. She handed Emma a worn-out textbook from a shelf to one side and motioned her toward the desks.

"Class, this is Emma Chandler," she told the assembled students who paid Emma as little attention as she paid them.

"Take any available seat."

Emma noticed right away that all the seats in the back of the room were empty, and she assumed the teacher required her students to sit near the front. With that philosophy in mind, Emma selected an empty seat in the last occupied row of desks.

"I hope you already have a fundamental knowledge of calculus," the teacher warned her. "We're partway through our second unit of study."

It took Emma a moment to realize that the teacher was speaking exclusively to her. "I'll be fine. Thank you for your concern."

"It's not *you* I'm concerned about," the teacher answered sharply. "It's what will happen to the rest of my class if you're behind."

Emma clenched her teeth and forced herself to answer politely, "I will not hold the class back, I assure you." She removed a fresh notebook and a pen from her backpack and placed them on the desk. The teacher snorted and returned to her lesson. It took Emma a few moments studying the work on the board to comprehend the lesson, but once she did, she managed to complete her homework while the teacher prattled on to lesser minds.

If Leader expected this school to provide an academic challenge, she was dead wrong. Emma spent her first three classes skimming the textbooks to get an idea of the course materials. She had learned some of it already, but she quickly memorized terms and familiarized herself with what the other students in the school considered to be difficult. Any time she was not being spoken to directly, Emma worked on homework, including previous chapters the classes had already covered.

Before lunch, Emma found her locker on the top floor. She managed to get it open with only a little trouble. Inside the locker door there was a picture of Amos pulling a face that she promptly tore down. Of course, Amos had been here to set up the creepy surveillance that allowed him to know what she said to Chastity. She shot him a quick text: **Funny.**

She could practically hear him laughing, although she got no response.

In her backpack, she found her lunch, packed that morning by Waylon. She glimpsed in and pulled a face. The trouble with nutritious food was that it did not keep well. She fished a few dollars from her emergency cash, then, thinking better of acting without Leader's sanction, she sent a text to her: **I'm using emergency cash to buy school lunch.**

A moment later, Leader's response came through: **Fine. They have a salad bar.**

Emma accepted that. Salad was what she would have selected, anyway, most likely. Hauling her backpack onto her shoulders and tossing her packed lunch in the nearest trash, Emma walked downstairs to the cafeteria.

Every cafeteria she had ever seen was practically the same. This cafeteria had few distinctions. Instead of round tables, like Sacred Covenant, the tables here were traditional long rectangular tables with matching benches. The cafeteria line was broken into three sections: the salad bar, the hot lunch line, and the drink section. Trays were dumped on the opposite wall, away from diners and food service bars.

Emma collected her salad quickly, paid for it, then glanced around for a place to sit. Like every high school cafeteria in the world, students sat in cliques at every table. As Emma moved through the room, she began identifying the crowds. Closest to the door were the jocks and cheer crowd. The other end of the room seemed to be the lair of the angry punk, goth, and potheads. In the middle, as if to separate the polar opposites, was a buffer of art kids, thespians, gamers, readers, and press. Unfortunately, the world had no table for Emma's kind. If there had been empty tables, she might have chosen to sit alone. But every table had occupants. She avoided the one where she saw Chastity heading. She had no interest in sitting with student government.

Emma moved to the buffer zone and a table of girls chatting and reading. She probably wouldn't make friends there, but at least she would not be bothered. "May I sit here?"

One of the girls nodded and scooted aside so Emma could have the end seat.

Partway through her salad, Emma felt a strong gaze focused on her. She looked up. The entire Student Council table was looking her way and Chastity spoke in a somewhat animated voice. Emma's eyes zoomed in on Scott seated in the sea of polos and button-downs. She stifled a gasp of surprise. Leader said Scott was at school here, but Emma had not seen him until now. If not for his sparkling gaze and sardonic smile, she might not have recognized him. His hair was clean-cut and parted, and he wore slacks and a polo shirt like the others at his table. Besides the dangerous grace of a martial artist, and the ferocity of the Guild in his eyes, he fit right in.

He was good at his job. He pretended not to know her. He listened intently to Chastity's obviously elaborated narrative and made eye intense contact with Emma several times. After a few minutes, he rose smoothly and spoke loudly enough for half the room to hear, "Who is she, Chastity? Let's have a talk this new girl."

Chastity seemed to be arguing with his plan, but still she pointed Emma out. When Scott crossed the room, he was followed by another young man and three young women. Chastity hung back, looking concerned. Emma took a long pull from her water bottle and let them come. She pretended to be unconcerned, but she was so happy to see Scott that it was difficult not to greet him exuberantly.

"Are you Emma Chandler?" Scott asked in a somewhat authoritative voice with a hint of patience he wanted detectable. She took a long look at him, starting from his brown leather shoes, and worked her gaze up his blue slacks, past the white polo, to his slicked-back hair. She wanted to laugh. He looked so unlike himself!

"Yes," she drawled. She looked past him at his posse and asked, "Are you car salesmen?"

Scott's voice lost its patience, "You're new to this school, so we're going to let slide that you haven't shown any kind of respect for rules or the student code. But you should know that everyone is dedicated to keeping Slope Oak a safe and clean campus."

"Not everyone," Emma argued, glancing up at him again. She slipped her fork into her mouth and pulled it out with a jerk. "I saw that the marquee out front has been decorated with spray paint. Do you really believe the vandals weren't members of this student body?" She shrugged. "That doesn't seem like a dedication to cleanliness and safety."

"Listen," the other boy added, stepping forward to capture her gaze. "All of us have to go to school here and we all want to have a safe learning environment. By attending this school, you made a commitment to abide by the student code. That means no foul language, no putdowns, and no troublemaking. It's not that hard."

Emma rose slowly so she would not be at such a disadvantage to the towering mass of tweed. Students all around them quieted to hear the heated exchange. Emma raised her brows and looked Scott's crony up and down in the most challenging way possible.

"Listen, Tiger. Why don't you and the rest of the PGA Tour mosey on back to your table before one of you bastards gets a wrinkle in your khakis?"

She knew Scott well enough to show his amusement, but he masked it well in anger. "This kind of behavior will not be tolerated at this school."

Oh, he was enjoying this! How excited must he have been to learn that Chastity's insults had come from Emma?

"I did not realize you were the campus police," Emma answered sarcastically. "I assumed from your clothing that you were the drama club. These are costumes, right? Are you doing a bit right now?"

Chastity joined them and stepped forward hotly. "Profanity and the need to insult others often stems from a lack of intelligence," she said feeling as if her words could not be construed as an insult.

Emma happened to be watching Scott, so she saw his brief smile and the pained widening of his eyes. Chastity could not have selected a worse hill to die on.

"Is that so?" Emma asked the girl quietly. "Your premise is that my need to insult you comes from my lack of intellectual prowess?" She saw the look of caution in Scott's eye as Emma's gaze swept past the student government clique. It checked Emma's diatribe, and she found herself offering the ridiculous girl an out.

"I'm going to do you a favor right now, Chastity, and warn you for the last time to stay away from me. If you want to match wits, I will annihilate you."

When Chastity's only response was a challenging snort, Emma gave a slow, cold smile. She heard Chastity's confrontational words once more, like a poem circling her mind, mocking her—well, *attempting* to mock her. It ripped away any gentleness she might have been capable of displaying.

"Let's work your hypothesis out to a conclusion then, shall we?" Emma did not speak softly now. Chastity and the student government had wanted a scene; she spoke up loudly and clearly. "Extrapolating from your appearance—*and* your puerile position on the student committee—I would infer that you have a deep need for other's approval. I must assume then that my immediate dissatisfaction with you as my guide initiated a self-reflection. This reflection most likely led you to the consideration that your self-estimation as a necessary factor in this school's ecosystem has erred all along."

Scott did not seem amused now. "Stop," he ordered her. Obedience to him was her first nature, but he had initiated this contact and she could not simply back down now.

"In fact," Emma went on, ignoring the dangerous look in Scott's eye, "I presume that upon closer inspection of the student body, you'll find that, instead of appreciated, your presence is merely tolerated. Instead of admired, you are endured. Your overcompensation with your peers at school clearly exhibits a phobia of being perceived as insignificant. This, I presume, is predicated on a lack of approval at home."

"Stop it," Scott repeated, ferocious now with his need to stop her. Emma rode over his words.

"Your desire for recognition and acceptance belies your belief that you have cloaked your insecurities in a veil of tweed skirts and hosiery. In fact, the only person deceived by your meager camouflage, ironically enough, is you."

Chastity seemed mostly confused, so despite Scott's fierce look, Emma clarified. "In other words, we all know your confidence is an act and that's why we don't like you." She shrugged as Chastity's face fell, comprehension coming at last.

"Keep it real, bitch," Emma concluded, and offered a peace sign as her final insult.

Chastity blinked, swallowed. She was obviously trying not to cry. "I . . ." She shook her head. "I don't think . . ."

"I know you don't," Emma interrupted her. She leaned toward Chastity, although the closer proximity to Scott was dangerous, as his gaze could have melted her with his fury.

"My IQ is over 160, Chastity. You're sporting somewhere around a 95. So, let's finish this. I reject your premise that my need to insult you stems not from a lack of intelligence." She held up an admonitory finger, but then lazily let it trail down, pointing at Chastity's outfit as it fell. "But rather from my deep abhorrence for tweed. And my use of profanity is just to piss you the hell off."

Chastity turned and strode quickly away, followed by two of the other Student Council girls with indignant expressions.

Scott let out a low, furious breath and shook his head at Emma. "She is a perfectly nice girl," he chastised. And he shouldn't have been, but he was talking to the Emma he knew, rather than the character she was meant to play at this school.

She responded with like sentiment, "Don't come onto the mats without your guard up."

The young man standing with Scott glared hatred at Emma. He said, "I will be reporting this incident to the disciplinary office."

Emma cocked her head at him, challenging him with his eyes. "Do it," she encouraged darkly. "I actually think it will come out in my favor. We're an anti-bullying school. I can probably find fifty or sixty witnesses that will claim I was eating my lunch, minding my own business, when the horde of you descended on me with an intention to bully me into conformity. And no offense, but I don't look good in tweed."

"Come on, Scott," the kid said, disgustedly turning away from her. As they walked away, he spoke to Scott in Spanish, "Es una piruja!" *She's a whore.*

Emma chuckled, "I speak twelve languages fluently. Tell me, do the Cheetahs only discourage profanity in English?"

Scott spun and pointed a menacing finger back at her. "Stop!" he ordered. She had reached the line. He would not allow her to go any further without some kind of retaliation. If he retaliated, they would blow their cover, and no one would be able to save them from Leader then.

Emma lifted one shoulder in a slight shrug and sat back down to finish her salad. The girls at the table watched her warily. She glanced at the table beyond them and saw the same sort of suspicion in its inhabitants. This was worse than her other first days at other schools. She had never managed to alienate half a student body in one day before. She would never make friends at this rate. She sighed at her salad in hopelessness.

Chapter Fourteen

"Hey," a girl said as she dropped her tray in the space across from Emma. She wore dark clothes but did not appear to be goth, she had several piercings. The ones in her brow and nose had been filled with nude studs to be less obvious, probably in accordance with the student dress code. Her hair had been dyed black. No girl outside a fairy tale could be as white as this girl and have been born with hair that dark. She wore a t-shirt with an angry-looking musician on the front, and jeans with various holes. Emma thought the holes must have been a fashion statement rather than an indication of wealth because she wore real diamonds in the first holes of both ears.

"Hi," Emma answered, drawing out the word to turn it into an impolite demand of *what do you want?*

"I'm Josie," the girl announced.

"Emma Chandler. What can I do for you?"

Josie smiled, and the result was that she became minimally more attractive, though no less fierce. "You did it already. Emma Chandler one; Chastity Monez zero."

Emma rolled her eyes. "I didn't do it for accolades."

Josie shrugged. "It needed to be done, whatever the reason. She walks around this school like it's her own personal kingdom. She threw a fit last year that the dress code allowed for patterned hosiery. She calls it slut leggings. They changed the dress code for her."

That seemed a silly reason for Josie to turn against the girl. "You have an affinity for slutty legwear?"

Josie's return snort spoke volumes of how little she really cared about the issue. "Of course not. I just feel sorry for the sluts who can no longer wear fishnets."

Emma smiled at that. She could maybe be friends with Josie. "When she announced that she would serve as my guide, I legitimately considered the possibility that she was an actress hired by the school."

The warning bell rang on the tail end of her words and Josie grabbed her tray and stood up. "You don't need one of those ass-kissers to show you around the school. Come on. I'll take you everywhere you need to go."

Josie's tour of the school was very different than any Emma might have received by the Student Council. She was shown the upstairs lavatory that was used mostly for smoking, the projection booth where druggies sold their wares after school, and the ditch room in the art hall where students sometimes hung out instead of going to class. The ditch room was really just an old storage closet where the furnishings had been piled along the walls to leave a small space in the center for loafers.

Another highlight of Josie's tour was the backdoor into the Attendance Office. "In case you don't get into class on time, and you don't want any hassle," Josie explained as she quietly filled out an Admit to Class pass for each of them. "If you come in the office and speak to the Attendance Officials, they require notes from parents and reasonable excuses for tardiness. If we do it this way, no one needs to know that you were hooking up with a hunky basketball player under the bleachers," she handed Emma the pass with a smile.

By the time the tour was over, Emma had completely missed her P.E. class. She knew what Leader would say about Emma skipping classes. Something akin to "Checkmate."

"I have to get to my Ethics and Values class," Emma told her guide regretfully. She was actually enjoying her time with the future criminal and was sad to leave. Josie had an angry sense of humor that Emma appreciated.

"Yeah, it'd be a shame to miss that," Josie answered sarcastically. "Do you have Johnson?" When Emma nodded at that, Josie said, "Downstairs to the blue hall, third door on the left."

"Thanks," Emma answered. She adjusted her backpack on her shoulders and turned to walk away. After a couple steps, she paused and looked back at the girl. "Can I eat lunch with you tomorrow?"

Josie gave an unconcerned shrug. "All right. See you around."

Emma hurried away.

Leader's car was in the front of the carpool line after last bell. Emma climbed in the passenger side but before she could greet her, Leader held up her hand. She was on the phone. That was a relief to Emma, who was tired from the long stressful first day. She did not want to talk about her day and Leader most certainly would have things to say. Her backpack fell to the floor with a weighted thud. She had stopped at her locker to collect all her textbooks for Leader's perusal, so her backpack was heavy. She settled back against the seat and closed her eyes.

"I can be there tomorrow," Leader was saying. She pulled the phone away and said, "Seatbelt." Then as Emma Obediently buckled her seatbelt, Leader returned to her conversation. "That won't be necessary. But I can't be there until tomorrow evening." She exited the lane and drove onto the side street. Emma watched the passing buildings as she attempted to unwind from the day. Springfield was such a little city compared to every other place Emma had lived with the Guild. The tallest buildings seemed to be the hospitals, and even those were no higher than ten stories. Springfield sprawled out rather than up.

Emma saw the strip malls and the frozen yogurt stands, the car dealers, and the restaurants typical of every city in America. Leader drove them through the business district up into a residential park. She wound through several streets and finally entered their neighborhood. She had been on the phone the entire time talking business in words Emma did not understand.

Emma knew it wasn't someone in the Guild on the phone because of the tone in Leader's voice. She was always commanding and direct, but to her subordinates she spoke with a brusque expectant quality. During this phone call she listened a lot, commented a little, and spoke in a semi-respectful manner.

They drove into the driveway and parked in one spot in the three-car garage. Emma had originally been surprised by their house. Usually, the Guild House was a massive ten to twelve thousand square foot building with a six-car garage, several floors, and often in a gated community. This house was diminutive in comparison. It was a basic five thousand square foot modern home with four bedrooms and three and a half bathrooms. Waylon and Adam shared half the unfinished basement. The other half had been spread with mats and turned into the training room. Emma was accustomed to a much larger training facility, but she found the basement to be just as effective at getting her focused and ready for her daily Guild tasks.

Leader unlocked the car door, allowing Emma out, but she stayed behind. Again, Leader pulled the phone away from her mouth and said, "I'll be in in a minute. Get started on your homework."

Emma sighed, "I don't have any homework, Leader. I finished it all at school."

"Excuse me," Leader said into the phone before pressing the mute button. "What's wrong? How was school?"

Snatching her backpack from the seat, Emma gave the phone in Leader's hand a pointed look. "We're going to do this right here, right now? Can we please just talk inside when you're done with business?"

"Yes," Leader answered with a stern look. "Get your books and homework out so I can look them over. And see if you can drop that attitude before I get in there."

Emma did not even bother to respond. She went through the garage door into the house. It was quiet inside. Adam was attending Missouri University and must have still been on campus. Piper was practically a ninja; she could be in the same room with Emma and, if she wanted, never be seen. The quiet, though, clearly displayed that Amos was out of the house, seconded by the fact that his car was not in the garage.

Obediently, Emma spread her books and notebooks out on the desk next to the office in the dining room. The desk looked bizarre and completely out of place there. When she recovered last week, enough to see the house, she had found her desk in the dining room. One look from Leader explained why. In the Guild, bedrooms were used for sleeping and studying. They were furnished only with beds and desks. But Emma had proved to Leader that she could not be trusted to Diligently complete her studying privately. Emma accepted the relocation of her desk without complaint. Leader could decorate her houses any way she wanted.

Leader entered from the garage while Emma was making herself a protein shake. "You made contact with Scott today?"

Emma spun around, "What?"

Leader sounded annoyed, as if she had just heard about it. Then Emma saw why. Amos followed her into the kitchen. "No!"

Leader presented Amos with a sweeping motion. "You're suggesting Amos lied to me?"

Emma set her shake down hard on the counter. "Amos needs to get his facts straight," she argued, shooting a withering look at the Number Two. "I did not make contact with Scott; *he* contacted *me*!" She glared at Amos. "Tell her!"

When Leader looked at Amos, he nodded. "That's true. Scott and his new friends approached her at lunch."

Leader shook her head, furious and frustrated. "What possible explanation can he have for making contact? I gave explicit instructions! To both of you!" she shot Emma a severe glance. "This kind of incompetence is going to be the death of me."

She dropped her phone and purse on the counter and swung on Amos. "I want to see the footage. Compile it!"

Amos held up a stalling hand. "I can pull it up right here," he promised, motioning at the laptop on Emma's desk. Emma's pink laptop that was never allowed off her desk. Leader motioned impatiently for Amos to get started.

"And what about you? You had nothing to do with it?" Leader asked, dark gaze boring into Emma. "You have nothing to report?"

Emma picked up her shake, attempting nonchalance, and said, "I skipped P.E. today." She took a quick drink.

Leader calmed, but not the good calm of gentle waters. She was the cold calm before the maelstrom of her fury. "You *skipped* P.E. You asked my permission to buy school lunch, but on your own you decided to *skip* P.E.?"

When Amos announced, "It's ready, Leader," Emma had never been more grateful.

Leader held up a finger and warned, "This isn't over." Then she swung around and locked her gaze on the screen. Emma slipped back, far enough to be out of Leader's reach but close enough that, if she was called, could come quickly. She perched on the edge of the kitchen table, drank the protein shake and waited nervously.

Emma winced once or twice while hearing the replay of her snide words to Scott and his friends. Her victory seemed pale now since trouble was looming, and she and Scott might both catch it for this. Her eyes slid closed when the recording came to the part where Scott told her to stop and she disobeyed. She really was good at obeying orders, but he had backed her into a corner. If she had backed down from the fight, she would have turned herself into a target for bullying in front of the entire school. If she was bullied, she would react violently, and she could not see how that would be good for the Guild. However, Leader had not instructed her not to be violent while she had been instructed to obey. A tricky tightrope to walk . . .

Amos stopped the show after Scott walked away, saving Emma from having to talk about Josie and the illegal tour of the school. Leader turned slowly and scrutinized Emma for a long moment.

"What was his provocation for approaching you?" she asked softly. "He mentioned a violation of the student code."

Emma shrugged over at Amos, who turned back to the computer and began typing away. "I was given Chastity Monez as my student guide," she said, to which Leader gave an abrupt nod. "I was a little mean to her. I said she dresses like her grandmother, and I think I used the word 'damn' in a non-biblical sense."

Leader raised one eyebrow, "Why?"

Emma shrugged, "She bugged me."

"I have that footage, too," Amos suggested, but Leader waved him away.

"So, Scott's in Chastity inner circle?" she asked him instead. "Does he have good cause for defending her honor already? Or is this just some ploy he concocted to play games with Emma while at school?"

Amos pulled a face. "I don't know. I mean, he is friends with the student committee and the honor society. I guess it is feasible he might approach any new kid who causes trouble and insults his friends. Leader, it was not going to be a good idea for Scott and Emma to become friends at school. At least this way she has a legitimate reason for keeping her distance."

Emma jumped to her feet. "I'm not going to hide from him! He picked a fight with me, and I clearly demonstrated today that I'm not backing down. I'm not going to stay out of his way like a frightened bunny rabbit just because he got in with the popular crowd."

Leader's hand shot into the air and made a summoning gesture. "You're going to do as you're told, Emma," Leader said as she trudged toward her. "If Amos says you're to keep your distance, you find a way to fit it into the character you have created for yourself at this school."

When Leader reached Emma's side, she patted her face twice with a firm hand. "However, I actually agree with you in this," Leader looked at Amos. "She can't stay away from him now that he's thrown the gauntlet. She has to stand up for herself. It's his hide that needs singeing. What is it exactly Julianne is doing over there? Throwing parties? If she gives Scott an inch, he'll walk all over her. She knows that."

"She does know that," Amos assured Leader. "I sent the footage on to her so she can analyze it. She'll take care of Scott."

"I want Scott to keep his distance from Emma," Leader ordered. "He has more power, being the initiator. He is to make every effort to keep his crowd away from Emma and let her get any education she can." Emma scoffed at that, winning her another hard pat on the face.

"I'll call Julianne right now," Amos said.

"Do that," Leader directed. "And I want to talk to her."

Amos removed his phone from his pocket and walked into Leader's office to make the call. Leader turned on Emma. "Am I to understand from your derision that you did you not find your academics challenging at your new school?"

Emma rolled her eyes and backed away from the woman's grip. "Are you joking?"

Leader provided a mean smile, "I was, actually."

Emma pointed at the desk spread with her books. "It's all right there. You can see for yourself." She let out a frustrated breath. "My Calculus teacher was afraid I was going to hold the class back. You should have seen her face when I turned in my assignment at the end of the period. It took every ounce of restraint for me to keep from saying 'neener-neener' at her stupefied expression."

"Well, that reaction certainly would not have served the purpose of demonstrating your intelligence." Leader thumbed through the books and she shot Emma a bland look.

"It doesn't need any more demonstration," Emma answered sullenly. She shuffled some of the papers around on her desk. "I did not want to demonstrate it in front of the school today. I would prefer it if my intelligence speaks for itself without my meager assistance. My hasty words make a muddle and, rather than smart, I mostly came across as a douche."

Leader murmured her agreement to that, but her perusal of the textbooks did not abate.

"At least I came off smarter than Scott," Emma added, and she felt little delight in her success.

"You are smarter than Scott by a landslide," Leader replied, looking up from the history book. "Your genetic profile assures me of that. In fact, you're too smart for this curriculum, for all they praise it to the sky. Good thing I have a backup plan for you."

Emma scowled. "First of all, I don't want to be homeschooled. Second, what if my genetic file lied? What if I'm really just a regular-level smart but you used your words to swindle me into believing I can be more?"

Leader snapped the book shut and leaned back against the desk. "If my words had that kind of effect, I would swindle you into Obedience and Diligence. And you'll be any kind of schooled I choose, Little Girl. Don't get cheeky." She tapped on the computer and brought up a website. "From today on you are to complete your homework at school so that your homework time in the afternoon can be spent here."

Emma moved closer, leaning down to look at the site. If it was supposed to be a college website, it missed. It was too dark and unwelcoming. The words Einstein's Workshop flashed across the screen periodically in what was supposed to be a bolt of lightning. The official website name was Stone University.

"What is this?"

Leader motioned toward the computer. "I built you a catalogue under your new username: Game Pawn. Two words. The password is NUMBERELEVEN, all caps, no spaces. You will be attending these supplementary classes online since your school cannot keep you challenged."

Emma thought she ought to be angry at the double work, but the website intrigued her. "Will this be able to make up for what my school lacks?"

Leader came to her feet again and looked down at Emma coolly. "You do think well of your abilities, don't you?"

"Shouldn't I? My Leader assures me I have superior intellect."

Leader chuckled and swatted Emma with a firm hand to the bottom. "It will challenge you. I can assure you of that, as well. Scott would find it hopeless, but I am sure you will persevere."

Emma would devote herself to perseverance in this. It had been a long time since she had faced an actual academic challenge. And any advantage she had over Scott was worth the effort since it was more to tease him with. He had the upper hand in so many other areas.

Thoughts of Scott returned her mind with concern about his choice of friends.

"Leader?" she asked, turning to look in her superior's eyes. "Did you assign Scott to this group of friends as some kind of mission?"

"Why do you ask?"

Emma pulled a face. "I can't think of any other reason why you would let Scott make friends with them. It's pathetic. Student Council is just a minor form of government, and I thought you wanted us to stay out of government." That seemed to amuse Leader, so Emma tried another tactic. "He's a nowf, you know, dressed like he is and hanging around with those kids."

"A nowf?" Leader asked, her amusement wearing thin. "What's a nowf?"

Amos suggested, "You would do better not to ask," as he leaned out of the office to offer Leader his phone.

When Leader continued to stare at Emma expectantly, she said, "A 'no-one-would—"

Amos cleared his throat, "She can infer the rest by context. Thank you, Emma." And he forced the phone into her hand. Leader gave Emma a stern look as she walked away, saying into the phone, "Julianne, what is going on over there that makes Scott think he can flout my orders?"

Amos grabbed Emma by the shoulders and shook her slightly. "Are you out of your mind? Leader is on a precarious edge of sanity today. Could you not push her all the way over?" He spun her toward the exit and said, "Go downstairs and do some forms. You missed P.E. today, so you can use the workout."

Emma sighed, but she answered, "Yes, sir."

"And Emma?" Amos called, drawing her attention back to his gentle smile and concerned eyes. "You don't have anything to worry about. Scott still belongs to you more than he ever will belong to that clique he joined. You know more than the character he has to play; you know him. At the end of all this, we'll be a unit again."

Emma rolled her eyes and walked away, but she was surprised by the level of comfort Amos' words supplied.

Chapter Fifteen

Leader left for Beijing the next morning. Her parting instructions for Emma were to "be Diligent" and that she'd want a full report upon her return.

Amos took her to school. "Either Piper or I will pick you up at three," he instructed as she climbed out. "Steer clear of Scott, okay? I don't want to deal with your insubordination on top of the rest of Guild matters while Leader is off."

Emma sighed at that. "I did not seek him out in the first place. You know that."

He made a soothing gesture at her. "I just don't want any unnecessary trouble."

"Okay." Emma picked up her backpack but before she could get out of the car, Amos grabbed her by the arm and pulled her close enough to kiss the side of her head.

"Have a good day, honey." She pulled away with a glare at him for the unexpected display of affection. He laughed but if he had anything else to say, she didn't hear it. She hopped out of the car.

Keeping away from Scott turned out to be more difficult on the second day of school. Yesterday, she hardly saw him but today he seemed to be everywhere. She passed him in the hall several times before lunch threw them into the salad line together.

"Are you okay?" he whispered.

His unexpected question made her stumble with the salad tongs. When she turned and looked at him, she saw Josie standing just beyond them waiting for her.

"Well, if it isn't king of the polo society . . ." Emma commented, looking him up and down scornfully. "Are you back to harass people minding their own business? Round two?" She moved away before he could answer. "Asshole," she said loudly enough for anyone near to hear. She followed Josie across the room to a table as far from Scott's cronies as they could get. She resisted the urge to look back at him throughout lunch, though she felt certain several times he was looking her way.

Academics were not difficult for her, but this school was the most challenging she had attended for different reasons. Kids here either glared at her or watched her tentatively. They either stood challengingly in her path in the hall or laughed at her as she walked by. There were few people who were nonchalant and most of them were people who sat near Josie at lunch. The faculty was nearly as bad. Her own teachers tolerated her, but other teachers scrutinized her as if expecting her to pull out a can of spray paint at any moment. Worse than the teachers, the student counselor always seemed to be around, beady eyes narrowing in consideration. Emma's only job at this school was to not be a troublemaker, but her first day sealed her fate with Mr. Berkshire. He saw how she had behaved with Leader, and then Chastity probably tipped him off about their interactions. Half the school witnessed the verbal altercation in the lunchroom. Berkshire seemed to anticipate trouble from Emma at any moment.

Even though she had several more hours of academics after school, she was never so happy to get back to the Guild House in her life. The Guild House became more and more of a safe haven with each subsequent day, even with Adam in it.

At home, her only real frustrations came from Leader's online courses. Emma found Stone University trying but not so much because of intellectual challenge as its perpetuity. As soon as she mastered a concept, it spat more at her. As soon as she passed a class, the next level popped into her catalogue. If she failed to pass a test with a perfect score, the program removed her from her high standing and returned her to a previous chapter, unit, and, once, to an entirely different class. She felt exhilarated every time she attempted to beat it, frustrating as it could be sometimes.

"Good evening," Leader said as she walked in late one night. She touched Emma's shoulder lightly. Leader had been gone for an entire week, and Emma really missed her this time. She often went away, but rarely for more than a couple days. Emma was accustomed to her presence in the Guild House, brusqueness and exactingness and all. No offense to Amos, but he wasn't Leader.

Emma smiled up at her from where she sat at the desk looking through her notes on an online reading. "Have you been good?"

"Yes, ma'am."

Emma scrutinized her. Leader looked tired. Dark circles around her eyes made her seem older than she was a week ago.

"How was Beijing?"

Amos joined them from the office. "Thank god," he breathed, shaking his head in relief at the sight of her. "Are you okay?"

Leader shot him an angry look and walked toward the stairs, "I'm fine. And there is no God, Amos!" She brushed him away with a flick of her fingers. "I don't want to talk about it right now. We need to have Summit with the other half of the Guild tomorrow afternoon while the kids are in school. We'll talk there." When Amos tried to argue, she spun around and shot him an arched look. Then she smiled over at Emma softly, "I'll take you to school in morning so I can get that full report. Sleep well." And she disappeared from view.

Amos sighed, grabbed the phone, and went into the office to make a call. Emma wondered what it was that Leader did not want to talk about, but she didn't dwell on it because Leader would never tell Emma anything until after her Loyalty was tested and she entered the Senior Guild.

Emma came down the stairs to the kitchen for her breakfast. Amos called "good morning" from inside the refrigerator, but when he turned to speak to her, his smile slid away.

"Is that what you think you're wearing to school?" he demanded, looking her up and down with barely restrained revulsion on his face.

She glanced down at her clothes before sliding up onto a bar stool. She answered nonchalantly, "Yes."

Amos leaned across the counter to meet her at her eye level. Slowly, with deliberate calm, he told her, "Think again."

She was a little confused by his vehemence and looked down at her outfit again. Emma found black fishnet stockings yesterday while doing laundry for the house. She assumed it belonged to Piper, but she could not resist pilfering it away when she remembered Chastity's hatred for patterned hose. In order to really show them off, Emma put on a pink skirt that was short enough to challenge the student dress code. It was a fabulous find from the laundry. She opted not to wear a bra so she could wear her off-the-shoulder black shirt. Her hair had some definition after dumping various products in, although it looked like she had just climbed out of a swimming pool.

When Emma looked up, she saw that Amos was staring at her expectantly.

"What?"

"You're not wearing that to school!" he snarled with clipped off words and flashing eyes. He flicked his fingers toward the stairs. "Go and change."

She shoved away from the counter. She had to obey him, but she didn't understand what he was in a snit about. "What is your problem?"

He raised his voice a little, "Go and change right now! Are you kidding me? You can't wear *that* to school. You look like a hooker."

Leader leaned out of the office to look her up and down, "Seconded."

"Purity culture? Really?" Emma shot back at them both although she was uncomfortably aware that she was arguing with her superiors. "What's wrong with it, anyway? It's well within the character I developed for myself at this school."

Amos snorted and Leader stepped out of the office with her brows raised. "Not within the character *I* created for you. Did you change her character description while I was away, Amos? Did you tell her she could dress like she was about to strip her clothes off and dance around a pole?"

She was being facetious, but Amos still held up a defensive hand. "No, I did not." His decibel level rose with each word. "Get upstairs and change, Emma! I swear to God!—" He cut off when she spun around and tramped up the stairs. At her back, he shouted, "And do something about your hair! People are going to think you're homeless!"

When Emma got back to her room and changed into jeans and a white sweater. A white knit hat with a decorative brim went onto her head since she didn't have time to do anything with her hair. She was furious, but not because Amos had shouted or that Leader had compared her to a stripper. She was furious that her well-laid plan to piss off Chastity was ruined.

Yesterday, Chastity held hands with Scott while walking down the hall. Blood thundered in Emma's ears watching them. She crackled with indignation and fear. She wanted to do anything, say anything, but she couldn't. The smirk on Scott's face was too hurtful. He stepped right over Emma's books sprawled across the hallway floor and snickered over his shoulder. If not for Amos' text at that moment that she had forgotten her lunch, Emma might have considered hitting Scott.

Her real trouble was that she couldn't approach Scott directly without getting them both into serious trouble with their superiors. He seemed to be deliberately trying to upset her, but she was not empowered to rise to it. She wanted to get to him in a way that kept her blame-free, and the best way to do that was through Chastity.

A repeat of yesterday's fury welled up in Emma as she stared at the fishnets. Chastity would be beside herself if Emma came to school wearing them. That was the whole point. Well, that and to see what Scott would say when she told Chastity that fishnets were probably the reason her father had knocked up her mother.

Since Amos had not mentioned her past several exchanges with Scott and his cronies, Emma wondered if he wasn't watching the daily school footage like he had the first day. Thoughtfully, and with her heart suddenly pounding furiously, she eyed the stockings. She glanced around the room and then plunged the whole forbidden outfit into her backpack. Perhaps Amos would fail to watch the surveillance today.

She was in a subdued mood, although nervous, when she got back downstairs.

"Is this more to your liking?" she asked, tugging at the sweater as submitted herself for Amos' scrutiny.

He handed her breakfast after giving her a cursory glance. "Eat fast," he ordered. Then he raised his voice, "Leader, you have to leave in five minutes if you're going to take Emma to school."

Once they were in the car, Leader watched Emma silently for a moment. When Emma ignored her, Leader smiled and returned her attention to the neighborhood road. "Tell me about public school."

"It blows." Emma might have left it like that if not for the demanding look Leader shot her that insisted elaboration. "The classes are easy, but my teachers hate me for no good reason."

"Probably because you're cocky."

Emma did not respond to that jab since it was likely true. "The students are mean."

That seemed to surprise Leader. "Meaner than you? I never thought I would see a kid outside the Guild that was meaner than you."

Emma gave a frustrated sigh, "Not all the kids *are* outside the Guild." She sat back against the seat hard and stared at Leader. "At every opportunity, Scott makes my life as hard as possible. Yesterday, he tripped me and his 'dedicated to safety' friends laughed their heads off when my books spilled across the floor."

Leader shook her head, a dangerous glint dancing in her eyes. "I hope he has a good reason for harassing you, and that it's not just some elaborate game he concocted to tease you."

"He does have good reason," Emma admitted unhappily. "Chastity is leading a hate fest against me and he pulls something whenever she's around. I can usually see it coming because he gets that light of mischief in his eyes before he does anything. My friend Josie shoved him pretty hard into the lockers after he tripped me. She got detention, but Scott walked away like nothing had happened, hand in hand with Chastity like lovers."

Leader studied her a moment. "I see," she said with a weighted tone.

"You see what?" Emma snapped back. She did not really want to know what Leader thought she saw. "The only thing you see is the vendetta I'm building against my best friend. When the Guild comes back together, he'll have to sleep with an eye open."

"I see you still have an attitude," Leader answered sternly. "Good thing a sweet disposition is not a Guild Skill."

"I want to be able to retaliate without fearing you'll destroy me," Emma insisted. "Up to this point all I ever do is make snide remarks and trip them up with my words, but if you allow me to engage them, I can end this. One quick jab to the nose and Chastity would back off."

Leader barked a surprised laugh, "I'm not letting you punch that girl, Emma. You insulted her and now you have to live with the consequences. Scott will be smart enough not to get into trouble because he knows I would eat him alive; he shouldn't be more trouble than you can handle."

"I can handle him," Emma snapped back. "If you let me handle him, I'll do it today."

Leader shook her head, "No. Keep as much distance as you can. Tell me about Josie."

Defeated, Emma settled back into her seat. "Josie's an angry girl in a foster home. She doesn't talk about anything personal. She has an opinion about everyone in the school and, with the exception of a few people, most of them are not complimentary."

"Is she a troublemaker?"

Emma shrugged. "Not really. She doesn't dress out for P.E., so the gym teacher calls her a menace. The office watches her pretty closely, but I think that's because she *looks* like trouble. She smokes. She skips classes she thinks are stupid. And, of course, she shoves the occasional jackass into lockers."

"Okay," Leader said, choosing to ignore the jibe about Scott. "As long as you're not getting into any trouble, you can maintain a friendship with her."

"Thanks," Emma said, but it came out more like a question than gratitude.

Leader cut someone off and slipped into the loading/unloading lane to a chorus of horns honking. "The only reason you're in this school is to keep up the current Guild pretense. In order to do that, you need to stay out of trouble."

Emma reached for the door handle. "I understand, Leader. It doesn't matter to you whether or not I have friends, or whether I get tripped in the hall by a bully who is supposed to be on my side but decided to be a nowf instead. It doesn't matter to you that the entire school hates me because Chastity exaggerates the truth. I guess it doesn't matter to you that Josie and the kids like her are the only ones who will even look at me. The only thing you can afford to care about is Guild business. You have made yourself imminently clear about that on more than one occasion."

Leader grabbed her face, the way the previous Leader used to do. But unlike him, the current Leader was not harsh. "Hey, I'm not trying to make you miserable, Little Girl. I want you to be able to have friends. But your *safety* is my top priority. Do you think I moved us to this town in the middle of nowhere for shits and giggles? I did it to keep you and everyone else in the Guild safe. I split the Guild to keep us safe. It's not permanent, so please try to make the best of it. All right?"

Emma pried herself out of Leader's grip. "All right," she answered. She offered a false smile and a sarcastic, "I'm so glad you're back."

Leader hit the unlock button and asked, "Aren't hats against your dress code?"

Emma growled out in frustration, "I'll shove it in my locker." Then she winced when she saw Leader's hand moving as if to strike her. Instead, Leader just flicked the brim of Emma's hat, sending it soaring into the backseat.

"Have a good day," Leader said with a smile.

Emma slammed the car door, hoping to shatter the window, but no such luck. Some kids hanging out outside shot dirty looks her way. She flipped them off on her way through the doors.

Chapter Sixteen

Emma's heart pounded as she approached the first restroom. This was her chance to change if she was going to do it. It was probably a terrible idea. Amos could look at the live feed of the school at any time. What would Leader do to her for disobedience? And there was no definition of Diligence that included wasting time thinking up mean things to do to Chastity. It would be Mr. Mitchell all over again, and Emma's pride was still not fully restored since Leader's last beating.

Emma took a painful step away from the restroom. It wasn't worth it, she told herself. Chastity wasn't worth Leader's retribution.

There she was! Chastity stood behind a table at the end of the hall. She was taking money for tickets to the Winter Social coming up next week. And, like the dedicated devotee that he was, Scott sat beside her.

Emma spun on her heel and entered the restroom so fast that she did not have time to talk herself out of it again. She stripped in the first stall and dressed quickly in the clothing Amos had forbidden. He might come to the school to physically remove them from her if he happened to glance in the camera at all today. She could not worry about him. She could not worry about Leader's retribution. She was dressed to antagonize Chastity, and that was all.

She left the bathroom with the full intention to approach Chastity right away, but the school principal was at the table, so Emma slipped up the stairs instead. She would probably see Chastity a dozen more times. No need to rush it. After all, it wasn't as though Emma wanted her to know this outfit had been selected just to annoy her. Or did she?

Josie was waiting beside her locker. One glance at Emma and she laughed out loud, "You look like a Playboy Bunny."

"I'm dressed," Emma argued.

"Barely," Josie answered on a chuckle. She tugged at Emma's stockings. "I'm pretty sure these are against the dress code. You wouldn't want to infuriate Madame Senior President, would you?"

Emma grinned. Josie was starting to know her uncomfortably well.

"With any luck. I looked up the dress code and the only thing the disciplinary office can do to you is assign a demerit to your record. You need five demerits before they make you meet with the counselor, and fifteen before you can be suspended. I'm not worried."

Josie sat down in the hall and tugged off her knee-length goth boots. "Switch me," she ordered. "You should be wearing these babies when you see Chastity. She thinks boots of any kind are a Satanic ploy to get boys to think about sex. She's so stupid; boys will think about sex without any inducement."

Emma was already wearing boots but hers only went above her ankle. Josie's would make more of an impact. She sat down and removed her own.

"Keep your legs closed," Josie warned her with a laugh. "Your skirt is awfully short."

Emma blushed and folded her knees around to remove her boots in a more modest fashion. Josie's boots were a little too tight, but they certainly completed Emma's look. Now only eight inches of the fishnets showed, but it would be enough.

"Please don't do this without me," Josie begged as she pulled on Emma's boots. "I gotta see her face when she sees you."

Emma shrugged, "It probably won't be until lunch."

Josie scoffed, "Yeah, right. She's been dogging you like she has a crush. Maybe she does." She shrugged at Emma. "Maybe that's her real problem."

Emma rolled her eyes, rejecting the idea completely. "She wears a golden cross around her neck and carries a Bible with her to most classes. I don't think she's a lesbian. Besides, I'm pretty sure she has a boyfriend."

"First of all, you can still be a lesbian if you're a homophobe. Second, that snot-nosed man-whore she wears on her arm looks like a beard if I've ever seen one. I would have busted him up if not for that obnoxious student teacher interfering." She looked thoughtful for a moment. "He's kind of hot, you know, for a prep. Too hot for Chastity by a long shot."

Talking about Scott was making Emma angrier, and she didn't have time to be angry. She had to get to her Calculus class on time or her frail old teacher would assign her double work. That was her tardiness policy. While Emma did not find calculus particularly challenging, she did not have time to do double work when she was expected to clock in on Stone University by four o'clock. There was barely enough time in class to do the sets she was already assigned.

"I have to get to class."

Josie grabbed her arm, "Just don't do it without me there, okay? I want to see her face."

"I'll try," Emma snapped. The warning bell rang and Emma jerked away. "See you later!"

Emma tried running in the hall, but the boots made running almost impossible. Besides, the teachers in this school tended to stand in the hall to monitor. They would reprimand runners. Emma walked as fast as she dared. The attendance bell rang when she was turning into her hall. She stumbled into class breathless, but her teacher still arched a brow.

"Looks like double work for Miss Chandler today," she said mildly. Emma just barely managed to keep from cursing. Her mischievousness had just become a lack of Diligence.

Josie stalked her. She popped up unexpectedly between classes, asking right off, "Has she seen you yet?"

After her second class, Emma sighed and said, "It will probably not happen until lunch." She was spending every free moment she had working on the extra calculus work, and Josie's interruptions were stealing her time.

Josie shrugged, "Just checking."

After her third class, Josie met her again to walk to lunch. Emma got a lot of glares and some sneers, but all Josie had to do was frown at kids for them to move along with their business and leave her alone. They got to the cafeteria without any trouble in the halls.

"I'm so happy," Josie announced as they came through the door. She seemed even more invested in this than Emma.

Emma got all the way through the salad line before anything happened. Chastity came through the door when Emma was at the payment register. Her mouth dropped open, and her eyes popped when she recognized Emma. Josie, standing beside Emma, chuckled slightly. Chastity walked immediately to the table where her cronies sat. Scott wasn't there yet.

"Let's take the long way to our table," Josie instructed, motioning toward the Student Council table with a jerk of her head.

"Okay," Emma agreed reluctantly. Scott's absence dimmed the thrill of this episode. She had wanted him to be there to see her tell Chastity to screw her stupid addendums to dress code policies.

They walked side by side toward Chastity's table. As they approached, the other kids fell silent, making the tail end of Chastity's words audible to Emma. "She looks like a prostitute!" Her friends' eyes were all on Emma, so Chastity turned slowly around to meet Emma's gaze. Her eyes reflected unease at being caught unawares.

"Josie?" Emma asked, but her eyes never left Chastity's. "Did you hear our Student Council president using a putdown? Correct me if I'm wrong, but isn't that against the honor society code?"

Chastity glared hatred at her, "I wasn't talking to *you*!"

Emma displayed a nasty smile and set her tray down on a nearby table. "But you were talking *about* me, Miss President."

Josie popped in a comment, "Gossip is frowned on, as well, I think."

Emma nodded, "Oh, I know that, Josie," she said, still smiling at Chastity. "And our president knows that, as well. She does have an average IQ, after all. She should at least be able to remember the student code."

Scott joined them at the table. Chastity sighed in relief. She reached out for his hand but to Emma's satisfaction, he didn't see the gesture because his gaze was glued to Emma's outfit.

"Holy God."

"You made me your deity?" Emma asked in her most obnoxiously sweet voice. "I accept. You can worship at my fishnetted feet." The skeptical look he shot her in return was more than enough reward for wearing these clothes.

Chastity gave up trying to hold Scott's hand and instead folded her arms across her chest. "Maybe you're not as smart as you think you are, Emma Chandler. Since you clearly could not remember the student code says you can't wear patterned hosiery." She motioned a disgusted finger toward Emma's legs. "You'll get a demerit for this kind of clothing. It's disrespectful to the rest of the student body."

Josie piped in again, "Did she just say she respects your body? That's so sweet, Chastity. I think she loves you, Emma."

Chastity flamed red in rage, "No! I said your clothes are disrespectful to the other students and faculty at this school. The disciplinary office will take care of you." The other kids at her table murmured in agreement when she shot them an entreating look.

"What is disrespectful to the student body is that *you* are our representative," Emma argued. She motioned a hand toward Chastity's pantsuit that included tapered legs and shoulder pads. "Who dressed you today? The '90s?"

Chastity's face colored more deeply. "My father selected this outfit. But even if I was dressed by 'the '90s' at least I don't look like a pimp buys my clothes."

A fitting comeback, Emma thought, but she could not walk away and leave Chastity with the upper hand. "That's true. He can pick out your clothes, but I guess your father's pimping days were over as soon as he had *you* to toy with."

Scott stepped between them before Chastity could fully comprehend the words, "Stop it, Emma. Don't be a bastard." His eyes darkened.

"Violent language is against the student agreement," Emma shot back at him. "You should be careful; it would be a shame for your pretty girlfriend to have to report you to the disciplinary office. You might miss your tee-time at the club if you're sitting in detention."

"Golfing?" he shot back ferociously. "That's your big insult against my clothes? I'm wearing a polo shirt, so that must mean I'm a golfer?"

"Actually, I would say you were a nowf," Emma replied, unconcernedly.

That angered him. He had made up that particular acronym to describe Mitchell when Emma started having trouble with him.

"What do you think your clothes say about you?"

"Well, I don't think I would be classified as a nowf," Emma shot back with a grin. No one else could follow the conversation now, but Chastity seemed pleased that Scott was fighting for her. "I think I look like liquid sex, according to the way your girlfriend keeps lusting after me."

He scoffed, "How the hell did you get out of the house in that?" he demanded, and his language surprised Chastity, who squeezed his arm in alarm.

"That's none of your damn business," Emma snapped back. The thrill of this prank had sped away now, and she only felt angry. She wanted him to screw up and blow his cover so Leader would destroy him. She wanted him to feel pain. She wanted to rip him away from this school and those obnoxious polo shirts, and Chastity with all her self-righteous purity. "Don't ask me about what's going on in *my* house! You want to ask anyone anything, ask Chastity about getting screwed by her father! *She* needs your concern; don't you dare concern yourself over me."

Chastity cried out in horror at Emma's words and Scott's stance shifted. That was all the warning she had that he was going to hit her. She struck first since she was always in her ready stance. Against Leader's direct order, Emma attempted to handle Scott. Her first strike hit true; she broke his nose. Unfortunately, he had received more training than she, and was bigger and stronger besides. He managed to keep his feet and her second jab contacted his block. He countered, and she was tossed off her feet.

He anticipated her springing to her feet since being on her back was a vulnerable position they were taught to avoid. She was fast enough she could have made it to her feet before he could kick her, but she wanted him off-balance. She rolled out of the zone of his feet and launched a kick to his groin. He was out of practice! Her kick contacted with painful force, and he doubled over.

When she rolled up to her feet and saw that both of her hits had caused substantial damage, she moved to his aid. But he either misinterpreted her movement or was too angry to accept her aid. He elbowed her to the ribs and slammed her against the square post in the middle of the lunchroom.

"What is your problem?" he screamed and slammed her again. She twisted herself free of his grip and knocked him to his knees with a quick sweep of her legs. He dragged her down with him, though, and managed to throw a punch that caught the side of her face. She moved away from his next hit and grappled to free herself from his practiced holds.

He was ripped off of her by one of the coaches. She was dragged to her feet ,as well, and held back from him by a pair of massive arms. She bled from the mouth, and her ribs throbbed, but mostly her heart ached. This was not at all what she had in mind when she pulled on the fishnets. Scott glared hatred at her from a few yards away where he was also being restrained. What a disaster!

Chastity wept profusely while her friends told the sudden swarm of adults what they had witnessed. Josie shouted contradictions to their versions of the story, and managed to get some support from other kids who witnessed the fight. Emma did not even care. She stared hollowly at Scott until he was dragged away from the cafeteria by the coach. Emma was pushed after him by her own captor.

"Get them to the nurse," said a stern voice Emma did not recognize. "Then bring them to my office."

Chapter Seventeen

Principal Morley was a cross man used to dealing with troublemakers and druggies. When Emma and Scott were delivered to his office, he brought them in directly and made them sit across the room from one another. Coach Munson stayed in the room in case Emma or Scott decided to make any more trouble. They wouldn't. Sitting in the principal's office was a surefire cure for any violence they might have been feeling since the fight. They had bigger problems now.

"Have their parents been called?" the principal asked his secretary.

"Yes, sir. I spoke to their mothers. They're on their way."

The principal nodded satisfaction before closing his door at the woman's back. He came around to stand behind his giant wooden desk. The secretary's words had doomed them both, and they knew it. Scott even had the foresight to sigh in anticipation. Julianne would be enraged, but her anger was nothing compared to Leader's.

"All right!" the principal said, pulling their eyes to him. "Mr. Jameson. Miss Chandler. What seems to be the problem?"

When neither of them spoke up, the principal cleared his throat, "There is a no-violence tolerance at this school," he admonished.

"A no-tolerance violence policy?" Emma clarified.

"God, you are a piece of work!" Scott snapped at her. "You knew what he meant. You don't have to correct every stupid thing anyone says."

"That's enough!" the principal snarled. "Knock it off, both of you! Now, Miss Chandler, I've heard a lot about you, and I have to say, it's not all complimentary. I understand you routinely violate the student agreements by use of profanity, bullying, and, evidently, the dress code, since your skirt is short enough you should have received a demerit for walking in the door in it."

"It's short enough she looks like she's for sale," Scott scoffed.

The man placed both hands on the desk and leaned across it to glare at Scott. "You will refrain from making any comments unless addressed, young man. Do I make myself clear?"

"Yes, sir," Scott replied, his tone humbled slightly. "I apologize."

The principal cleared his throat again, "I have heard a lot about you, too, Mr. Jameson. And so much of what was said *was* complimentary, I find myself surprised that you're involved in this at all. I guess you can't believe everything you hear."

"You can't believe it when it's coming from Chastity Monez," Emma piped in. "She's been against me since my first day here. She, Scott, and all their student committee cronies approached me on my first day and attempted to bully me, but I don't suppose she admitted that to you. No! Scott she praises to the sky, but I'm a pariah because I wasn't the person she wanted me to be."

The principal leaned toward her now, "That's enough out of you—"

"No," she answered back. "I'm not going to sit here and let you talk down to me when you're already prejudiced, Mr. Morley."

He held up a halting finger, "My prejudice is strictly based on today's events, Miss Chandler. And in that you are equally culpable."

Scott snorted, "She sucker-punched me."

Emma's mouth dropped open in surprise and she turned wide eyes on him. "No *way* are you going to play innocent bystander, Scott! No way! You were getting ready to hit me. As far as I'm concerned, I reacted in self-defense."

Scott pointed at the bandage on his face and shouted, "You broke my nose! And self-defense? You accused Chastity's father of molestation! What if it's true, Emma? How could you say something like that?"

"It is true. I could smell that trauma on her the instant I saw her, but that's beside the point. You were going to hit me, and I was faster. Self-defense."

The principal pounded a fist on his desk, "Enough! It doesn't matter who started it. We have a no-fighting tolerance and that means you're both suspended equally for three days."

Emma felt the confines of suspension gripping her heart, and fear made her nasty. "Shouldn't he be given more days for being beat up by a girl?"

Scott came out of his chair, but the coach stopped him from moving toward her. "You sucker-punched me, you little bitch! I'll kill you!"

"Sit down!" the principal shouted. "Sit down right now, Mr. Jameson! We do not make threats of any kind at this school. If it happens again, I will call the police. Do you understand me?"

The idea of the police being contacted cooled Scott and Emma both. Neither of them would sit for a month if the locals got involved with Guild business because of them. They were on a precarious enough ledge as it was.

Scott sat down.

"A three-day suspension is my handbook guideline for first offenses, but I think you two need a week to cool down and pull yourselves together. I know you have only been here a couple weeks, but we have strict rules that I expect you to follow. We have to make Slope Oak a safe campus, and that takes everyone working together."

He would have gone on but a tap on the door interrupted him. "Come in," he invited, and his secretary opened the door.

"Mrs. Jameson is here. Shall I let her in?"

"Please," the principal said with some exasperation in his tone. Scott slid back and looked down at his feet for a moment, gathering himself to face his doom. Emma was scarcely less worried.

Julianne came through the door hurriedly, clutching her purse under her arm. She greeted Mr. Morley with concern tingeing her voice and worry on her face. "I'm Scott's mother. Is he all right?"

The principal nodded once. "He needs to see a doctor," he recommended, nodding toward Scott. "His nose is broken, but he seems okay other than that."

The coach dismissed himself at this point, assuming Scott would not attempt a fight with his mother in the room.

Julianne spun to look at Scott and drew breath in alarm. She took the two steps to his side and grabbed his head in her hands. She got one hand on the bandage to look at the damage before suddenly turning back to look at the principal.

"How did this happen?" she demanded. She happened to glance around then and spotted Emma. She drew a sharp breath in surprise. Obviously, she had not yet seen the footage. She had no idea Emma was involved. She wasn't supposed to know her, but Julianne peeled her gaze away with some difficulty. Her next look at Scott was angrier.

"What happened?" she repeated, and her tone was much cooler this time.

"Your son got into an argument in the lunchroom today," the principal informed her. "I haven't been able to get a straight answer from either guilty party about how the argument started, but it resulted in a fistfight. We have zero-tolerance for violence at this school."

Julianne muttered in Chinese, but so quickly Emma could only translate the words, " . . . protect and keep us . . ." before Julianne switched to English. "I am so sorry, Mr. Morley. I am shocked that this happened. Shocked!" her repeated word was said a little more firmly and it was meant for both Emma and Scott. She looked at them both as her eyes scanned the room. Then her hand clenched Scott's shoulder as she demanded, "What is this about?" but again, she was speaking to both of them.

"She sucker-punched me," Scott said quickly. He held up a closed fist. "Jab! Straight to the nose!"

Julianne swiped his fist away and turned a surprised look on Emma, who sneered, "You were going to hit me. I defended myself." She looked up at Julianne pointedly. "Anyone *watching* could see he changed stances!" Julianne got the covert message to watch the footage, but it wouldn't matter once Leader got her hands on them.

"You *broke my nose!*" Scott snapped back.

When Emma sat forward to argue, Julianne said, "Stop it!" and Emma obediently settled back. Scott also calmed down.

"I am so sorry about this," Julianne told the principal. "This will not happen again."

"It can't," Mr. Morley replied. "Your son has been suspended for a week. I expect him to abide by all rules and agreements when—" he cut off at another knock on the door. Leader. Emma's stomach sank. "Come in!"

This time the secretary did not have an opportunity to announce the newcomer. Leader strode in, powerful as ever. Unlike Julianne, she took in the entire room before greeting the principal. She did not move one step closer to Emma, but rather remained equidistant from Scott and Emma both as she approached the desk.

"I would say good afternoon, but I don't suppose it applies," Leader said, offering her hand to shake Morley's.

He responded with a heavy sigh, "No, it does not. Were you informed of why you were called?"

Leader nodded, "Emma was in a fight, I was told."

"Yes," he replied. "During lunch, she engaged in an argument that turned into a fight. She has been suspended for one week."

"Both parties have been suspended?"

"Yes." If the principal noticed how silent the rest of the room was, he did not make any indication.

"For one week?" Leader asked into the silence. "I thought school policy was a three-day suspension for first-time acts of violence."

The principal cleared his throat again, "It is. But they seemed unable to get themselves calmed down, so I decided they needed five days at home instead of three. I believe they can pull it together by then." Emma winced. If he had any idea how fast Leader could enforce them pulling it together, one afternoon suspension would have been all he needed.

Leader nodded slowly, taking it all in. "I see. Has an official report been filed for Emma?"

"No," Morley replied. "I have to sign it first."

"I'll wait," Leader said. "I want to see it before I leave."

"It may be some time, Mrs. Chandler," he answered. "I'm happy to fax you a copy."

"I will wait," she replied coolly. She shot a glance Julianne's way.

"I'll see Scott's, as well," Julianne announced. "If it's not too much trouble, Mr. Morley."

It was but he pretended it was not. "They're in the front office. I'll just go and get them." He left the door open as he went hurriedly. Leader turned slowly around, looking at her subordinates each in turn. Emma could not meet her eye. When Leader's gaze rested on Julianne, she said, "You follow my car when we leave here."

"Yes, Leader," she agreed. She let out a defeated breath. "I was blindsided by this. I am thoroughly ashamed of myself."

"No," Leader cut her off. "We are not doing this here. You follow me when we leave, and we'll do it someplace where we can really do it." The threat in her voice made Julianne recoil. Scott slipped further down in his chair. Emma sat tall. She somehow hoped that if she sat still enough, Leader would forget she was there and would leave without her. No such luck. Leader glanced at her, gaze traveling up from Emma's boots to her disheveled hair. Leader sucked in breath between her teeth and looked away. Emma closed her eyes and prayed for death or deliverance. But Leader was her only deity and she was going to crush her in almighty hands.

When the principal returned, he held two yellow slips of carbon-copy paper. One he handed to Leader, one to Julianne. Julianne held hers carefully within Leader's sight while pretending to peruse it. After a moment, Leader said, "Is this all?"

"A more detailed report will be available tomorrow," Morley answered, returning to his desk though still not sitting. "I can email it to you, if you would like."

"Yes. May I keep this?" She presented the yellow carbon page.

He nodded, "It's your copy."

Leader folded the yellow paper and slipped it into her jacket pocket. "Thank you for your time and your prompt attention," Leader told the principal. "This will never happen again."

"It *can't* happen anymore," the principal replied. "As I was telling Mrs. Jameson, we are a zero-tolerance school when it comes to violence and bullying."

Emma knew she should cut her losses and keep her mouth shut, but she couldn't help it. "I have been bullied at this school *every day* in the week and a half I have been here!"

Leader held up one finger. It was a gesture used in training, demanding silence and attention. "This will *never* happen again," Leader repeated slowly, and though her eyes never left Morley, Emma felt very small under the threat of her words.

"I'm sorry your daughter feels she is being—"

Leader waved a hand dismissively at whatever he was going to say. "Mr. Morley, this incident will never occur again. My daughter will be back next Wednesday and will prove to be as good a student as you have ever seen. There will be *absolutely* no more trouble."

Julianne piped in, "That stands for Scott, as well."

The principal did not seem to know what to say, so Leader took charge. "Let's go!" she ordered, snapping her fingers at Emma in the way that made the sound reverberate in her ears. Emma picked up her backpack and quickly followed Leader from the room, Scott and Julianne right behind them. If Morley was surprised by their sudden departure, he said nothing. Leader had that effect on people.

Chapter Eighteen

Leader's car was parked in visitor parking outside the office doors. She pushed the keyless entry on her keychain as they crossed the parking lot. Julianne and Scott walked beyond them, on toward the drive thru where Julianne was parked. As Julianne passed Leader, she handed her Scott's yellow report, and Leader slid it into her pocket next to Emma's.

"Get in," Leader ordered as she walked around to the driver's side. Emma's heart beat painfully as she reached for the door. She could not make her hand close around the handle; it was trembling too hard. Her legs felt weak but at the same time they pulsed with the need to escape. She hesitated only a moment before doing as instinct dictated. She ran.

Emma was fast, but Leader was faster. She shed the heels and was after Emma in a split second. She caught her in under ten. When Emma felt Leader's hands close on her shoulder and her arm, she crumpled in a tearful heap. She had never been under any illusion she could get away from the Guild, but her quick recapture was a painful reminder of Leader's vast superiority. She could never escape. Leader would never allow it.

Emma's weight was nothing to Leader, who could probably lift a car if she felt like it. She hauled Emma to her feet and hissed, "Walk!" in her ear. Emma walked. Leader would carry her if she had to—Emma knew that—but life would be so much harder for her if she made Leader do it.

This time, Leader escorted her all the way to the door and pushed her in. She buckled Emma in, triggered the manual child lock inside the door, and slammed it shut.

Leader slipped back into her heels and climbed in the car, not even winded. She tossed Emma's backpack into the backseat. Slamming her car into reverse, Leader backed out of the spot, and squealed out of the parking lot. In a matter of seconds, Julianne was right behind them, following through the streets of Springfield.

Emma slid down as far as her seatbelt would allow and cried silently against her arms.

They drove toward the Guild house but took an abrupt turn onto Kansas Expressway and headed north. Several miles later, they reached the outskirts of the city and Leader spoke.

"What is it you're afraid of, Emma?" she asked as she took a turn onto a less-traveled road. When Emma did not immediately answer, Leader snapped, "Sit up and look at me!"

Drawing a breath to calm herself, Emma adjusted her seatbelt and sat up. It took another calming breath to look at Leader, who watched the road but shot an occasional glance at Emma.

"Answer my question," Leader said when a glance at Emma proved she was sitting up.

"I don't know," Emma spoke softly, tears still on her face.

"You ran from me," Leader shot her a surprised look. "You *ran*. What are you afraid of? Where were you going to go?"

Emma bowed her head and covered her face with her hands. "I don't know," she replied miserably. "I wasn't thinking ahead. I was just scared."

"Why?" Leader snarled back. "I'm always the same, Emma. There are no surprises with me."

"I know," Emma replied through her tears. "That's what I was afraid of. You said you never wanted to be called to the dean again. You said not to engage Scott. You said I needed to stay out of trouble. And . . .?" She shrugged helplessly.

"You're forgetting I also told you not to wear those clothes," Leader replied crossly.

Emma slipped further down in the car seat. "I didn't forget," she replied miserably. "It was just a ploy to upset Chastity and engage Scott."

Leader let out a breath through her nose, not quite a scoff. "You think I don't know that? I know you, Emma!" She turned the car onto a dirt road and jumped immediately to a deadly speed. "Do you think you're the only person in my Guild to have ever done something stupid for attention? Well, you have my attention. 'Welcome back from Beijing, Leader. Now watch me disgrace myself!'"

Those words brought on a fresh round of tears. "I'm not even sorry," Emma admitted in bitter anger. "That's the trouble with all of this! You're going to expect me to be sorry, like Julianne is. Like Scott is . . . but I'm not sorry. I wanted to punch Scott and I did it. I did it."

Leader let out a mirthless laugh. "Emma!" She reached over and grabbed Emma's leg in an intense grip. She shook her in furious frustration, fingers painfully digging into Emma's thigh. "You're not supposed to be sorry! If you make a deliberate, practiced violation, you should at least have the self-respect to stand up for what you did! Running away from me is not standing up!"

Emma pried Leader's fingers off her leg with some difficulty. "I know! I know! It's just you can do anything you want to me. I ran because I was scared of what you would do."

Leader shook her head in frustration and decelerated, "What did you think was going to happen? I may *want* to strangle you sometimes, but I never would! The worst thing I have ever done is take a strap to you."

Emma wiped her face on the shoulder of her shirt, but more tears quickly replaced them. "That's not the worst thing you've ever done," she muttered. Leader looked aside at her, but she did not ask. Emma was glad, because she didn't want to talk about the time this woman claimed death was "the price of disobedience."

At the fork in the road, she veered right, and Emma steadied herself by grabbing the handle suspended from the ceiling. They drove in silence for several minutes. Emma concernedly watched Leader's driving. Emma had not yet had a driving lesson, but she imagined it was generally frowned on to drive angry.

"*Are* you going to take a strap to me?" Emma finally asked. The not knowing was worse than any punishment.

"Give me one good reason why I shouldn't," Leader snapped back. Emma shrugged slightly and looked out the side window. "Can't think of any reasons why not? Me neither!"

Emma glared back at her through her tears, "I *do* have a reason. Beating me didn't work last time. What makes you think it will work this time? Einstein said that insanity is doing the same thing over and over and expecting different results."

"Don't you use that condescending tone on me, Emma! Maybe beating you is just to appease my anger and is not meant to correct your behavior at all. What do you suppose Einstein has to say about that?"

Emma hated the idea that Leader would hurt her just because she was mad. She wiped furiously at her tears again. "Does that mean you're going to?"

"Why wouldn't I?" Leader raged. "Can you prove to me in any way that you have been Diligent? And don't let me even get started on Obedience, Number Eleven! Obedience is a skill you should already have mastered. Yet here you sit in the clothing Amos forbade you to wear! You engaged Scott when I gave you direct instructions to stay clear of him."

Emma's tears finally gave way under her forming anger. "*Scott* engaged *me*! And I have been Diligent, Leader! Up until today, I have completed my work at school as instructed, and gotten onto Stone University daily to face that staggering workload. I have done everything you asked me to do!"

"Diligence is more than just doing as you're told, Emma!" Leader shouted back. "Diligence is living up to your potential. Is *this* your potential? This sniveling, frightened girl who dresses like a whore to attract attention? And runs from her Leader to avoid a beating?" The wheels to Leader's car spun as she made an abrupt turn down an unmarked lane.

"Maybe that is who I am!" Emma shrieked back. "Maybe the magical potential you see in me is a fictional, imaginary delusion you created to convince yourself you're a good leader!"

The car skidded to a stop in front of a worn-down old farmhouse and barn. The abruptness made Emma wince, afraid for a moment that Leader had only stopped the car to confront Emma's nasty remark. But then Julianne's car came in behind them.

"That's very convenient!" Leader shot back, eyes afire. "You get to play the role of picked on heroine forced to do the bidding of the big, bad, scary

Leader. You get to turn me into the villain. If you do that, you can convince yourself that you don't deserve a beating."

"I don't!" Emma parried. "I don't deserve it!"

"It's not up to you!" Leader replied forcefully. "Get out of the car!"

Emma drew a deep breath, attempting to tame her fury. Through gritted teeth, she explained, "I can't. You threw the child lock."

Leader looked hard at her for a long moment before climbing out and stalking around to the passenger side. She opened the door for her and held it so when Emma climbed out, she had to pass very near her.

"Are your Amos-approved clothes in your backpack?" Leader asked coolly as Emma stepped beyond her. Emma flinched when she slammed the door.

"Yes," she answered in a controlled calm.

"Good," Leader replied. Then she withdrew a knife from somewhere on her person. Startled, Emma backed away into the side of the car with a squeal. Leader gave her a challenging look as she approached. Emma squeezed her eyes shut in fear, but Leader took the knife to Emma's shirt, not her person. Emma cried out again in shock this time as her shirt fell to the ground in scraps. She covered herself as best she could and watched in horror as Leader's knife rent the skirt, as well. It was a sharp enough blade that when Leader took it to her stockings, it cut through them and the boots at the same time. With the exception of her panties, which were a very chaste classic-cut pair, Emma stood bare against the car, staring in horror at Leader. Another challenging look from Leader followed and she tucked the knife away.

"Are you crazy?" Emma snarled, glaring and blushing furiously. Scott was in the car behind them. Could he see her? "It's forty degrees out here!"

"Thirty-eight, actually," Leader answered. "And Einstein very well might call me crazy." Those words sent a chill down Emma's spine. "Would you like to get dressed in appropriate clothing now?"

"Yes!" Emma snarled.

Leader jerked her head toward the backseat and Emma moved faster than perhaps she ever had before. She dove into the backseat and tugged her sweater and jeans out of the backpack. Her hat was still there on

Leader's backseat, so she put that on, as well. Once she was dressed, she sat up in the seat but remained where she was. Leader and Julianne were walking together toward the barn and clearly arguing. When she heard Leader raise her voice, Emma slipped down to lie across the seat. If not even Julianne would be spared today, Emma did not stand a chance.

Several minutes later, the door at her feet opened. She jerked to a sitting position to face Scott. He stared at her with no expression for a moment. He looked ghastly without his bandage. Both his eyes were black, and his nose was swollen. She had done that to him. He was her best and most trusted friend, and she had blackened both his eyes, broken his nose, and done some possible damage to his testicles. She couldn't bear to look at him; she looked beyond him toward the woods in the distance, trying to think of what to say.

Scott slapped her with an open palm. She cried out and looked at him in shock. Before she could demand an explanation, he coldly said, "That's for not stopping when I told you to."

He shut the door and walked back to his car without another word. Leader and Julianne had not seen their exchange, so engrossed were they in their own conversation. Emma curled back up in the seat. She would never tell them, because saying it aloud would have been impossible. *Scott had struck her!* He had never used his authority in such a way, even when he hated her. She bit back tears. She was relatively sure nothing Leader could do to her now could be as painful.

Julianne collected her from the car several minutes later with a stern, "Follow me." She collected Scott in similar fashion. They went to the farmhouse and into the kitchen. It wasn't really a kitchen at all, Emma realized as she looked around. It was an exam room one might find in a clinic or hospital. She motioned Emma to a chair and situated Scott in front of her on the exam table. She scrutinized his injury with the fierce intensity she used when attending ailments. She asked him questions, but Emma did not listen. She looked out the window over the sink at the backyard and thought about this horrible day. She winced when Scott cried out suddenly under Julianne's ministrations.

"There!" Julianne announced. "You should heal up pretty now. Is there anything else you want me to look at before I'm done?"

"No," Scott snapped bitterly.

"Are you sure? I know she kicked you."

"I'm fine!" Scott retorted and hopped down from the table with a wince. He now had a nude-colored clip on the bridge of his nose, but with the shadows under his eyes, he was still a painful sight.

Julianne snapped her fingers. "You're up, Emma," she ordered, and patted the surface of the exam table.

"I'm fine," Emma replied.

Julianne spun to face her with an arched brow. "I did not preface my statement 'if it suits your fancy.'" She snapped her fingers again and pointed to the exam table. "Right now." Emma Obeyed. Scott walked across the room and leaned against the doorframe, looking out into the adjoining chamber. He looked as tired as Emma felt.

Julianne examined Emma from head to foot, prodding once or twice at bruises and asking various questions. Julianne's careful fingers crawled over her scalp, and across her jaw. Emma winced and shied away from her hands when they examined her bruised ribcage, where Scott had been most effective. Julianne bandaged her up, slathered her knuckles with an ointment to ease the pain she did not even know she had. Several times Julianne shook her head and said, "I can't believe this." She seemed truly mystified by Scott's and Emma's attack on one another. Emma still had trouble believing it herself.

Leader came through the door as Julianne let Emma off the table. She gave Julianne an expectant stare.

"They're both bruised up," Julianne answered Leader's implicit query. "As you could see, Scott's nose was broken, but I found no other injury he would allow me to attend. Emma's ribs are bruised, but without an X-ray I can't determine if there are any fractures. Her jaw is a little swollen and she has a couple nasty lumps on her head. They certainly did not restrain themselves."

That wasn't true. If they hadn't restrained themselves one of them would be dead; they were trained killers. But Emma opted not to correct her.

"But they're okay?" Leader's voice was hollow, but Emma thought she was genuinely concerned.

"Yeah, they're okay," Julianne answered unhappily. "But not for lack of trying to destroy one another."

Leader gave a thoughtful nod, "You can go back to the house when Piper gets here."

Chapter Nineteen

Leader made a summoning gesture at Scott and Emma and walked into what was probably originally a living room. It had various types of high-tech equipment Emma did not recognize. There seemed to be no semblance of order to it all. Leader wove through it with practiced grace and went up the stairs at the end of the room. Scott followed behind and Emma brought up the rear.

The upstairs led into an open space with several couches, chairs, a television, and a bar on one wall. The table across the room was where Leader led them. With a peremptory order to sit, Leader walked around to the head and sat down. It was a much smaller table than Scott or Emma were accustomed to, only seating five. Scott and Emma took the chairs farthest from Leader but incidentally across from one another. Even at such a small table, their regular habit kicked in.

Leader sat cocked in her chair, looking at them but resting her head in her hand, propped up on the back of the chair.

"Emma doesn't think I should beat her," Leader told Scott. "She doesn't think she deserves it for this. What about you? Think I should let you off the hook?"

Scott wet his lips and sat forward in his chair, folding his arms on the tabletop. "I will accept any punishment you deem appropriate, Leader; that goes without saying, but, incidentally, I think I don't deserve it either. I did not knowingly disobey, and I have not shirked even for one second since we moved here. Everything I am supposed to be doing, I am doing. My Guild responsibility is Confidence, and if I did not display great tact or delicacy today, I most certainly cannot be accused of a lack in Confidence." He shot Emma a quick glance.

Leader drummed her fingers on top of her head as she studied him, "I think you have a better case than she does."

Emma glared at Leader through her lashes, "You don't need to strike me to make your point, Leader. I understand already. But Scott can defend his time and his actions to you, and I cannot. I disobeyed Amos. I disobeyed you. I disobeyed Scott. I was tardy to Calculus and so have extra homework I could not complete in class, which I knew you would count as a lack of Diligence."

"You don't think it qualifies?"

Emma pressed the palms of her hands against her eye-sockets. "It qualifies," she miserably conceded. Her hands fell into her lap. "You told me you would push me, and I don't assume you changed your mind." She looked up at Leader. "I can't defend myself to you."

Leader shook her head in agreement, "No, you can't. Amos sent me the footage of your day and I must say you're well on your way to another disappointing term. I don't like to be disappointed."

Emma turned her face away, looking toward the stairs. She wished she could walk away, like normal teenagers in normal houses. She did not want to hear what Leader had to say. She did not want to deal with anything else today.

"The thing is, Emma, I can be pretty forgiving," Leader explained. Emma knew that. She had asked a Leader's forgiveness before when she had desperately wanted it, and it had been graciously granted. "I understand better than anyone how trying it is for the Guild to be separated. I know it is difficult for you and Scott to be in different homes and unable to speak to one another regularly, as you are used to. It is difficult that Scott's mission placed him in the Student Council crowd and your aversion to Chastity pushed you away from it.

"When I feel as guilty as I do for separating the two of you, I am extremely prone to forgiveness. Most of my anger is at myself and I can't honestly blame you two." When Leader paused, Emma glanced her way.

She had no idea Leader felt guilty for separating the Guild. Why had she done it?

"As I was walking with you to the car, cooling down, I was even thinking of what I could say to the two of you that would be strong enough to convince you of my displeasure, but at the same time assure you of my appreciation of your troubles at school. Some things happened in Beijing that reminded me of my responsibility to you all and of frailty of youth." Leader's eyes took on a distant expression as she floated through her memories. "Sometimes the simplest parts of life are overlooked in the Guild's need for precision and perpetuity. Simple things like friendship and love." Her eyes refocused. "Your friendship with one another is too important to me to let it rot away because of today's events."

Emma peeked up at Scott thoughtfully.

"You can't order us to be friends," Scott said doubtfully.

Leader spun forward in her chair and looked sternly at Scott. "You are friends already. If you're trying to back away now, it's out of fear or anxiety and you aren't permitted to balk at those considerations, Number Ten. Or do we, indeed, need to discuss Confidence?"

Scott took the warning and looked at Emma. "I think we'll be fine, Leader." He really believed it. They had already had their face-off at the car. "Emma?"

She nodded in answer, "We'll be fine as long as you admit you changed stances and were planning to hit me in the lunchroom today." Her stipulation appeared to amuse him. "I was acting in self-defense."

"I was going to hit you," he admitted. "But you were *not* acting in self-defense. You walked into that school today with the full intention of pushing my buttons."

Emma could not very well deny that truth. She nodded and grudgingly conceded, "That's a fair assessment."

Leader nodded in satisfaction. "Good. Scott, you are going to stay here with Piper until the end of your suspension. And before you get it in your crazy head that it's going to be a party, let me tell you what it's going to be: seven days of cleaning, organizing, painting, lifting and carrying, cooking, and lots of other endless chores. And don't think you're going to be spared,

Emma, simply because you're going home. You'll get the same and on top of that delightful menu, you will be expected to maintain your time and attention on Stone University, with increased results since you aren't using your brain power on thinking up ways to press Scott's buttons. Scott, Amos will come each morning to train with you. He is to double your Mat time, since you clearly need the practice." She shook her head at him. "Beat up in the cafeteria by a girl in heeled boots . . ." Her disgust for that was palpable. "That means Thomas hasn't been working you hard enough."

Scott agreed in as grudging a way as Emma had before.

"I will be giving Piper strict instructions with regards to your care," Leader went on. "I am not taking this suspension lightly, and I will see to it that she does not either. That goes for you, too, Emma."

"Yes, Leader," Scott and Emma said on top of one another.

Leader rose slowly from her seat. "I think that means I'm done with you for now, Scott. Amos is in the barn. I want you to go down there and tell him I said to work your forms until you're bleeding or crying."

Scott sighed, "I guess this means you decided not to beat us."

Leader pulled a face, "I can beat you whenever I want, Scott. I may wake up tomorrow and decide you need it. But as for now, I decided not to beat you."

Scott opened his palms. "I want you to forgive me, Leader," he replied with Confidence. "I don't want the idea of your anger hovering over me all week."

Leader seemed to consider this, "I forgive *you*."

Emma caught the slight emphasis on the pronoun and looked up in concern. "What about me?"

Leader shook her head, almost disgustedly, "You neither asked my forgiveness nor deserve it, Emma."

"But . . . why not?" Scott came to her aid, sounding actually angry on her behalf.

Leader held up a hand at them both to stall any more arguments.

"Because . . . I am willing to forgive the premeditated disobedience, the sloth, and the wonton disregard of your missions. Even though it rankles, I am even willing to forgive your disrespect to yourselves and to each other." Emma listed those things in her mind. That seemed to be everything Leader could be harboring against her. Then Emma saw the look in Leader's eyes, the implacable accusation masking deep-seated pain, and she knew before Leader said it, "I am not willing to forgive running away."

Scott seemed confused for a moment, but then he turned a horrified look on Emma. "You ran away?" He was the only person in the Guild who she might have hoped to take her side in this, but he clearly did not.

Emma felt small in her chair, facing his censure and Leader's threats. "Less than ten whole yards."

"I'm surprised you made it that far," Scott snapped back. "What were you thinking? Where were you going to go?"

"I wasn't thinking," Emma raised her voice over his. She looked at Leader and opened a beseeching hand to her. "I thought we already established that I wasn't thinking. I was just acting on impulse."

"You don't get to have impulses that make you run," was Leader's caustic reply. "You are a fighter! I trained you to be a fighter! You don't run away from me."

Scott shook his head in disapproval, in complete agreement with Leader.

Emma shot back, "I think you're holding me to a Confidence standard."

Leader said, "Yeah, you're probably right. But I would hold even Victoria accountable if she tried to run away. For the *second time*."

That was the key, and Emma knew it. She had run away before, but back then, the woman before her had not been Leader, and had not had to take it personally.

"Scott, Amos is in the barn," Leader reminded as she sat back down in her chair.

Scott sighed on Emma's behalf. "Yes, Leader." He walked away and left Emma to her fate.

For a long time, they just sat there in silence with their thoughts. Emma stared at her own hands on the table. She could understand Leader's anger now. Back when Emma had run away from the previous Leader, her crime had been much more severe. She had tried to catch a train to another state. That fateful attempt had resulted in the death of the then Leader, and the current Leader had replaced him. It had been left to Leader to discipline her for running away, but she let it slide, considering her punished enough by the consequences of her defection. But today was personal. Emma could see that.

"I wasn't running away from your discipline," Emma admitted in a whisper. "That's not what I am afraid of." She had Leader's attention now and, though she did not want to go on, she forced herself to continue, "I was afraid of the look in your eyes that you gave me when we were parked outside Sacred Covenant on my last day there. The day you said I wasn't living up to my potential and you were going to push me. After everything that happened today, I was afraid I failed to measure up again. I was afraid that you would start talking in the car and you would say I was a fool to fight with Scott. I was afraid you would say I was jealous of Chastity and that I had behaved like an idiot."

Leader looked hard at her. "I would never ridicule you for that. I understand your sentiments, Emma. When you told me you wanted to punch Chastity and Scott, I kind of figured you would find a way to do it. This may surprise you, but I had similar altercations when I was your age under similar circumstances. When I said, 'I see,' this morning in the car, I thought we both understood that I could see your frustrations and the cause of your distress."

Emma vaguely remembered. "I just couldn't bear to hear that you were let down."

"Let down?" Leader replied skeptically. "Emma, as your parent, I was proud. You beat up a kid that was twice your size; a bully that, frankly, had it coming."

Emma buried her face in her hands for a moment to draw a breath and push away the tears that threatened again. "I would do anything to keep from disappointing you, Leader," she whispered and looked up into Leader's eyes. "I wasn't running from your discipline, I was running away from your disappointment."

An expression of cold irony crossed Leader's features. "Unfortunately for you, Emma, today you have to face both."

The welling emotions of pain and shame put Emma's head down in her arms. She no longer attempted to stifle her tears. She had earned them.

Chapter Twenty

U sually, Amos was a pleasant man. He often attempted to make Emma's life a little sweeter than it had to be. In her childhood, Amos was the one she went to when she struggled with Guild or school or social expectations. He was the voice of validation at home, where she was certain to receive little, if no, compassion from anyone else. Amos was always the one to reassure her, to smile her out of her gloom, and remind her that she belonged to someone. Usually, Amos was patient and understanding and forgiving.

"Evidently, I am too lenient," he snarled when he, Leader, and Emma headed home from the farmhouse in the Volvo. "What I say can be overlooked, I suppose, because I'm a nice guy." He shook his head in disgust. Emma sat a little smaller in the backseat, keeping her gaze glued to her lap.

"It's a good fault to have, Amos, being a nice guy," Leader answered in a soothing tone. But Amos was having none of that.

He turned in the passenger seat to glare back at Emma. "Does my pleasant disposition make it easier for you to ignore my commands?"

Emma's eyes maintained their focus on the hands in her lap. She did not dare meet his gaze, furious as she expected to find them. She did not need his anger to humble her, humbled as she already was by Leader's previous demonstrations of power. She winced at Amos' question but was afraid to answer with the truth. In fact, it had been Leader she had been most concerned to upset. When Emma placed the forbidden garments in her backpack, Amos' words had flickered through her mind, but she discarded them easily. She knew him to be gentle, and that certainly made him easier to disobey.

"Well?" Amos demanded, not giving her the option to maintain silence on this issue. He expected her to tell him if she thought his kindness made him an easier target for disobedience.

Emma made tentative eye-contact. "Yes," she admitted, though it pained her. She caught Leader's grimace in the rearview.

Amos turned back to face the road. For several moments, he sat quietly, only drawing deep breaths. Then he screamed out a single profane word and punched the dashboard, demolishing the cover to the glove compartment.

Emma flinched from his outburst, totally unprepared for his display of violence. Leader was not. She signaled and pulled the car over to the roadside.

"Let's talk, Amos," she instructed as she killed the engine.

"I hate him! I just hate him!" Amos snarled, clenching and unclenching his fists. Emma stared at the back of his head in horror. She could not imagine who he could hate, if not her. Yet, the pronoun "him" suggested it was not Emma. "And I hate him even more because he was right." He launched a slap at the rearview mirror, but Leader intercepted his hand. She grabbed his face in both of her hands and forced him to look at her.

"He is dead," she told him in a voice that was both firm and gentle. Emma flinched again, because now she understood. Leader. Leader before the current Leader. He often accused Amos of being too soft.

"It doesn't matter!" Amos shouted back, jerking out of her grip. "He was right. You almost died in Beijing and then what would have become of the Guild? 'Everyone can just do whatever they want! Never mind what Amos says, because he's a milksop, pansy, weakling!'" He punched at the dashboard again.

Leader grabbed his hand and insisted, "Let's talk about this outside. If you sit in here, you'll demolish my car."

Amos jerked from her grip and tried to open the door, but the child lock was still on.

"I'll get it," Leader assured him. But he didn't wait. He launched his elbow through the passenger window before she had even fully exited the vehicle. The glass shattered, cutting Amos' arm thoroughly as he reached through and opened the door himself. He stalked away from the car toward the empty hayfield. Leader stared at the car door for a moment, sighed, and followed him away.

Stunned, Emma sat in the silence, staring at the broken window in horror. Then she leaned forward to look at the glove compartment. She regretted that movement immediately when her freshly welted backside throbbed with her change of position. She returned to a position that caused less pain, but there was none that ensured she could be comfortable.

She watched Amos and Leader out in the field. She heard the murmur of their voices but could not identify specific words. Leader seemed to attempt to console him, but Amos continued to shout back furious responses. Since it seemed like it would be a long time before they returned, Emma unbuckled her seatbelt and rolled onto her stomach on the seat.

Leader returned by herself almost ten minutes later. She climbed in the driver's side and sat back against the seat with a sigh. After a moment, she turned her head to look down at Emma stretched out on the back seat. A flash of annoyance appeared in her eyes, and she launched a generous smack to Emma's backside.

"Really?!" Leader demanded. "You couldn't have just kept your mouth shut?"

Emma jerked up to her knees with a pained cry. "He asked me a direct question and I told him the truth. I thought I was required to tell the truth!"

"You are," Leader growled.

Emma glared at her. "Then I'm getting mixed signals here!"

Leader smiled slightly and chuckled. "You get sassy with me, and I may hit you again," she warned but without any significant threat.

Emma grumbled "Don't!" and returned to her stomach.

For several minutes they sat like that, Leader lying against the driver headrest and Emma sulking in the backseat. Then Emma shifted onto her elbows and asked, "What did he mean, you almost died in Beijing?"

Leader let out a small breath and turned to look at Emma again. "There was an attempt on my life. But I'm okay. I'm smart and I'm fast."

The idea that someone had tried to kill Leader pained Emma. Life was so precious and so quickly lost. "Who was it? Arrow Guild?"

Leader shook her head and made a doubtful face. "Nah. Those poseurs took several pretty damaging hits when they confronted us last. They lost half their complement in one year. They won't be strong enough to come after us for at least a decade. Probably longer. Their only hope—their strongest link—is only a child right now." Leader turned her body to look at Emma more directly. "You aren't still worried about Arrow, are you? Amos and I subdued them the day they shot Eric. We took you home and then attacked their main base. They're not coming around again for a while. They're weak sauce."

Emma did not know what Leader meant by saying that she and Amos had "subdued" the Arrow Guild, but the fact was that Emma was afraid. Arrow Guild had played with her heart and convinced her to betray Guild secrets. They had seemed powerful to Emma when one of their youngest members had turned a gun on her.

"I am worried," Emma admitted unashamedly. "Someone tried to kill you, and someone concocted a disease to infect me and Scott. What is it they want, Leader? Why do they want to hurt us?"

Leader's answer came after a tut and a sigh. "There is so much you don't need to know. You should have your childhood and as much innocence as you can while you still can. Just let me take care of the threats. You don't need to worry."

Emma sat up with only a few cringes. "Are there many threats? I don't understand why!"

"You're not meant to."

"But this is why we moved here, right? It's why you split the Guild this time? We're under some kind of threat. It's why I'm in public school instead of private." When Leader didn't answer, Emma said, "I know I'm right."

"You are right," Leader answered finally, but her voice now had an edge to it. "But you don't have time to waste thinking about things that aren't your business."

Emma was frustrated by that and sat forward to complain, a movement only spoiled by her sharp intake of breath when she felt pain. "But if I knew what it was I was facing, I might be able to help. I most certainly would be better at Obedience if I knew why I had to Obey."

"Well, that's not a luxury I'm willing to give you," Leader shot back. "You're just going to have to learn to trust me and to Obey because you trust me."

Emma made a frustrated sound. "I do trust you, Leader! If you and the Senior Guild would just learn to trust the Junior Guild, we could all be on the same page. It would be easier for me to do what you ask if I know why you're asking it."

Leader scoffed. "What makes you think that?" She leveled Emma with a glare but then immediately shook her head and turned away. "No, it doesn't even matter. We're not talking about this. Your mission is to attend school and Stone University. You have no reason or right to question me. You do as I say . . . and not just me!" She jerked her thumb toward Amos' direction. "Everyone! You do as everyone above you tells you to do, because their superior experience is worthy of your respect and attention. Is that clear?"

"It's stupid," Emma shot back. "If you have the chance to have a twelve-man army, why would you settle for six? Or a single-handed battle? Because I know you fight solo more than you need to. Otherwise, no one would stand a chance trying to assassinate you."

Leader watched her with her brows raised expectantly, eyes darkening with Emma's every word. When Emma cut off, Leader asked, "Are you through?"

When Emma tried to argue, Leader said, "You're through." and turned her back.

"Fine," Emma said and gingerly settled herself back against her seat. A minute later, she said, "I just think you can trust me more than you think you can."

"I can't even trust you to Obey me *right now*." She spun around and fixed Emma with a look of carefully controlled anger. "I just spent an hour striping your backend like a tiger's and here you are, not even thirty minutes later, arguing with me and continuing to argue even after I tell you to stop. If I cannot trust you to do something simple, how could I possibly trust you with more?" Emma recoiled from those words, but Leader went on. "Guild Business is not a walk in the park. I don't treat it like a joyride. It is the single most important business in this world, and I entrust it to those who are Obedient, Diligent, Confident, Controlled, Courageous, and Loyal. You have a long way to go."

"Yes, Leader," Emma answered in a small voice.

"Buckle up. Here comes Amos."

"Yes, Leader," Emma whispered. She shifted her weight again, wincing with every movement, and buckled her seatbelt as instructed.

Leader turned again before Amos got all the way to the car and pinned Emma with her fierce stare. "I will expect you to toe the line from now on, Emma. And I will be watching very closely to see if you need any more demonstrations of my authority, or reminders of the importance of your subordination."

Under that fierce gaze, with her backside on fire, Emma felt very small. "Yes, Leader."

Amos climbed in. "Let's go home," he suggested in a voice devoid of emotion.

"All right," Leader agreed and turned the car on with a flick of the keys. "I don't think we're going to have many problems with Emma for a while, Amos. She's going to be Diligent in showing her humility and respect for her superiors."

"Glad to hear it." He did not sound at all glad. When he took a moment to look over his shoulder at Emma, she saw that his eyes were nearly as fierce as Leader's. He was the Senior Guild member home the most. During her suspension, he would likely be the biggest enforcer. She felt even smaller.

Chapter Twenty-One

Emma toed the line. Her suspension was filled with exhausting amounts of academic work and chores. Leader was rigid in her expectations, pushing Emma as she promised to do several weeks ago. She was not unkind. As far as she was concerned, Emma had been soundly punished and all was forgiven, if not forgotten. Leader pushed Emma because she required her to live up to a potential she saw in her. And so Emma trained, worked, and studied harder than ever before. She awoke at six o'clock each morning, ran hard all day, and fell into bed exhausted at nine each night. She longed to return to school, although Leader promised her that she would not stop pushing even then.

It was Amos, though, who made the suspension difficult. Thursday afternoon, Emma was standing at the bar in the kitchen eating a sandwich when he suddenly appeared on the stairwell.

"Did you finish cleaning the downstairs bathroom?"

It was one of today's many chores. She scrubbed the floor with a brush for almost an hour, cleaned the tub, sink, and toilet, and even wiped down the walls and floorboards. If Amos went in that bathroom, he would see it was clean.

"Yes. A few minutes ago."

"Do it again," he instructed firmly and turned to walk back up the stairs. She was puzzled. Had he checked it and found it wanting?

"Why?"

He spun around and was down the stairs and across the room to her almost before she could blink. "Don't question me!" he snarled, pointing a furious finger in her face. "Just do as you are told!"

Emma put her sandwich down and said, "Yes, Amos," in a contrite voice, and slipped past him to the stairs. He followed her like a menacing guard dog as she collected her cleaning supplies and water bucket from the supply room and entered the bathroom. She looked up several minutes into scrubbing the already clean floor to see him walk away. She sighed.

At dinner, he was still as cold as a mountain stream. He called her to set the table when she was on Stone University.

"I'm in the middle of a quiz," she told him. "I'm almost done."

"I did not say 'set the table when it please your highness,' Emma," he snapped back. "Right now." When she Obeyed him, she timed out and failed the quiz, resetting her to her previous settings and ruining three hours of academic work.

She tried to take her meal standing but Amos told her to sit down though no one else came to eat. Even Leader was absent. Amos took five bites of the food he had cooked then stormed out in a fury.

"Do the dishes!" he shouted at her back. The feeling of anger he brought into the house was like a heavy presence. In the loneliness, she finished her food and did the dishes as he ordered. After the dishes were done, she went into the study where he sat reading. If she talked with him and apologized, maybe the presence would be banished, and he would return to the congenial person she knew he was.

"Go away, Emma," he said without even looking up from his book.

"Amos," she began. That's as far as she got.

He slammed his book shut. "What!? What is such an emergency that you think you can override my order to go away?" She stepped back. "Well? Is your time more valuable than mine? Is what you have to say more important that what I might be doing?"

"No," she answered, stepping back again. "I'm sorry."

"No, *sir,*" he corrected her ruthlessly. "I'm sorry, *sir!*"

She dropped her gaze. "No, sir."

"You don't get to *choose* when to Obey me!" he railed on, despite her obvious humility. "You have to Obey every time! You won't be safe if you don't Obey. I thought you of all people would have a testimony of that." His reference stole her breath away and caused tears to sting her eyes. Her disobedience two years ago when he chased her into the city to retrieve her from Arrow Guild held weighty consequences. He had to kill in order to protect Emma then. And, of course, Leader had died to save her.

"I do," she whispered through a voice heavy with unshed tears. "I'm so sorry, Amos."

"Move the laundry!" he snapped at her back. There was not an ounce of compassion in his voice though she had obviously been affected by his words.

"Yes, sir."

Emma hoped by Friday morning that his mood would improve. It didn't. He returned from training with Scott shortly after eight. Emma stood up to the bar again, this time flipping through notes and some books. Amos came in through the garage, looked around, and said, "I thought you were supposed to mow the lawn today."

Emma watched him warily. "I am," she admitted and showed him her list of chores on the counter. *Mow the lawn* was prominent on the list.

"Why isn't it done?"

Emma frowned. "Amos, it's 8:15 in the morning. I trained for two hours, took a shower, and ate breakfast. I haven't had time."

Amos' expression changed to confusion. "Oh," he said in a tone that resembled understanding but had an undercurrent of sarcasm. "I'll just go ahead and take any excuses you offer me, Number Eleven. It's not as though I have any particular reason for telling you to mow the lawn today. In fact, why don't you blow it off completely and do whatever the hell you like?" He stood there in the doorway, keys in his hands, staring at her expectantly.

Emma did not know what he wanted from her. She knew his question was sarcastic, but she was not certain how to answer. If she said "Great, thanks!" as she was sorely tempted, she had the feeling it would not go off very well. She also considered arguing her point that she had not yet had time to mow the lawn, and what was the big rush if she had all day to complete the list of chores? She even considered apologizing since he seemed to be waiting for something, but she did not know what she would apologize for since she hadn't done anything wrong.

Hoping he did not go off on a crazy tangent about how she ought to have finished already, she finally said, "I'll go right now."

"You think?" he snarled, snapping his fingers, and pointing toward the garage where the mower was stored.

It took her two hours to complete the task. She came in sweaty and tired to get a drink in the kitchen. Amos was there, sitting on the bar counter flipping through a cookbook. He looked up at her when she came in, staring intently. Emma stopped in her tracks, looking back at him, trying to figure out what he could possibly find fault with.

"I'm done," she told him at last when she said nothing to her. "Did you want to check it?"

He closed the cookbook with a snap. "Do I *need* to check it? If you don't have confidence in the job you have done, perhaps you ought to try again."

"I am confident my work will meet with your approval," she shot back, a little more bite to her tone than she had dared use with him yesterday.

He clenched his jaw and responded with slow malice, "Don't get cheeky, Emma."

Emma let out a sigh and approached him appealingly. "Amos, I don't know how to please you! I know you're angry with me . . ." She cut off when he looked away, snapping the cookbook open once more and returning his attention to it.

"The boxes in the garage need to be sorted," he advised almost absentmindedly. "It's not on the list, but I want it done today." He looked up at her as if daring her to argue. She didn't.

"Yes, sir," she answered and went immediately to sort the boxes.

The extra chores ensured Emma logged on to Stone University late, lowering her score. Amos was in the kitchen while Emma tried studying all afternoon. Her frustration with him and with redoing work she had already completed yesterday, combined with his angry presence and the noise of dinner preparation, resulted in a poor score for her work a second time in a row.

One of the nasty little surprises Stone University had to offer was its emergency plan. It shot a message to Leader as soon as Emma's score dipped below her set parameters. She received a text message from Leader almost instantly: **Diligence?** She screamed internally.

She kept working until Amos called her to set the table again, an interruption that infuriated Emma. She slammed the laptop closed as she pushed away from the desk and consequently heard it crack.

Amos was across the room in an instant. "What the hell, Emma?" he demanded as he opened her laptop and saw the screen cracked and breaking away from the base. "You think laptops grow on trees?"

Emma could not bring herself to answer respectfully this time. "Yeah, Amos! My thought was: break the damned laptop 'cause I can just go pick another one off a laptop tree!" She removed her phone from her pocket and launched it across the room. It hit the wall and shattered. "I guess I'll pick a new phone while I'm at it!"

Her screamed words echoed through the house, bringing Adam up from the basement, eyes wide with alarm.

Amos stared at the pile on the floor that used to be Emma's phone and at the laptop broken in his hands then slowly lifted his gaze to Emma's. She stared back defiantly.

"Go to your room," he ordered and at last his tone was not harsh.

Emma let out a scoff that was almost amused. She stormed away. "Fine with me!"

"I'll be up when I calm down," he warned her. She flipped him off, and when Adam seemed surprised by the gesture, she flipped him off, too.

Emma paced in her room until she calmed down a little. Then she sprawled out on the bed on her stomach and watched the clock. She could smell dinner; the tantalizing aroma wafted throughout the house. But she was not invited to join. She could not remember in all her time in the Guild ever missing a meal. Leader was strict about proper nutrition and body training. Healthy meals were supplied three times daily and nutritious snacks were always readily available. While she waited, she heard the definite sounds of Leader entering the house, dinner being served to Waylon, Adam, Leader, and Amos. She heard the clean up afterward. Dishes clinked as they were washed by hand in the sink. Water ran to rinse them.

By the time she heard footsteps on the stairs, dinner had been over for an hour and it was coming dangerously close to the time she should be preparing for bed. She waited, stomach grumbling, still simmering in her fury, but no one came. The footsteps moved on down the hall without pausing by her door.

Emma considered going out, but she thought better of it. Amos had told her he would come up when he calmed down. The implicit instruction was to wait until he deigned to show up. At 8:30, after more than two hours in her room, Emma got up and prepared for bed. She had her own bathroom in this house, for which she was grateful. It was attached to her room, so she supposed it would not be a violation of Amos' intention for her to prepare for bed. She brushed her teeth, washed her face, and moisturized. She dressed in her warm pajama pants and a soft t-shirt. She folded her dirty clothes and placed them beside the door. The laundry chute was in the hall. At 9, she shut off the lights and climbed into bed, deciding Amos had forgotten about her.

He hadn't. He came in five minutes later.

"Sit up," he ordered and flipped on her overhead light. She blinked at the sudden brightness and sat up carefully. She thought he did not appear any calmer, though he had promised he would not come in until he was calm. "I decided you don't get to have a phone or a computer. You don't really need either one. Leader wanted to be sure you had access to us in case you're in a dangerous situation, so I offered her this." He held up a one-inch square metallic box. "It can clip easily on your keys. It's a panic button. If you're in danger . . ." He flipped open the box and showed her the rubber button inside. ". . . just press this button. It's simple."

She nodded uneasily. She never imagined they would take away her phone. Everyone in the Guild carried a phone, even Victoria. Emma remembered being given her first phone when she was in kindergarten. Multiple times, Emma had deliberately lost her phone and it was always returned to her. She could not imagine not having access to texts from Amos and Leader. She received countless instructions via text messaging.

"How long will I go without a phone?" They would have to give it to her when she went back to school, but that was still four days away. Could she *go* four days without a phone? It seemed an excessive amount of time.

Amos shrugged at her question. "Maybe Leader will buy you a new one before your birthday."

Emma recoiled. "That's ten months away!"

"I can count," he answered firmly and placed the cube on her bedside table, on the pad that charged her phone each night.

"Amos, I need a phone," she told him earnestly.

His head lifted and he peered down at her thoughtfully. "No, you don't."

"Yes, I do," she insisted.

He moved toward the door. "Don't argue with me. You're not going to win."

Emma looked away from him before she said something she would regret. "Fine," she said in frustration. "If I don't have a computer, how will I complete my online catalog? It's pretty demanding."

"You'll use Leader's desktop computer," he informed her. "I moved it to your desk so you may begin using it tomorrow." That was fine. The only benefit of the laptop was that she had been able to put it up at the bar yesterday and today to avoid sitting. "I don't think I need to tell you that if you mistreat Leader's computer as you have your own, she'll throw a fit."

"Yes, sir," Emma answered. That was true enough.

Leader leaned in through the door. "Amos, I need you to go to the farm. Piper called in a panic and said 'the machine' was blinking at her. She said you told her to call if that happened."

"I did," Amos said. "I'll go now. I'll take the Porsche."

"No way," Leader countered. "You have to drive the Volvo until you fix it."

His smile reminded Emma of the old Amos, the person he had been before this heinous suspension had begun. "I'll fix it tomorrow," he assured Leader and slipped out the door. Leader patted his shoulder blades on his way out and watched him fondly as he walked away.

Her eyes were hard when she turned back to Emma. "You know the dictionary definition of idleness? Groundings. Being sent to your room so you can waste my time lying around? That is idleness."

Emma stared at her in surprise. Was she really chiding her about this? "Amos sent me to my room, Leader. It's not like I could tell him no."

"Of course, you couldn't," was Leader's acidic reply. "The key would have been to avoid throwing a tantrum like a child and being *sent* in the first place." She approached with two menacing steps. "You're not thinking, Emma. In order to be Diligent, you have to think ahead and know that your actions will have consequences. Throwing a tantrum resulted in Amos sending you to your room, which meant you wasted my evening holed up here like a panicky little bunny."

Emma stared at Leader, not even trying to hide her incredulity. "Are you serious? You are really turning this around on me? I did not ask to go to my room and spend three hours up here doing nothing. Amos *sent* me."

Leader slapped Emma's ear. "You're not listening to me, Emma. Listen to me. Sometimes things don't go as you plan. Sometimes things get in the way. That's part of life. You don't have to control your attitude if you don't want to, but if Amos chooses to control it for you, you are still responsible. Whatever circumstances led to your grade dipping today may very well be important to you, but I only care about results."

"I had less time to work today!" Emma said and Leader hit her on the other ear.

"Listen to me! I expect you to fight against all the odds and raise your score at least a percent every day. I do not want to listen to excuses or whining. I want results. So, tomorrow, when Amos still has his panties all in a twist and keeps heaping work on you, you better work like a soldier, Emma, to get him off your back. You will need to perform like a scholar when you log in to the university. I am not playing with you about this. You better learn to work hard while you're at home, because even when you return to school, you will be expected to live up to my ever-mounting expectations for you."

Emma wanted to argue, but she resisted. She bit back her angry words and excuses, answering, "Yes, Leader." She tried to keep her tone from betraying her bitterness and failed. Leader ignored it. She walked to the door.

"You owe Amos an apology for how you behaved today," she added as she flipped out the light.

Emma remained sitting, glaring after Leader. "I hardly think so," she muttered when the door was safely closed.

Leader still heard her. "I'm not asking," she said coldly through the door. Emma wanted to throw something again, but the only thing close to hand was the panic button cube, and what would he do to her if it, too, was broken by a tantrum? Not wanting to imagine it, she slipped back down onto her belly and closed her eyes, willing herself to sleep even though her stomach grumbled angrily.

Chapter Twenty-Two

The following day, Leader worked Emma as hard as she ever had on the mats. By the time it was done, Emma was sore, tired, and near tears.

"That was a good warm up for what's to come," Leader informed her as she stretched into a backbend as if this workout had not been difficult at all. Emma sat on the mat with her legs splayed, supposedly stretching out, but really feeling like she was going to vomit.

"Why are you doing this?"

Leader sat down, adjusted her ponytail, and smiled. "That's a silly question. I already told you I was going to push you." Leader let that sink in for a moment and then stood up and crossed to the weaponry wall, calling over her shoulder, "Get cleaned up." She selected a set of swords from the wall and moved to the center of the mat. Emma pushed herself to her feet to do as she had been told but couldn't help watching Leader's forms. Leader had perfect poise. Her sword-form was so precise that Emma watched it out to its completion. It was like a deadly dance. Afterward, Leader spun and, with pristine control, swung the blade so that the tip was at Emma's throat, causing her to stand very still and resist breathing. She stared into Emma's eyes. "Clean up," Leader reminded her and pulled the sword away.

Emma hurried upstairs.

At breakfast, under Leader's intense scrutiny, Emma apologized to Amos. "I am sorry about how I behaved yesterday, Amo—"

He interrupted her. "No, you're not." He dropped her plate in front of her. "Listen, Emma, don't bother trying to make nice with me until you're prepared to be sincere and accept my complete authority. You're a smart girl and I suppose that means you think you know best. You may not think much of my intellectual powers, but I am still your superior."

Emma pulled a face. "What is that supposed to mean? What does my intelligence have to do with anything? It was not *intelligence* that prompted me to put on slutty clothes and flaunt myself in front of Chastity. Obviously."

"Eat your food," Amos shot back. He dropped Waylon's and Adam's plates on the table and stalked away. Leader was already eating. Furious but Obedient, Emma picked up her fork. She did not even get it to her mouth before Leader cleared her throat. When Emma met her eyes, Leader glanced significantly in the direction of Amos' retreat.

"He told me to eat," Emma answered. "I'm trying to be Obedient."

Leader took a bite of her food while staring Emma down. Then, almost imperceptibly, she nodded her head toward Amos' direction. Leader was higher in the Guild and her orders, therefore, were superior to his. Emma shoved back from the table and went after Amos.

She found him in the laundry room downstairs, tossing in every manner of clothing without respect to color or cloth type. She reached past him and cancelled the wash sequence. Her delicates were in the pile and would be destroyed if he succeeded.

"Amos, I am sorry," Emma declared and she realized it was true. She was not sorry about how she had acted yesterday, but for disobeying him and certainly for telling him it was easier to disobey him because he was a nice guy.

"Are you?" he asked with a bite of condescension. He moved toward the exit.

Emma kicked the door shut and stood in front of it. Even if Amos had to destroy her to get out, he was not leaving until they resolved this one way or another. If he was surprised by her action, he showed no evidence of it. Instead, he glared down at her with dark eyes that reminded Emma of something she could not quite place. Emma had never quite appreciated the size of this man. He was tall, taller than Leader. His chest was wide and strong, and the muscles in his arms rippled as he crossed them on his chest. She had known him all her life, but this was the biggest he had ever seemed to her.

She found it was suddenly difficult to form words. She recognized the look in his eyes now. It was the same look of determined passion that had resulted in his killing Emma's first boyfriend. To be fair, the boy tried to kill Emma first, but still, Amos shot him in the streets in broad daylight.

"Are you sorry, Emma?" Amos snapped in bitter sarcasm. "Are you really?"

Emma could see it: the connection between this week's events and that deadly event two years ago. Amos was her protector. He knew her boyfriend was dangerous and would try to hurt her. He came to the rescue, tracked her down, followed her, and pleaded with her. He tried to be nice and the boy ended up pulling a gun on Emma. If she Obeyed Amos in the first place, she would never have been in danger, and he would never have been forced to kill.

"I am so sorry," Emma whispered. "You have every reason in the world to be disappointed in me. I should never have disobeyed you. It was wrong for me to think I knew better or had a superior understanding."

He looked at her thoughtfully and she could see his anger receding. "I know it feels like purity culture, but we have to deal with the hand we were dealt. I want you to dress in a way that will make people take you seriously."

"I'm not talking about that," Emma replied. He fell silent. She swallowed. "Not exclusively, anyway."

He seemed to understand suddenly what she was talking about and shook his head. "It's fine. You're fine. Everything worked out fine."

Emma shook her head in frustration. "No, I'm not. God, Amos! Do you think I wake up every morning and think 'What can I do today to piss off my superiors, cause fights with my best friend, and in general cop a real attitude?' I'm not *trying* to be a pain in the ass; I just sometimes can't help it. The fear and the pain combine inside me and create this boiling magma of rage. It makes me want to be mean and destructive."

He took those words with a speculative nod. "You do seem to have a bad attitude these days. I just assumed it was teenaged rebellion."

Emma looked away and shook her head, but she said, "Maybe it is."

For two years, she had tried to accept who she was and be okay with her position in the Guild. For two years she had tried to forget about the look of hatred her first love had turned on her. She tried to stifle the urge to scream that sometimes welled up in her when she remembered the moment he pulled out a gun. She tried to forget it, but it replayed in her mind every day: Amos following her through the streets, ordering her to come home, arguing with the boy who claimed to love her. She replayed the guns appearing, shots being fired, and bodies in the street as if it had happened yesterday. She replayed Amos' dejection, his shock that he had been forced to kill a child. And there was rarely a moment in Emma's life when she did not see the blood on Leader's shirt, realizing all over again that her disobedience had killed him. Sure, her boyfriend had shot him, but it was Emma's disobedience that had killed him.

"Emma," Amos said, moving toward her to grasp her shoulders in a firm grip. "You can't beat yourself up about the past. You have to move on from it."

She glared up at him, fighting the tears. She hated tears! She hated how they made her feel and what they made her look like! "Have you moved on? You killed a seventeen-year-old boy! Did you just forget that?"

Amos' grip tightened painfully. "No, of course not. I'll never forget it, Emma. I have made eight blood kills in my life, and that one is by far the most painful. But I wouldn't change it, Emma. Even if I had known what was to come, I would have killed him again. My well-timed shot was what threw him off balance enough not to get you through the eye. And if I had to kill a dozen more like him to keep you safe, I would do it. I would."

That was the real problem, Emma thought. Amos really cared about her and wanted to protect her from the harsh world. It was something he could not do successfully, and they both knew it. She leaned forward and put her head on his chest, willing herself not to cry.

"You shouldn't have to do it."

"But I would," Amos answered firmly.

"You shouldn't *have to*!" she argued against his chest. "If I had only listened to you, it never would have been necessary. I really thought he could not be the person you knew he was."

Amos slid his arms around her. "Emma! I had access to the Fourth Layer of Disclosure. That's most of the Guild clearance. You were running off your feelings! That's what you're supposed to do when you're in the Junior Guild."

Emma clutched at his shirt. "I wanted you to be wrong."

"I know. *I* wanted to be wrong." But he wasn't. Emma's boyfriend was a rival fink. Getting close to Emma was his mission, and Amos had killed him for it.

"I'm sorry," Emma said, no longer able to hold back the cascade of tears that immediately soaked the front of his shirt. "I'm so sorry."

Amos' hold tightened. He held her against him for a moment like he would never let her go.

"Me too." Not for being a jerk and throwing a tantrum all week, but for being the one who had broken her illusion of her beautiful boyfriend. He told her no one could be trusted and made her see why love was a fairy tale. He was sorry he took away her childhood. And his apology made her cry even more.

The rest of Emma's suspension was not any easier, but it was certainly more peaceful after she made up with Amos. She still had the endless chores, painful training, and rigorous academics, all intensified by Leader's demanding standards.

"I push you because I know you can be better than this," Leader told her after Mat training Tuesday morning. It had been the most extreme training yet. Emma wanted to scream but was too exhausted, sprawled out on the mats beside Leader.

"Why don't I see you pushing anyone else? What about Waylon? And Adam. Especially Adam, who just does whatever he wants!"

"Because you can be more," Leader answered intensely.

"More than what?"

Leader grabbed Emma by the front of her shirt and dragged her closer, pulling her up to a sitting position.

"You can be more than all of them!" she hissed, not angry, just insistent. "And I will see that you have the opportunity."

Emma thought that sounded more like a threat than a promise. When Leader released her, she collapsed back onto the mats with a frustrated sigh.

"What makes you say I can be better? Is it my genetic file again?" She had to wonder. The previous Leader had been intensely interested in her aptitudes, too. He had said he would push her into science, although she had many talents. He always seemed to know more than he let on. Now, the current Leader seemed to have the same passion. What could possibly be in her genetic file that made them believe she could become more than all the others?

Leader smiled at Emma as she backed away to cross the room.

"Get cleaned up," the woman ordered, eyes twinkling. She moved toward the weaponry wall to continue her personal training. With a sigh over her questions being ignored, Emma Obediently got herself up and left Leader to her workout.

In the afternoon, while Emma was attempting a dangerous chemical reaction in the kitchen with a lab set Waylon had brought home a few days earlier, Amos followed Leader down the stairs with concern in his eyes.

"When are you leaving?" he asked as he pursued her.

"In a few minutes."

Emma postponed her experiment in favor of watching her superiors. Being home all the time made her insatiably curious about Guild Business, but she knew better than to ask anything. All they ever did was look at her doubtfully or scold her for a lack of Diligence. Instead of asking questions, Emma watched, hoping to see or hear more than they intended.

Leader strolled through the kitchen with a glance at the experiment but no comment. That was unlike her. Another hazard of being home was Leader's constant nagging presence, and the myriad of "pushing" comments she made about Emma's work. If she had nothing to say about this lab, she must be preoccupied.

Leader went into the office, but when Amos followed, he failed to close the door. This was convenient for Emma, whose hands hovered over her experiment, though she did not move a muscle. She barely even breathed, eager as she was not to miss anything.

"Leader, this is not safe!" Amos ranted. "You were captured and tortured in Beijing last time and that was before the bombings near Tangshan. If you're discovered there, you'll be hunted down!"

"I know very well what the risks are, Amos," Leader replied smoothly. She did not sound concerned at all, only preoccupied. "Can you pull up my Atlantis file? It's not responding to me."

"Yes. You're putting in the wrong sequence. It's five-seven-five-gamma-niner. No, not like that . . . Get out of the way!" There was a sound of movement and shuffling. Then Amos continued, "I think you should be more concerned than you are, Leader. That wasn't a drill when my machine registered imminent danger. I created it for this exact purpose! It was a warning for us to lay low. I don't know why I even have to tell you this! You're the one who told me to put Piper in dirt. Do you know that today alone our satellite has been hacked three times? Well, not actually hacked, they were meager attempts. But still . . . attempts! You're fighting a losing battle on a plane that is already going down!" He paused for a moment. "Here. Is this your file?"

"Yes, thank you. I hear your concerns and I know they're from the heart, Amos. But I am not asking for your advice about this. I have a mission to finish."

"They tried to kill you!" Amos shouted back.

"I know," Leader snapped. "I was on the receiving end of that attack. They tried to kill me. They failed. And now they think I'm defeated, but I know what they're capable of now."

"Leader, this is insane—"

"Amos, the Research I need is in that city! Some fools took something that belongs to me, and I want it back. I cannot risk anyone else getting infected because these Rogue idiots—or whoever they sold it to—want to play cat and mouse with me. I'm not easy prey."

"Cat versus mouse. Hunter versus huntress. What difference does it make if you come home in a body bag?"

Emma flinched at the words and dropped the beaker she held. It shattered on the kitchen floor, bringing Leader out of the office just far enough to see what the noise had been. Emma met Leader's gaze and no matter how she tried she could not keep the fear from showing in her face. Leader sighed and glanced significantly at the substance that seeped into the kitchen mat under Emma's feet. When Emma realized what she had done, she cursed and jumped into the act of cleaning up her mess. The solution had already begun eating at the fibers of the rug.

When Amos tried to speak again, Leader ordered, "Shut up!" in as sharp a tone as Emma had ever heard her use with him. The office door slid closed and Emma could no longer hear their words.

They returned twenty minutes later after the mess was cleaned up. Emma did not finish her experiment. Instead, she sat on the kitchen bar and waited for them to emerge. Leader did not seem surprised, although Amos looked a little pained at her presence.

"Look, Emma," Leader began, but Emma interrupted her.

"Where are you going?"

Leader let out a slow breath. "Back to Beijing."

"Why?"

Leader grabbed Emma's knees and squeezed them gently. "Business," was her answer and she pulled Emma off the counter. When Emma fell, she landed on her feet, looking up into Leader's eyes.

"Dangerous business," she shot back.

"Yes," Leader confirmed. "But you don't have anything to worry about, Em. I'll be fine."

Emma scoffed. "What did he mean: they tortured you?" Leader shrugged that off as if Emma had asked about a hangnail. Emma grabbed her arm to keep her from escaping. "Please, Leader! Just tell me!"

Leader grabbed her face in both hands and leaned forward to kiss her on the head. "I'm going on a trip to finish what I started in Beijing two weeks ago. As always, my business trips are above your disclosure level. You are not qualified for more information." She kissed her again. "I'll bring you a souvenir."

Leader pulled away, slugged Amos in the arm hard enough to make him grunt, and then walked to the stairs. Emma followed her like a buzzing insect.

"What if they try to kill you? What if they succeed? What will happen?"

Emma could not bear to lose Leader. The idea caused pain in Emma's chest. She found it difficult to catch her breath.

"I'll be fine," Leader cheerfully reassured her as she marched up the steps. "You have work to do."

"No," Emma croaked out against the tightening of her throat. She wanted to anger Leader. She wanted to do something that postponed Leader's trip. "No, I'm not doing anything! Not until you talk to me." Amos, behind Emma, tried to speak, but Emma shouted, "No!"

Leader stopped on the top step and spun around, a hand on either banister, larger than life and as powerful as ever.

"I am going to Beijing to pick up what I went to get in the first place, and to kill the people who tried to kill me. While I am there, I thought I would also like to kill the man who attempted to torture me. When all is said and done, I'll probably be back in a couple weeks with a few bumps and bruises."

Emma swallowed. To listen to anyone discuss murderous plans while standing tamely on the steps would have been sickening. But when it was Leader, who had the means, skills, and probably the experience to follow through, it made Emma need to fight even harder to draw a good breath.

"But . . . if they kill you," Emma choked out.

Leader's razor-sharp gaze pounced on Amos. "Boy, are you lucky I have a flight to catch," she toned dangerously. When she looked back at Emma, she said, "You have nothing to worry about, Emma. I am not going to be killed. I know their strategies and I know where they are holed up. But even if I was killed—although I won't be—Amos knows what to do. You will always be safe."

Emma tried to speak and found she couldn't. She couldn't catch her breath. She needed Leader to stay safe. Emma could not imagine life without her!

"Emma!" Leader cried in alarm. "Amos, I think she's panicking!" The last thing Emma saw was Leader jumping nearly the entire flight of steps to try and reach Emma before she fell. Amos caught her from behind when she blacked out.

Emma came to and backed away from the sharp smell waved at her nose. Amos held her in his arms on the floor while Leader squatted above. She patted her face and waved a sharp-smelling herb under her nose.

"Emma," she was saying urgently. Emma met her gaze and Leader let out a relieved breath. "Hi," Leader said, tucking the herbs away. "You're a lot of things, Emma, but never boring."

"Did I . . .?"

"Have a panic attack and pass out?" Leader finished for her. "I think so, but I'm going to have Julianne meet you at the farm to find out for sure if you're okay. And then I'm probably going to break Amos' skull for him."

"But you're not going to Beijing?" Emma begged. When she tried to sit up, Amos restrained her.

Leader was mixing the herbs into a cup of water beside her on the floor. She lifted the cup to Emma's lips and ordered, "Drink this." Emma obeyed, but she had not forgotten her question, and she would not forget it.

"Beijing, Leader?" Emma repeated, gagging on the drink. It was not water; it was vodka, and it had a bite and a bitter aftertaste.

Leader got down low so she could stroke the hair from Emma's face and kiss her on the temple. "Emma, listen to me! You have nothing to worry about. When you wake up, I'll already be gone. But I want you to remember that I said I will come home safe. I'll probably be back by Christmas." Emma tried to protest but found her tongue seemed too heavy to work properly. "Be good. Be Diligent. I'll be checking your scores every day, so I will know how you're doing in on Stone U." Emma's eyes felt heavy and she realized Leader drugged her. The last thing she heard was, "Don't worry about me."

Chapter Twenty-Three

Emma awoke to Adam shaking her roughly. "Get up!" he snarled at her. "Amos said you have to be up before I leave for class, and I'm already late. Get up, dammit! Get up! Leader will kill me if I'm late for another class."

Emma blinked away from the harsh sunshine streaming in through the window of her room. And then, when she was able to process Adam's words, she shoved his hands off her.

"Stop it," she admonished, though it rasped out of her throat, scratchy and dry. "What time is it?"

"Seven," Adam growled in response, hand hovering above her, as if he was still deciding whether or not to keep shaking her. "I tried to wake you up thirty minutes ago, but you went back to sleep. I cannot be late for class." He held up a threatening finger. "I will toss you in the shower and turn on the cold water if you go back to sleep again."

She shuddered at the threat. She had no memory of him waking her at all. In fact, she was having trouble remembering anything. Her head felt cloudy. Attempting to comprehend Adam's words was hard.

"Am I late for training?" Training usually started at dawn. What time had he said it was? She let her eyes close as she tried to remember.

"There's no time for training," Adam growled, shaking her again until her eyes opened once more. "Don't go back to sleep, Emma!" He swore violently and jerked her to a sitting position. "You need to get in the shower! Amos is picking you up for school in ten minutes!"

"School?" Emma asked, trying to shake the grogginess from her mind. What did school have to do with anything? She could not focus on the idea.

With a cry of frustration, Adam hauled her over his shoulder and lugged her to the shower in her bathroom. He dropped her in the tub. Still foggy, and not entirely certain what was happening, Emma tried to formulate a question. But Adam only turned the faucet onto its coldest setting and aimed the nozzle at her head. Emma shrieked when the water hit her. She tried to grasp the nozzle from Adam's hands, but he shoved her away.

"Are you awake, Emma?! You have to go back to school today! Wake up!"

"I'm awake," she shrieked at him. It did not stop him. He aimed the water at her again to drown out her shouts. Unable to stop him, she huddled on the floor of the tub, trying to turn her back to the icy stream as she shouted at him to stop.

"You awake?" he demanded when he finally turned the water off.

"Yes," she cried, glaring hatred up at him. The glare was somewhat spoiled by the dripping hair over her face and the involuntary tremble in her jaw. Her entire body gave a shuddering shiver in response to the icy cold.

"Good," he shot back as he walked away. "You have to be ready to go in five minutes."

A warm shower helped her clear her head. It also restored her memories. She recalled the events which caused Leader to drug her yesterday. She had gone into hysterics, but Leader was still going to Beijing. The horrible fear of losing Leader—the one that had overtaken Emma yesterday—returned with a painful tug at her heart. Emma sat on the floor of the tub, this time in a warm stream, to try to calm her fears.

Some of the tears she had not been able to shed yesterday worked their way to her face, but the steady stream of warm water kept evidence away. She wrapped her arms around her knees.

This is why Leader doesn't share her business with Junior Guild, Emma realized. She was not yet strong enough to handle the idea that Leader might never come home.

"Emma!" Adam roared from the next room. "You are killing me!"

He stormed into the bathroom.

"What are you doing?" He ripped the curtain aside. When he saw her there, naked and huddling, he shut the water off. His voice softened minimally. "Amos is going to be here any minute, Emma. You have to get ready to go."

"I know," Emma assured him. She remained where she was, though, arms wrapped around herself to keep covered.

"Hey!" Amos' stern call entered their conversation. "What are you doing in here, Adam?" He grabbed Adam by the shirt and dragged him out of the bathroom. Once they were gone, Emma jerked the curtain back into place and turned the water on again. She heard Amos reading Adam the riot act, but she felt smug about it. That would teach him to turn the cold water on her.

A minute later, Amos leaned in and said, "Are you okay, honey?"

"Yeah," she lied, hoping her tearful voice was muffled in the stream of water. "I'm getting ready for school. Please tell my *you're* taking me and not him."

"Me," Amos agreed. "We'll talk in the car."

When Emma got to the garage, Adam squealed out of the driveway in the Charger, looking as angry as Emma had ever seen him. Amos stood beside the Porsche shaking his head, murmuring, "Self-Control, Adam. Self-Control," though Adam certainly could not hear him. Amos smiled up at Emma when he saw her waiting.

"Morning," he greeted and clicked the button on his key ring to unlock the passenger door. "Ready for school?"

"No. Not at all." She shook her head, still feeling a bit foggy. "What was it Leader made me drink yesterday?"

"Sleep tincture," Amos replied as he climbed into the car. Emma followed his lead. She stuffed her backpack in the backseat and buckled in as Amos explained, "It's to force the body to calm down. In many cases that means the subject falls asleep. Although, a Leader I knew once used it on someone in shock, and she did not fall asleep, so who knows."

"I'm guessing it's not over-the-counter."

Amos laughed. "No! It's a highly toxic poison if it's not used exactly right. I do not even have the clearance to touch it. Leader keeps it on her person at all times."

Emma squinted against the painful rays of the sun as Amos backed out of the garage. "So, did she knock me unconscious because she didn't want to deal with my hysterics?"

Amos clicked his tongue. "You know that's not why. You had already passed out once, and she wanted to make sure you were safe. The sleep tincture forces the body to be at rest or, in your case, comatose. You did not even wake when Julianne did a once-over. You have slept nearly fifteen hours."

Emma let out a sound that was half whine, half growl. "Mean," she accused.

He chuckled. "Not intentionally mean. Leader has called several times to check up on you. She was getting worried that you weren't responding. But here you are, bright eyed and bushy tailed."

"And hungry," Emma complained. "The last meal I had was lunch yesterday. And I feel gross because I didn't train today. Why didn't you get me up in time to train?"

"I was at the farm. Adam was supposed to wake you at six. He slept in."

Emma scoffed. "And he'll probably walk free, but when I fail to do something, it's the goddamned end of the world."

"What did you fail to do?" Amos asked suspiciously as he handed her a meal-replacement shake from the center console.

Emma pulled a face at his question and then at the shake. "I don't know, but it will happen." She tasted the shake and nearly gagged. "What is this?"

"Double potency," Amos replied with an innocent shrug. "Julianne tested your blood sugar yesterday and she's concerned. She's making you a meal plan. Today is probably your last school lunch."

Emma tried another swallow and pushed the cup away. "I can't drink this, Amos. It's horrible. Please tell me you have another plan? I'm so hungry."

He studied her for a long moment and then swerved into a fast food lane. Emma was shocked. Fast food had never been sanctioned in her life. It did not seem much more appetizing than the shake, but she was hungry enough to try. He pulled up to the drive-thru sign.

"Excuse me?"

"Would you like to try our new breakfast burrito?" asked the disembodied voice coming from the menu sign.

"No, thank you," he answered in a tone that spoke his raging doubts. "I will take the heart-smart breakfast and a yogurt cup to go, please."

Emma finally smiled. "You're in the drive-thru, Amos. They probably package it to go."

He shushed her and said, "Is your orange juice 100 percent juice?"

A long pause followed his question and then a different voice answered, "I don't think so."

"All right, no juice. What's the total?"

"First window, please," answered the voice. Amos studied the menu for a moment and shook his head, murmuring about inefficiency as he drove around.

"Is Leader going to kill you when she sees a charge for fast food?" Emma teased him.

"No," he answered. Then his voice changed to a lighter tone and he shrugged. "I'm using cash and I'll lose the receipt. In case I get audited, let's call this 'batteries and paint thinner.'"

Emma laughed softly. "No way! If you get audited by Leader, you stand alone with your batteries and paint thinner. I'm washing my hands of this entire illegal venture."

Amos, true to his word, paid with emergency cash. They collected the bagged food at the last window. It smelled like starch, but Emma was hungry enough for just about anything. The heart-smart breakfast did not seem very smart, but she ate most of it. The yogurt was so sweet she couldn't take more than a couple bites. She felt greasy and once again wished she had time for a proper meal and training.

"When does Leader land in Beijing?" Emma asked as they pulled into the carpool line. There were no other cars anywhere to be seen. School had already started.

"I'm not permitted to speak to you about that," Amos answered apologetically. "I am only allowed to say she is safe and healthy."

"How could you possibly know that?"

He lifted one shoulder and offered her a closed expression. "You will have to trust me."

She sighed because she didn't want to but had no other choice.

"Do I need to walk you to the Attendance Office or anything?"

"No." Emma unbuckled and reached back for her school bag. "But the school probably already contacted my 'mother' to find out why I am not in school. They have insane attendance policies."

Amos pulled a face at the idea Leader had been contacted, but then he shot Emma a smile. "Are you well enough to go to school? You look a little gray."

"That's because my skin resists coloring. It's a genetic condition, not an indicator of health." When he looked concerned, she smiled and said, "I was joking, and I'm fine. I'm just not in a hurry to go in. I'm late for Calculus, so I'll probably have double homework in there, even though I mastered the subject online last week and should not even have to sit through the class. And the stupid Winter Formal is next week, so that's what everyone will be talking about, and I think it's dull, dull, dull. And Josie is probably going to want all kinds of details about my suspension that I will have to make up on the spot, and I have never fully mastered the craft of lying."

He patted her leg affectionately. "Sounds like you have a big day."

"On top of all that," Emma added, still not wanting to exit the car. "Chastity will have had five entire days to spread rumors about this fight. I am going to be a pariah because I threw the first punch, and an entire cafeteria full of kids witnessed it." She rested her head against the seatback and closed her eyes. "Additionally, the tincture has left me feeling a tad foggy and I'm not sure I will be up to the inevitable confrontation between me and Chastity today."

Amos chuckled. "It sounds like the tincture evened the score a little. She may stand a chance."

Emma rolled her eyes. "She would not stand a chance of defeating me if I was still unconscious. Have a little faith!" She opened the door but before climbing out into the cold, she said, "Amos, is she going to be okay in Beijing? Am I going to see her again? If not, I hate that the last thing she said to me was 'be good' or whatever."

Amos looked extremely confident when he said, "Emma, she'll be fine. She's been doing this a long time. And the very last thing she said to you was 'Love you, Em,' as she put you in the car to head for the farm. She'll come home to us soon. Now go to school. And be a good girl, okay, Emma? I don't want to come down here and pick you up from the principal's office today."

"Okay," she agreed on a sigh. Then she grinned mischievously at him. "I'll defer my misbehavior to tomorrow." She climbed out. Amos nodded as if her answer were acceptable. With a grin, he waved to her and pulled away from the curb.

Chapter Twenty-Four

Emma checked in with the nasty people in the Attendance Office, got an Admit to Class pass, and went to her locker to collect her morning books. The Calculus teacher hardly even acknowledged her entrance but held up two fingers to indicate double homework. Emma didn't even care. She did not need the lesson, so she worked on homework until the bell rang.

She had been right that everyone was talking about the Winter Formal. The walls were plastered with signs and posters advertising the event. Everywhere she went, people were discussing dresses and dates. But Emma was wrong that everyone would treat her as a pariah. There were certainly some, and a lot of people whispered about her, but more than anything, she noticed respect. They gave her respectful distance, respectful nods, and some guys even said, "Respect, Cobra." She had no idea what they meant, but she nodded in return.

"Hey," said Josie, sneaking up behind her between classes. "You're back."

"Yeah," Emma answered.

Josie looked her up and down. "You look normal. What happened to my boots?"

Emma winced. "About that . . . How much did they cost? Because my mother destroyed them."

Josie laughed. "Nah, we're good. Consider them my gift to you for kicking Chastity in the emotional taco."

Emma rolled her eyes. "I hate her, but I'm pretty sure my mother will skin me alive if there's another incident at school. She promised the principal I would be every teacher's dream student. And if I get suspended again, I may rather slit my wrists than go home to my father."

Josie pulled a face. "I guess they didn't think it was so funny that you beat the snot out of that kid?"

Emma shook her head. "Not funny at all."

"You looked like you really knew what you were doing," Josie replied appreciatively.

Emma paused in the hall and looked up at Josie. "My father is a martial arts black belt, and he has been training me since about kindergarten. I do know what I'm doing, but I should also have the discipline not to engage in pointless fights. He made that very clear to me this week. I think I had better stay away from Chastity and her posse for a while."

Josie pulled a face. "That won't be easy. Every kid in the school has heard about the fight, and most of them have given the win to you."

Emma was confused. "Why? We both got suspended."

"Yeah," Josie shrugged that off. "Nobody cares about that. The numbers are pretty evenly split between the people who think he was an idiot for losing to a girl, and those who think he's a pig for even fighting you in the first place."

Emma opened her palms in question. "Why? If he had not fought back or defended himself, I would have clobbered him."

"Most people think you did, anyway," Josie said and she was immensely pleased. "They're calling you the Cobra."

Emma rolled her eyes again. "Yeah, I heard that. What does it mean? Am I supposed to be impressed that they are comparing me to a hooded venomous snake from the Elapidae family?"

Josie said, "Don't be pretentious. It's a compliment. It means they think you're fast, scary, and deadly. Or it could be after a video game ninja. I don't know."

"Or it could mean I'm sneaky and easy to attack with a garden hoe," Emma replied, reaching for the door to her classroom.

"Have you ever killed a cobra with a garden hoe?" Josie asked sarcastically.

"No," Emma answered. "The only time I have ever seen a cobra was through heavy panes of glass in an aquarium."

"Exactly," Josie replied with a satisfied smile. "You're untouchable."

Emma shrugged. "I guess I can't count on a date to the Winter Formal then." Josie's response was a recoil and a face that suggested she would rather be bitten by a cobra than attend the Winter Formal. Emma actually agreed with her.

"See you at lunch," Emma said and ducked into class.

Emma was relieved when she got to lunch and saw Chastity stuck behind a table selling last-minute tickets to the Winter Formal. She noticed Emma, of course, and managed to shoot her a dirty look and turn up her nose. Emma walked past with only one comment, "Glad to see you're working toward your aptitudes. One day you'll make a great makeup peddler." It wasn't particularly brilliant but Chastity did not have time to answer before Emma walked away.

Emma said quietly, "That's all. I promise," in case Amos was watching. She collected her lunch and looked around for Josie. She saw Scott at his customary table. He nodded to her as if they were old friends, which of course they were, but the parts they were playing weren't, so she looked away. For the first time since she came to this school, people invited her to sit with them. Before she saw Josie and crossed to her, she had gotten three invitations and had been called Cobra twice.

Lunch went off without a hitch. Not that there was really a chance of anything happening; the cafeteria was monitored by a handful of adults today. They watched her like she could sprout horns and a forked tail at any moment, yet they gave Scott as little attention as any of the other kids in the lunchroom. So much for the principal's lack of prejudice.

It wasn't until after school that she even saw Chastity and Scott again. They were kissing against her locker, despite the student handbook forbidding public displays of affection. Emma chose to ignore them;

although seeing him kiss that Bible-thumping bimbo was almost enough to make Emma want to punch him again. She walked on.

"Hey, Emma," Chastity called in jovial hatred. "Do you need to buy tickets to the Winter Formal, or is your pimp already getting them?"

Emma was wearing a jean skirt with a perfectly respectable knee-length hem and black leggings. Her shirt was black with the French word *"belle"* all over it in various colors and fonts. Over that she wore a knee-length white sleeveless sweater. She was dressed respectably enough to be president of the celibacy club. But she said nothing of all that.

"Of course, he's not," Emma replied coolly. "Your dad knows better than to show his face around here."

There was a chorus of "oooh's" as if Emma was performing in a melodrama for kids passing in the halls.

"Don't," Scott said in a quiet voice, a worried look of warning in his eyes.

Emma would have walked on, but in a voice filled with mocking concern, Chastity said, "Oh no! Poor little Emma! Did no one ask you to the Formal?"

Emma turned to face Chastity. The warning in Scott's eyes became more forceful.

Emma let out a sigh, "Chastity Monez, no matter how many times we do this you are always going to end up weeping in a little ball of tears somewhere in the school. Why would you do that to yourself? Despite your horrible personality and clothing that should be returned to a fifties secretary, you manage to be respectably popular. And even though your boyfriend's testicles will probably never drop, he's moderately attractive. You are president of the student committee and, to some people, that's a noteworthy accomplishment. On top of all that, it is even rumored that you have friends and—though I find this hard to believe—talents. Is there some reason you need me to destroy every shred of dignity you manage to scrape together each day from the carnal wreckage that is your home life?"

Chastity's eyes glittered dangerously. "So, no one asked you, then?"

"No," Emma answered honestly, then she elaborated. "They saw what I did to Scott after he asked me. Can you blame them?"

The chorus of onlookers laughed at that, but Chastity did not seem at all alarmed. She seemed smug. "I can't say I'm surprised. You're a horrible person. You would be a horrible date."

Emma smiled and Scott's eyes warned her off even harder. He said, "All right, Chastity. That's enough. Let's go."

"Is your daddy bringing you to the Formal?" Emma whispered. She wanted to be sure the other kids in the hall did not hear, but some of them did anyway, and another echo of "oooh's" surrounded them.

"My dad is not a pedophile!" Chastity screamed.

"Well, that's the official word," Emma conceded.

Chastity was breathing heavily now and she said, "You are a despicable, malicious person and the only way you can feel good about yourself is to tell lies about other people. You're just mad that no one asked you out and everybody hates you!" She wrapped her arms around Scott's and snapped, "Have fun at playing Solitaire and wishing you had a date as attractive as mine."

They went to walk away, and all the nasty words Emma could have said to destroy the girl flew out of her head. She grabbed Scott's arm, jerking him to a stop, and demanded, "You're taking her to the Winter Formal?" Emma had no idea why it hadn't occurred to her sooner. He was actively playing the part of her faithful boyfriend, and Chastity was expected to attend. Leader had never let any of the Junior Guildies attend extracurricular activities. Emma could not remember Adam, Laura or Scott ever attending a dance or fundraiser. Of course, this year, Scott had played on the football team, so all things were possible. But to Emma's mind *this* was not. Kissing Chastity was bad enough. Walking linked through the halls was bad enough. Standing tamely by her side like a devoted lapdog while she attacked Emma was bad enough! He could *not* take Chastity to the school dance.

"Yes," he said, quietly and with a significant glance toward their audience. "I bought the tickets today."

But Chastity laughed a big, nasty laugh and said, "Oh, is Emma jealous of a girl she can't even admit has talents? How sad!"

"Don't," Scott warned when he saw the intention in Emma's eyes. He got a little louder. "Emma, don't!" But she couldn't help it. Chastity had hit on the one and only thing she could ever have used to insult Emma: jealousy over Scott's attention. It didn't even matter that Chastity had stumbled on the insult by accident; Emma was incapable of holding in her rage.

"EMMA!" Scott screamed as Emma's stance shifted. "DON'T!" But Emma did. One full-armed jab to the mouth and Chastity crumpled to the floor, unconscious. It had been a hard hit and Emma backed away with a sharp intake of breath for the immediate pain in her hand. Time slowed down for Emma as normalized thinking returned and she realized what she had done.

"Oh god," she breathed out, aware in that moment only of Chastity on the ground, possibly with a very serious injury, Scott sliding to his knees beside her and shouting for someone to get the nurse, and the throbbing pain in Emma's hand. "Oh god," she said again. She thought this might be as good a time as any to hope there was a deity to have mercy on her soul.

Normal time returned and the kids all around reappeared, and so did the principal with eyes on fire, and Amos, who was walking nonchalantly into the school at that very moment, probably wondering why Emma had not met him at the carpool line. But it was the hand of the school police officer that ultimately closed on Emma's shoulder. He said, "Miss Chandler, please come with me." Emma felt as if the walls were closing in on her, but she obediently went where the officer directed her.

She was hollow. During her interview with the school police, she was hollow. They filled out a police report and Emma had no idea what that meant exactly. During her interview with Principal Morley, where Amos sat in reflective silence, Emma was hollow. The principal suspended her again, this time up to winter break, another five days away. He also notified her that he was recommending to the district her expulsion from school or anger management courses. She heard every word, but she was hollow. She should have been scared; Leader was going to destroy her for this. She should have been angry that they were calling this "unprovoked assaultive behavior" when it was most certainly provoked. Above all, she should have felt concern that an ambulance had been called and Chastity was in the hospital. But all Emma felt was emptiness.

Amos was not nearly as agreeable with the principal as Leader and Julianne had been, but he said Emma would attend anger management and there was no need to involve the district. He said, "You're suspending her for nearly two weeks, Principal Morley, after which she will have two and half weeks of Christmas vacation. I think by January, after she has attended anger management and several rounds of family discipline, she will be ready to return to school."

"I will still be making my recommendation to the district," Principal Morley answered.

They were escorted off the campus by the school police. This time, Emma had no desire to run. She got in the passenger side of the Porsche without a word and buckled herself in. Amos thanked the police as he climbed in. He said nothing until they were several blocks away.

"Couldn't wait until tomorrow, huh?"

Emma bit her lower lip and looked up at him with giant eyes. He was only teasing her, perhaps trying to lighten the mood, but there was nothing that could do that now.

A sobbing breath escaped from her. She wished she felt sorry enough for what she had done to ask about Chastity's condition. But she could not do it. All she felt was hollowness and the pain of realization that Scott was taking Chastity to the formal. She was a stupid, silly girl, after all. What would Leader's disappointment taste like this time?

"I'm so glad Leader is in Beijing," she whispered, even though she wasn't at all glad. Amos let her cry until the tears dried up.

By then, they were on a painfully familiar dirt road. Emma sighed when she saw it. "We're going to the farm?" She was certain nothing good could ever come from being at the farm.

"Yes." Amos shot her a dire look. "This is the end of the road, I think, Emmalyn Stone. We might be able to look the other way when you attack a big kid who knows better and is threatening your safety." He shook his head and clicked under his breath. "But we can't ignore your behavior once it escalates to attacking unarmed civilians. One of the reasons we demand

Obedience and Diligence is to protect the innocent." He glanced toward the hand she was cradling in her lap. "And to protect you."

She flexed her hand. She knew it was broken. The pain was bearable, but the movement was not quite right.

"I didn't want this to happen."

Amos sighed and shot her a sad smile. "And yet, here we are."

When they drove up to the farm, Julianne was pulling up, too. She got out of her car and glared back toward Emma and Amos.

"Everybody hates me," Emma murmured.

Amos gave a sigh that was almost a scoff. "We *love* you, honey. If we didn't, we wouldn't care this much. They both looked at Amos's phone on the car charging panel as it lit up with the word **LEADER** flashing menacingly. With a shake of his head, Amos leaned forward and picked up the phone. With a grave glance at Emma, he jutted his chin toward Julianne. "Go on."

He answered the phone as Emma got out of the car. It wasn't even on speaker, and Emma heard Leader's snarl, "Beat the living shit out of her!"

Amos answered in an exhausted tone, "Leader, the answer cannot always be 'beat the living shit' out of people." Emma shut out the rest of their conversation with the slam of her car door. Then she walked Obediently to Julianne's sharp summoning gesture.

The doctor raised a brow and pointed toward the door to the farmhouse. Emma preceded her into the kitchen that was really an exam room. "Getting yourself damaged like this is…" She shook her head. "I really should beat you."

Emma let out a breath that was nearly a cry. "That's the prevailing opinion." She blinked tears away. "Maybe it would hurt less."

Julianne's eyes were hard, but her touch was soft as she reached for Emma's hand. "Is it in a lot of pain?"

Emma shook her head. "Not much."

"Well, you have a high pain threshold, so…"

"I do?" Emma had a hard time believing that was true. Her mind kept conjuring the image of Chastity's smug expression, and her own devastated realization that Scott was going to a dance with her. Chastity had Scott. It felt like being kicked repeatedly when she was already bleeding.

Julianne's gentle hand touched her face, turning her to meet her gaze. "Did she get you?"

Emma shook her head. "No. She didn't have a chance. I punched her once and that's all it took." And it hadn't been enough to erase the agony of Chastity's enigmatic hold over Scott. "It was all me."

Julianne looked at her thoughtfully for a moment, then opened a cabinet and started preparing a syringe. "I'm going to give you a painkiller." When she looked over her shoulder, her gray eyes were softer. "Of course, it will only help the hand. I'm afraid we don't have an authorized cure for heartbreak."

Emma drew a shuddering breath and felt tears prickling again. "I'll be fine," she lied Diligently.

Chapter Twenty-Five

Leader promised to be back before Christmas day, and she was true to her word. On Christmas Eve, she pulled up in the driveway and honked her horn. Even Amos was surprised when he looked through the blinds and saw Leader standing outside in the snow with a Christmas Tree tied to the roof of her Volvo.

To Emma's memory, they had never celebrated Christmas in the Guild. It was a holiday that made little sense to her. The house was usually decorated so they would look the part of a normal Midwest family. Considering Emma's serious suspension and Leader's absence from the Guild House, no one had been in the mood to go fight Christmas crowds and buy decorations for a sham. Emma was not even allowed to put a foot out the door to pick up the daily newspaper, much less go to the store for festivities.

Amos, Adam, and Waylon went out to get the tree and the boxes of decorations Leader had in the trunk. Emma waited inside, per her restrictions. When Leader came in through the front door, her cheeks were pink from exposure to the bitter temperatures. She carried an umbrella and a wooden box. A studying glance from Leader seemed to be both affectionate and stern. It tugged at Emma's heart and tied her stomach in knots.

"I promised you a souvenir, I believe," Leader said brusquely and passed over the little box. Then, before stowing the umbrella in the coat closet, she smacked Emma sharply across the legs with it. "I'm sure you and I have a lot to talk about."

Emma winced at the strike, or rather at the threatening promise to "talk," but she was relieved to see Leader looking so healthy. Things must have gone well in Beijing.

"I'm glad you're back."

Leader smiled in answer and nodded toward the box.

Inside the box was a pair of Neiliansheng cloth shoes in beautiful pink satin. They had tiny, embroidered flowers and Chinese written characters on them. They were lovely. Emma smiled up at Leader. "They're beautiful. But I thought 'Guild constituents shall not accept gifts.'"

Leader raised a stern brow. "Am I Leader or not?"

"Thank you, Leader," Emma said sincerely. She always had everything she needed, clothing and supplies, to pull off a given character mission. These shoes, though, were a true gift. The Guild Book had many things to say about giving and receiving gifts—but it all mostly boiled down to "Don't." Emma was pleased that Leader would challenge an edict for her.

"You're welcome," Leader said, and she meant it. She patted Emma's face once, sharply. "Did you Obey me and not worry about my well-being?"

Emma shook her head unashamedly. "No, ma'am. I worried about you every day. But when I did, I smacked myself on the hand for not being Obedient."

Leader pulled a face. "Well, aren't you a funny girl? Ritual suspension has turned you into a funny, funny girl."

Emma humbled at once. "No, ma'am. I broke two bones in my hand, fractured Chastity's jaw, and knocked out several of her teeth."

"And I understand—to spite you—she still managed to attend the Winter Formal as Scott's date," Leader answered with no emotion in her tone. There was no way to reply to that, so Emma made no attempt. Leader made an affirmative sound and wrapped an arm around Emma's shoulders, squeezing her once.

"I missed you," Leader said and then walked away.

Emma smiled slightly. She hated Scott and Chastity. She hated the Winter Formal. She hated school. But she loved Leader.

"Help me with the lights and ornaments," Leader ordered her as Waylon brought in a handful of boxes and dropped them on the couch. "Let's make it look like we celebrate this pagan holiday."

Emma spent most of her winter break training and studying. She managed enough academic points to graduate to a new level on Stone University. Leader said that she basically graduated from high school.

"You're still going back to Slope Oak in January," Leader told her firmly before Emma could get her hopes up too high.

Emma was not really surprised. She was glad to get out of the House again, if not at all excited to return to school. Leader's anger management courses were painful and taxing. Emma would have been willing to face much worse than Chastity Monez for a few moments away from Leader's expectations and scrutiny.

"You were in school at Slope Oak for four weeks, yet somehow managed to only attend ten days. I don't think I need to warn you what will happen if you get suspended again, but I think I had better." Leader held up one finger. "First of all, I will give you a refresher course in Obedience. That includes establishing my authority, removing your comforts, and making you prove yourself to me all over again. Then, when I feel you are adequately schooled in Obedience, I will move on to Diligence. And I do not think you would like the way I teach Diligence when I think it's being ignored in my Number Eleven."

"I will control my impulses, Leader."

"Perhaps a better plan is to focus on your mission." Leader presented Emma with an open hand. "Focus on being the character I created for you. Don't worry about Scott. Lay low, be Diligent. That is your task at school. That is your entire task. It's not going to be easy to return to that mission now you have managed to alienate the entire faculty and alarmed the student body. But I have amazing faith in you, Emma. Well, *some* faith. But a strong belief in your desire to avoid punishment."

Emma tried to do as Leader instructed. Her first week back at school, she presented an official apology to the principal and the Disciplinary Office. She avoided any place where she might see Chastity or Scott, including the cafeteria. Most days, she ate in the commons area in sight of the office or with Josie in the ditch-room. But Emma found it impossible not to focus on Scott. On the occasional day when she saw him in the hall, all the raging emotions came rushing back and she found she had to walk quickly away or risk becoming violent again. The sight of Chastity had similar effect. And when she saw them together it was sometimes all she could do to calm her trembling hands out of fists.

She was given a phone again at the end of January when it became an inconvenience for Emma to be without one. After such a long time without, it took Emma a little while to get used to having a phone on her person again. She had it confiscated in three classes her first week in February when it chirped because she forgot to turn it off.

Having her phone turned out to be a blessing. One time when Emma saw Chastity and Scott in the hall, Chastity stroked a hand through his hair while looking deliberately at Emma as if to provoke her. Stupid girl. And Emma was stupid, too, because it worked. Fortunately, her phone rang just then and, since she was between classes, she answered.

"Walk away now," Leader instructed her firmly. Emma drew a breath and did as she was told. "Good thing I happened to be watching your live feed."

"Yes," Emma agreed in a hushed voice.

"Do you need to come home early?"

Emma considered it—*really* considered it. She knew Leader was offering it mostly as a threat, but she did not care. "I think I will be okay, Leader, but thank you."

"Be Diligent," Leader ordered.

Leader's observation was very rare, Emma knew. Emma had made friends in January that Leader would surely disapprove of. Some of them were Josie's pothead friends, and others were just general troublemakers with bad attitudes. Emma felt linked with them in ways she did not understand. She even, with thoughtful intent, selected darker clothing from her wardrobe in order to blend in with them more thoroughly.

She smoked her first cigarette on Groundhog Day. Josie taught her how to do it. She hated the experience but also felt a little thrill. She was almost disappointed when Amos and Leader said nothing about it.

Leader left the first week of February and was back only days at a time between then and the end of March. She still had access to surveillance and Emma's online education, as she frequently demonstrated through emails and texts. Her promise to push Emma was not neglected even when she went away for weeks at a time.

How did you fail that test? Did you not study adequately? Messages of the like were common when Emma was not doing well. When she was doing well, the texts were: **Good progress today. I expect to see you beat this score tomorrow.** She never had any rest.

Emma began to be sneaky. Through her rigorous education, she learned some computer skills and managed to hack Leader's security layers on the computer she was using at home. She got into the Guild Book, but it was unfortunately in Arabic, a language she did not yet speak or read fluently. The security layers slapped down harder once it was clear there had been a hack. Emma was even pretty sure the Senior Guild had meetings about the incident. She did not confess.

The second time she attempted a hack, she got into a file called **Peas and Carrots**. It was in English, fortunately. In her quick, nervous perusal she saw tags and files numbered through twelve. She went straight to Eleven. There was a lot of information she did not understand but that her flawless memory promised to store for her until she could make sense of it. But she was pretty sure this was her genetic file. One section was labeled "Genetic Basis and Experimentation Log." The very first line had her IQ: 164. Below that, it said: **Potential IQ 212.** Emma stared in shock at that then nervously looked toward the stairs in fear Amos would come down and catch her. She did not think IQ had levels or potential. She thought IQ was an absolute that did not fluctuate. How could she have a *potential* IQ? She needed to consider this.

As much as she wanted to read more about her genetic basis, she scanned the file for what she wanted to know most: where she had come from. She came to a scanned document several hundred pages down. It had the words: **Emma, age 4, delivered to the care and constant guidance of Eric Stone, Leader of Stone Guild International. Emma: heretofore subject to the Nursery/Hereafter to the Guild.** One signature line had a name she could not recognize, but the other line had one solidly written word: **Leader.**

Emma hungrily moved to the next page, hoping for more. This page was titled: **Birth and Placement**. But Emma read only *Smithfield, Rhode Island* and the date of her birth before a sound behind her jerked her around. Leader stood against the kitchen bar apparently at ease, She slapped a leather belt into the palm of her opposite hand, making a dangerous, rhythmic thud. Emma would never have tried hacking her systems if she knew Leader was home.

"Know what I mean?" The words were more menacing than the thud of the belt.

Emma reached behind her to press the escape key.

"What does your schedule say are you supposed to be doing right now?" Leader asked in a dangerously cold voice.

Emma drew a shaky breath. "Stone University."

Leader slapped the belt against her palm again. "Let's go in the garage for a while and discuss my meaning of the word Diligence." She used the belt to motion toward the door.

It did not take long for Leader to discover that Emma was the culprit of the original hacking, as well. Leader removed her own computer from Emma's desk, and Amos replaced it was a computer that was barely sophisticated enough to get onto the University website, much less anything else. Despite the very stern punishments, Emma thought Leader was impressed with her ingenuity.

In the middle of February, Leader opened Emma's backpack and found a baggie of weed.

"Emma?" Leader snapped. "What is this?" She removed the baggie and held it for her to see.

Emma pulled a face, giving herself away instantly. "It's not mine. My friend Cameron had a locker check today and he asked me to hold it for him."

Amos was in the room, as well. He asked, "It's a drug?" in a somewhat scandalized voice.

"Marijuana," Leader confirmed, but her black gaze never left Emma. "Are you going to stick to your little story, Emma, or would you like to get the truth on record before I beat it out of you?"

"It *is* Cameron's," Emma repeated.

"It's a drug," Amos accused. The Guild had very strict policies about harmful substances. Alcohol was permitted only at parties where Guild business was being performed, and only when drinking was completely unavoidable. But there was no tolerance for drug use or the possession of drug paraphernalia of any kind.

Emma rolled her eyes. "Oh, please! It's not even addictive." She held up a condescending hand. "Wait! That's wrong. It's one percent addictive. Call rehab! Emma might be one percent in danger!"

"It's one hundred percent not okay!" Amos snapped back.

"I was holding it for Cameron so he didn't get in trouble," Emma shot back. "I've never smoked it!"

"No?" Leader asked. "Is my surveillance going to confirm that, Emma?"

"Okay, once," Emma admitted. "But I did not care for it, and I won't do it again." She did not enjoy any kind of smoking.

"What do you think Diligence means, Emmalyn Stone?"

"Please!" Emma shot back furiously. "You can't possibly pin this on a lack of Diligence! I am acing my classes, and I haven't even spoken to Scott since December! How can you finagle your way into proving I haven't been Diligent?"

Leader looked outraged. Emma felt perhaps she may have crossed a line. But it was Amos who hit her. He smacked her across the ear with the flat of his hand. "Don't you dare take that tone with Leader! What has gotten into you? Marijuana is a drug, and it is addictive. Even if it wasn't, it slows down cognitive function and affects development in the growing brain. Are you so smart, Emma, that you can afford to kill off your brain cells and stunt your potential?"

Emma barely heard him over the ringing in her ear.

"Well, I was certainly right that public school would challenge you," Leader murmured thoughtfully.

Emma glared up at her and snapped "Go you!" in sarcastic celebration of Leader's success at challenging her.

Amos hit her again. This time she cried out and dropped into a chair, head in her hands and elbows on her knees.

"That's enough," Leader told Amos gently. He backed away. "I'm going to let you choose what to pin it on, Emma. You can choose to tell me that you're carrying these drugs and trying them out is a matter of you not living up to your potential, thwarting your mission, carelessly consuming harmful substances into your body, and in general failing to abide by Diligence as I have taught it to you. Or you can pin it on disobedience. The Guild rules state: *no drugs of any kind*. I believe you were taught that when you were Twelve."

Emma glared up at Leader through her fingers. "How can you pin it on disobedience? You never told me I couldn't smoke weed."

"Leader told you."

"He's dead!"

Leader shook her head. "Oh, Emma! Leader never dies. I may not be the same person, but I am Leader."

Emma exhaled in frustration. She most certainly did not want to pin it on disobedience, although it truly belonged there. She knew what the rules were about drugs and harmful substances. If she claimed a lack of Obedience, Leader would instruct her again, and she did not want that.

"By partaking of harmful substances—however little harm may have occurred—I have neglected to abide by the Guild's high standards for health. That is a Diligence offense."

"Yes, it is," Leader agreed. "Amos, get rid of this." She tossed the bag through the air and Amos caught it.

Emma winced when he upended the bag in the sink. "That's an entire quad!" she cried out. "It's worth so much money!"

"A shame your friend entrusted it to you then," Leader answered. "Let's you and I go to the farm." She grabbed Emma's upper arm to pull her to her feet and toward the garage.

Leader chose to reinstruct Emma in the glories of Diligence. It was a painful lesson that kept her from school the following two days. She remained on the farm with Leader through the weekend. When she was sobbing on the training room floor at one o'clock Monday morning, begging Leader to please let her return to school the following day, Leader said, "I do hope for your sake you find a different coping mechanism than rebellion." Emma gave her a shuddering promise that she would.

Chapter Twenty-Six

On March 3, Emma was stuck in a seat near her Calculus teacher when Chastity introduced the school-wide safety assembly. Emma listened in growing fury as Chastity thanked everyone for attending—failing to mention it was mandatory—and acted like a mini celebrity on stage. She put back her shoulders and said in her obnoxiously pandering voice, "Before we get started on the important safety information, I have an important announcement."

Emma felt every muscle in her body tauten.

"I am so pleased you entrusted me to be your Student Council President this year. It's been a great one so far. Your Student Council has worked hard for you. We were able to address many of your concerns."

Emma rolled her eyes and looked down at her hands in her lap, twisting each other in fury.

"We are cracking down on school bullying and passing new rules to make Slope Oak a safer and cleaner campus."

Emma clenched her teeth. She knew from experience that Chastity's idea of cracking down on bullies did not include herself or her mob of sycophantic followers. And the rules they passed only furthered purity culture and the patriarchy. Emma's fury made her heart pound and her ears ring.

"I am pleased to take this opportunity to announce that I am running for Student Council President again next year so we can continue the important work we started—"

The ringing in Emma's ears raised to a screech until she found herself on her feet in the middle of the packed auditorium. She interrupted Chastity's nauseating pandering and shouted, "The Cobra will run against you!"

The principal and several faculty members started. They threw each other shocked, angry looks. Her Calculus teacher, though, grinned.

"You have moxie," she said up at Emma with the sound of laughter in her tone.

Emma's announcement met with at least as much applause as Chastity's. The Cobra nickname had stuck since her attack on Scott and was certainly aided by her subsequent attack on Chastity. Kids who never voted would come to the polls for this election. All the kids Chastity alienated in her tenure would rise from the background to support Emma's platform. Emma had no desire to become president. She did not want to be involved in politics or lead assemblies. She did not want to have to pretend that she cared about Slope Oak. The one and only desire was to knock Chastity off her perfect little throne.

Chastity was obviously alarmed by the outburst, but she followed the rules. She did not deviate from her approved script. She carried on with the assembly as if Emma's outburst had never happened, though Emma was pleased that her face was flushed in either anger or embarrassment. She hoped both.

Emma sat back down slowly. It was an act that reminded her—via the pain of contact with the bench—that she needed Leader's permission to make mission-altering decisions. Emma's approved persona at the school was not one who was likely to run for student council. She pulled out her phone.

May I run for student council? she asked in a quick text to Leader.

Leader's immediate response was: **Stand by . . .**

Emma waited nervously, not paying much attention to the assembly. As it was winding to a close, Leader sent her another text. **After you fire the gunshot, it's a little late to ask for a death warrant.**

Emma pulled a face because that was not an encouraging answer. She picked up her phone to formulate a response several times but could not think of any that would be appropriate. Finally, Leader sent a new text: **Get the lavatory pass and excuse yourself from the assembly.**

Obediently, immediately, she turned to her teacher and asked, "May I be excused to use the restroom?"

The teacher shot Emma a knowing glance and eyed her phone.

"I have to call my mother," she explained with a sigh. "I have been in a lot of trouble at this school, and I don't want her to think I am running for Student Council behind her back. That means I need to call her. Please?"

The teacher narrowed her eyes and said, "Do you know what to do in case of fire or tornado?"

Emma nodded and innocently said, "Run around and scream in panic?" The principal had just explained that running and shouting was not ever safe.

"Very good," the teacher teased back. "Go ahead. Be quick."

"Yes, ma'am," Emma agreed and slipped away from the auditorium. As soon as she walked into the nearest restroom, her phone rang.

"This is Emma."

"Why do you want to run for Student Council?" Leader asked.

"I thought that would be obvious," Emma replied as she paced the short distance across the empty restroom. "Chastity is doing it, and I don't want her to win. If I win, she won't."

"Do you think you have a shot?" Leader did not sound like she thought that was remotely possible.

Emma thought about the question for a long moment, and then said, "Yes."

"Emma, you realize we can pick up and move at any time," Leader said firmly. "You could be sworn in and then I could move us to Tahiti the next day."

"Please move us to Tahiti," Emma laughed, stopping to examine herself in the bathroom mirror. Dark makeup and hopeless eyes stared back at her. She looked nothing like a Student Council President. She sighed. "It would be perfect, actually, because I'm not convinced I would be a great president."

"Then you shouldn't run," Leader replied sharply. Emma slid dejectedly against the bathroom wall until she hit the floor. She tried to swallow Leader's decision, but it was like a pill that refused to go down. In the deserted restroom, Emma choked on Leader's disapproval. She choked on the lack of Leader's belief in her.

"I already said I would run," she whispered. But Leader knew that.

"Emmalyn, if you don't want to be president, why do you want to run?" Her tone was exasperated but affectionate.

"I don't know," she answered petulantly. She did know. She knew that she wanted to cause Chastity pain. Running, even without winning, would cause her so much pain! But winning would be the best prize because then Chastity would be completely dethroned.

"Emma, you can do anything you put your mind to," Leader assured her, and her belief in Emma warmed some cold places in her heart. "If you run, you can beat her. And if it means this much to you, I will not forbid it."

A flood of relief made Emma's eyes prickle, but she did not cry. "Thank you, Leader!"

"Wait!" Leader answered on a chuckle. "My support is conditional, Little Girl. At no time may the election process affect your education. You are to be Diligently moving forward on Stone University, and keeping up your excellent grades at Slope Oak. Next, you may not use psychological warfare in this fight against Chastity. You must and will maintain a diplomatic platform. Even if she hits you with slanderous campaign, you fight her without it. Finally, you must allow me to see all your signage and speeches before you use them and will abide by my ever-ready veto."

Emma was dismayed not to be able to launch a character attack against Chastity, but she figured that would happen all on its own. So many people hated Chastity that almost anyone could have run against her and gained support. As soon as Emma launched her campaign, the haters would smear Chastity's name without any help from her official platform.

"I agree to your terms."

"I will still be holding you to the high standards of Diligence I have for you. I plan to read your daily diary tomorrow, so I expect to find it is up-to-date and accurate." Leader's warning made Emma grimace. She was horrible at keeping up with her diary. "I also expect to see your personal writing tonight. Since I graciously added time for writing into your daily schedule, you should have plenty."

Emma pulled another face. She had not been able to write anything worthy of Leader's notice since Scott started dating Chastity. Most of her poetry was just an angry hate campaign against Scott.

"I don't have any."

"Why not?" Leader replied coolly. "You have a talent for this. Are you neglecting your talents?"

Emma kicked at the paper towels on the floor in frustration. "I haven't had any time, Leader! I have spent all my scheduled writing time keeping up with Stone University work. I have hardly picked up a pen since we moved!"

"My schedules are not up to interpretation," Leader replied caustically. "We'll talk tonight." Leader ended the call.

Emma let out a frustrated breath but said nothing. She had a feeling Leader was watching her right now, and she did not want to give her any reason to make the "talk" tonight more memorable. She was also grateful Leader agreed to let her run for president, and she did not want her to change her mind. Diligence would certainly be the hinge pin of Leader's support.

Emma pushed herself up from the ground, looked in the mirror, and tried once again to imagine herself as Student Council President. She certainly did not look like Chastity, or really anyone who had ever been in student government at this school. She put her shoulders back when she realized that she was more like the majority of students. She was relatable. She was rebellious, angry, and stubborn like most kids in her school. She was misunderstood and desperately searching for herself. The Cobra, though, was a dangerous, sleek, enigma. The Cobra could be their president.

Emma left the restroom.

On her way back to the assembly, a hand reached out from a crossing hall and grabbed hold of her. The smell of Scott warned her off attacking barely in time; she recognized his aftershave. He wore his customary khakis and polo shirt with his hair in a cut far too short. He looked more like a president than Emma ever would.

His voice was low and urgent, "What are you doing, Emma? You can't run for Student Council!"

Emma dislodged herself from his firm grip with a twist Leader had taught her last week. She was too angry to care if he was her Superior. He wasn't supposed to seek her out at school. He was not supposed to talk to her.

"Don't touch me."

"Emma," he pleaded, his eyes wild with fear. "I can't let you get away with this! You'll destroy my mission. I'll tell Leader."

The anger she spent months trying to repress began, like acid, to slowly leak out of the sealed compartments in her mind. She backed a few steps from him and slid into a defense stance. Her stance alone warned him that she was prepared to fight if he got in her way.

"Stay away from me," she warned, not trying to conceal her fury. Her hands came up into a defensive waiting formation and she glared at him. Her eyes dared him to touch her again.

He came nearer, but not within striking distance. He was a fool, but not foolish enough to approach her when she was coiled and ready to strike. Like a true cobra.

"Emma, I won't let you do this!" he snarled. "Everything I am working for—"

His phone rang, startling them both. Emma knew it was Leader. She dropped out of her defensive stance immediately. She did not wait around for confirmation. She darted past him and ran away.

Instead of returning to the assembly, Emma went into the ditch-room. From her backpack, she retrieved her writing notebook and forced anger through her pen onto the clean white sheet. Rage became organized letters on the page.

I emerged from the darkness of somewhere,

Before me. Before Them. Before

now. I was something else completely.

Not a child, because we are never children
in this Guilded Cage. The foaming rage
at my mouth like an animal:
Wild, rabid eyes glitter in the light of day.
I don't have a say
over how my life is lived. How my life
flows
one moment into another.
No mother to comfort me. Nor father
to offer certainty. I glide like
a bat on Training wings. Shifting at the echoes
coming back to me
from somewhere far
from here
where I am me. A glittering
truth that fills me
with hope.
Then I periscope
back into the creature they made me.
Breaking
beneath their expectations
of perfection.
No inspection truly sees
what I am when I return to the darkness of
somewhere.

In her mind, Emma was aware of the time passing, the bell ringing, and of Leader's probable scrutiny. She remained where she was until the rage subsided. When it left, there was emptiness for a while. She shut her eyes and imagined Scott being reprimanded by Leader for approaching Emma at school. She imagined him in pain. She pictured him being forced to break up with his girlfriend as punishment for failing to be Obedient. It brought her enough satisfaction that it stoked the anger again like a fire. It burst forward, its warmth shoving the emptiness and despair away.

With a smug smile, Emma titled her work "Anger Management." She looked at it in satisfaction for several moments.

Leader texted her: **Nice touch.**

"Stop it!" Emma snapped aloud. She shoved her notebook into her backpack. "Don't you have anything better to do?"

Chapter Twenty-Seven

Emma entered the administration office clutching the summons in one hand and her backpack in the other. "Excuse me," Emma said politely to the secretary. She proffered the note. "I received this in gym."

The lady looked at her suspiciously. She took the note, glancing over it. "All right, Miss Chandler. Have a seat."

"Yes, ma'am."

She turned to take one of the many empty chairs but then turned back and asked, "Do you know why I was summoned?"

The lady smiled this time. She really was a gentle person. She just didn't trust Emma because of all the trouble she had caused this year. "No, dear. You're running for president of the Student Council, right? Did you fill out all the forms?"

"Yes. Last week."

"Maybe you missed a signature," she suggested. Emma nodded as if accepting that notion, though she really rejected it. If she had missed a signature, Amos would surely have caught it. And if both of them missed something, Leader would have caught it when Amos emailed it on to her.

Emma sat down to wait. She was not sad about missing gym; it was a soccer day and Emma always had to pretend she was menstruating to get out of contact sports. Emma knew there was a debate over whether soccer was classified as a contact sport in general, but it was spelled out very nicely in the Guild Book: *Any sport in which there is a fight for space or a single ball/puck will be classified among Contact Sports and avoided by Guild constituents.* Leader would not allow Emma to participate yet refused to sign an excuse waiver.

"You should learn to lie with precision," Leader said by way of explanation.

Emma got her homework out and started on it while she waited. She could not concentrate well. Thoughts of the coming election knotted her up inside and, as Leader hinted it would, caused her to be less than Diligent with regards to her homework. It was difficult not to think of the election all the time.

Josie had laughingly volunteered to be her campaign manager at lunch the day of the assembly. "We'll hit her with everything we've got! We can demand she step down from her reign of terror."

"I don't want to fight with fire," Emma lied. The truth was that Leader would not allow her to. "I think I can win on my own merits."

Josie pulled a face at that. "What merits? You're a bully and a rebel, and people like us don't get elected to Student Council." She pointed her fork over at the prep table. "*They* get elected. Don't tell me you plan to change your image just to win an election."

"I am a rebel," Emma said thoughtfully. Then she smiled. "That's who I'll be. You know, you're wrong about rebels; they get elected. America was founded by rebels. Jesus was a rebel and look what he managed to do? Thousands of years later, there are entire nations of people dedicated to him. Rebels get things done."

Josie still seemed doubtful. "How do you plan to do this?"

Emma studied her for a long moment and said, "Thoughtfully."

Her campaign design shaped quickly after that. She turned herself into the dark heroine, leading the rebels to storm the castle of an evil dictator. Her first poster, designed by Waylon, was a pink castle in the background with smoking towers and a black silhouette of a cobra in front. Bold words said: **Cobra for President! A Rebel with a Cause.** People speculated that the castle was representative of Chastity's dying leadership. Others said it held the smoldering remains of Chastity's body after the Cobra's venomous attack. Emma had only meant the castle to stand for general decadent leadership.

Other posters that followed showed the Cobra image on top of a pink wall. Words across the top said: **Student Body, Tear Down This Wall!**

Her favorite poster, though, had the most direct attack on Chastity that Leader allowed. It had a princess looking up with a surprised expression, holding up the edge of her pink dress to show black fishnet stockings worn underneath. Stretched across the bottom was the Cobra symbol with the words: **Cobra: Not chaste but not hiding it.**

Chastity ripped those posters off the wall every time she saw them. People constantly asked her to pull up her skirt and let them see, which infuriated her. If not for Scott's constant intimidating presence, they might have said much more.

Josie, who never wore pink, showed up at school several days later wearing a pink t-shirt with the words **Daddy's Princess is Going DOWN!** in black on the front and **Vote for the Cobra** on the back. Under the words in the back in fine print was **Emma Chandler did not approve of this t-shirt**. It was amusing and, though Emma could not wear one without angering Leader, she was pleased to find that Josie had ordered an entire box. She passed them out all day long. By the end of the day, there were even mean boys on the wrestling team wearing them.

As Emma sat waiting in the office, her mind churned over upcoming events. The first rally was supposed to be tomorrow and Leader wanted to see a speech. Emma knew Chastity would supply all the inspiration she needed in the moment, but Leader had forbidden her to go off-book. In a phone conversation just last night, Leader said, "Speaking is just reading what you have written as if you were thinking it up on the spot! You're a decent writer, Emma. You should not be having a problem with this."

"It's just that I don't know what kind of attack Chastity will make on me, Leader, so I do not know how to prepare a rebuttal. In the moment, I will know better what to say. If I try to write it out, I'll be floundering on the spot."

"You will either submit your speech to me or you will take a sick day, Emma. I'm not playing with you."

Emma sighed and relented, "Yes, Leader."

But she did not know what to say. Chastity's campaign was malicious. All of her posters were an attack on Emma. She did not seem to even bother with the other candidates. **Snakes get Exterminated. Vote Chastity**

for Another Safe Year! And **Use your Voice, not your Venom! Vote Chastity!** And **EmmaChandlerIsAHorriblePerson.com and .org . . . Need I say more? Vote Chastity.**

Chastity was sure to use hatred to drive her comments at the rally tomorrow, but Emma had no idea how she could plan a speech around words that had not yet been spoken. If she simply stuck to her platform, as Leader recommended, she would be clobbered by spiteful comments. If she went off-book, she would be clobbered by Leader. There was no way to win.

"Emma Chandler?" the counselor came into the waiting room to greet her. The summons had not specified who she was meant to see, only that she was required to appear in the administrative offices right away.

"Mr. Berkshire," Emma greeted, rising to her feet to meet his eye.

He smiled in a congenial way, but he neither liked nor trusted her. "So, running for Student Council President," he said, rolling up onto his toes slightly as he spoke. "Big job."

She nodded. "It probably seems so to small minds," she answered without thinking. She had meant it as an insult to Chastity, but his face darkened.

"Big responsibility," he added in a cooler tone.

"Yes," she agreed. "Representing the student body is a big responsibility. I look forward to when it may be done well." She shifted her backpack onto her shoulder. "Was it you who had me summoned? Did you want to talk about the campaign?"

"No," he answered, but she did not know to which question. "Come with me, please."

She followed him into the office hall, past Principal Morley's door and his own office. There was a teacher's lounge and copy room beyond that where she saw Chastity making copies and chatting with a faculty member. They sure loved her. Chastity looked up as Emma walked through, giving her a haughty look that said Emma did not belong there. She didn't. Emma hated teachers, counselors, and principals.

The last door in the long hall had no plaques or windows to identify it. The counselor rapped on the door soundly and waited. The door lock clicked and the counselor turned back to Emma.

"I need to hold your phone and your backpack, Emma," he instructed.

Emma had a painful moment of concern but she agreed. "Here," she passed over her backpack and showed him the side pocket where her phone was held.

"Anything in your pockets?" he asked.

"My house keys," she said, removing them from her jacket pocket. He held out his hands to take them and she said, "I am required to have them on my person at all times. House rules."

His hand remained open in front of her. "I'll write you a note," he promised her coolly.

In the private schools she had attended, she had never been asked to surrender her keys or empty her pockets. For that matter, she had never been led to an unmarked door in any administrative offices before. She felt a wave of nervousness she had never associated with school before. She had felt such feelings when she knew Leader was angry or when she thought she might get caught doing something she should not be doing. But this was public school, so perhaps counseling sessions required her to turn over her belongings. She tried to quiet her fears and placed the keys in his hands.

"Go on in," he encouraged. She stared doubtfully at him. Wasn't he joining her? "Go ahead." She supposed not. Emma took the door handle in hand, turned it, and stepped through the door.

The room smelled like fresh paint. It was small but had a couch, a chair, and a coffee table. The only window had frosted glass so it allowed in the light but not the scenery. There were two men in the room in black suits. The skinnier blond man was seated in the chair and fiddled with his wristwatch. The other, taller man stood near the door. He closed it as she came through, and then locked it. Emma's fears escalated. Were these social services men? She had heard that sometimes kids were pulled out of class and questioned by social services about possible abuse going on in the home. What would she say?

The blond man stood up. "Hello, Emma," he greeted with a smile. "How's school?"

She watched him walk around the chair and her eyes narrowed slightly. He was no social worker. His stride was too smooth. He was trained in hand-to-hand combat. Emma realized suddenly that the man behind her also had the deadly grace that spoke of regular rigorous practice. She wished suddenly that she had not handed over her keys. The panic button was still attached, and she could have ensured Amos' immediate attention, if not Leader's, who was in Canada today.

"Sit down, Emma," the taller man instructed, pointing at the couch. Emma glanced at him, looking at the way he held himself and moved. He was carrying. So was the blond man. Social workers did not carry firearms; they were definitely not social workers. She moved to Obey, but partway through thought better of it. What if they were rival Guild? What if they had come here to kill her?

She forced her panic down. If they came to kill her, they would probably not take her out of class or bothered to invite her to sit. They wanted something. Probably Guild secrets, since that was what Arrow Guild had been after two years ago. She just had to play it cool. She had to stick to the character she was given by Leader and not let them know anything.

Emma sat down on the edge of the couch while holding herself in position to be able to move quickly. She also scanned the room for any items to use as possible weapons. The window had no blinds, so no cords or turning rods. The couch and chair were of sturdy construction, so no help there. There were no pictures or any adornments in the room at all. At this point, Emma's only option was the belt she happened to be wearing, although it was mostly decorative and not very sturdy. When her eyes moved to the coffee table, she saw a pile of flat metal discs no bigger than the end of her pinky. She had seen them before, in the main room of the farmhouse. They were part of Amos' endless security systems.

The tall man nodded. "That's the surveillance equipment from this room," he confirmed. "We did not want to risk being overheard."

Emma drew a sharp breath. They were going to kill her. She was just going to be a message from their Guild to hers. It probably was Arrow fighting back, declaring war for the loss of their people.

The blond man reached forward, and it took every ounce of control Emma had not to wince. But he just offered his hand to shake hers. "I'm Agent Caldwell," he said. He nodded his head toward the man behind him. "That's Agent Peterson. We're here to talk with you."

Emma refused to take his hand, but she looked into his eyes, trying to see more than he was saying. "Which agency?" she asked, watching him closely to see if he would lie to her.

"Central Intelligence," he answered freely. He appeared to be telling the truth.

CIA. Emma swallowed. Why would the CIA want to talk to her?

"How old are you now, Emma?" Caldwell asked, seating himself in the chair across from her.

She could find no reason not to answer him, but she was scared. Had Leader been watching when she came into this room? Would she be able to find her without surveillance up and running? Emma wondered if there really was a microchip in her spine that served as a tracking device; she had been told once that there was. Today was the first day she hoped it was true.

"Sixteen," she answered.

"How many years have you been in Stone Guild?" Peterson asked.

Emma's heart may have actually stopped beating for a moment at his question, but she recovered well.

"I'm sorry?" she asked, feigning confusion. "In what?"

Both men smiled as if they had expected her to lie to them. "Well, you're certainly well-trained," Caldwell said. "My compliments to Leader."

She continued to feign her confusion. "What do you mean?"

Caldwell shrugged. "Look, Emma, we know you moved here in November under the alias 'Emma Chandler.'" He dropped a photo on the table in front of her and, despite herself, she looked down at it. It was a picture of Sacred Heart in Virginia. "Yeah," Peterson said. "We went to your old school and talked to all your teachers and Dean Parish. A

Mr. Harrison Mitchell was able to give us a very detailed account of your exploits in Chemistry. It sounds like you're very bright."

Not bright enough to have recognized this for the trap it was! She forced her mind to be calm. "I don't know what you're talking about," she lied. "I did move here in November, but I came from Paris. I went to boarding school there."

Caldwell nodded as if he believed her, but another picture he tossed on the table showed a still image of Emma and Leader walking through an airport. "Mrs. and Miss White," he said. "November 21 of last year. Cincinnati/Northern Kentucky Airport. I believe that's you in that photo, Miss White."

She could hardly deny it, so she said nothing. How much did they know?

Peterson spoke up in his deep bass voice. "Look, Emma, we know you have been taught to lie and not to reveal your identity to us." He crossed his arms on his chest. "We know this school is bugged worse than a Spanish bodega." He smiled at his pun, but Emma made no reaction to what was, at the very least, a racist comment. "We painted the room in case our friend the engineer was sneakier than we remembered and did not make his surveillance detectable to the naked eye. We also know that this man," he nodded at Caldwell to put down another picture. It was Leader, the previous Leader, before he had died. "stole a pretty important nuclear file from one of his contacts in Homeland Defense. That is why we are here, Emma."

She could not continue to pretend she wasn't the girl they clearly knew she was. She stared at Leader's picture, even picked it up. The last time she saw him, he had been lying on the street covered in his own blood. He had been the hardest person she knew, but somehow her heart still ached when she thought of him, of his death. Most of her memories of him were filled with frustration and pain, but she remembered one sweet image of him carrying her in his arms. She was a little girl and could see the whole world from high up in his arms. He laughed at her for some reason she did not understand, but she did not care.

"You ready to come to the Guild?" he asked, carrying her to his silver Porsche, the car Amos had remodeled and now drove regularly.

"Yes!" she had answered. She could remember her excitement, and how it felt to wrap her arms around his neck. She kissed him and he laughed again.

Emma shook her head to dispel the memory, and she dropped the picture back onto the table. "I don't know anything," she said, telling the truth finally. She looked first at Caldwell and then Peterson. "I don't know what kind of intel you have, but I don't know anything about files or nuclear anything."

"Is that so?" Caldwell asked. He clearly did not believe her. "Emma, you came to the Guild at what? The age of four? Five? Would you like me to believe that in twelve years, you have never been able to get any information? What would induce you to be loyal? Why would you live under an alias, switching schools approximately twice each year of your life? If you're sitting in the dark, why agree to that farce of a family when you have a perfectly good family of your own waiting for you?"

Good questions. She did not answer right away. Did she have a real family? Someone suggested that possibility to her once before, but she rejected it. Wouldn't her face have appeared on a missing children's website if she had been kidnapped? Wouldn't these agents have an obligation to return her to her family if they knew of one? But their questions were provocative. What *did* induce loyalty? Why didn't anyone from the Junior Guild ever go to the police or the CIA? Was it fear of being caught and punished? Emma had been punished this year more than most Guild members were in a lifetime, and she still felt the need to be loyal to Leader.

"I'm a robot," she replied with a shrug. "I was programmed to be loyal."

It was a hypothesis she and Scott had created a couple years ago; that somehow everyone in the Guild was a robot, devoid of emotion and programmed to kill. It had been a fantasy Emma used to cope with grief over losing Leader, but robots did not have grief or jealousy.

"Yeah, I just bet you have," Caldwell replied, not at all kindly. "Well, you are one of the kids. It's unlikely they trust someone implicitly, so there must be a system for advancement. And you're one of the smart ones. Einstein's own."

Emma sat back against the couch now. She could not run from them and she had no information. They were at an impasse, but at least she would be comfortable.

Caldwell reached forward and picked up a handful of the tiny metal surveillance pieces. "You know, Emma, for people who claim to be sophisticated, you're not very smart. You don't cover your tracks and you always show your hand." He motioned toward the door. "We know Scott's here somewhere, under a different name. Sloppy of you both to come to the same school. We know Thomas is working in a corporate firm somewhere here in the city. We are pretty sure Victoria is at the private school on Republic Road. We know Monique took the Guild jet to Canada today. We also know you have a safe house within driving distance. There is a lot we know about your crime network because you're sloppy."

"So, the Central Intelligence Agency isn't actually good at what they do," Emma replied sarcastically. "They just get lucky when we leave them breadcrumbs."

Peterson interjected, "You're awfully cheeky for someone who doesn't have any information."

"No," Emma answered sharply. "I'm cheeky anyway. It's part of my M.O."

They sat in the quiet for a minute then Emma said, "Look, gentlemen, you're wasting your time with me. I don't know anything. I can't even tell you why I am compelled to be loyal."

Caldwell glanced at Peterson before saying, "That we might be able to tell *you*. We know a lot of the ingredients for soup, but we're looking for buried treasure."

Emma stared at him. It was code, obviously, but it meant nothing to her. She stared at him for a moment, narrowed her eyes. Both men waited. They thought they had something she wanted and were offering to trade.

Peterson said, "We've been to your workshop, Einstein. We know what you're capable of. We're highly fascinated with your abilities."

Emma felt her blood run cold. They weren't just looking for information. They were recruiting! But why? What did they want?

"Einstein," she said quietly. "You have been on Stone University." Peterson winked and Caldwell pointed at her and tapped a finger to the side of his nose. Her hands reached up to cover her face for a moment. Not long. She could not afford to not watch them. Stone University was a Guild-protected program. The only ways they could have gotten in were: 1) they had Guild clearance; 2) they had an informant on the inside; or 3) they hacked in. 1 was impossible. 2 was unlikely. They must have hacked into the satellite stream and accessed high-frequency files. That was the only thing that made sense. Amos mentioned in December that there were hacking attempts. Had he mentioned it since?

"Which of my abilities fascinates the US Government?" Emma asked doubtfully. If they had even glimpsed at her records in the University, they knew she had a genius-level IQ. She was through her first year of college already. "I don't suppose you're interested in the solution for my super strong adhesive that has the ability to glue a teacher to his chair?"

"We know the ingredients for soup," Peterson repeated. "We want buried treasure."

They were willing to give her something in return for what they wanted, but she did not know what they had or what they wanted. This conversation was pointless.

"Gentlemen," Emma said, rising to her feet. "I have nothing to give you. My loyalty is to the Guild."

"Is it now?" Caldwell asked, eyes shining. He removed a picture from inside his suit jacket and offered it to her. Emma took the picture, but she did not know the person. She studied the woman's face thoughtfully. She seemed familiar, but Emma could not place her. Her eyes were blue, and she had short blond hair in a riot of curls.

"That's your mother," Peterson informed her.

Emma drew a sharp breath. That was what was familiar about her: she looked like Emma herself! Older, matured, with a scar on her chin and no trace of fear in her eyes. It had to be Emma's mother. There was no other explanation! She pressed the photo to her chest.

"I have to go," Emma announced, moving around the coffee table. Peterson stepped aside for her to reach the door. She struggled with the lock and the handle in her one-handed rush. Nothing short of the apocalypse would wrench the photo from her hand. Neither man tried to stop her as she sprang free of the room and cruised down the hall. It, too, had been painted, she realized. How much of Amos' network was down? Did he know yet? If so, why hadn't he burst in?

As she reached the copy room, she halted. The agents' words floated through her head, and she looked back over her shoulder at them. *Ingredients for soup . . .* The men were standing in the doorway of the room, waiting. They knew they had her.

"Peas and Carrots," she announced. She took several steps back toward them. "The ingredients for soup are Peas and Carrots." Boy, were they ever satisfied! "You piggybacked on my hack into Leader's files. You want me to hack her system."

"So, I guess the rumors are true," Caldwell smiled. "You are a genius."

They knew who she was! The whole story, assuming they had Leader's personnel file. That was why they had mentioned so many names. She was the reason they knew all those names. And they were willing to tell her all of it. They were willing to reunite her with her mother. They were willing to help her if only she led them to top-secret Guild information.

Hope flared in Emma. It was a painful hope; reminiscent of the last time she had allowed herself to believe there was life outside the Guild. And that had ended in bitter tragedy. It had not been worth the trouble then, but this could very well be legitimate. She was holding a picture of her mother. She always dreamed of a normal life with a loving family and birthday parties and driving privileges. She could have real friends. She could grow up to be a real adult, with a job—not a mission—and a family—not the Guild. She imagined a life that was not filled with fear and death. But could she trust them? She had trusted before, and she had lost. And people had died.

"I don't know," she said out loud, moving back toward them. "I need to think about it."

Peterson nodded. "Tell you what, Einstein, you decide you're interested, come up with an excuse to use the office—your campaign might work—and call us from the counselor's phone. It's been returned to safe mode." He proffered a business card. "We'll be waiting."

Emma took the card and pocketed it. She turned to leave again, but stopped and looked back, "Leader can never learn about this," she warned them. Or perhaps she was warning herself. Leader was almost the only person in the world she respected. Emma would be mortified if she thought for one minute that she had betrayed Leader.

Was it betrayal? Emma had begged Leader to tell her more, to tell her why they were there and what their purpose was. Was there a purpose or was the Guild, as these agents suggested, just an elaborate crime network with sloppy clean-up skills?

Caldwell laid a finger beside his nose in a promise not to tell. "We look forward to your call."

Chapter Twenty-Eight

While Emma was still in the painted hall, she tucked her mother's photo carefully into the center of her Calculus textbook. It was safe there since Leader had already seen the text and approved it. Besides, ever since Emma began Stone University, Leader seemed much less interested in her high school homework. There was no other hiding space Emma could think of where Leader would not see it. She considered her locker or the ditch-room, but Amos' surveillance was everywhere. Everywhere except this painted hall.

Emma made sure the picture was securely held near the binding and then returned the book to her backpack.

By the time she got to gym class, it was time for showers, so Emma went on to her next class of the day. Her mind was preoccupied again, but this time with thoughts of her mother and the agents' proposition. She found herself daydreaming, an activity that had been broken out of her in childhood. She imagined returning to her mother's house in Rhode Island, walking through the gate and approaching the door. She imagined Caldwell knocking, and the door opening, the woman in the photo stepping onto the porch.

Caldwell would say, "Ms. Ackerman?" Emma imagined she had a last name like Ackerman, a name she could keep forever and never give up to hide her identity.

"Yes?" the woman would answer, a little confused.

"We wanted to return your daughter to you, ma'am," Peterson would jump in. "This is Emma." And he would present her.

In Emma's mind, the woman's breath would catch and when she finally breathed, it was to expel a tearful sigh and draw Emma into an embrace. "I had nearly lost hope!" she would say. Sometimes Emma imagined her saying, "Where was she? Where has she been all these years?" And she would vow never to let Emma out of her sight again.

"Miss Chandler?" The economics teacher's voice broke through and reality came screeching back. "Did you hear me?"

Emma looked into the man's face and tried to recall his words. Finally, she had to admit, "No, sir. Sorry. I was distracted." He appeared to be surprised by that, but he repeated his question, and she answered it. Several minutes later, the same thing happened. She inwardly cringed, begged his pardon again, and tried hard to focus from then on.

When he gave the class a silent reading assignment, he crossed the room to her. "Are you all right, Emma?" he whispered, careful to make sure no one else could overhear. "You seem like you may not be feeling well. Do you need to see the nurse?"

"No, sir," she replied, embarrassed that she caused him concern.

"If you change your mind, I have a pass already filled out for you on my desk," he promised.

"It won't be necessary, but thank you," she answered and refocused on her work.

She was similarly distracted in her final class of the day, and it won her a threat of detention but, thankfully, no follow through. Waylon picked her up in the carpool line, but as he was on the phone the entire trip home, he did not notice how preoccupied she was.

Stone University proved impossible for her to do. At five, Leader called.

"Are you ill? Why aren't you getting any work done?"

There was no way to answer. If she said she was preoccupied, Leader would assume it was the campaign. That would anger her but was, Emma realized, a nice cover. But then Leader might make her drop out of the race. The funny thing was that Emma did not care as much about the campaign now that she had a mother to daydream about. But what excuse would she use when she went to call the agents in the office if she dropped out of the race?

That was when she realized she intended to call the agents.

"I'm sorry," she told Leader, trying her best to hide her bubbling anxiety. "I'm really tired today. I wish I could say it's not because of the campaign, but it probably is."

Amos, who was in the kitchen making dinner, looked up in concern.

"I told you that this campaign could not affect your work, Emma!" Leader snapped.

"I know," she replied, contrite. "But I have done really well up until now. The rally tomorrow is weighing on my mind. I'm afraid she'll attack me, and I won't be prepared to defend myself. And I can't lose to her, Leader. I can't."

There was a long pause while Emma waited in fear. What if Leader had backup surveillance? What if she knew about her meeting with the agents and was waiting for her to tell about it to prove her innocence? Emma just about blurted it all out.

"I understand," Leader answered in a gentler tone. "You may log off and focus on preparing for your rally. I know this is important to you."

Leader never ceased to amaze Emma. Just when Emma was sure she was going to fly off the handle, she softened. Just when Emma expected no mercy, Leader granted it.

"Thank you," she breathed, truly grateful.

"Put Amos on," Leader ordered. "And get to work on your rally speech and possible rebuttals. I want them emailed to me before dinner."

"Yes, Leader," she agreed and handed the phone to Amos.

Despite her lies, the rally that earlier seemed so important was suddenly not. Emma had a family. If she left tomorrow, nothing here had to matter. Scott could kiss any stupid bimbo he wanted! Chastity could run for President of the United States and pass federal laws outlawing patterned hosiery for all Emma would care! If Emma left tomorrow, maybe this passionate self-loathing she had carried since Leader's death two years ago would finally go away. She could leave it behind.

When Amos ended the call with Leader and returned Emma's phone to her, he said, "You can go in the den if it will help you focus."

Emma felt relieved. Doing work in the kitchen—the main hub for activity in the house— was difficult even on a good day. She retired to the den, closed the door, and attempted to write rebuttals to possible attacks by Chastity. She got very little done. In the quiet privacy of the room, she found herself retrieving the photo of her mother and imagining what she was like. She tried desperately to remember what happened before she was put into the Porsche that day so long ago—the first memory she had of the Guild. Where had Leader picked her up from? Why did her memory seem casual and relaxed if indeed Leader was kidnapping her? Had her mother given her up for adoption? Had the Guild adopted her? If the Guild had adopted her, she belonged to the Guild even if her birth mother attempted to make contact.

That idea effectively shut down her joy. She managed to write a respectable amount of her rally speech while refusing to think about her mother.

But thoughts came back and Emma pulled out the picture again.

"I want you to be real," she whispered at the woman's photograph.

She managed to stuff the picture away in time for Amos not to see it when he stepped into the room. "Dinner's ready. Do you have a speech to submit to Leader?"

Emma glanced at the notebook where she was writing random thoughts about what to say to Chastity. "Not really," she admitted. Amos cocked a stern brow. Emma added, "I'm not feeling very inspired, Amos."

He came across the room, picked up her notebook, and looked over her words. He made a couple thoughtful sounds. "It's a good, clean start, Emma. Come get some dinner and I will delay Leader for you. Maybe some food will clear your mind and help you look at this another way."

Leader did not agree. She told Amos to send Emma to the mats to train for an hour after dinner. *"Forms 83 through 97 should jumpstart her, and if it doesn't, I'll be home tomorrow,"* Leader's voice rang through the speaker phone Amos held up for her. The threat was unmistakable. Leader would tolerate her inattentiveness no longer.

Forms actually did help her. They refocused her mind on the fact that people lie, and the agents might not have anything for her at all and want only to use her. The picture of her mother could very well not be her mother at all, but just some woman who looked similar enough to Emma trick her into believing they were related. The forms reminded her that her muscles stored her anger at Chastity for being close to Scott when Emma was forced to be away from him.

She fought the boxing bag for a long time and then she sat down and wrote a speech that would both please Leader and obliterate Chastity's platform.

Unfortunately for Emma, thoughts of her mother did not go away. She continued to have doubts, but she also continued to have hopes. When at breakfast Adam harassed her, she thought about how happy she would be to escape him. She thought about seeing him for the last time and felt no pangs of sadness at all. However, Leader walked in the door suddenly and announced her intention to drive Emma to school, with an encouraging smile and a "It will give us time to catch up!" Emma felt overwhelming doubt. The idea of seeing Leader for the last time was painful enough to make her reconsider everything.

"You're very contemplative today," Leader said when they were in the car.

"Yes," Emma agreed, uncomfortably aware of Leader's scrutiny. Not for the first time Emma wondered if she knew about the agents' visit and was simply waiting for Emma to tell all. It was entirely likely; it wouldn't be the first test Emma had undergone in the Guild.

"Are you nervous about the confrontation with Chastity?" Leader wanted to know.

She wasn't but she lied. "A little. Her campaign is clearly geared toward tearing me down, so I can expect a ruthless attack."

Leader chuckled. "Well, you can hardly blame her, Emma." Those words, apparently filled with judgment, cut Emma deeply. She looked up into Leader's eyes. Did Leader want her to fail? But Leader continued. "You are the only adversary she has in this race. The other two kids who are running will only split her ticket. You are the person to beat." Emma relaxed. It had not been a judgment at all, but a backward compliment. She was saying Emma was a worthy opponent.

"You're going to do fine," Leader encouraged her. "This will give everyone a chance to see how nasty Chastity can really be. Playing it nice during this race may have been your most strategic move so far."

Emma rolled her eyes. "Since you forced me to play nice, you have to say that."

Leader patted her leg. "What time is the rally? I think I might like to come."

Emma shot her a pained look. "No," she begged. "Please don't do that! Just watch it on surveillance like you always do. If you're in the audience staring me down, I will never be able to do a good job."

Leader shot her an arched look. "What time?"

"Eleven," Emma grumbled back.

Leader smiled. "I think 11 will work well. I can move some things around and maybe even Amos can join us. It would be appropriate for your family to come. Will Chastity's family be there?"

Emma sighed. "Probably. We were all encouraged to invite people we love. Chastity will probably have an entire posse: aunts, uncles, and grandparents."

Leader smiled at the derogatory tone in Emma's voice. "I can scrounge you up a posse, too, you know. I have a few connections."

Emma's response was only a long look of disdain. "No, thank you. Maintaining my image as the Cobra is dependent on a mysterious quality you would destroy by bringing a fan club to the rally. And I would appreciate it if you did not bring Amos, either. He will try to hug me and it will ruin my street cred."

Leader snorted. "I'm sorry," she shot back sarcastically. "I had no idea I was ruining your 'street cred.' I'm not sure I was even aware you had 'street cred.'"

"I do at school."

Leader chuckled at the idea. She reached into her center console and pulled out a small box. "Maybe this will help keep up your image," she suggested, passing the box to Emma. Emma stared at it doubtfully until Leader arched her brows. Emma took the box in hand and opened it carefully. In the box was a silver serpent charm strung on a black cord. The serpent had chiseled black stones for eyes that shone in the shifting light of the car. It was really a beautiful piece, Emma thought, if haunting.

"Put it on," Leader encouraged.

Emma removed the necklace from the box and studied it a moment before tying the cord around her neck. The serpent hung just below her collar, peering out at the world in a defiant way. It was the very image of rebellion, Emma thought. It was perfect for her campaign.

"Thank you," she said quietly, and she meant it.

"You're welcome," Leader answered with a smile.

As an afterthought, Emma added, "I'm not actually supposed to accept gifts, you know. It's against Guild rules."

Leader only chuckled in response, not rising to the bait.

When they pulled into the drop-off lane, Leader leaned to try and hug her. It was not a real hug; it was only in response to Emma's apparent aversion to familial affection in sight of her peers. Leader was trying to ruin her image.

Emma shoved Leader away from her and snapped, "Get off!"

Leader laughed; a twinkling musical sound Emma so rarely heard from her. Usually Leader's laughter was less jovial, more image-driven chuckles and sarcastic scoffs. She was enjoying teasing Emma this morning.

Emma pointed a stern finger at her, grasped her backpack by the handle, and jumped out of the car.

"See you at 11, shnookums," Leader teasingly called before Emma managed to slam the door. She saw Leader's laughter continue as she pulled away from the curb. Emma watched her go and was suddenly not so sure she would call the agents.

CHAPTER TWENTY-NINE

The rally was an optional assembly for students, but it was better attended than any presidential debate in the school's history. When Emma and the other three candidates walked out onto the stage to take their places, Emma could not help looking around at the size of the crowd. Her stomach clenched. She had never felt this kind of strange nervousness before. Stage fright? She heard of it before but never thought it would affect her. Emma faced rage, deception, murder and attempted murder, and various other forms of violence. It never occurred to her, with all that baggage, that she would have a perfectly healthy fear like stage fright. It was about as rational as a fear of the dark. She tried to fight the nervous sensations.

Josie sat in a crowd of rebels in the very front row. Most of the kids with her never sat on the front row for anything. Emma amusedly wondered if they had managed to get the front row by skipping classes in time to be early. Almost the entire group wore their pink **Daddy's Princess is Going Down!** T-shirts. The show of support ought to have made Emma less nervous, but their show of solidarity only heightened her anxiety. There was so much riding on this debate. What if she went down in a brilliant flame in front of the entire student body? What if her nerves overcame her senses and she found she could not defend herself against Chastity's attacks?

In a desperate attempt to be grounded, she searched the auditorium for Leader. Leader had the ability to give confidence with a single glance. But she was nowhere to be seen. Instead, Emma saw Caldwell and Peterson standing in a doorway at the back of the room. They stood with the two school police officers and looked like they could be faculty. If anyone on faculty had the ability to look that dangerous, anyway. Caldwell's little smile made Emma feel sicker. What were they doing here? What if Leader spotted them? Would she know them for what they were? Did she already? Was that why she wasn't there?

Principal Morley welcomed the students and visitors and gave a short speech about the importance of the debate, detailing its long, rich history as if the people watching cared. They didn't. They were bored. But Emma wished his speech would never end. Her mind could not focus on the words she had written for this event. She could not remember her platform. No matter how many times she discreetly wiped her palms on the thighs of her black pin-striped pants, they never seemed dry.

She did not want to be president, she realized. She did not care about beating Chastity. She wanted to jump off the stage and walk out the door and never look back. Would Leader care if she dropped out halfway through the race? It did not exactly demonstrate the dedication Leader had insisted was part of the Diligence skill. Did it matter what Leader thought?

Yes.

Emma searched the crowd again. *Where are you?* she asked in her head. One look from Leader and Emma would be okay. One glance, and she would know Leader supported her dropping out of the race. And if she did not support it, one glance would buoy Emma up enough that she could get through the rally. Her breath came in quick gasps. If Leader was there and she saw the agents, she could tell Emma if they were liars. She could claim Emma belonged to the Guild and take away the temptation to betray it. If Leader were there, where she had said she would be, Emma could relax and focus on the task at hand.

I want to leave! she screamed in her head. She glanced at Chastity. The girl looked as chaste as her name implied. She wore a red suit jacket with a matching skirt, black high heels, and pearls. She looked like a student body president.

In contrast, Emma wore a t-shirt with *Nirvana* printed across it. It was Adam's shirt; she had found it in the laundry. She could not represent the students. She hated the students! Besides, Chastity needed this. It was the only thing she had going right in her life. Was it right for Emma to steal that from her?

The moderator stepped up to the podium and explained the procedure of the debate, but Emma was no longer listening. She was panicking. She recognized the feeling; it was the same way she felt when she thought Leader might be killed in Beijing. The day she *begged* her not to go and she went anyway! To Beijing. With the Atlantis file.

Buried treasure.

The agents wanted *buried treasure.* They wanted the Atlantis file! Emma had no idea what it contained, but she remembered Leader asked Amos to open it for her. It had been under critical lock. She knew that because he announced a code to open it. Her eyes flashed across the room to the agents, but they were no longer there.

She could do it, she thought. She could hack Leader's system and get to the Atlantis file if she happened to get access to the office when Leader wasn't home. She could do it and *then* decide if she wanted to barter with the agents. She could do that much easier than she could stand in front of an entire school full of people with no idea how easy they had it. She couldn't represent these whining, infantile idiots! Chastity deserved them!

"Miss Chandler," the mediator said in the first question launched her direction. "Miss Monez says you do not have a solid platform and that your constituents will be disappointed in your leadership. Would you please outline your platform for this panel?"

Emma stared at the moderator and beyond her at the student panel that was responsible for directing the questioning. This whole thing seemed so trivial in the face of her real-life dilemma. There was nothing in the Guild holding her there except fear. She could walk away. There was a home waiting for her. If Leader ever asked her again, "Where were you running to?" she could answer, "My mother."

"No," she answered, eyes searching the crowd. Her gaze contacted Scott as it scanned and doubled back to him. He sat in the third row, eyes on her intently as if to ask why she wasn't answering the question. He mouthed "What's wrong?" at her and made a small gesture with his hand to encourage her to answer. He would understand that she did not want to do this. He would understand that she wanted to lose.

Then her gaze traveled down to his shirt and she saw the words: **Snakes bite. Emma hits. Don't let her destroy our school!** It was a **Vote for Chastity** shirt. She had seen six or seven of them in the past few days.

Suddenly, the rage returned and with it all the reasons she had started this campaign. Her fears fled. Her nerves were squashed by the compelling anger. She wanted to taste blood today. And since Scott was off limits, Chastity would do.

"I'm sorry, Miss Chandler," the mediator asked in surprise, "Did you say that you will not outline your platform?"

"That's right," Emma replied, floundering for a way to recover. "The trouble with my opponent is that she is obsessed with platforms, agreements, and committees. It isn't committees that change the world. It's one person at a time choosing to make one change at a time. It isn't lists of rules that make a school safe. Rules have never been successful; not since the beginning of time. I can even use an example she would accept in the story of Adam and Eve. They were only given one rule and they could not follow it.

"The only way to maintain a safe environment is by every student dedicating him or herself to upholding one. It is a personal commitment to the good of a community over the immediate need to satisfy one's personal grudges. It is not possible to lecture and punish someone into making a change. People change when they choose to change."

Her words stirred in her heart. Leader had tried to change her. Leader tried to make her behave and had failed. Leader enforced the rules with strict discipline, and still Emma was slipping through her fingers. She would not Obey Leader out of fear anymore! She needed more, but when she asked, Leader refused. The agents were offering her more.

One of the students on the panel spoke quietly and the moderator turned the microphone over to him. "Could you explain how you intend to institute this change in students?" the boy asked with a respectful nod.

Emma pulled a face. "I don't intend to institute anything," she answered dismissively. "What the students in this school want, and what they deserve, are some options. Since when did the wearing of patterned hosiery affect a student's ability to learn? This is not a prison and it's not a communist country—it's a school. The faculty focus should be on education, not on dress-code infractions."

Her words received wild applause from the audience. Options. That was all anyone really wanted. Every free country in the world was built over the carcasses of oppression. That was all Emma wanted, she realized. It wasn't so much that she hated the Guild. She was fond of Amos and Waylon, Julianne, and Lara. She felt real affection for Victoria. Despite her dislike of Adam and Ilene, her indifference toward Thomas and Piper, and her current hatred for Scott, her heart belonged to the Guild. But she wanted to believe she had some influence over her life. She wanted to believe that she could wake up tomorrow and decide to walk away from it all if she chose to. The not-being-able-to-choose part was the most difficult thing about belonging to the Guild. But now she could choose! She could choose the CIA, trusting them to keep her safe, and walk away from the Guild forever. It was something she could *choose*, not something that was chosen for her!

But she did not know if she could do it. Her *soul* belonged to Leader. There was no one in this world who meant more to her or that she wanted more to be pleased with her. Would she feel the same way toward a mother she had never met?

Chastity's rebuttal came in time, "As an active member in my community and in this school, I find that rules make me feel safe. My opponent seems to be suggesting that we turn toward anarchy and free reign. I defy that any student in our school would feel *safe* under such an arrangement.

"Furthermore, there are many studies that suggest dress codes are one of the fastest and most effective ways to equalize a student body. Schools that enforce a strict dress code are safer and have higher graduation rates. I welcome my opponent to find research supporting her claim that anarchy creates a safe and harmonious learning environment."

The mediator allowed the other candidates to weigh in, but it had already become obvious to the entire congregation that this rally was a fight between Chastity and Emma. Unfortunately, Emma could not focus on the debate because her mind raced through the pros and cons of betraying the Guild.

"Miss Chandler, did you wish to make any statements regarding your view of the School Beautification Initiative?" asked the Mediator.

No. But Emma said, "I think it's absurd. We have a beautiful building, and it is moderately well-supplied. This initiative, designed to repaint and resupply the school, is a drain on resources and a waste of time. We would do better to spend our money on a tutoring program for students who need help and really want to succeed. Instead of beaming around at a freshly refurnished cafeteria, we could turn our attention to a hot lunch program that would allow students to eat who usually hide in the restrooms during lunch because they cannot afford a meal. Or we could always fund an experiment to show that pantyhose have little to no effect on academic performance." She looked directly at Chastity. "And that a code of ethics is a far more practical than a book of rules."

More cheering. Emma wondered, though, why they supported her. Was it because they agreed with her that painting a school and repaving the parking lot was a waste of precious school resources? Or were they hungry for discord? Wasn't the entire reality TV phenomenon based on a love of discord? And what about Emma? Was she a friction junky? In her heart-of-hearts was she really eager to meet the woman who had given her life? Did she really want to walk away from the Guild forever? Like people who jumped out of airplanes or rafted over waterfalls, was standing on the edge of betraying the Guild just Emma's way of feeling alive?

The moderator moved on to other topics. She asked each candidate to name one change they would like to make if they were elected president and describe, if they could, how they planned to accomplish it. As the incumbent, Chastity was the first to answer.

"As pleased as I am with this school and its wonderful student body," she began. Emma barely managed to refrain from rolling her eyes at such blatant flattery. "I believe I would like to institute a stronger anti-bullying program. Students could sign a new agreement stating their intention to abide by a no-bullying tolerance. That would include, as always, deliberate physical assault and use of violent words, threats, and foul language, but I would like to go above and beyond that to the more ambiguous mental assaults of sarcasm, veiled insults, and verbal attacks. I also think bullying should be considered an act of aggression and handled with appropriate detention or suspension of guilty parties."

Emma could barely contain her laughter. She smirked. She was the last of the candidates to answer the panel's question. She managed with some difficulty not to respond until invited to do so.

"Miss Chandler?" the moderator prompted.

Emma nodded to acknowledge the prompt but for a moment she allowed the audience to wait in awkward silence. There were so many changes she would make if she could. If she could change her life, she would never have moved here where Chastity's bullying turned her into this catty person. If she could change anything, she would change Leader's trust policy to include her. She would change Scott's attraction for Chastity that she could not understand. She would change the Guild split. She would change the fact that she was nearly six months past driving age and had yet to be behind the wheel of a car. No. If she could change anything, she would go back in the past and change the trajectory of the gunshot that killed Leader when he protected her. If she could change anything, she would ensure that the shot hit her instead, as it had been meant to do.

"Miss Chandler?" the moderator repeated. "Did you understand the question?"

"Yes, of course," Emma replied. She never met a question she did not understand. "But it's a big consideration. I would have to say that the most important change that needs to be made will be completed with my election as president."

"Please explain," one of the panelists prompted.

"This school is living under the puritanical rule of a ruthless dictator who likes to throw out new rules when she is inconvenienced. My election will ensure her fall from grace and power. That is the most important change I can imagine."

Her response got a lot of reaction from the audience. The **Vote for Chastity**! camp booed and cried unfair abuse of the debate process. The Cobra camp stomped feet and gave cheers and thunderous applause. They chanted, "Cobra! Cobra! Cobra!"

Principal Morley stepped to the microphone and had to ask twice for order. "Miss Chandler," he rebuked coolly. "This is not a forum for attacking our current student committee and its elected officers. You have one last opportunity to answer the question in an appropriate manner."

Emma gave him a comical salute and said, "Once I become president, I would like to work toward getting rid of detention. To my understanding, it is an ineffective punitive process that yields few positive results. I feel detention is an uncreative establishment meant to sweep problems under the rug rather than deal with them directly. Despite what others may believe, students do not want to be in trouble. They do not break rules because it's a thrill or they want to upset the teachers and the system. We break rules because we are reaching for a level of control the world believes we cannot handle.

"I understand that getting rid of detention will require a lot of work and would have to go through the district. It would require a lot of minds to be reprogrammed to imagine a different corrective procedure. It would require a stronger dedication on the part of the students to uphold the high academic and character standards of this school. It will take much more effort than adding a new line to the student handbook no one ever reads and enforcing a student 'agreement' no student ever actually agrees to. But I believe in the power of the dedicated teen."

She had won over the student body. The teachers glared cold hatred at her, and the administration probably wished she never transferred into their school, but the students were hers. She knew it. She looked at Scott's miserable expression and saw that he also knew it. And Chastity knew it. Although there were no points awarded at this debate, and there were still at least thirty minutes of questions to go, Emma had won.

Chapter Thirty

Emma sat backstage in the dark auditorium long after it emptied. Lunch came and went. Her P.E. class began without her. Emma sat against the wall in the dark behind the curtain, using the light of her phone to look at the picture of her mother in her backpack.

Leader did not come to the rally.

Emma touched the photo with a delicate finger and tried to make sense of how she was feeling. She neither asked Leader to come to the rally nor wanted her there, but Leader insisted she would come, and then she didn't.

Emma did not need anyone to hug her and tell her she did a great job. She knew already. She clobbered Chastity and wiped the floor with her opponent's ideas and assertions. She knew she represented her constituents well. The angry kids, and the partiers; the sexually free, the morally deprived; the judged, scorned, and misunderstood—all were represented by her direct words and fearless answers. Unfortunately for Chastity, that was eighty percent of the student body.

Yet, Chastity stood backstage after the rally, wrapped in the comforting arms of two parents. No matter how dysfunctional Emma sensed their household was, they were there to support their daughter. They repeatedly told her she did well, generously lying to say she was the strongest candidate. They hugged and kissed her.

Emma saw the families of the other candidates come back to congratulate their brave efforts. They, too, lied. They encouraged. They were parents.

Emma had no parents. Pretending did not make it real. No amount of pretending Leader was her mother made it so. A parent would have been here. A parent would have been sitting in the front row, beaming proudly as Emma squashed her competition like a bug. A parent who supported her child would come backstage to quiet her fears and reassure her. But Emma stood completely alone.

At one point when the stage door opened, Emma's heart leapt and she hoped it would be Leader. It was Scott. When he came into the room, she entertained the smallest hope that he came to congratulate her and celebrate her success, but he barely even glanced at her. He walked to Chastity who was already wrapped in a circle of acceptance. He took her hand, whispered, "You did well," and then kissed her on the cheek. That was when Emma realized no one was coming for her.

"You can go on to lunch, Emma," Principal Morley said as he bustled past her. But Emma ignored him. She was a fool, but she waited. When she was in grade school, she was in a school play. No one had shown up then, either. In fact, Emma was left on the school steps late into the night until someone remembered to pick her up. She waited now as she waited then: desperate, but not really hopeful.

In junior high school, Emma won the state spelling bee. She smashed her trophy against the school wall when she realized no one came to watch her. That earned her a trip to the administrative offices and a call to her "parents." When her "mother" arrived to pick her up, every word out of her mouth was scornful and furious. Emma still wondered to this day if they ever learned she won an award.

When Chastity and her group left the backstage area, Chastity snorted and said, "What's the matter, Emma? No one came to congratulate you? Even with your filthy heart, *someone* must love you."

Those were the only words Chastity ever said that stung. Scott tried to catch Emma's eye but she looked away. Determined not to give Chastity the satisfaction of appearing emotional, Emma walked off. She went all the way to the back of the stage and sat behind the curtain. And there, in that place, for several hours, she fought against the emotions. She would not cry. She did not cry! She always knew that her whole life was pretend.

She sat staring at the only thing that brought her any comfort. She looked at the photo. She hungered for the end of pretending. Sliding down to her side, she drew her knees up under her chin. She held the photo safely inside her backpack and allowed herself to dream.

She imagined her mother saying, "You did wonderfully! Were you nervous, Emma? Because at first you seemed nervous, but as soon as you started speaking, your face lit up and I could see that you truly had a passion for what you were saying."

Emma shut the phone and placed the photo back into her textbook. She pulled her backpack under her head and closed her eyes. She dreamed of her mother laughing.

"I thought Chastity would swallow her tongue, the way you attacked detention! You should have seen her face, Emma! She was visibly angry."

Emma rolled so her back was to the curtain. She felt the cool cement wall against her knees. Her breath bounced on the wall and came right back to her.

"I hope you really wanted to be president, honey, because it looks like you're going to win this thing. It's not too late to drop out, if you change your mind. I don't care what you choose as long as it makes you happy. I always support you."

Emma squeezed her eyes shut, forcing back the tears. Swallowing her pain.

She retrieved the business card hidden in her bra and entered the digits into her Guild phone. She knew the number could be tracked, that her text would be recorded, that she should use a safer phone, but she did not even care. She texted: **I'm in.**

And then she allowed herself to cry.

*

Emma expected to get caught. She waited for it, even. After all, the Guild was naturally suspicious of everyone and everything. It did not trust easily or well. While lying in the cold dark behind the curtain, she expected Leader to come storming in, eyes on fire, claws unsheathed. When she didn't, Emma was a little disappointed.

She pulled herself together before her final period, but instead of going to class, she stole some paper from a supply room and went to the upstairs lavatory where teachers never ventured. In the last stall, she locked the door and sat on the floor and wrote words Leader would never receive. Angry poetry and furious words scattered across the pages. And then, when the final bell rang, she tossed the work into the trashcan and went out to meet her ride. She felt a small sense of satisfaction for throwing the work away. Leader made demands; she wanted to see all of Emma's written work. Tossing it in a trashcan was like stealing from Leader, and it made her feel powerful.

She recognized the feeling. It was this emotion that Leader warned her about last month. *"I do hope for your sake you find a different coping mechanism than rebellion."* Screw you, Leader!

Emma furiously hoped the Volvo would pull up, but it was the Porsche. The window rolled down and Amos gave her a smile. "Hi, Emma! How was school?"

She just looked at him, stared at him. He did not know. He must not have been watching surveillance today, or he would not have even asked her. He would know she skipped all her afternoon classes to sit in the dark. He might not be able to see the photo, since she held it carefully inside her backpack, but he would know she wasn't Diligent.

Amos pulled a face when she said nothing. "Not good, huh?"

She tossed her backpack in the backseat and climbed in after it. Amos gave a chuckle. "There is a perfectly good passenger seat right up here." He patted the seat. "I'm not a chauffeur, you know."

Emma slammed the back door shut and pulled her seatbelt across her lap. "Yeah, you are," she answered coldly and looked out the side window.

Amos turned partway around to study her, right arm across the passenger seat, expression curious. When she continued to ignore him, he turned back around and put the car into drive. For several minutes, they rode together in silence. Emma looked out the window, but she saw nothing. Her head was full of images of how to crack Leader's security. If she got into the system, could she circumvent Amos' surveillance? If she did that, it would make meeting with the agents much easier. She would not have time to play around, though. It might not take Leader long to discover the system had been hacked. She would have to get in, download the file, and get out.

"Emma, did the rally not go well?" Amos asked, a hint of concern in his voice. She did not answer and after a minute he asked a little more sharply, "Emma?"

She did not bother to look at him, but she said, "I do not want to talk, Amos. I thought ignoring you and sitting in the backseat would make that clear, but apparently not. Will you please just leave me alone?"

He glanced over his shoulder but did not answer. Instead, he leaned forward and touched the dashboard. It came alight with numbers and colors in various patterns. It startled Emma. She knew the Porsche had a serious computer built in, but she always thought it was accessed through the screen where the stereo used to be. But this was the entire dashboard. Amos watched the road with one eye while he moved images and symbols around on the dashboard with his free hand. After a few moments, the surveillance from the rally pulled up in a ghosted image across the right side of the windshield. Emma could still see the road beyond the image, but it was the image itself that captured her attention. It started out on the frontal view of the stage, but it changed at random every few seconds, to endless points of view, including a fairly disturbing one that appeared to be from Emma's own eyes. She realized after a nervous moment it was from the silver serpent necklace Leader gave her that morning in the car. She tore it from her neck in fury. Nothing with Leader was ever what it appeared.

Suddenly, the speakers in the car blared with the moderator's voice and the entire rally played for Amos. He watched from the corner of his eye, still watching the road as they drove along. Despite her desire to be taciturn, Emma could not help sitting up and watching the scene unfold. It may as well have been a professional feed; very rarely was a camera view obscured by a passing body or an unfortunate angle.

They reached the house long before the replay of the rally finished. Amos opened the garage door and pulled in, but when Emma tried to get out of the car, he clicked the lock, trapping her there without a word. She sat back against the seat and waited quietly for him to release her. He didn't.

When the rally ended, Amos reached forward and tapped a few more symbols on the dash. The ghosted image disappeared. For a moment, he sat staring forward through the car window at the wall of the garage. Finally, he turned in his seat and stared at her with very serious eyes.

"You almost bolted. At the beginning of the meeting, you looked ready to run. What stopped you?"

She did not want to tell him it was hatred for Scott, so she shrugged.

He nodded, accepting that. Emma was suddenly grateful Amos picked her up today rather than Leader. Leader would never accept shrugs as an answer. She would make Emma dig deeper, tell all. Emma wanted to be left alone.

"I don't know why you're so moody," Amos said doubtfully. "You did remarkably well. It seems to me you have this election in the bag. Is that not what you wanted?"

Emma looked away. "It is. Can I go inside now?"

"No," he answered firmly. "I need to talk to you."

Her stomach clenched. *He knew!* She drew a long breath and scolded herself to calm down. She stared at Amos, desperately trying not to look guilty. She said, "About what?"

He pulled a face. "'About what?'" he mimicked. "The Guild, silly. What else would we ever talk about?"

Emma swallowed. He sounded pretty jovial for someone who was about to condemn a traitor. She answered with her normal disdain, "Of course. What *about* the Guild?"

"We're probably going to move," he said as he turned his body and pulled his legs up to rest in the passenger seat. "Soon."

That sent her into mixed emotions. If they moved soon, would she have a chance to get at Leader's computer? Would the agents need to find her again before she could give them what they wanted? Or were they moving *because* Emma was betraying the Guild?

"We haven't been here very long," she muttered.

"I know. And twice in a school year is a lot. You're almost at the end, though."

She scoffed and shot him a dark look. "Is that supposed to make me feel better? This school year was a complete waste! Are you at least permitted to tell me why?"

His eyes narrowed, but not in anger. He seemed to be speculating. "We're being tracked," he finally replied. Her stomach clenched again and she had to concentrate on breathing and behaving normally. "It's not a real big deal. Normally, I can get rid of stalkers with minimal trouble, but these particular ones are determined. You may or may not know this, but we've had three security breaches since we moved, and a couple in Virginia before." She must have made some kind of expression because he put up a pacifying hand. "We'll be okay. In fact, it was the major reason Leader went to Beijing last year. She had to get a handle on it all."

He gestured toward the windshield and the upgraded system. "We have a new Upgrade, so we should be able to secure everything and get on top of the attacks soon. But it will be a lot safer for us to initialize in a secure location."

Emma glanced at the windshield, remembering the ghosted image of the rally. "And this Upgrade will make everything fancier?" she tried to make her tone nasty, but she was awed.

Amos said no. "It is primarily designed to improve our security systems, but there are some fun and fancy elements. I have been adding more and more as I study and understand the Upgrade." He tapped the dashboard. "This is my most advanced addition so far, but I'm not through examining the full Upgrade, so who knows what more there will be? The point is: Leader put the actual upgrading process on hold because she wants us to be in a completely secure location when we initialize the full change over."

It made a weird kind of sense. "Why not change over here and *make* this area secure? At least then Victoria, Scott, and I could stay in school until summer." Then she narrowed her eyes and said, "Unless, we're not *all* moving. Just us? Or the whole Guild?"

He snorted. "The whole Guild, Emma, of course. This has been nobody's ideal situation."

She shook her head. "I don't understand why the split was even necessary. It doesn't seem like we're any more secure apart than together."

Amos shook his head. "We're separated mostly for a mission, not just security reasons. We're off subject!" He cleared his throat and said gently, "This is a busy season for Leader. And now she's off again researching the most current threat to our establishment." Emma just barely managed to keep up a normal breathing pattern at that revelation. Leader was researching the most *recent* threat? Did she know? "Anyway, I don't know when she'll be back, but tomorrow I have to leave for D.C. and I can't leave you here with only Adam and Waylon. You have to have someone from the Senior Guild heading the House."

Emma was puzzled. "So, you're taking me with you?"

He laughed. "No, of course not. You would be bored to tears in D.C., stuck in a hotel room for days on end."

Emma let out a frustrated breath. "Amos, are we in sight of the point of this conversation? I'm running low on caring." Really, she was just nervous and the idea that Leader and Amos would both be gone made her realize she might just have a shot at their computers.

"Stop it," he warned about her tone and her attitude. "The point is that I won't know if we will be moving until I get back. While I am there, I will learn a little more about how this Upgrade affects our systems, and I will be better able to determine if we should leave or if we can stay until summer vacation."

The thought that they might move and leave Chastity behind only served to please Emma. Scott would lose his obnoxious little girlfriend. But the idea that Amos might come back and upgrade the system concerned her. She might not be equipped to hack it once the Upgrade was in place. It was hard enough as it was from an inside computer on the same network.

"I'm hoping that if I immediately initialize then the threats will go away. Leader seems to think our location is already compromised, so it might not matter." He smiled at her. "But I would like you to stay in school at least long enough to destroy Chastity's chance at reelection." She wanted that, too. The polls opened Monday one week from now.

Amos drew a heavy breath. "With Leader gone, and since I am going to Washington, I am bringing Piper back to run this house. Ilene will go to the farm to protect our work." Why was he telling her all of this? No one ever explained anything to her before.

He must have read her expression because he said, "I am telling you this because I want you to understand what I expect out of you. Piper is relatively new to the Senior Guild. She's tough, as we all are when we get to her place, but she's inexperienced. I think you already know this, but you can be a lot to handle sometimes, Emma. I do not want Piper to have any trouble with you while I'm gone. That includes, but is not limited to, trouble at school, idleness, disobedience, and general bad attitude."

She sniffed. "You're telling me not to have a bad attitude? Do you really think you can control that?"

He reached back and grabbed her arm, jerking her toward him fiercely. "Emma," he said sharply. "I am not doing a bit with you right now. I am serious about this. You need to figure out how to improve your attitude or become a better actress because Piper is not going to have to put up with this while I am gone!"

She looked into his eyes and tried hard not to cry out against his vice-like grip. "Okay," she whispered. He held her for a moment longer than was strictly necessary. When he released her, she slipped back against the seat, massaging her bruised bicep.

"Okay," Amos said, and he sounded satisfied with their conversation. "That's what we needed to talk about."

Emma looked up at him through her lashes, angry but trying to hide it. "Can I go inside now?"

"Yes. And tell Waylon I went to the rendezvous, and I'll be back after dinner." She pulled a face at the idea that he would not be there to cook for them. He smiled, but he said, "I want his full report when I come back. I'll get Scott's while I'm out."

Amos readjusted himself in the driver's seat as Emma grabbed her backpack and slid to the door. Before she got out, she looked back at him. "Amos, where did Leader go?" she needed to know. She felt a pang of hopeful fear. Maybe Leader was called away on emergency business. Maybe it was life and death. If she didn't make it to the rally because she was saving a life, Emma could hardly be annoyed with her.

He shook his head slightly, but he said, "Russia."

Her voice mirrored her surprise, "Why? Emergency business?"

Amos shook his head. "No. She was planning to leave tomorrow, but she came out today and said she decided to leave early. She did not say why."

Emma nodded, pretending not to care, but she did care. No life to save, just an extra day in a hotel. No urgency. Emma tried to push down her irrational anger. She did not even want Leader to come to the rally. It didn't matter!

Emma grabbed the door handle and had half climbed out the door when Amos said, "Wait," and pointed at the screen. It said: **Incoming call—Leader**. "She probably wants to know about the rally."

Emma unhappily settled back again as Amos touched the panel to accept the call.

"This is Amos," he declared.

"Emma's with you?" Leader did not sound like she was going to have a friendly chat about the rally. She sounded angry. She knew!

"Yes," Amos replied in a guarded tone. "We're in the Porsche. She's in the backseat."

"Give her the phone," Leader ordered.

"You're on speaker," Amos said. "She can hear you."

"Emma!" Leader demanded. "Why did I receive a call from your school saying you didn't sign out before you left early today?"

Emma barely managed not to pull a face when Amos turned around to pin her with an arched look. "You left school? When?"

"I did not leave the school," Emma snapped back. "I just skipped my afternoon classes. God! They're like fucking prison guards."

Amos went to speak, but Leader beat him to words, "Why didn't you go to class, Emma? What possible explanation can you give me for that?"

The rebellious anger came rearing forward and Emma retorted, "I thought I would go to class and, in fact, even planned to. I said I would go, but I changed my mind. Or is that only allowed for the Senior Guild?" She swore at Leader, and then at Amos when he looked back in surprise.

There was silence for a moment and then Leader said, "So, you're mad," in a calmer tone of voice.

"I'm fine!" Emma's snarling voice dripped with venom. "How is Russia?"

Leader sighed. "I'm still in the air. Emma, I'll have Amos send me the feed of the debate. I did not think you wanted me to come!"

Emma pulled a face. "I don't care. Do whatever you want!" She reached for the handle to open the door, but Amos grabbed her arm.

"What is the matter with you?" he demanded. Then he looked at her thoughtfully. "Did you get your period today?"

Emma let out a disgusted breath and jerked out of his grip. "Are you kidding me? Will you both please just leave me alone?" And she stormed out of the car.

She thought better of her tantrum as soon as she was through the door. What if Leader decided to watch the feed, but she did not stop, as Amos had, and continued to watch Emma sit in the dark all afternoon? Would she see the photo? If she did, she would probably have Amos comb the previous feed for where she got it. But it was too late now. On her way through the living room, she saw Waylon kneeling on the floor in the middle of a pile of papers.

"Amos says he's going to the rendezvous, but he wants your full report when he gets back," she snapped as she walked past. On the bottom step, she turned around and said, "He's getting Scott's while he's out." Then she hurried upstairs before he could try to engage in conversation. She locked herself in her room, sat down on her bed, and did nothing at all productive. Diligence be damned!

Chapter Thirty-One

Emma still expected to get caught. When she came downstairs in the evening, she expected Amos to be waiting for her with surveillance footage of her meeting with the agents and of her text to them. She had no idea how she thought Amos could acquire such footage since the agents had disabled his network in the school, but that was still what she expected. Instead, Waylon was cleaning the kitchen and pulled a plate of food out of the refrigerator for her. He turned on the stove to heat it up.

"May I use the microwave?" she asked softly. She repented of her previous tone when she saw he saved her some dinner.

Waylon gave her a soft smile. "Okay," he agreed and shut off the stove. They were almost never permitted to use the microwave, although Leader never explained except to say, "It's in the Guild Book." It must not have been a terribly strict edict if Waylon was willing to overlook it. He was in the Junior Guild, like her, though. He probably didn't know all the answers.

She heated the food and sat down at the bar. Waylon was rinsing out the sink, but when she got settled, he leaned over and wiped the counter like a bartender. "What seems to be the trouble, darlin'?" he asked in a mock deep voice.

She smiled at him shyly and said, "I'm sorry I yelled at you earlier."

He cocked his head to the side and continued to wipe the counter. "I'm guessing you had a bad day."

She shook her head. "No worse than any other day. I'm just having a bad . . . life."

He chuckled. "I get that. There are plenty of trying days in the Guild. It's a hard life, for sure." He tossed the dishrag in the sink and leaned back against the opposite counter, watching her. "You're going to make it, though. You're smart. You're strong." He gave a slight laugh. "You're certainly forceful. You're going to make it."

Emma nibbled at her food while she digested his words. "What if I don't want to?" She darted a look up at him.

He let his legs slide a bit farther forward, using his arms to prop himself against the counter. "Well, I don't know what you mean by that exactly, but I'll explore it with you." He narrowed his eyes in thought. "When I was at your position in the Guild, I was younger than you are, so I don't know if it's the same. I remember life being hard. Leader is always exacting. The Guild does sometimes squeeze every ounce of joy from your life. I remember thinking 'This cannot be real!' every other day or so." He grinned at the obvious dismay on her face. "I can give you the advice Piper gave me when I was struggling: stop expecting to get answers to your questions."

She snorted and looked away. Waylon laughed again. "Yeah, it didn't help me, either. You know, when I was in Diligence, struggling to figure everything out, stuck in the dark with unrelenting expectations all the time . . ." He shook his head in commiseration. "I think I just kept expecting to wake up one day and be back in my bed at the Nursery, surrounded by comfort and familiarity."

His mention of the Nursery made Emma narrow her eyes. "How old were you when you became the Twelve and entered the Guild?"

"Nine," he answered.

She dropped her fork. "Nine? Do you remember things from before? Do you remember where you came from?"

He studied her for a moment before nodding. "A little. Nothing particularly significant. I remember being anxious to come to the Guild House and get my real life started. I remember the day my phone rang for the first time. I picked up and said, 'This is Waylon?' like a champ, but I was nervous."

Emma had no idea what he was talking about. "Who was it?"

"Leader," he replied simply. "The Leader back then. She was like a goddess; the most amazing person I had ever seen." He laughed at that a little. "I suppose our Leader now is pretty impressive, too, but I've long since been over the awe effect that strikes civilians."

Emma pulled a face. "The 'awe effect?'"

He stood up straight. "You know what I'm talking about. It's the impression everyone in the Guild makes on civilians. You have to have noticed it. You walk through a crowded room and people move out of your way like drones. You make a suggestion, like 'I bet it would be hard to jump over that parking meter,' and suddenly you have ten volunteers willing to demonstrate."

She did know what he was talking about! It happened all the time. Just like when she had been sent to the dean's office at Sacred Heart and the kids in her class had revolted against the teacher on her behalf. She supposed this "awe effect" could also be responsible for how easily she managed to obtain committed voters. Everyone in the Guild had that influence on people? She noticed it with Leader of course, and once in a while with Amos, but everyone?

"Why?" Emma asked.

He stepped toward her and tapped her nose with a gentle finger. "Because you're special. You wouldn't be here if you were not."

He started to walk away. She said, "Can you tell me about the Nursery where you came from? Did I come from there, too?"

He shrugged. "Emma, when Leader brought you home to the Guild the first time, he said 'This kid is going to rock the Guild's foundation and change the world.' That's all he said about where you came from. And, trust me, it was a high compliment from him.

"It doesn't matter where you came from, though, you know? Even if Leader collected you from under a toadstool, you're here now, and this is definitely where you belong."

Her heart beat hard as she looked at him. She wanted to believe him, but she wasn't sure. If she truly belonged here, why did she have a picture of her mother upstairs in her backpack?

Amos came into Emma's room when he got home. She was already in bed, but she sat up when he walked through the door, panicked for a moment that he knew her secrets. He stood against the doorframe, backlit by the hall lights. Even though she could not read his expression clearly, his body language was not angry. She relaxed.

"Hi again."

"Hi," she answered, squinting in the dark to try and see his face. The shadows played with his features, but he did not look cross.

"I'm sorry I asked you about your period," Amos told her gently. "Leader informed me that at no point is that an appropriate question to ask an upset girl. And also, she has your cycles recorded in her planner, so she knows you're not menstruating."

"Wow," Emma said on her exhale. "She has them recorded? I just don't even . . ." There were no words to express how violating that information was. "Is there something you need, Amos?"

He shook his head. "I just wanted to check on you. Waylon said you two talked and that you seemed reserved but not angry. He says you're having a hard time."

And that was what she hated most about the Guild: nothing was sacred or private. Her conversation with Waylon was a free discussion, as was, apparently, her menstrual cycle. "I'm fine," she lied. "I had a bad day. Is Leader going to throw the book at me when she gets home? I got nothing accomplished today. No classwork. No homework. No University. And in the way of chores, I did not so much as fold a pair of socks."

Amos sighed. "I know. And Leader knows. I think she's forgiven you for your lazy day."

"Good," Emma answered and she laid back down. "Can I sleep in tomorrow? It's a Saturday."

Amos cocked a brow at her. "Better not push it."

Her phone buzzed on her nightstand. He glanced at his watch and looked up at her in surprise. Nervously, she reached for the phone and checked the number, afraid it would be the agents and Amos would demand to read the message. He did not leave, of course. He would want to know who dared to contact her so late in the evening. She almost sighed in relief when she saw it was just a message from Leader. It was one word: **Yes.**

She pulled a face but then realization dawned, and she proudly lifted the phone to present it to him. "Leader says I can sleep in!" she crowed. "Thank you, Leader." It was creepy, but at least if Leader was spying on her, the answer was yes.

Amos came forward to verify her claim. He chuckled when he saw the word. "I'll need an order direct from her before I'll let you sleep past six." And he walked to the door. Before he made it into the hall, his phone rang. He laughed, but he picked up. "This is Amos," he said as he reached for her door handle. Whispering, "Good night," over his shoulder, he closed her door and walked away.

Emma was extremely grateful she was given permission to sleep in because she could not fall asleep. She heard Amos secure the house, shut off the lights, and go to his bedroom. She heard the neighbors come home drunk after one in the morning. When two o'clock wound around, Emma climbed out of bed and got her backpack. She removed the picture of her mother and crawled back under the covers. Using her phone to light up the image, she stared at the woman in the photograph. She finally fell asleep with the photo pressed to her chest.

Emma had mixed feelings as she watched Amos drive away in the Porsche the next day. Her mood improved enough that she thought she would miss him. She could smell an inedible lunch cooking and that made her miss him already. His leaving opened up some other possibilities, though. She felt the pull of the office behind her. If she had perfect timing, she might be able to break through the security and get the information the agents needed.

Yet, that would be the point of no return. If she chose not to do it, she could still be in the clear with Leader and live out her life in relative harmony. The moment she hacked Leader's system with traitorous intent would be the end of her peace of mind. She was already jumping at shadows. Once she actually stole information from the Guild, a severe look might be enough to make her wet her pants.

If she was going to do it, though, she needed to do it soon. Leader would probably be in Russia at least through tomorrow, and Amos had said that he did not expect to be back until Tuesday. If she was going to do this, she needed to do it before they returned. They were too vigilant when they were home.

"Kid," Piper called from the kitchen. "What are you supposed to be doing right now? And I'm pretty sure 'standing at the window staring into oblivion' is not a Diligent answer."

Emma drew a breath and walked into the kitchen, to her desk. "I did not get anything done yesterday. I have work to do today."

Piper nodded. "Hop to," she ordered and returned to frowning at a cookbook.

Emma logged in to the University, but instead of going to her catalog, she explored the site. She was careful of what she clicked into and what she spent time in. Leader had access to her exploration minutes. But she did spend a few minutes exploring computer sciences and coding, and programming. Just in case Leader looked at her records, Emma also went into social sciences, political strategies, and the studies of war. She had gone into them with the sole purpose of throwing Leader off her trail, but she found things that interested her in every category. The final site made her decide to go to the library and pull Sun Tzu's *The Art of War*. She perused it thoughtfully.

Piper came in, gave her reading material a glance, and chuckled. "Looking for a way to defeat that bratty girl Scott's dating?"

Emma rolled her eyes. "I wouldn't need a book to do that, Piper. I defeat Chastity with my words about every other day. This is the required reading for a course on Stone University I am considering taking."

Piper seemed mildly surprised. "You're taking courses on Stone U? Wow, kid!" When Emma looked confused, Piper went on. "Stone U is really challenging. I'm trying to remember the last person who used it. Probably Thomas. You know, he's a grade-A genius like you. Like Leader."

She did not know that. "I know he's in business, but I do not know his aptitudes."

"He has four PhDs," Piper explained. "And none of them are in business. He does the business end of things because he's so smart, and because Leader doesn't like to. He said that Stone U is a pale reflection of what is really possible in the world, but he did not explain what that meant."

Emma had no idea what it could mean. More than anything, the program just frustrated her with its rigorous schedules and impossible expectations. "It's a lot of memorizing, logical thinking, and planning. Sometimes for hours I will just complete puzzles that seem to have nothing to do with anything. Number puzzles. Letter puzzles. It doesn't seem to matter what they are about but, at the end, I somehow have all the countries in Africa memorized, or I can logically think through how to deactivate a bomb. Occasionally, instead of going into my catalog, I visit pages from various fields of study and try to figure out what I'll be expected to learn next. There seems to be no rhyme or reason to the way I am scheduled, but I'm sure Leader knows what she's doing."

"You can deactivate a bomb?" Piper asked skeptically.

Emma blinked at her. "Depending on the type and its origin, yes, I'm reasonably certain I can." She shrugged as if it was nothing and said, "I'd rather not have to."

Piper did not seem to enjoy the idea that Emma could deactivate a bomb. "What is the University for? To create trained psychos?"

"Thanks," Emma said dryly.

"All I mean is: aren't there more important topics of study for a teenager?"

Emma closed her book and said, "That's what I'm saying, Piper. I don't always know what I'm studying. Everything I do seems to be very difficult or exhausting, but not a lot of it makes sense until I'm in the application part of the unit. I'll be given a sequence of hundreds of numbers and symbols to memorize, and I'll input them over and over. If I make a mistake, I start over. If I hesitate, I start over. Sometimes, I will wake up with the sequence going through my mind. I have no idea how it applies to anything. And then I get to the application part of the unit and I find that I have spent days memorizing a star map, or a government's entire leadership history, or a complex engineering schematic, or a musical score—that one was pretty surprising! But the part that surprises me most is that I look back and actually understand what I have been doing for the entire unit. It all makes sense suddenly. And I can think of hundreds of ways to apply what I have learned. I connect information in bizarre and sometimes random ways, and it feels like I should have known it all along. Or that maybe I already did, and the exercises on Stone University somehow unlocked the information."

She realized she sounded crazy, and Piper's expression was certainly quizzical. Emma's face flushed and she looked away, muttering, "Never mind. All I know is it's bloody hard, and it's never ending."

Piper nodded. "So, you won't get a PhD on there."

Emma scoffed. "Not one that would be recognized in this country."

"So, Thomas got his degrees at an actual school," Piper said with a thoughtful nod.

Emma rolled her eyes. "He was probably on a mission and just got his degrees on the side."

Piper made a non-committal noise. "Well, whatever. Amos wants you to wash the Volvo, including vacuuming. He wants it spick-and-span—his words!—when Leader returns and he doesn't know when that will be." She jerked a thumb in the direction of the garage. "I pulled it into the driveway for you."

Emma placed the book on an end table with a little sigh and went to the cleaning closet for the car washing supplies. Maybe she would not get a chance on the office computers while Amos and Leader were away after all.

Chapter Thirty-Two

Emma went in the middle of the night when she could not sleep. She moved as quietly as she ever had, aware that Piper was asleep in the room next door. She knew Leader was very likely awake in Russia, but it was unlikely she would be watching surveillance of sleeping Guild members. Amos was probably asleep, too. Even if he wasn't, he would probably not be watching, and for the same reasons.

She moved on the steps as quietly as she could, relieved that none of them had a squeak. Several of the training forms taught her to walk lightly, so she was able to move quickly and silently across the kitchen. She glanced around in the dark, listening for any indication that Waylon or Adam downstairs were out of bed. It would be just her luck that they would come upstairs for a drink when she attempted to hack Leader's computer.

Taking the handle lightly in her hand, she turned it carefully so it would not make any sound. It hit a stop and would go no further. Locked! Of course, it was locked! And Piper probably had the key, if not Amos himself. She pressed her lips together, fruitlessly trying the handle again. There were probably a thousand ways to get around a simple door lock like this, but Emma did not try. She had no idea what other security Leader had inside that room. What if Leader had a transmitter in there that somehow detected the turning of the door handle and sent her a message about it? It was highly unlikely, but Emma did not want to risk it.

She went instead to her own, worthless junk computer and turned it on. It did not come on soundlessly as the other computers in this house since it was about a million years old in technology time. Emma listened for any sounds of movement, aware even as she did so that anyone in the Guild could avoid being heard if they chose. Especially Piper, who was superior in the Guild at stealth.

Emma spent half an hour trying to get more out of her computer than it was capable of, and then she very discreetly, very carefully, infected it with an irreparable virus. She shut it down. At least now she would have a legitimate reason for requesting a better machine.

Several minutes after Emma returned to bed, Piper opened her door and looked in. She said nothing. Emma lay still and concentrated on regular breaths until Piper walked away, but Emma was not certain Piper really thought she was asleep.

Emma's phone rang at four-thirty in the morning. She was startled, but she rolled over and grabbed it. The caller ID said **Andrew Turner**. She did not know any Andrew Turner. But when she studied the number, she realized it was one she had dialed at school. The CIA agent! Her heart beat painfully. She answered the call hesitantly, "This is Emma."

"This is Andrew from school," Caldwell said from the other end. Every hair on her arms rose and she felt a wave of fear. *"I'm calling because you went a little off book, but you still seemed to make an impact."* She swallowed back her fears. He must know that Leader would get a record of her calls. He was speaking carefully.

She cleared her throat. "Yeah, I do make an impact on people. Andrew, it's early in the morning on a Sunday. I don't have anything to say about the election until school Monday, if you're lucky and I am able to talk with you. When I'm home, I'm not running for class president; I'm being my mother's daughter." Was that clear enough? She had nothing to report yet, and please do not contact her at home again.

"I just thought maybe you needed the chance to talk," Caldwell replied coolly. "I thought maybe you wanted to know my impression of your performance. It seemed risky." That was clear enough. Her text to him the other day had been incredibly risky. She knew that!

Emma rolled her eyes. What did he think *this* call was? A good idea? "A risk that evidently paid off," she snapped back. "I won over almost the entire student body. I think I have a pretty good chance of winning this thing. But I'm not going to talk about it right now. I have work to do. Maybe I'll talk to you about this tomorrow at school."

"All right," he drawled. "But you do understand what's on the line, don't you, if you don't win this thing?"

"Yeah," she snapped, really getting angry now. "I know you have a lot of eggs in my basket. And you need this. But guess what? I have a lot of other things in my life besides this one little election. It's not as important to me as it is to you. I don't think it can be until I know exactly what I'm getting in to. It's hard to know from my perspective. I have never run for president before. I'm proceeding as best I can, but I'm starting to think the benefits will not outweigh the risks."

A long pause followed as the agent attempted to decipher her meaning. Then Caldwell said, "There are plenty of benefits for you. Are you in this to win or not?"

"I'm in," Emma answered. "But you have to let me win my way. I will talk to you tomorrow at school. Do not bother me at home again." She hung up the phone and stared at it uncomfortably.

The door opened. It was difficult to see Piper in the dark of early morning, but anger flowed on the chill of her words, "Who was that?"

"A kid from school," Emma groaned. "His name is Andrew. I don't know why he called me at home. I warned him off doing it again."

"Leader texted me to let me know you were on the phone," Piper snarled back. "At four-thirty in the morning, Emma! What the fuck?"

The phone in Piper's hand came alight before Emma could apologize again. Piper growled in her throat. She flipped the light switch, and the sudden assault of light on Emma's eyes made her cry out. Piper held up her phone and snapped, "Leader says, since we're already awake, we may as well start our day. At four-thirty in the . . ." She drew a breath to calm herself. "Get up," she ordered and spun around to walk out the door.

Emma groaned, but she moved quickly enough when Piper shot a furious glare back over her shoulder. "You wouldn't be so tired if you weren't climbing out of bed all hours of the night to play around on your computer. Or getting up to talk in code to your boyfriend at four-thirty in the morning!" Emma recoiled more from the realization that Piper knew she had been on the computer than that she realized she had been talking in code with "Andrew." Piper went on, "You better come down to the mats ready to work hard because I'm not in the mood to do any relaxation forms." And she stormed out.

Emma made her bed and got dressed quickly. Piper was already waiting on the mats when she came down. True to her word, there were no relaxation forms. She was at least as demanding as Leader. Piper knocked her off her feet repeatedly but did not call an end to the session until there was blood on the mat.

"Kid," Piper sighed, squatting around her and grabbing both sides of her face to examine her nose, from which the blood came. "You're too slow. You're smart. You're strong, but you're too much inside your head. Come out here in the world and join us in the moment."

Emma glared at her and said nothing.

"Just like that. You're feeling something but you're trying to keep it inside as if you're afraid of what my reaction will be. You think too much! Sometimes you just have to react. You'll never make it this way, kid. It's as if you don't trust yourself or anyone else. What do you think the Guild is designed to do? Alienate twelve people from the world *and* from each other? We're here to be a team."

"Go team," Emma hissed furiously and shoved out of her hands. Despite Piper's attempt to comfort her, Emma felt only rage against the Guild machine. She had to figure out how to get the Atlantis file soon. Much more time in the Guild and she would deplete her reserves of temperance.

"My computer is not working," Emma told Piper later in the day.

Piper was in the den around the corner, but she came out at Emma's complaint. There was a strain in Piper's eyes from the phone conversation she'd had with Leader an hour ago. Emma had no idea what was said, but Piper had been quiet and focused ever since.

"What do you mean? You were just on it in the middle of the night. What did you do to it?"

Emma rolled her eyes. "I was just on it to see if anyone uploaded videos of the debate yet."

Piper let out a frustrated breath. "I can get you a video of the debate from surveillance. Anyone who put a video online will have taken it from their phones and it will be sloppy."

Emma shrugged. "Amos wasn't home, so I couldn't ask him," she lied. "But my computer is . . ." She tapped aggressively on the keyboard. ". . . dead!"

Piper crossed the room, withdrawing a set of keys from her pocket. "*I* can get you the video feed, Emma."

"That's not the point . . ." she cut off as Piper unlocked the office door and walked in. Emma got up and followed her. Leader's office in this house was much smaller than her old one, but it was still quintessential Leader: glass-top desks and tables, black and white modern décor, and couches no one ever sat on. There was an addition to this office, though. There were framed photos on the wall of every member of the Guild. It looked like a family collage one might find in any house in America. Emma idly wondered if it wasn't risky for Leader to hang portraits of all of them, even those living in a different house across the city.

Piper went to the desk and tapped on the glass surface. Emma felt awed as she watched a ghosted image rise from the desk like a hologram. Piper sighed when she saw it and shook her head. "Damned Upgrade," she muttered, but she began to move symbols around on the glass surface of the desk. There seemed to be no pattern to it, but Emma watched carefully for any clues that might help her recreate it later.

The holographic image changed and Piper scowled. "No . . ." she said under her breath. She went back to moving symbols around, but before she managed much, a still image of Agent Peterson flashed into the stream. It was gone a moment later. Emma managed just barely to keep from reacting. She watched Piper for any sign of recognition. Piper only glanced at the man and murmured, "No . . ." She did not seem to be alarmed. Worse, she did not seem confused, either.

He disappeared a couple taps later. "Ah," Piper suddenly announced. A black image appeared in front of her. She tapped a few more times. "Eureka!" she said with a smile as the rally appeared before them. So, Piper had been in the surveillance feed all along. That means Peterson was on Guild surveillance. Why? Did Leader know?

"What did you want to see?" Piper asked with a triumphant smile.

Emma shrugged. "Comments and status updates about the debate."

Piper made a frustrated sound. "I thought you wanted to *watch* the debate!" She presented the still image of the stage.

Emma shrugged again. "I watched it Friday. I was just wondering what people were saying. That's why I looked online. If someone got something up on YouTube or Facebook, there will be comments. There is no way to know definitively that I succeeded until I know what people are saying about the thing."

Piper rolled her eyes, tapped one symbol, and the entire image disappeared. "You could have told me that before I fought with the system."

Emma only managed to keep from rolling her eyes because Amos' photo on the wall reminded her that he had threatened her about her attitude. "I gave up looking last night when my computer started being annoying. Now, today, it's not working at all."

Piper motioned to the door in a command to exit. She said, "You will just have to wait until tomorrow and actually talk to people at school, Emma."

Emma did not budge. "That's not my immediate concern, Piper! I have to make some serious progress on Stone University today, but my computer is not working! Leader is going to expect me to increase an entire percent today, and I can't get into the program."

That seemed to deflate Piper's superiority. She looked a little frustrated and said, "I don't know what to tell you, kid. I don't know how to fix computers. Leader and Amos are both unreachable today, and Thomas is not allowed to come over here while the Guild is split."

Unreachable. Hope blossomed in Emma's heart. "Piper, I have to get this done!" she made herself sound frantic. She needed access to a computer while Amos and Leader were for sure not watching. "I have spent the past few days accomplishing nothing, and Leader is going to hang me out to dry if I can't prove even an ounce of Diligence to her when she comes home!"

Piper sighed. "I'll call Thomas," she promised, but she seemed unhappy about it.

That was the last thing Emma wanted! If Thomas was as smart as Piper claimed he was, and he had spent any time on Stone University, he would be able to recognize the virus Emma gave her computer. He would recognize it as her work even if he did not pull up the surveillance feed to substantiate his suspicions.

"Just forget it!" Emma cried, storming out of the room in her best imitation of a teenaged fit. "I'll take what I get!"

"Emma!" Piper called after her. "Get back here!" When Emma did not immediately return, her voice sharpened, "Right now!" Emma came. She was trying hard to look furious and scared at the same time, although what she felt was hope.

"What?"

Piper pulled a laptop from Leader's top desk drawer and offered it to her. "Use this," she ordered. "I'll have Waylon look yours over in the meantime and see if he can't figure out what's wrong."

Emma took the laptop and mumbled a "Thanks" in a voice she hoped sounded contrite and moody at the same time. What she actually felt was a surge of relief. She walked away, tamping down her excitement so she appeared irritable at least until she was out of Piper's line of sight. Leader's laptop was better than she had hoped!

Chapter Thirty-Three

Emma casually entered the administrative offices during her lunch period. She waited while an adult and then two students spoke to the secretary. When it was her turn, the secretary's smile slipped away a little. She recognized Emma and, like all the adults in the school, was unhappy Emma was running for president. The students would definitely vote for Emma, but the faculty was rooting for her to fail.

"Good afternoon," Emma greeted respectfully. She said no more than that before Chastity suddenly burst into the office and walked up to the counter. She seemed distressed. There were tears on her face and her coloring was pale. She ignored Emma completely.

"Mrs. Gray," Chastity interrupted. "I need to call home!"

The secretary turned all her attention to the distressed child. "All right, honey. You can use this phone." She pulled a corded phone up onto the counter. "Go ahead."

Chastity's hands were shaking as she picked up the receiver and attempted to dial the number. Tears leaked down her face. Obviously distressed, she could not punch the numbers correctly.

"Don't you have a cell phone?" Emma asked doubtfully when she tried and failed to dial correctly a second time. A mobile phone would have the number programmed already.

"I left it at home!" Chastity screeched. She tried dialing again. Emma heard the standard misdial message: *The number you are calling is not a real number. Please check the number and try your call again.*

"Here," Emma ordered, snatching the base from under the girl's unsteady hands. "What's the number?"

Chastity did not argue, which was assuredly a measure of how upset she was. She told Emma the number.

"There. Is it ringing?"

Chastity nodded, and then turned her back on Emma. Emma turned and smiled at the secretary as if Chastity had never walked in and interrupted them. "Good afternoon, Mrs. Gray. I was wondering if I could see the counselor. I need to ask him about the debate."

Mrs. Gray continued to watch Chastity in concern, but she glanced at Emma in annoyance and said, "He's with someone right now. I can send for you when he's available."

Chastity cried harder as soon as someone on the other line picked up. She whimpered, "What's happening? Scott showed me the news report!" That caught Emma's attention. Emma could not make out the words of the person on the other line, but whatever was said made Chastity cry even more.

"Is he in jail?" she squeaked. Well, Emma was intrigued by that. Who was in jail? Scott? No, because he had shown the news report.

"I didn't say *anything*," Chastity wept. Her knees buckled slightly, and Emma supported her before she fell.

"Here," she suggested, motioning toward a chair a couple feet away. As Chastity moved, Emma grabbed the phone base and followed her. "I didn't. I didn't," Chastity murmured miserably. Emma sat beside her on an end table.

Looking up at the secretary, Emma demanded, "Can we get water and some tissues here?" Before the woman even knew what she was doing, she jumped up to oblige. She returned a moment later with a paper cup from the teacher's water cooler and a floral print box of tissues. Emma relieved her of the supplies and forced the cup up to Chastity's mouth in an urgent command to drink. When she obeyed, Emma then handed her a couple tissues. Chastity did not more than murmur quiet words and cry while the person on the other end of the line shrieked at her. The secretary hovered concernedly nearby.

When Chastity spoke again, she said, "Mother, I'm sorry. I just . . . I'm so sorry!" She was gulping in too much air. She hiccupped softly while she sobbed on the phone. Emma pulled her phone from her pocket and opened a browser. Using a search engine, she typed in: **Monez news**. The first yield was a developing news story about the preacher Alexander Monez being arrested during preschool Bible study that morning in his church. The charges were listed as molestation and child pornography. Emma was a little horrified, but not really surprised. The photo attached was of Chastity's father in handcuffs. Emma put her phone away, a tad guilty that she ever accused the man based on only a gut feeling. It was little comfort that she was right.

The woman on the phone screamed at Chastity and the poor girl no longer seemed able to speak. Emma reached for the phone, "Give it to me." When Chastity resisted, Emma snatched it out of her hands.

"You were always a worthless daughter in the first place, and he was too good to you!" the woman on the line shouted.

"Hey!" Emma snarled back. Everyone in the office started at the commanding tone. "Hey! What is the matter with you, lady? Your daughter is a perfectly nice kid, and a victim in all this. You should be so lucky to have a daughter who respects you and is concerned with being a decent human being! You and your bastard husband don't deserve someone as beautiful as your daughter!" She hung up the phone.

Chastity stared in horrified shock at Emma.

"What? You don't sit there and let people talk shit about you, Chastity! Stand up for yourself!"

The girl crumpled over on her knees. Emma sighed. She had to force another tissue into her hands. Looking up at the secretary, Emma snapped, "She needs to see a nurse!" Wasn't it obvious to the worthless woman that Chastity needed care?

The secretary hurried away to call for the nurse and Emma rolled her eyes at all the incompetence. She awkwardly patted Chastity on the shoulder.

The girl sat up and shoved Emma's hands away. She shrieked, "You're just loving this, aren't you! You are just eating this all up!"

Emma rolled her eyes again. "Despite what a horrible, soulless person you think I am, I actually do not like seeing people in distress." She shoved the water cup at Chastity. "Drink this."

Chastity glared murderous hatred at her, but she obeyed. This was the awe effect in action, Emma realized. Chastity would not have been willing to take a hundred dollar bill from her under normal circumstances. Under normal circumstances, the secretary would have dismissed Emma and all her suggestions without a second thought. The other office faculty would have taken over comfort of the distressed young woman. But Emma was somehow in control of the emotions in this room. The faculty left them alone.

When the nurse came in, Emma relinquished Chastity to the woman's care. She waited until the secretary returned and the office went back to its relative state of harmony. Then she returned to the counter and said, "Now, about seeing the counselor."

The awe effect did not last as long as Emma hoped.

"He's busy," the woman snapped. "I told you that already."

Emma nodded. "Please leave a message for him," she replied sweetly and walked away. It did not matter. She had nothing yet to report to the agents. Leader's computer was tighter than the Pentagon. It was impossible to get through stealthily. She tried every way she could imagine. She could probably make it through on a direct assault of the system, but that would get to Leader so fast, it would be like announcing her work over a loudspeaker. That had to be saved as a last resort.

She saw Scott in the hall at the end of lunch. He watched her as she walked by. For someone whose girlfriend was experiencing life-altering stress and emotion, he sure seemed well-pleased. She could recognize that jaunt in his step any day. She watched his back doubtfully as he walked away.

Emma felt relieved when she was pulled out of gym with a summons to the counselor. She gave her teacher an apologetic shrug and walked away. Josie followed her to the door of the gym, "What does he want?"

Emma shrugged. "I asked to see him." When Josie looked doubtfully at her, Emma said, "It's about the campaign. No big deal. I just know he wanted to understand my platform and so I agreed to meet with him today."

Josie made a disgusted sound and said, "Prep," like an insult as she walked away to sit on the bleachers. Like always, she was not dressed properly and would sit on the sidelines and receive a zero for the day's class.

Emma went to the office. It was as busy as ever, but this time the secretary greeted her immediately, although no friendlier than before. "Emma, you can go right on back." Then she watched her as though she expected Emma to pull out a can of spray paint and start tagging the furnishings.

Emma walked through the office. She nodded at Mr. Morley in his office. His eyes darkened at the sight of her, so she knew he saw her, but he pretended not to. That was slightly amusing. For a man so concerned with respect and proper conduct, he was sure a terrible example of correct social procedures.

Mr. Berkshire met her outside his office when she approached the counselor suite. "Good afternoon, Emma," he said with a polite nod. He was no more trusting of her than the secretary or the principal, but at least he was polite.

"Good afternoon, Mr. Berkshire," Emma replied in kind. "Thank you for agreeing to meet with me. I was interested in your opinion of the rally and of my unaltered intention to run for Student Council President." That explanation was as much for the surveillance as it was for the faculty within earshot. No one ever expected the Cobra to tamely meet with the school counselor to discuss her future or her personal life. She did not confide in anyone, not even Josie, who was supposedly her best friend. Josie would not have been comfortable as a confidante, anyhow.

He opened his door and motioned her through. "It just so happens that I have some thoughts on the matter. Come on in."

The smell of fresh paint was the first thing she noticed, followed directly by other changes. The furnishings had all been replaced since her first day in school when she met him in his office. There were no longer any books on the shelves or frames on the wall. His desk was new. It still had Styrofoam and cardboard squares under the feet. There was nothing in the room she recognized from her first visit. Well done, agents!

He nodded toward the phone on the desk as soon as he closed the door. "Dial nine to get the outside line."

Emma felt a wave of relief. She had been afraid she would have to somehow convince him to allow her the use of his phone. He sat down behind his desk and removed a novel from his top drawer. Opening to his bookmarked place, he began reading silently as if she was not even there. She picked up the phone and dialed nine. She heard a series of clicking and then a dial tone, but before she could actually dial a number, another soft click sounded.

"Hello, Emma," Caldwell said on the line in his silky voice.

Emma's pounding heart picked up intensity.

"Agent Caldwell."

"Do you have something shiny for me?" he asked in his amused tone.

"No, but I did say I would speak to you today, so I called," Emma was very aware of Berkshire's presence, so she spoke carefully. "I used my shovel, but so far nothing has turned up. I'm having trouble even breaking ground."

"Well, we did not expect even you to have an easy time with it, Einstein, but we're patient. If you have nothing for us, why are you calling?"

Emma glanced askance at Berkshire. "I need to clarify my end of this agreement."

Caldwell chuckled. "I was wondering when this would come up. Name your price."

That was a relief to Emma. "The entire kettle of soup."

Caldwell laughed again. "We were planning on that, Einstein. I did not think you would want to stay in the boat when it sunk. And besides, once you get to what we need, you'll be in danger where you are. We'll have to move you for your own protection."

Emma thought about that. Was he meaning she would be in danger from Leader? Or an outside source? Perhaps he meant both, and it could certainly be true. She had no idea what was in the Atlantis file. There very well could be a dozen people who wanted to get their hands on it.

"I want to meet her," Emma said, still watching the counselor. "Can you arrange that?"

A long pause. Emma worried when he did not immediately agree to her request. Meeting her mother was the entire reason she was willing to betray the Guild. If she had no home to go to, she did not want to jeopardize her relationship with Leader.

Caldwell finally agreed. "Yes. As soon as the file is in our possession, we will move you out. We'll get you to safety and bring your mother to you in a safe house. If we could introduce you before then, we would, but we can't risk taking you away from the Guild until you have the file. We won't have many windows to get you out. And then, once we do, we have to move you to a safe location. We can't just show up on her doorstep. The Guild will be waiting for you at an obvious place like that. You will be held in safety for a very long time. Your identity will need to be changed and we'll need to alter your appearance."

They all seemed like sensible precautions. She could not imagine after betraying Leader that the Guild would rest until Emma was found. Changing identities was something she was good at, fortunately. It would all be worth it if she got to meet her real mother and have a real family.

"Okay," she agreed.

Caldwell's voice intensified. "We will have only the one opportunity to get to you. Once you have the file, there's not going to be any playing-around time. Monique is suspicious of her own shadow. If she has any indication that you are on the dirty, she'll put a bullet in your head so fast, you won't even have a chance to cry out."

Those words chilled Emma. She had a hard time believing it could be true. Leader was always brusque and demanding, but never murderous with the people in the Guild. Emma knew she killed without blinking, but always outsiders. Always dangerous outsiders who threatened her life or her Guild . . . Emma was a threat to the Guild now. She was planning to steal from them and then run away.

I can't forgive running away, Leader told her when she had tried to run away before. She only made it half a dozen steps before she was caught. If she stole an important file with the intention of giving it to Leader's enemies and then ran away again, Leader very well might choose to kill her and be done. No more bad attitudes. No more teen drama. And then

Leader would just move Victoria up to Diligence and kidnap a new kid to be the Number Twelve. Emma would be replaced in the blink of an eye, as Leader had been two years ago when he was gunned down on the street.

"I understand the risks," Emma breathed.

"Do you? An entire nation may be resting on your ability to succeed in getting me this file. You fail, and millions of lives may be at stake. You don't get out fast enough, and Monique will bury you in the floorboards and walk away like you were never there."

"I understand," Emma snapped back. But her head started ached and her heart beat too fast. Her vision blurred on the edges. She had to calm down before she had another panic attack.

"Call us again tomorrow. And if ever you're in imminent danger, or you get the file, text us. We can be to your side quickly enough to prevent her attacking you. Probably."

Emma drew a steadying breath. "Way to calm down your informant," she congratulated sarcastically. "I'll talk to you tomorrow." She hung up the phone.

Berkshire looked up. "Finished?" he asked as if he had not been listening in the whole time.

"Yes, thank you. I'll need to call again tomorrow. Can you get me out of a different class, though? If I miss too much of one class, it will be easily detected."

He nodded. "How about fifth period?"

"Okay. Thank you for your help."

He smiled and walked to the door. "Any time, Miss Chandler." He opened the door for her. "Thank you for your time."

She returned to class in time to sit with Josie and flunk the day in gym. As they were leaving, Josie questioned her about her meeting with the counselor. Emma shrugged it off and sarcastically said, "I needed advice about my pregnancy."

Josie laughed uproariously, but unfortunately, they happened to be walking in front of Chastity at the time, and she scoffed.

"Slut," she said and veered off down a side hallway. She did not look much recovered from the ordeal of finding out about her father's arrest.

Her eyes were swollen from crying, and she was still carrying tissues. Emma rolled her eyes. Helping her dial the phone and drink water was clearly not as big an impression as Emma being right about Chastity's abusive father.

Chapter Thirty-Four

After school, Piper stood outside the Range Rover with her sunglasses on, leaning against the passenger-side wheel well. Her shorts were ridiculously short for early spring and her shirt was little more than a bra. "Hey," she greeted when she saw Emma approach.

"Hi," Emma answered. She felt relief at seeing Piper. Surely, if Leader had found out about Emma's clandestine meetings with the agents, she would be there herself.

Emma removed her backpack to toss it in the backseat but paused before opening the back door when a hopeful thought blossomed. "Piper, can I drive?"

Piper pulled off her sunglasses and shot Emma a skeptical look. "What?"

"I'm sixteen," Emma replied with a timid smile. "Thomas was going to teach me last year, but then . . ." She could not mention the split directly. She shouldn't have even mentioned Thomas. She half-expected Piper to feign confusion.

She pulled a horrified face and spoke in a scandalized voice, "You cannot let Thomas teach you to drive. He drives like a grandmother!"

More hope. "So, does that mean you'll teach me?"

Piper looked guarded. "Why hasn't Leader taught you?"

Emma honestly did not know why. "She mentioned my trouble in school, but that was back before we moved, so I don't know. I'm doing well in school now. And, if you taught me to drive, I could just drive myself to and from school. No more need to pick me up and drop me off. I'd be free."

Piper gave a chuckle. "Free, huh? I don't know about that. It's a pretty ambiguous term. But . . ." she tossed the keys and Emma had to drop her backpack to catch them. "Okay."

Emma was stunned. "Really?"

Piper jerked her thumb toward the car. "Sure. Hop in." Piper got in the passenger seat and adjusted it while Emma excitedly collected her backpack, tossed it in the backseat, and climbed in the driver's side.

Emma started the car, but before she went anywhere, she looked at Piper. She was worried now that driving was a reality.

"What if there is some reason Leader did not teach me to drive? I don't want you to get into trouble for teaching me."

Piper waved away her concerns. "Buckle your seatbelt and adjust your seat, mirrors, and steering wheel. You let me deal with Leader."

Emma smiled. Those had been orders, and she was obligated to Obey orders. Obediently, she buckled, adjusted her seat and steering column, then her mirrors. "I'm ready."

Piper nodded. "Keys in the ignition, foot on the brake, and turn it on."

Emma Obeyed again but she admitted, "I'm nervous."

"Good," Piper answered, reaching over to shut off the suddenly blaring rock music. "That will keep you cautious. This is a more than two ton violent weapon on the road if you're being stupid, cocky, or distracted." A car behind them honked. Piper flipped them off out the side window.

"Okay," she went on unconcernedly. "Ten and two." Emma adjusted her hand positions. "Very slowly let off the brake and you will roll forward. Good. Push on the gas a little." She laughed. "A little more, kid, or you'll never go anywhere. Good. The turn signal is right there next to your left hand. Flip it up to signal right and stop at the sign to check traffic."

Emma's heart pounded as she approached the stop sign leading from the carpool line. There was some traffic in the distance, but Piper said, "Pull out into the nearest lane." Emma calmed her mind, remembering what she had learned about distances and speed. The cars would not overtake her before she got out into the street. She went.

"I'm driving," she announced when she was cruising along Primrose.

"Yes," Piper agreed with a playful smile. "Accelerate to the speed limit. You're at least going to want to be going twenty."

Emma Obeyed nervously. The cars up ahead seemed to be braking and Emma said, "I'm scared."

"It's fine," Piper said unconcernedly. "They're a long way off, but when you get closer, you'll slow down. You want to keep at least one car length for every ten miles per hour between you and the cars in front of you. That means you have to be two car lengths." She leaned and looked at the speedometer. "Almost."

Emma Obeyed every instruction but her nervousness never went away. Her hands were clenched on the wheel as if at any moment the car could run wildly out of control. Piper did not seem concerned in the least.

Emma's phone rang. She panicked a little. "What do I do? It's in my pocket."

"Ignore it," Piper replied dryly. "You don't answer the phone while you're driving; it's not safe."

Emma thought about that and then said, "Everyone in the Guild talks on the phone while driving."

Piper nodded. "They're idiots. Driving is dangerous, and it requires all your senses. Your reaction time is immensely decreased when you're on the phone. It's dangerous and I intend to teach you to drive well, not distractedly."

The phone rang again. "What if it's Leader calling?"

In a sharp voice, Piper said, "Emma, worrying about who is calling is a distraction from driving. If you are not ready to focus on what you're doing, signal and pull over to the side so I can switch you."

Emma ignored the phone and promised, "I'm focused."

"You're approaching an intersection," Piper said, completely unconcerned as her own phone began to ring. She silenced it. "The light is red, so slow down. You're going to stay in this lane." Usually they turned here, but Emma was grateful not to have to turn onto the much busier Campbell Avenue. "When you're stopped, you want to be able to see the back tires of the car in front of you through your windshield. If you can't see them, you're too close."

Emma did as she was told but driving through the intersection was stressful. She was certain that at any time a car from the crossing lane would run its light and smash into the Range Rover. When the light turned green, she crept slowly through the intersection to the sound of car horns honking behind her.

"Ignore them," Piper ordered. "You're doing fine. We'll be in a neighborhood soon enough and there won't be as much traffic. That will be easier on you, I think."

Emma felt relieved once they were driving slowly down Westview. It was much easier to drive in a neighborhood than on the busier streets. Piper told her to slow down and pull over slightly to let the impatient drivers behind her pass. Once that was done, Piper had her drive to the end of Westview and stop at the stop sign. She looked both directions since cross-traffic was not expected to stop, and slowly pulled onto Broadway.

"Good," Piper said with a smile. "You're getting the hang of it. There are some kids on the roadside up ahead. You'll want to watch them very carefully. Kids aren't too bright, and they often walk straight into the road without looking. Just slow down a little and be sure they're going to stay put. Good."

Emma watched the kids, and the road, and drove along. Emma did exactly as she was told. When, for no apparent reason, Piper told her to turn into a dead-end road, she went. When they reached the end, she followed Piper's instructions for stopping, reversing, and getting the car turned around. They parked several times and Piper explained things to her. When they merged into traffic on Republic Road, Piper told her to increase speed to fifty, and she Obeyed, nervous and exhilarated to be moving so fast. She was not as nervous at her next intersection. Driving was getting easier as Emma became more confident in Piper's instructions and in her own ability.

Piper directed her all the way home, though she went a winding route designed to give Emma a very long practice session. Piper opened the garage door, but she instructed, "Park in the driveway, kid. I'll pull it in."

When Emma was parked and she pulled the emergency brake, Piper nodded. "Good run. Turn off the car and hand me the keys." Emma Obeyed. "How do you feel?"

"Good," Emma said. She removed her hands from the wheel only to find they were sore from clutching it so hard. When she got out, her legs were a little wobbly. Piper gave a laughing snort as she came around to the driver's side.

"You did good," she complimented. "You can drive to school tomorrow."

"Really?" Emma asked. "Do you think Leader will be mad you taught me to drive without asking her?"

Piper shrugged. "Nah! You knew how to drive already; I just put you through the application process. I'll have Leader email me a permit and you can drive with me from now on. I don't want you ever driving with Adam, since he's a maniac. But I think I trust Waylon with you, too. He's a little fruity, but he'll be careful. Will you listen to him well?"

"Yes, ma'am," Emma agreed immediately.

"Good," Piper said. "We can probably have you ready for a license before Leader even gets home."

That caught Emma by surprise. "I thought she would be home tomorrow."

"Nope," Piper answered. "She called today. Amos will beat her home by several days at least. He'll probably want to take you out, too, just to make sure we haven't corrupted your driving skills. Fair warning: he's pretty strict about following traffic laws to the letter, including speed limits."

"I would not break the traffic laws," Emma answered in shock. The idea of it was horrifying. People died when they broke traffic laws!

"Well, I did warn you," Piper said dismissively. "You better probably download a copy of the diver handbook and study it because Amos is likely to give you a quiz before he ever lets you sit in the driver's seat."

"Okay," Emma agreed. She had read the Virginia driver handbook, and she could not imagine there was much different in Missouri, but it couldn't hurt to find out.

Emma went inside, got a drink of water, and went to her desk to get started on Stone U. A couple minutes later, Piper came through the door carrying Emma's backpack. She dropped it on the kitchen bar.

"Get your homework done," Piper ordered. She shook her phone at Emma and added, "I'm telling Leader now that I took you driving, and if I know her like I think I do, she'll say 'no driving unless she's on top of her schoolwork.' And probably other stuff about Diligence. Are you being Diligent?"

No, but Emma said, "Of course."

Piper scowled at her doubtfully. She tapped a button on her phone and walked away into the office and shut the door.

Emma grabbed her own phone from her backpack pocket. The call she had missed while driving was from an unknown number. Afraid it was one of the agents, she checked the message.

"Hi, Emma. you don't know me. My name is Sailor. I know what's going on in your life right now and I want you to be very, very careful. You can't play for two teams. I do not usually interfere with these matters, but in this case, I think it would be best to put you on your guard. Cobras may be fierce and deadly, but they are still subject to weaknesses. While you are outgrowing your old skin, do not sleep with the mongoose." The woman's voice was replaced by an automated male voice. "This message will be deleted from your files and your phone memory will be cleared. Please do not attempt to contact this messenger for any reason." And a click sounded the end of the message. True to the word of the automated voice, the message disappeared from her phone memory, and her entire call history was deleted as soon as the message ended. Emma stared at the phone in eerie alarm. Had it been a trick of some kind to get her to drop out of the race?

Emma looked up in alarm when Piper emerged from the office. She almost asked her about the message, but then thought better of it. Until she could decipher the meaning of Sailor's words, she wanted to keep it to herself.

"You okay?" Piper wanted to know. "You're white as a ghost."

"I'm fine," Emma lied. "What did Leader say?"

Piper pulled a face. "A lot of 'You should not be making these kinds of decisions without *first* consulting me' and other whining nonsense."

"But . . ." Emma was confused. "You're in Initiative right now, aren't you? Doesn't that mean you can make these kinds of decisions? Besides, you're in charge of the Guild House until Amos comes home, so I belong to you."

Piper held up a hand and said, "No, you don't. Even in charge of everything as I am, you never belong to me. You belong only to Leader. Everyone belongs to Leader." Then she shrugged to lighten the mood. "But, until someone comes to tag-team me, this is my decision. You're ready to drive. You can drive."

Emma nodded along, but she did not hear anything after, "You belong only to Leader." Life was getting complicated. She belonged only to Leader, but she had a photo of her mother, to whom she had belonged first. She had a random deleted message from Sailor, whoever that was, warning her against mongoose. She had agents who claimed millions of lives were on the line if she could not access buried treasure. If that was not stressful enough, she could not figure out how to get into Leader's secure files. She closed her eyes to focus on breathing exercises. *Calm,* she told herself firmly. She had to be calm or she could never do any of this.

Emma couldn't sleep. In the middle of the night, she lay awake with no hope of calming her thoughts. She wondered about the message from Sailor so hard that her head hurt. Whoever it was, she could not be on the Guild's side. The Guild could not really be "the mongoose" she was warning about, either, because the message seemed to suggest that was a newer development. For a while, Emma thought it must just be some kid at school talking about the election somehow. But logic won over that hypothesis. A kid at school would not have access to technology that could remotely delete her phone history and messages. Presumably, that precaution had been taken to keep the message from being heard by anyone else. If that was so, then the Guild must be the mongoose. But how could it be, when the warning had been not to sleep with the mongoose, when she had been with the Guild most of her life? It made no sense!

When Emma could move away from the message, her mind fell on her current mission. Not her Guild mission which was, as always, to blend in, be Obedient, and Diligently live up to her potential. The mission assigned by the CIA was to hack Leader's files. She had done a few maneuvers during homework time, but with no luck. The way Emma had taken before was closed and locked up tight. Emma was going to have to use a battering ram to get around the security, and Leader would know right away if she tried anything aggressive.

On top of all that, Emma was afraid to betray the Guild. Not the Guild as much as Leader. Doing this the slow way was agony. If she could just get into the files right away, she would not have all this time to second-guess her decision. But it was almost too late to turn back. Even if she told Leader what she was doing, Leader would never trust her again. And Emma would always have doubts about the Guild forever. She would always doubt the Guild's purpose.

She wrapped up in her blanket, imagining she was cold. What she wouldn't give just to be a normal kid whose only problem was defeating the other more-qualified candidates in the school presidential race!

She fell into a fitful sleep sometime after midnight.

Emma dreamed. She dreamed of long ago in the Guild House in Utah County when she was afraid of getting caught consorting with the young man who became her first boyfriend. She could not bear to think of him even in her dream. The image of his face was blackened out of her memory and the place where his name used to be was just "he" and "him." "He" had betrayed her, but before that he made her fall in love. He made her believe there was something more to life than constant fear and oppression in the Guild. "He" was her only hope back then.

And then her dream filled with the old Leader, tall and fiercely handsome, as if he was sculpted from raw materials, formed for the sole purpose of setting hearts aflame. He was not attractive to Emma, though. He was frightening. In her dream, he rebuked Amos.

"Have you decided to start rallying for my position? You'll have to beat out Monique, and you know she'll have her viper fangs in you before you usurp her authority."

In Emma's dream, she watched the two men face off across her room. It was light enough she could see them both, but it was also somehow intensely dark. Leader's anger seemed to make it dark. Emma watched as Amos spoke, pacifying Leader.

"I went for a drive. I did not steal your car. I wanted to go for a drive."

Those were not exactly the words Emma remembered from the memory of this moment, but the dream was very clear.

"You rerouted my satellite," Leader replied. The dark was getting darker all around them, and Emma was certain she would be swallowed.

"Help me," she cried, but they ignored her.

"I was spying on Emma," Amos answered. The darkness closed in on them. "I had to use the car because it was the only place I did not have to hack your system too extensively to access the satellite."

"Help!" Emma screamed as claws and fingers reached from the darkness toward her. She tried to move away, to kick at the reaching tendrils, but they were only shadows. Shadows that could kill her.

"Your incompetence is going to destroy us," Leader railed, but Amos was gone now. He descended on Emma, getting bigger, blacker, reaching out into the darkness, becoming one with the shadows.

"Leader!" Emma screamed, trying to fend him off. But then she was no longer calling for him. She was screaming for the only person she knew who could rescue her. "LEADER!"

"Emma!" Leader's feminine voice broke through the darkness. "Emma, don't go! Don't go!"

"Emma!" the shadow called, reaching tendrils into her hair, claws toward her heart. "You cannot betray me! I will never let you betray me! Your incompetence is going to destroy us!"

Emma sat up in bed, screaming for Leader. Adam was by her bedside with wide eyes. He shook her violently and said, "Emma! Wake up! You're dreaming! Wake up!"

She collapsed in his arms when realization came back. It had been a dream. She had been dreaming.

Piper came into the room with her phone pressed to her ear. "I tried to wake her, Leader!" she was saying. "She wouldn't . . . She's awake! Oh, thank God!" She shoved in beside Adam and grabbed Emma's face in her hand. "Are you okay, kid? She's white, Leader. I have never seen her so pale."

Emma trembled, but she submitted freely to Adam's embrace and Piper's handling. Waylon watched with intense concern from the doorway. He was also on the phone but said nothing.

Piper released Emma and stood up. "I don't know what's wrong, Leader. She was hysterical, but she would not wake up. Waylon got Amos first and he's checking her vitals now, but . . . What did he say?" Piper looked confused. "What does that mean? How can someone be trapped in their subconscious? Yes, ma'am. Yes. Here she is." Piper put the phone up to Emma's face. "Talk to Leader."

Emma swallowed, trying to force moisture into her mouth. There was nothing there, and swallowing made her throat sore. It was strained from screaming.

"Leader?" she croaked, pulling out of Adam's arms. He climbed off the bed and walked away, shaking his head.

"Emma?" Leader asked. "Are you okay now? Are you reoriented?"

"Yes," Emma said, but it was hard to get words out.

"Piper said you seemed out of sorts yesterday. Are you feeling ill?"

Her head pounded enough to jump off her shoulders, and her throat felt raw. But she said nothing because images of her dream began to return. Leader became a shadow. He wanted to kill her. He wanted to kill her for betraying the Guild. Her eyes stung, and she squeezed them shut. Was it really betrayal to steal information from an organization that kidnapped children from their families?

Piper took the phone from Emma and said, "She's crying, Leader. I don't know what to do." Piper sounded frustrated. She was not very affectionate on a good day. She liked things to be steady and even-keel. Drama was not part of the life she enjoyed.

Waylon shut his phone down and crossed the room to Emma. He pulled her out of the bed to her feet. Sternly, he said, "Form twenty-nine." It was a relaxation form. Emma immediately Obeyed the order. When Adam reappeared in the doorway holding a glass of water, Waylon took the drink from his hands and offered it when she finished her form. She took a drink and Waylon said, "Form twenty-seven," in a calmer tone. Emma Obeyed.

Piper walked out of the room to finish her conversation with Leader.

Waylon continued to give her relaxation commands until she was clear-minded and asked to stop. Then Piper came back.

"Leader wants me to take you to the farm. She'll have Julianne meet us there. But according to Amos, your only illness is an increased activity in the brain where fear is located, and he said you have a hypertension in your heart." Piper narrowed thoughtful eyes at her. "It's anxiety. You had an anxiety attack. Again."

"I'm okay," Emma assured her. She felt numb. "I had a nightmare. But I'm okay now. I'm tired."

Piper grabbed Emma's shoes out of the closet and said, "You can sleep in the car."

The car. Everything clicked into place as if she had been working on a puzzle on Stone U. Suddenly the picture came clear and Emma knew exactly how to get to the satellite files. She could access them from Amos' car. If Amos did it, Emma could. She felt a surge of confidence, and if the shadows at the corner of the room seemed a little menacing, Emma ignored them.

Chapter Thirty-Five

Julianne found nothing physically wrong with Emma, but she held her at the farm for observation for two days.

"I need to watch your blood pressure, Em," Julianne said in concern. "I'm very worried about your anxiety." She studied Emma's eyes. "Maybe this presidential campaign is too much for you on top of your Guild duties."

"No!" Emma exclaimed, panicked more for the loss of an excuse to call the agents than any lingering concern about the election. "It's almost over now, Julianne. Please! I just want to finish the race." She did not expect to be president at all, because she expected to be rescued by the agents as soon as she got her hands on the Atlantis file.

Julianne's face continued to harbor concern, but she nodded. "You need to keep working on your breathing exercises and relaxation forms. Every day, multiple times." She murmured under her breath about anxiety meds as she walked away.

Emma was left in Ilene's care, though the woman had little tolerance for her. She was always icy and often unkind. Emma could not prove anything, but she thought Ilene still harbored anger at Emma for being instrumental in Leader's death two years ago. Despite their age differences, Ilene and Leader had been in an intimate relationship. Ilene never recovered from her grief at losing him.

If not for the fact that Julianne came several times each day to check on her and do an exam, Emma's time with Ilene would have been unbearable. The second day, after Julianne ruled out neurological disorders, she allowed her to drive the farm truck around the fields for a couple hours of driving practice. Emma was still nervous, but without any other cars to crash into her, she felt safer and more confident than her first driving lesson.

By Thursday, Julianne gave Emma a clean bill of health. She sent Piper to the farm to pick her up for school.

When the Range Rover drove up and honked, Ilene handed her a sack lunch at the door. In her icy indifference, she cautioned, "Stay out of trouble."

"Yes, ma'am," Emma replied, and happily walked away. Losing Ilene to the other house was the one good thing about the Guild split. Emma was not going to miss her when the CIA came to take her away.

School was a regular, mind-numbing blur. She saw Scott a couple times, and he always watched her carefully until Emma worried he might be looking for signs of betrayal. When she actually thought about it, though, she laughed at herself for her paranoia. Scott had to know Julianne was at the farm taking care of her. He was just watching to see if she was okay.

She managed to go almost the whole day without seeing Chastity. The only time was when Emma was summoned to the counselor during her fifth period. She crossed Chastity in the office. Chastity's eyes narrowed at her hatefully, but Emma ignored her.

"Good afternoon, Miss Chandler," Mr. Berkshire said when she reached his office. He held the door as she came in. When he closed it, he said, "Dial nine."

She nodded her thanks. She dialed nine and waited this time.

"Hello, Einstein," Caldwell said in his mocking tone. "We were starting to get nervous when you did not call Tuesday. Did you get cold feet?"

"No," Emma replied. She wasn't going to bandy words with him today. "I may have found a better shovel. I won't know until Amos comes home, but I expect him soon. I will not make contact with you again until I have something shiny to offer. You're going to need to be ready with my kettle."

"We'll be ready," Caldwell promised her.

Emma was picked up by Waylon after school. "Hi!" he greeted as he walked around to hand her the keys and get in the passenger side. "You're driving."

"Thanks," Emma said, happy to oblige. Once she was in the car and everything was adjusted, she asked, "Where's Piper?"

Waylon smirked. "I'm not going to take offense to your obvious desire for someone else to pick you up." Emma tried to argue but Waylon only laughed and brushed it away. "She's reporting. Amos came home, and he goes on a conference call with Leader and some other people in . . . five minutes ago. He wanted an entire report before that started, so Piper sent me."

Emma turned the car on. "I am pleased it's you," she said as an apology for her hasty words. "May I put the car into drive?"

"When you're buckled," he said with a nod.

Emma scoffed at herself for having forgotten. In the Guild, people did not drive ten feet without a seatbelt on. When they pulled the car out of the garage to park it in the driveway for washing, they probably wore a seatbelt. She fastened her belt and put the car into drive. Waylon did not have her drive all around like Piper had. He made her take the most direct route home. There was a lot of school traffic on every road, so she had to be vigilant. She even asked Waylon not to talk when he asked her about school.

"I can't think about anything except driving."

"It's fine," Waylon answered. "Speed up a little, honey. You're pissing off the people behind you."

Emma nervously accelerated, but she said, "Piper said to ignore the other people and just drive."

"Piper's a bitch," he replied, as if that explained everything. But Emma did as she was told. She drove home, and even parked in the garage next to the Porsche when directed to do so, though she was extremely nervous about driving into that enclosed space.

"Well done," Waylon said with a smile. "You'll be driving yourself to school in no time."

Before they climbed out of the car, Emma said, "Does Scott drive himself to school?"

Waylon gave her a quizzical look. "Who?"

Emma sighed. She was not as good at this split Guild as everyone else seemed to be. Emma tossed Waylon the keys and grabbed her backpack. Over his shoulder, he said, "Your dad is in a conference call, so you'll want to be quiet when you get in." He looked back at the garage and gave a thoughtful frown. "I guess Piper went back to the farm." And he walked through the door, hanging the keys on a hook by the door with the other keys of the other vehicles.

Emma was slow about getting her backpack and moving to the house. The keys were hanging there in easy reach. Amos was busy. Leader was occupied. Piper was gone. Waylon trusted her to come right in and get started on her homework. Adam was still in class downtown. This was Emma's chance! If she was going to attempt to access the Porsche computer, it had to be now.

She set her backpack down on the steps and grabbed the Porsche keys from the garage hook. She winced when the car beeped as she unlocked the door. She inserted the key in the ignition and sat down. Point of no return . . .

She turned the key. Nothing happened. She had geared herself up for this act of rebellion. It was bitter disappointment to fail so quickly. But then she read the words near the speedometer above the wheel: **Retinal Scan Required.** She sighed, looking around for what could read her eyes, although she imagined she would be denied access. She was wrong. A light on the dash column gave a bright flash and Emma blinked in surprise when the car suddenly started.

Welcome, Emma! A message across the dashboard read cheerily. Emma was not so cheery about it. She had had no idea the car would be programmed to recognize her. She almost got out and walked away. But she couldn't. She was so close!

She recalled what Amos had done to access the computers. She glanced at the door to the garage, careful to be sure no one was watching, and then she reached out a hand to touch one of the symbols. It let out a musical chime and her hand jumped away. When Amos touched it, it did not do that.

Incorrect. Please input 84-character passcode.

Emma sank back against the designer leather seat with a defeated sigh. Eighty-four characters was an impossible sequence to guess. The characters on the dashboard ranged from numbers and letters to glyphs Emma did not even recognize. She experimentally reached forward to touch a few. They gave off sounds, but when she pulled her hand away, the negative message flashed onto the dash again.

This had been Emma's last hope for getting to the files undetected. If she tried to break in on Leader's laptop, she would be discovered immediately and would never get a chance to run. Hopes of meeting her mother faded and she was filled with the darkness from her dream. Her life would be in crime and secrecy, filled with demands, no explanations, and endless mind-numbing drills on Stone University until she wanted to die!

Emma sat forward again so fast that she hit her head on the visor. The drills! She experimentally tapped the symbols and laughed. Musical! She had memorized an entire musical score on Stone University. The first movement was a short eight-four note set.

Carefully, cautiously watching the garage door from the corner of her eye, Emma began to play the music on the mathematical symbols in front of her. She did not slow, nor pull her hands away until she had played the entire first movement correctly. It took several tries.

Correct. The dashboard console announced in flashing orange letters. And she was shown the operating system. Emma moved quickly, finding her way through the new system with some effort, but it was actually easier than the old system she tried to hack for the past week. It would not have been easy for just anyone, she realized. Stone University had given her a multitude of puzzles that helped her mind work through the difficulties others would find on the operating system. Leader's files were encrypted, but that only took a few tries to override.

She surfed through the files, pausing only once on Peas and Carrots. She could look, but then she would run out of time. She would never be able to free herself from the Guild without the CIA to help.

She glanced repeatedly up at the door as she moved through Leader's obvious file locations to places that were less obvious. She found the satellite codes under a file called **The Lady**. She forced her mind to work quickly, memorizing the repeating codes. She would need them to access the satellite, and she imagined the satellite files would be where Atlantis was held. There was no mention of anything like Atlantis in Leader's files. She repeated the sequence to herself again and again, like she always did on Stone University. And then she exited out and moved toward the satellite entry.

Amos came into the garage.

Panicked, Emma did the quick shutdown, exiting completely from the program and turning the car engine off. Amos came down the steps to the passenger side. She rolled down the window at his gesture to do so. He leaned on the window frame.

"What are you doing?" he asked, eyes narrowed. Had he seen her? Did he know?

Emma gave a nervous smile. "I was imagining what it would be like to drive your Porsche."

If he knew what she was really doing, he gave no indication. His warm smile spread across his face. He reached through the window to unlock the door. "Let's take it for spin," he said and got in the passenger seat.

Emma smiled, more in relief than excitement, but she let him think whatever he wanted. If he knew what she was doing in his car, he would have made some kind of indication by now. He would not simply be taking her out for a driving lesson.

Emma repeated the satellite access codes over and over in her mind. She slept with them and ate with them. When she got to school on Friday morning, she walked the codes and heard them in the birds' chirping in the treetops. She did not have the file, but with the access codes, the agents could get to Atlantis on their own. She was overjoyed to be so near the end of this conspiracy. The fear of discovery was overwhelming! And Leader would be home any day to look at her sharply and know she was up to something.

She carefully avoided Scott. He knew her too well. He would be able to sense rebellion in her now that she could practically taste freedom. He could identify her emotions with one look. The few times she passed him in the hall she kept her head down and walked on without even looking in his direction.

Emma wasn't careful enough of other people, though. As soon as Josie saw her, she said, "You okay, Cobra? You look . . . ish."

Emma smiled at Josie's weak description. "I'm fine." She changed the subject. "Voting day is Monday. How do you think we're doing?" The race was the best cover she had for behaving strangely. It might even work as an excuse for Leader if she happened to be watching surveillance.

"I know of thirty kids at least that are coming to vote even though they never have before. They'll vote for you. Monday, we're all wearing our t-shirts and fishnet gloves in support of the Cobra. We're going to win this."

Emma did not immediately answer. Her thoughts already fled away to possibilities outside of Student Council. With the access codes and any high-tech computer, the agents would be able to get to the file they wanted, then Emma would be on her way to a safe house. She would be kept safe for the rest of her life because the Guild would always search for her. It would only be worth it if her mother could be with her.

"Don't you want to win?" Josie asked, forcing her back into the conversation.

"What? Oh, yeah." She did want to win, if for no other reason than to watch Chastity fall from power. "Of course, I want to win."

Chastity approached them in the salad bar line. "Don't bother talking shop with her, Josie. She's a little preoccupied." And she walked away with a dismissive toss of her head.

Josie looked doubtfully after Chastity's retreating form. "She's getting desperate." Josie turned her scowl on Emma. "What is she talking about?"

Emma shrugged. "I never know what she's talking about."

Josie leaned close to her. "Are you on the up-and-up, Emma? Because if you're breaking any student codes or agreements, she can get you thrown out of the race like *that*!" She snapped her fingers for emphasis. "And with everything going on in her life right now, she would not hesitate to throw you under a bus." Josie leaned closer. "Did you hear about her dad getting arrested?"

Emma nodded. "Yeah." She walked away to pay for her salad. Emma wanted to call the agents, not gossip about Chastity's life troubles.

Lunch was a passing of time with no significance, except for the cold stares from Chastity across the room. Emma watched her with growing concern. It was hard to know what her problem was today. Chastity always seemed angry after her father's arrest. Today, however, she did not gossip about Emma to her Council friends or try to talk to students about the election. That was her pattern; Emma had grown accustomed to it. Instead, every time Emma looked at her, the girl seemed glare with suppressed hope.

"Where's her lapdog today?" Josie wanted to know when she noticed Chastity's uncharacteristic brooding. "He's usually hanging all over her."

Emma stood up. "I don't care," she lied. Emma did care. She was intrigued, but she had to distance herself from all this drama. She had to somehow distance herself from Scott, and Leader, and everyone. She was going home to her real family, and nothing else in the world could be as important.

Emma sent a text to "Andrew." She did not know any other way to communicate with him. Sending an innocent text seemed a less obvious communication than contacting the counselor. The surveillance in the school still worked everywhere else. If Leader happened to be watching, she would wonder why Emma instigated a conference with Mr. Berkshire. She had to be careful.

Andrew, my prospects for this race are shining, she sent. And she hoped it was a clear enough message for him while still veiled enough not to seem suspicious to Leader and Amos. Thoughts of her superiors made her feel nauseated and she had to shove away her emotions or be swept over by them.

She waited impatiently for a response, and even risked keeping her phone in her pocket in class. When it vibrated several minutes later, Emma asked for a lavatory pass and left class. She could not bear to wait.

It's looking dicey from my perspective, but I have polled different people was Caldwell's reply.

Emma sat clothed on the toilet seat, hoping for more. She could not reason through what the message might mean. He seemed to be warning her, but she could not imagine about what.

She replied: **Are you sure? I'm feeling like I'm all that and a bowl of soup.**

It was a little less coded than she should probably have sent, but she was nervous and growing impatient.

I'll think of something to fix this. Trust me.

She didn't trust him; that was the problem. She did not trust him or anyone else. Straddling the fence between the two worlds was too hard. She wanted to get down. Her phone rang. She scowled. What was he thinking? He could not call her on her Guild phone! Texting was dangerous enough!

But then she saw the flashing number was Amos. Hands shaking, she picked up. "This is Emma." She was pleased that she managed to sound normal.

"What are you doing texting when you're supposed to be in class?" His voice was stern.

She drew a steadying breath. "I know."

"Emma, Leader will be home next week, and she is not going to be pleased to find you have failed to be Diligent while she was away. You know, last night she called me and mentioned that your Stone University scores are slowing down. She thinks it's the class president thing." Good.

That was what she was supposed to think. "With your spiking anxiety, and your recent inattentiveness, she's bound to pull you from the race if you're ditching class to text your friends."

"I'm sorry, Amos," she said in her best repentant tone. "But the race is over Monday, and I swear I will never cause another problem."

"I would believe those words more from the CIA than from you, Emma." He meant it to be playful, but Emma was alarmed. She had to steady herself against the bathroom wall to keep from shaking. When she did not answer right away, his laughter faded. "Emma?"

"I'm going back to class," she assured him in a rush.

"Just try to keep your mind on your work, Emma. Okay? I think Leader is being lenient where your presidential race is concerned, but she only has so much patience in store."

"I know." She did know that. That's why she had to act before Leader came home.

"Back to class."

She hung up the phone and Obediently returned to class. But she was no more focused in this class than in any other. The access codes kept playing in her mind. They had the tune of rebellion.

Chapter Thirty-Six

Halfway through Emma's fifth period, the door opened. Chastity walked in with a note for the teacher. She walked out again right away, but not without shooting Emma a scathing glare. Emma returned a challenging stare. Since they were in the presence of thirty-five other witnesses, Emma could not afford to seem cowed by Madame Committee President.

"Emma Chandler, you're needed in the principal's office," the teacher advised. She held the note out for Emma to accept it.

Emma felt a sense of relief that her waiting was over. She collected her supplies, put them in her backpack, and accepted the note that would serve as her hall pass to the administrative offices. "Thanks."

Chastity waited in the hall.

"What do you want?" Emma snapped as she strode past her.

The girl's eyes narrowed hatefully. She matched Emma's stride. "I hope they expel you."

Emma did not grace that comment with a reply. She kept walking, but Chastity pursued her. "You think you're so great, Emma Chandler? With your clandestine meetings with the school counselor?" Emma almost missed a step at that, but she did not bother looking at Chastity. She would not acknowledge the girl's misplaced hatred. "That's right. You can pretend to be a regular student living a regular life, but I know all about you and the CIA."

Emma stopped dead in the hall. What if Amos was watching? "Get away from me, Chastity. I swear to you, if I hit you again, the doctors will not have enough pieces to put you back together." She glared aside at her.

Chastity did not seem to be affected by the threat. "Are you allowed to run for Student Council when you're working undercover?"

Emma felt herself panicking, but she attempted to appear natural. She turned and kept walking. "You're crazy, and you're still hysterical about your father's arrest."

"I know they were in the school, Emma," Chastity answered, impervious to Emma's words. "I saw them with my own eyes. And Mrs. Gray in the office tells me anything I ask. I know you have been meeting with them in the counselor's office." When Emma turned down a side hall, Chastity jumped into her path, blocking her way, wild hatred in her eyes. "I know you're not who you say you are."

Emma stared at the girl, really seeing her for the first time since that memorable first day in which Emma attacked her character with almost no provocation. Emma had been angry at life, at Leader, at the Guild. She took that out on Chastity when the girl was only trying to be kind and do her Student Council duties.

Chastity's hair, which once was perfectly styled, was slightly askew. Her eyes were bloodshot and still swollen from crying. Her cardigan was half off one shoulder, revealing a purpling bruise she obviously was attempting to hide. This girl, who offended Emma for no reason except daring to wear tweed in her vicinity, was losing everything in front of Emma's eyes.

Chastity's problems were not over now her father was in jail. Clearly, she was suffering several forms of abuse by various abusers. A glance at her on the first day gave Emma more information than she had any right to. Like the patterns on Stone University, things clicked into place for her a lot of the time. Unlike Stone U, she did not have to work for it out here in the world. Emma knew abuse well—it was like her constant companion. She could see the reflections of abuse in others' eyes. In their stances. In the way they walk. Emma knew that the moment she saw Chastity, the girl had made her uncomfortable because of the reflection between them. And instead of using her click-into-place knowledge to help enrich the girl's life, she used it to kick her when she was already down.

Emma knew her own abuse and Chastity's took different forms. She recognized the patterns and flavors of sexual abuse on the girl within moments of meeting her. That should have been enough to gain Emma's compassion. Instead, stuck inside her own bubble of anger and grief, she lashed out at a defenseless, broken girl.

Shame swept over Emma. She was ashamed that she had ever exposed this girl's weaknesses to the student body. Chastity's life was difficult enough without Emma's interference. Chastity certainly turned into a bully over the past months, but Emma started this war. Emma took an apparently weak young woman, insulted her pride, and disgraced her in the one facet of life where she had formerly been safe. She threatened and attacked her in her only sanctuary. It was no wonder Chastity hated her! Emma hated herself. They both hated themselves so much that the reflection of that hatred in the other's eyes was too much to bear.

"What is it you want, Chastity?"

The girl knew nothing about Emma except what she pieced together from snippets of information. Being on the office's good list had its perks, and evidently for Chastity that meant finding out information no one should have. But Chastity didn't have any idea how dangerous this information was. She had no idea that they were being recorded from several different angles just standing here in the hallway.

The girl's rage grew while they stood there, gazes locked. Emma felt a sense of danger that she learned to recognize on the mats as an imminent threat. Emma did not attempt to protect herself. But Chastity was not like the people in Emma's life; she did not react with violence. She lowered her voice.

"I'll tell everyone who you are," she threatened softly. "Everyone in the school will know and then you'll have to leave because your cover will be blown."

Emma's heart beat painfully fast. Her vision clouded. Anxiety, she knew. The signs were dangerously obvious.

"I'm going to leave anyway," Emma whispered. If Amos was watching, or in any way caught wind of this conversation, he would not rest until he combed every surveillance feed for justification of Chastity's claim that Emma was meeting with CIA. She was leaving one way or another. If the agents did not save her, Leader would kill her.

Chastity's fists balled up at her sides, but again she did not resort to violence. "Then why are you running for Student Council?" Her words were fierce. This was the angriest Emma had ever seen her. But it made sense. The Student Council was Chastity's sanctuary. It was the only place in her entire life that was free from abuse and criticism. Emma was taking away the only diversion Chastity had in her small, hopeless world.

So, Emma chose to be honest. "I was jealous."

Making that admission was as painful as any physical assault. If Chastity reacted angrily or violently, Emma might have endured it better. Anger and violence she knew well. She was trained for it.

Chastity only looked at her helplessly and shook her head, tears finally cascading over her lids in frustration. Her voice cracked as she asked, "Do you really think you'll be a good Student Council president?"

Emma looked away, not able to meet the other girl's eyes any longer. Even if Emma was staying at Slope Oak, she would not be a good president. She did not care about student issues. Things like the cleanup initiative and patterned hosiery were a waste of her energy. Everything she said in the rally was only to get a reaction from the crowd. That was what Emma was good at: getting reactions. She wasn't good at taking care of people. She was not good at caring about what other people cared about.

"No."

There was no other appropriate answer. They both knew Chastity would be a better president. She did care about people. School dances, activities, and issues were important to her. Her life was spent trying to make her little world a better place for everyone. Chastity's atrocious clothing and perky personality offended Emma that first day because she seemed to have everything Emma did not: the ability to be content in a world full of abuse and terror.

Chastity's fierce anger was unaffected by the tears streaming down her face. "Drop out! You don't belong in the presidential race. You have no business stealing votes from deserving candidates. Some of us really care about what happens in this school. You don't, Emma Chandler! Drop out!"

If this was only about the race, Emma would agree. Chastity deserved to win. Chastity *needed* to win. For Chastity, this race was the most important thing in her life. But Emma couldn't drop out with the CIA using this race as a cover. Not that Leader would let her drop out after she came so far. It wasn't a Diligent thing to do. "I can't."

When Chastity only stared hatefully at her, Emma whispered, "I'm sorry." She slipped past Chastity and hurried down the hall toward the offices.

At her back, Chastity cried, "I'll tell everyone about your double life! I'll tell people you're some kind of a cop and that you're working here undercover with the CIA. I'll force you out of this school before you can ruin it!"

Emma's steps halted. Chastity had no idea how dangerous that would be. If, by some divine grace, no one in the Guild caught wind of this conversation, any mention of Chastity's CIA story would send Scott running to Leader. And it was unlikely Chastity would keep such a juicy tidbit of news from her boyfriend.

"Please don't." Emma did not turn around. She could not bear to be vulnerable to this girl she spent so many months despising. But her life literally depended on this. Chastity stalked up to her, shoes thumping on the tiled floors.

"Tell me one reason I should not!"

Emma glanced over at Chastity, standing taller and prouder than Emma, especially in this moment. She knew she had Emma over the flames now. For the first time since Emma enrolled at Slope Oak, Chastity had the upper hand. The fire in her eyes showed how much she was enjoying it.

"It's more than my life is worth." It was an admission of Chastity's power over her, and the most painful words she had ever spoken.

Chastity's eyes narrowed. "Did you get my father thrown in jail?" The question was barely above a whisper, but she was so menacing, she reminded Emma of people in the Guild.

"I did not," Emma answered truthfully. "My speculation about his activities and his character was from my highly tuned observations of you. It's a gift I abused."

Chastity stared down at her, considering the words. Whether she believed Emma or not, there would be no love lost today.

"Drop out of the race or I'll blow your cover and force you out." Blackmail.

Emma turned her head, eyes closing briefly.

She did not get a chance to answer. A school police officer strode purposefully down the hall toward them, and Chastity strolled away as if she had not tearfully blackmailed another student candidate. Emma took a shaky step down the hall. She flashed the hall pass at the officer without a word and walked on. She expected at any moment to receive a call from Leader or Amos. But she did not feel soothed when they didn't call. From now on, Emma was certain she would never feel relaxed again until the agents took her away.

In the office, Principal Morley waited with his characteristic scowl. He barely greeted her as he instructed her to follow him. She was surprised. She assumed the summons was for the counselor, therefore really for the agents. But Morley led her into his office and motioned her to have a seat in one of the many vacant chairs.

"Miss Chandler," he said at his most formal. "I have some concerns about your being Student Council President." He folded his hands on top of his desk and leaned forward. "My biggest concern is that I do not think you're an exemplary student, despite your high-achieving academics. I think you're unfocused, undisciplined, and a bad example to your peers. What do you have to say to that?"

Emma could smell fresh paint. She noticed that the furnishings had been changed. In one glance around the room, she saw that he, too, was taking orders from the CIA.

"Did Agent Caldwell or Agent Peterson have me summoned here?" Emma supposed she could be a little less cautious since Chastity was about to out her to the entire school. Both of her CIA and Guilds cover would be blown simultaneously. Chastity thought Emma was some kind of cop, but Leader would know the scent of betrayal when she caught a whiff.

The principal seemed startled. Most people would not have noticed his disturbed state, but Emma could see the tightening around his eyes and the thinning line of his mouth. He scrubbed a hand through his hair.

"Beg pardon?"

Emma rose. "I don't think you have to worry about me for Student Council, Mr. Morley. May I use your phone?" And without waiting for permission, she picked it up and dialed nine. The familiar clicking sounded in her ears.

"Miss Chandler," Morley started. "I did not ask you in here for you to be disrespectful and distracted."

She held up a hand to stall his words when Caldwell spoke in his regular irony. "Einstein, I hope you have good news for me, because there's plenty of trouble."

"I know," she answered. "My cover here at the school is basically blown, and I only have the access codes. Not anything else."

"Peterson is dead."

That announcement made Emma sit down hard.

"When?" she asked. "How?"

The principal tried to speak and she waved an annoyed hand at him.

"Not important," Caldwell answered. "Put that blowhard on the phone, Emma. He can't listen to you, but he'll listen to me."

Emma looked up at the principal and handed over the phone. "He wants to talk to you."

She waited while Caldwell did all the talking. She could not hear his words, but she saw Morley's face go from angry to speculative to resigned and then he passed the phone back to her.

"I'll be outside" He walked around his desk to the door.

"If we're going to act, we need to act now," Caldwell said once Emma had the phone in hand again. "What are the access codes?"

Emma pressed her lips together for a moment. His partner was dead, and he felt nothing. His voice was devoid of concern. It was the opposite of grieving. He moved on without a beat.

"Tell me what happened to Peterson, or I give you nothing."

Caldwell gave a sigh. "You don't really want to know, Einstein. Trust me."

"Stop telling me to trust you. I *don't* trust you. I'm not going to trust you. I don't trust even my own two hands most of the time. Tell me about Agent Peterson, or I walk away right now."

"He was killed by one of your Guild cronies," Caldwell answered. "One single shot to the head. They're well-trained, your criminal friends."

Emma leaned forward, head between her knees, trying to breathe at a normal pace, trying to calm herself down. Her panic was going to get her pulled out of school if nothing else did.

"The access codes?" Caldwell returned abruptly to the topic.

Emma could not think about access codes. "Who was it? Leader?"

"No. The young gay man with the nice hair. Peterson was on your street, in position to collect you when you got home from school today, and your gay friend shot him at point-blank range. It was an assassination. There was never supposed to be a fight." He paused and then said again, "Give me the access codes."

Emma squeezed her eyes shut. *Waylon?* Sweet, even-tempered, charming Waylon had killed a CIA officer without any provocation? She could not bear it!

"Access codes!" Caldwell did not sound ironic now. He was getting short with her.

"You're not even slightly concerned over the murder of your partner?" It was alarming. She was shaken to her core, and she hadn't really known the guy.

"Death is part of the action, Einstein. Give me the codes!" Caldwell's words doused Emma in chilly recollection of the response to the previous Leader's death. Like that, this was not a normal reaction. When people died, especially people she knew, she could not pick up and walk on without a single concern. That Caldwell *could* made her shiver was a Guild reaction.

"No," Emma answered, sitting up so abruptly, she smacked her head against the desktop. Rubbing it with one hand, she repeated in a milder tone, "No. You can have me and when I'm at a safe distance, I'll give you the codes."

"That's not the way this works." Caldwell's voice became even less friendly. "If they're not the right codes, what are we supposed to do then? I won't be able to return you to get the right ones if I take you now."

Emma grabbed the edge of the table for support. "Your partner was just killed by the mildest member of the Guild! If they suspect me, I'm done for! And you wouldn't have a chance to get the codes anyway. You take me or no codes."

"I'm not in the state," Caldwell replied and Emma felt all of her hopes burst. They splashed around her in the wreckage of her peace. Her vision blurred again and darkened around the edges. She could not fight her panic attack and the Agent at the same time. "Peterson was supposed to pick you up. He's dead. I won't be able to be there until Monday at the earliest."

Emma shook her head. This could not be happening! "I'm not giving you a single code until you pick me up. If Leader gets to me first, you lose."

Caldwell snapped back, "She's going to get to you first! Her jet left its hangar this morning. She could be just about anywhere by now. If she was headed home, we're screwed. Just give me the codes, and I'll get you as soon as I can get a flight."

Emma hung up the phone. There was nothing more to say. Frantic, fearful, Emma burst from the office, stalked past a spluttering Morley, the school counselor, and several other administrators to get to the hall. The bell rang before she made it down the first hall, and she was no longer alone. The halls filled to bursting.

Emma ignored the other students. She shoved past people who tried to high-five her in support of her campaign. She pushed her way through a group of slow walking girls. She managed to knock down a kid who was reading instead of paying attention to hallway traffic. Although it was an accident, she did not even slow to apologize.

Chapter Thirty-Seven

There was nowhere to go. There was nowhere safe. If Waylon could kill a man in cold blood, there was no safe place on the planet for Emma to hide.

"Hey!" Josie called as Emma shoved violently past her in the hall. She grabbed Emma's sleeve. "What's wrong, Cobra!"

"I'm not a cobra!" Emma snarled back, breaking the girl's grip. "I never was. I have always, *always* been a mouse!" She jerked away violently and stalked on.

When Emma got to the upstairs lavatory, there were several girls inside talking to one another in front of the mirror. Happy girls, whose only life problems included what type of makeup to wear to match their skin tones and who was going to ask them to prom next month.

"Get out!" Emma ordered as she dropped her backpack to the floor with a heavy thud. When the girls turned in surprise at her insistence, but did not immediately act, Emma raised her voice to somewhere between hysterical screech and furious scream. "GET OUT!"

The girls went.

Emma stood in front of the mirrors, controlling her breathing, controlling her fear. Fighting down the panic. Panic for Leader's life had once caused Emma to have an anxiety attack. Panic for her own life could very well make her hyperventilate.

Emma saw Waylon in her imagination, pulling a gun. But his face contorted in her mind, and he became another man, a boy really. Emma's first love. He held a gun and pointed it at her. This gun would carry the bullet that killed her, but his betrayal had already stolen her life away.

Benjamin. His name floated up from where she had it buried in her mind, and she screamed in rage at it. She attacked the mirror in front of her, wanting to break the image of herself losing control. Her entire life was about control, but she couldn't stay there now. Caldwell was just like everyone else she knew. He was cold and distant from the very real reality of death. It was as if his partner's life meant nothing, as Leader's had meant nothing that cold day two years ago. It was as if he never mattered. The Guild was able to pick up and carry on as if there was nothing special or significant about him at all. Would Peterson's death be as insignificant as that? Would it mean as little as Benjamin's had when he died alone on the street?

Emma screamed out again, launching a direct hit to the mirror. It shattered, splintering her image for a moment before the glass fell from its frame in thousands of tiny shards. But there was nothing more of her image to mock her pain and anger.

The mirror had been loose on its frame, she now saw, and behind it in several places were hiding spaces for contraband. She grabbed the nearest, a half empty pack of cigarettes, and stared at them. When the door opened, and a young woman tried to come in, she only stepped one foot through the door before Emma launched her phone at the girl and shouted, "Get out of here!" The phone crashed against the door and bounced on the floor, but it did not break. Amos had basically made it indestructible.

Emma went to the door and leaned back against it to keep anyone else from coming in. She considered the cigarettes, then removed one slowly and put it in between her lips. She took the lighter from the plastic wrap around the outside of the package, lit the cigarette, and coughed once when she tried to inhale. Then she slid down the door to her bottom and smacked her head back against the painted wood surface. She was not a talented smoker. In fact, she was horrible and did not even enjoy it. But she wanted her nerves to calm down and she heard that was why people smoked. Besides, it gave her something else to focus on than Waylon's kill.

Another drag left her choking.

Emma's eyes slid shut. She could hear the commotion in the hall. The girls she kicked out were surely spreading the news already. *The*

Cobra strikes again! Emma couldn't care about that now. She had bigger problems than people hating her. Her problems at this point were even bigger than the possibility that Amos was watching her on Guild surveillance. Emma wrapped her arms around her knees and rested her head against them while holding the cigarette between her fingers, letting it burn to ash in her hands.

She had no idea what she was going to do now. She counted on Caldwell and Peterson to get her out safely. Keeping a calm, straight face at home among cold-blooded killers would be impossible. She could not do it!

Emma's eyes stung but she kept herself from crying. She was too cold to cry, too hurt, too frightened.

Glancing at the backpack in the middle of the bathroom, Emma thought about the mother she might never meet. And that made her colder. She lit a second cigarette and ground the first one into the tile beside her.

The door was pushed partially open, but Emma held it closed with her body. "Go away!" she snapped, pressing herself against the door to keep it from opening.

The inward force against the door stopped, but the person did not go away. "Emma, let me in."

It was Scott.

"Go away. This is a girl's restroom." He was the last person in the world she wanted to see right now. But Scott was unaccustomed to being disobeyed.

He shoved hard against the door, and said, "Let me in right now."

He could get in if he wanted because he was stronger and was on the outside pushing in. She had too much space to be able to use the side wall for extra leverage. She slid forward slightly, Obedient because her only other choice was to fight him.

Scott slipped in through the small space she offered and glanced around the room. He blinked in surprise but otherwise showed no distress over the state of the bathroom, with glass all over the floor, and her backpack and phone lying discarded in the middle of the room.

"Bad day?" he asked as he surveyed the scene. Then he looked at her and his voice went from amused to stern. "Are you smoking? Give me that!"

He snatched the second cigarette from her hand and tossed it in one of the sinks. Then, seeing the pack in her hand, took that, too. She did not fight him. It wasn't hers, and he seemed intent on getting it. "This shit'll kill you!" He crushed the pack in his hands and tossed them in a trash can.

Eyes narrowing, he peered at her. He approached tentatively when she refused to look him in the eye. She missed Scott! But it was too late to make nice now. She hugged her knees. Anything she said to Scott now would be reported to Leader. If Waylon, a nice and respectable person, could kill an innocent man without provocation, what more was Scott capable of? He wasn't a nice guy. He was like Emma. Twisted.

He slid down the wall at a right angle from her and crossed his arms on his chest. When he spoke, it was with soft curiosity. "What's going on with you?" She glanced up at him and saw the intense concern in his eyes. She shook her head. Not in refusal to talk to him as much as she had no idea how to begin. There was nothing she could say now that would not incriminate her in his eyes.

His foot nudged her slightly. "Come on, Emma. Don't make me get authoritative. I don't feel like bossing you around." He tried to make it sound like he was joking, but she heard the sincerity behind his words.

"We're not supposed to be talking to one another," Emma reminded him, finally lifting her head to look at him directly. He looked beautiful, even dressed in his prep clothes.

"I don't care about that." He adjusted the collar of his shirt to stand up straight and stretched his legs out long next to her, being sure to smooth his pleated slacks as he did so, accentuating the offensive garments. If it was anyone but Scott blocking her in next to the door, she might have felt trapped. But she felt safer with Scott than with most people. She did not want to feel that way. She wanted to withhold all her trust from everyone because every time she trusted, the world blew up around her.

"You're falling apart, Cobra. I saw the girls you kicked out of here, and you're not getting any votes there."

Emma expelled an exhausted breath and looked away with a shake of her head. "I have to drop out."

"What? No way! You're going to blow Chastity out of the race! It will be a spectacular defeat like no one has ever seen before. These country rednecks could use a little more controversy."

She rolled her eyes at him. "I don't want to be Student Council President, Scott. I never wanted to be." She sat up tall. "Yours is the only vote I ever cared about but I didn't think it would be fair to ask you to vote for me when you were dating my competition."

He read into her sarcastic joviality. "You don't seriously think I would *choose* to date a girl like Chastity Monez. Come *on*! I've been on a mission this whole time. You're supposed to be pretty smart. You had to have figured that out.

"The voting booths are private. No one, probably not even Amos, will see who I vote for. I can lie straight to Chastity's face. My vote is always with you." He nudged her with his knee and lifted his chin as if in dismissal of Chastity and the rest of the world. "There's always going to be a mission, Em. Other people are going to come and go in our lives, but you and I are all we really have. We're stronger than family."

Stronger than family was a bold claim. Emma glanced toward the backpack where the picture of her mother was safely held. Dreams of family were stronger than her and Scott this year. Unsubstantiated dreams of her mother led Emma to betray the Guild. Her life was on the line because of "family."

She glanced upward at the flickering fluorescent lights. Her feelings were confused, but she did not actually regret her complicity with the CIA. If Caldwell was anywhere nearby, she would be on her way away from this school forever. That idea still filled her with hope. She could live the rest of her life without seeing Leader's eyes darkened with disappointment and anger. The obligation to live up to Guild potential could easily be something Emma never dealt with again. But the idea of walking away from Scott did not bear thinking about.

"I never really wanted to be president. I just wanted to have a legitimate reason to be at war with Chastity. I hate her."

"I know you do." He pulled a face. "I don't know why. That girl's about one more trauma away from a psychiatric lockdown. Why would you choose to start a war with *her*? She's not worth it."

"You know why."

Scott did an amazing impression of Leader, with one brow raised in a stern look of expectation. "I want you to say it out loud."

Emma rolled her eyes again and looked away, but when he continued to say nothing, she finally sighed and admitted, "I was jealous of your attention."

He gave a self-satisfied smile that made her want to throw something at him. She kicked him hard in the leg since there was nothing within easy reach. He grunted, but his smile grew.

"I hate you."

He laughed , not at all concerned it might be true. It wasn't. She wanted to hate him, but she could not do it. Scott was her best friend, for good or for bad.

"What drove you in here?" Scott asked, glancing around the room again. "And I will believe you if you say a herd of elephants."

Emma gave a sad laugh. "No. I keep my elephants at home. This was . . ." she looked all around, ". . . insanity."

He presented the room with an open palm. "They're going to suspend, if not expel, you completely for this. I guess you won't have to drop out of the race then. Morley will never put your name on the ballot once he sees this vandalism."

"Yeah," Emma agreed on a sigh. She wished she could have this empty and pointless conversation for the rest of her life. It was just right. They were talking as if no time passed and no preppy girls came between them. They were mocking her bad choices, as they always did. Ignoring his, of course, because he was a baby about his mistakes. They were making light of the impending doom of Leader's retribution. But Scott did not know how heavy that doom was, nor the extent of her crimes. She couldn't tell him because, though he felt their bond was stronger than family, his loyalty to the Guild was stronger still.

"Emma, what's going on with you?" Scott's voice changed abruptly to concentrated interest. His gaze sharpened. Emma looked away and said nothing even when he added, "Tell me!" in a commanding tone.

She shook her head. "You should go, Scott. When the school police get here, you should not be sitting among the rubble of my disastrous life. You should go. Amos probably watched me throw my little fit and is on his way any moment. I don't want Julianne to skin you alive for sitting in here talking to me when you were ordered to keep your distance. You *were* ordered to keep your distance." It was almost a question.

Scott scoffed. "Screw them all. I finished my mission. The Guild cover is already blown everywhere else by everyone else. Why should we continue to pretend? We were never very good at it to begin with."

Emma leaned forward against her knees, resting her head on her legs for a moment. "That's because we don't belong anywhere, Scott. We're always alone even in the middle of a crowded room. We never fit in even for all we're trying to pretend we do." She looked up at him. "Do you remember that football game you played in? We could not have been more out of place."

He gave a snort of laughter. "What are you expecting? We're not sporty, and we're not . . ." he touched his shirt. ". . . preppy. We don't even own a TV, for crying out loud. How can we talk about apps or television that other kids talk about? When I started driving to school alone this year, I actually listened to music, and I still don't know if I like any of it. I can't be like 'Yeah, I love that new song by Monkey Toadstool' or whatever the stupid band names are. I don't have the slightest idea who in the world is considered cool, or if 'cool' is even a word they use, or if we just got that from our superiors. We're not really supposed to fit in, Emma. If the purpose of the Guild was to fit in, we wouldn't flaunt our wealth at everyone."

Emma looked up at him in surprise. "Flaunt our wealth?"

Scott shook his head at her lack of perception. "Emma, Leader drives the most expensive Volvo you can get on an American lot. Amos' Porsche is so pimped out it shouldn't even be allowed on the road. Every article of clothing Ilene buys for us has a brand name featured prominently." He pointed at her backpack and said, "That has a tag on it that says it was handmade by a backpack designer in Europe. *Nobody* has a one-of-a-kind designer backpack! No one in the world, except us. You have to read between the lines sometimes, Em. We were never meant to be part of the group, because we're different."

She stared in surprise at the designer label on her backpack. She never noticed it before.

"You're never alone, though, Em. In the crowded room when everyone gives us wide berth, I'm standing beside you. And so is everyone else in the Guild."

She stretched her legs out, sliding them beneath his crosswise. She sat back against the door to consider him. He really believed it. He really thought the Guild was his family.

"Don't you ever wonder where you came from or who you were? Don't you ever question your purpose here? Don't you want to know who you are?"

He squeezed her knee. "Every day." When she stared hard at him, shocked by his answer, he laughed. "You're such a narcissist, Emma! Do you really think you're the only person ever to have problems with Guild Disclosure Levels? The most infuriating part of life in the Guild is not the isolation from the world, it's isolation from the facts. Adam has a meltdown every couple of months because his only pre-Guild memory is playing with a dog in the yard and being called to come in for dinner by someone affectionate."

Scott held up a finger. "Lara almost died a few years ago because she went outside the Guild for information about her previous life. She was manipulated because she was so desperate, she was willing to do almost anything. She was abused and nearly killed, and still, the other day, she made contact with a missing children's network to see if her picture ever showed up." A second finger joined the first. "Yesterday in school, Victoria asked her teacher if every family has a Leader. When the teacher tried to explain that everyone can be a leader, Victoria insisted 'not in my family.' The teacher wrote a very long and disturbed letter to Julianne about oppression." His third finger rose.

Emma looked at those three fingers as he shook them at her: Adam, Lara, and Victoria.

"You think you're alone, but we all feel it."

Emma grabbed his hand and lifted another finger. "What about you?"

He slowly removed his hand from hers and shrugged. "I don't know. I guess I don't care as much about who I used to be as I do about who I am right now." She watched him, hoping he would say more. After a moment, he added, "I guess you don't remember a few years ago when Amos picked us up from grade school. You would have been in third grade then." Emma tried to remember, but school days were a blur. "He never picked us up before because Julianne or Ilene almost always did. He was the most senior Guild member at home, and he picked us up early."

Emma remembered. Her name was called over the loudspeaker and she was asked to collect her belongings and report to the office. Her teacher was annoyed because they were in the middle of a spelling test. When she got to the office, Amos smiled brightly and announced he was taking her home early. Scott was standing behind him, furiously brooding as, to Emma's eyes, he always seemed to be.

"I remember."

He drew a pained breath. "He picked us up from school early because I called social services during lunch and told them I had been kidnapped and was being held against my will. I said I was routinely beaten as part of my slave training and that if I was not removed right away, I might disappear and never be found again."

Emma did not remember any of that. When they had gotten to the car, Amos pleasantly told her to get in and buckle. He asked her politely about school and friends. Scott sat beside her, continuing to be moody. When they got to the house, Amos walked them in with no trouble, although he followed Scott to his room.

"What happened to you?"

Scott smirked. "Well, social services did not have a chance to show up because, as you may remember, the previous Leader was unhealthily obsessed with surveillance. Amos was almost always watching. Amos heard my entire conversation on the school phone and he came right away to get us. If I was gone, they would certainly have questioned you, so he picked us both up. I thought Amos was going to kill me, but . . ." He shrugged. "You know Amos. He has to be forced to swat at a fly. He took me to a safe house for a couple days until he could smooth things over."

"Were we ever investigated by family services?"

Scott nodded. "Yeah. When we went back to school, but by then Leader was back from one of his multitudes of business trips and able to charm them into believing it was a prank call."

Emma scoffed. "Why don't they just tell us something and then we won't be tempted to look other places?"

"I don't know. There must be a reason."

Emma turned her body so she sat across from him with her back against the opposite wall. She was going to say more, but then she saw his hand up and he wiggled his last finger suggestively. When she pretended not to know what he was doing, he said, "What about you? Haven't you ever done anything stupid or crazy for information or in retribution for not being told something you wanted to know?"

Yes. But she looked away rather than answer. He nudged her with his leg and said "Tell me" in a mock-threatening tone.

She looked at him. "Didn't Chastity tell you I was meeting with the CIA? You're her boyfriend. I thought she would have told you right away."

Scott laughed out loud. "Of course, she told me! She tells me everything. I thought it was funny. Central Intelligence at a Springfield High School? Really? What were they doing here, walking around waiting for students to volunteer information about cow tipping?" He laughed again. He clearly did not believe Chastity's story.

Her eyes narrowed at him for his doubt and laughter. "It's true," she told him in a stern voice meant to cut off his mirth.

It worked. The emotion that replaced it was confusion. "Wait . . . What?"

Emma wanted to tell him. She wanted him to know that she really was different from the rest of them. Emma did not do anything small. When she chose to betray the Guild, she did it with fanfare and fireworks! She went to the CIA and never looked back.

"It's true. I met with the CIA last week here at school. I have spoken to them on the phone. I don't know what kind of access to the offices Chastity has, but enough that she either saw them in passing or heard the counselor talking about them. They were here, though. Chastity is certainly right about that."

Scott shifted his position, clearly uncomfortable with her admission of guilt.

"That's not all," Emma went on when he tried to speak. "I spoke to one agent earlier and he said his partner was killed by Waylon today. Point-blank assassin gunshot. I have no idea why he was killed, but I think I can safely say my life is in danger. The CIA was supposed to pick me up when things got dangerous, but the other guy slipped town apparently and now I'm stuck here." She pressed her hands to her eyes and let out a heavy breath. "I can't believe Waylon killed him."

Scott leaned far forward and grabbed Emma's arm, jerking her hands away from her face. "You're serious," he said, not quite questioning. "You have been meeting with CIA agents and talking to them about running away. What do they want from you? What can you offer them?"

Emma swallowed at the fearful force in his eyes. "Information."

Scott shook his head, horrified but trying to hide it. "What were they offering in return?"

Emma stared into his eyes and saw the genuine concern there. He was truly worried about her. So, she had been right that Leader would probably end her for this. This was worse than anything anyone else had ever done for information.

Emma got up, stepped over his legs, and approached her backpack. She dug through it until she came across the photo of her mother. She withdrew it, holding it carefully against her chest as she returned to him.

"They said they would reunite me with my mother," Emma said. She felt no guilt over the admission. She knelt by his side and handed the photo over. "This is her."

Scott seemed shocked or perhaps amazed as he took the photo. His eyes locked with hers for a moment before his attention was captured by the beautiful woman in the photo. The image startled him further, but his surprised expression made the hair on Emma's arms rise. He recognized the woman in the photo. His expression gave him away.

"What?" she asked, concerned by his recognition.

"Emma," he looked up and pinned her with a very serious look. "You have to tell Leader."

"She probably already knows!" Emma pointed toward the mirror, shattered on the floor, indicating the hidden surveillance all around the room. "Waylon made a cold kill today. Do you think he did not tell her about it? 'Hey, Leader! FYI, I just killed a CIA agent.'"

Scott shook his head emphatically. "I don't think the men are who they said they are." He looked back down at the photo with real worry on his face.

She grabbed his arm in a crushing grip, demanding his attention in her desperate gesture. "Don't try to protect me, Scott; just tell me what you know. Who are they?"

He shook his head. "I don't know." He passed the photo back to her hands. "But she's not your mother."

Emma's hopes plummeted. She had so wanted Caldwell and Peterson to be legitimate, but she should have known. She should have at least suspected they were not who they said they were. But it seemed legitimate when they came to the school and spoken with the counselor and the principal. It did not take much to manipulate her. A show of authority, a little smoke and mirrors, and a simple picture of a woman they claimed was her mother. And she took their word for it.

"Who is she?" she asked, desperate to know but afraid for the dream to die.

Scott looked into her eyes and said softly, "I called her Leader."

The rock of Emma's hope shook, and she looked away, pained beyond imagination. Was there nothing sacred? Was no one safe from the grip of the Guild? Emma slid onto her back on the glass-strewn floor and crumpled the picture of the former Guild leader in her fist. Her entire life was one conspiracy after another.

Scott moved closer to her. "What did you tell them? What do they know?"

"Nothing," Emma answered helplessly. "I told them basically nothing. I was supposed to give them the information today, but I refused because he wasn't going to help me. The information was my only real leverage with them." She felt utterly foolish. Caldwell had tried so hard to get her to give him the information. He had never meant to help her at all. He had manipulated her with the sole intention of stealing Guild secrets. "I don't even know what kind of information I was bargaining with. The Atlantis file."

Scott's brow gave a quizzical twitch. "I don't know what that is."

Emma sighed. "Me neither. I heard Amos and Leader discussing it one day, but nothing about what it contained."

Scott leaned his body down over hers and caught her eye. "If Waylon killed one of these men, they were a danger to the Guild. You have to tell Leader about this."

Emma pushed him away and stood up. "No!" She tossed the photo in the trash. "I'm not talking about this anymore. I'm going back to class, and you should, too."

Scott gripped her arm in an almost painfully tight hold. His tone was urgent. "Emma! You can't just pretend this didn't happen. This other agent could be on his way to kill you."

Emma wrenched her arm from his grip. "And?! What's your point? It doesn't much matter who kills me, Scott. Caldwell may not even bother, but if Leader finds out about this, she definitely will. I don't think she'll smile fondly upon my willingness—my *intention*—to betray Guild secrets. I hacked her files! I infiltrated her systems. She's not going to let this slide by as if I failed a Chemistry exam."

His face betrayed that he agreed, but he said nothing.

"If Leader doesn't know, she probably won't find out, and I'll be safer. I'm going back to class." She picked up her backpack and slung it on her shoulder. She felt him watching her, wondering if he should report this. He should. It was really a Guild duty to be explicit about threats to their safety. She knew his loyalty to her warred with his loyalty to the Guild. She also expected to come out losing in that race.

She moved to the door, but he stepped in front, blocking her in. "If I don't tell a soul about this, will you swear to me you won't turn outside the Guild again without speaking to me about it?" When she did not immediately answer, he grabbed her face with both hands and insisted, "Please?!"

The desperation in his voice was what made her surrender. He was choosing to protect her over his loyalty to the Guild, and if she denied, it might destroy him. "I swear."

He stepped back, away from her. "I'm going to hold you to that," he warned her. It was a serious sacrifice for him to agree to this in the first place. She had no doubt that he would hold her to it severely. She nodded in acknowledgment of his sacrifice.

When she turned to leave, he called her to wait. "Here!" He retrieved the photo from the trash and smoothed it on his leg. "Keep this. She may not be the person you thought, but it's always nice to have a dream."

Emma just barely managed to keep from glaring. "I don't want it. I don't want the dream or the reminder."

Scott arched a brow and offered it to her. "Then keep it because I told you to and you're Obedient to your superiors." He held it in his hand until she snatched it away, stuffing it irreverently in her pocket.

He nodded with a significant glance at her pocket. "I'm going to hold you to that, too."

She did roll her eyes this time and walked out of the room.

Chapter Thirty-Eight

Emma's body convulsed in fear when she stepped outside and found Leader waiting in the hall. The woman leaned against the opposite wall, arms crossed below her chest, one heeled boot tapping the floor in mild impatience. Her hair was down in a beautiful mass around her shoulders. She looked as if she came straight from the plane because she wore jeans and a blouse rather than her normal business suit. Her beautiful eyes stared hard at Emma. It took every ounce of control Emma had to attempt to appear nonchalant, yet appropriately surprised. *Did she know?*

"Afternoon," Leader said in a neutral voice.

Scott came out and nearly treaded on Emma's heels until he saw what halted her. His breath caught in a sharp inhale. Leader raised one brow slowly, dangerously, first at Emma, then at Scott.

"What are you doing?" It was almost casual, a tone Emma was not accustomed to in Leader, and did not enjoy. It grated against the word "Checkmate" in her mind.

Scott did not even attempt to speak. Emma was numb just from finding her there. She hoped Caldwell was wrong about Leader's imminent arrival. But even if he hadn't been, she certainly had not expected Leader to show up at her school midday. Amos sure, but not Leader. Leader was rarely even home these days.

Emma glanced up and down the hall in both directions, hoping for witnesses. But everyone was in class, and for a wonder there were no campus police or nosy faculty anywhere in sight.

"Not feeling talkative?" Leader asked, but her ironic tone made it rhetorical. She looked at Scott. "I called ahead to Victoria's school to have her released from classes today. Go get her from her school and go to the farm."

Scott stepped around Emma with a nod. "Yes, Leader." He walked away. Emma watched him go, feeling her heartbeat getting heavier and more painful in her chest. His retreat left her alone with Leader. A parting look over his shoulder, perhaps an attempt to convey strength or calm, did not make Emma feel any safer. It had the opposite effect. If Scott had simply walked away, Emma might have been buoyed by his nonchalance, but his need to convey comfort made her realize how much she really needed it.

Leader ordered, "Let's go."

Emma shifted her backpack and followed Obediently, but her anxiety mounted with every footstep. Leader would never remove her from school early without a really good reason. So, unless the Guild was moving today, Leader probably knew about Emma's betrayal. She should never have trusted the agents. As well as they thought they knew Leader and Amos, they probably had never been able to circumvent all their surveillance. Leader kept a tight fist on her Guild. She knew. There seemed to be no other reason for her to come here straight from the plane.

They stopped at the Attendance Office to sign Emma out for the day. When asked why she was removing her daughter from school, she said coldly, "I don't think that's any of your business." Those words did not make Emma feel any safer.

Emma followed Leader through the front entrance and to the parking lot where Leader was parked in the handicapped parking space although she had not bothered to put up the hanger this time. Leader snapped a pair of designer sunglasses into place and clicked the auto-start and the unlock button on her keys as she walked around to the driver's side. Emma had the urge to bolt, but she thought better of that, too. If Leader knew about the agents, all Emma could do now was beg for forgiveness and hope for a miracle.

She climbed in the car and buckled, dropping her backpack to the floorboard between her feet. She watched Leader from the corner of her eye. The woman seemed colder than Emma remembered. She was distant and seemed full of unsaid words.

Leader pulled out into traffic.

"Emma," Leader asked, glancing aside at her. "What is going on with you?" Emma forced herself to maintain a normal breathing pattern and not look alarmed.

Emma turned her face to study the older woman. Through the dark shades, she could only make out the outline of Leader's eyes and not any of the emotion there. This was her chance! If she was going to admit everything, now was the time to do it, and to apologize and swear she would never attempt to betray the Guild again. Maybe Leader would spare her life. But what would her life be after her dream of a mother and a family had been ripped from her hands?

Emma said nothing.

Leader let out a frustrated breath. "Do you think I am an idiot? I know when your IQ is so much higher than everyone else, it is difficult to imagine anyone should be able to tie their own shoes without help, but I am not an idiot."

"I know," Emma replied softly. She did know that. Leader was perhaps the only person in the world who did not frustrate her with incompetence.

"*Do* you know?" Leader snapped back. She turned onto the highway and accelerated. They were not headed to the Guild House or the farm. Emma's heart beat harder. "I think sometimes you don't know what I'm capable of."

Emma swallowed and looked out the window. She felt real fear now. Leader knew. And there was no going back. She whispered, "What are you going to do?"

Leader shook her head. "Before I do anything, I want to know why, instead of asking me for what you want, you're trying to go behind my back." Emma felt the heat of Leader's gaze through the dark shades of her sunglasses. "Can you tell me that?"

Emma couldn't. She did not know why.

"Emma!" Leader demanded, waiting impatiently for an answer. When Emma only glanced at her again and said nothing, Leader shook her head. "You're killing me here, Little Girl. You're inside your head and so far out of reach it's sometimes hard to know if you're still with me. Are you still with me?"

Emma did not want to answer that. She lied, "Yes, Leader."

"You may be as smart as a world chess champion, but I still have the last move. I went through the surveillance feed and saw what you did to your computer. Piper may not have recognized it, and even Amos was baffled, but you can't fool me. I've been on Stone University. I recognize the sequence."

Emma looked aside at her in confusion. "You mean the virus?" Leader had been through the surveillance feed and the *virus* was what she fixated on?

Leader challenged her with, "Should we be talking about something else?"

No way. Emma was content to talk about the virus. She deliberately created a virus with the sole intention of being given access to a newer model computer.

"My computer was utter shit, Leader. You know that. It was barely adequate, and I knew feeding it a virus was the only way I could get a better one."

Leader took the exit onto another highway, leaving Springfield behind completely. "You need to ask for what you want! Don't just take things from me."

Emma felt no remorse for her action, but she answered, "I apologize. I will never kill a computer again without asking you for permission."

Leader snorted. "Cute that you think that's all I was talking about." Emma felt cold again, but she did not answer. Anything she said could be wrong. Leader was driving her out into the country, away from the farm, away from the Guild House and any and all witnesses.

"Let's talk about what it is you were really after," Leader ordered in a tone that sounded like a suggestion, but Emma knew it for what it was. Any time Leader became icy or brisk, Emma remembered who she had been before she became Leader; cold and firm, demanding, intimidating, and violent. Her tone sometimes reverted when Emma screwed up.

Emma sighed. "If you already know, and you're here to take care of me and my threat, do we have to talk about it?" She glanced up at Leader. "There's not a lot I have done this year that I'm proud of. I don't want to talk." She sat up straight. "But if we're going to talk, let's talk about your orders. I have a hard time believing Waylon killed Peterson without some kind of order from you."

Leader stared at Emma long enough that her car drifted onto the shoulder before she could correct the direction.

"Oh my god," she whispered as if in prayer. She shook her head and then stomped on the accelerator so forcefully it jerked Emma back in her seat. Emma reached a painful realization: Leader had *not* known,

"You're the informant?!" Leader demanded. She scoffed. "Of course, you are. You're the only smart person stupid enough to be drawn into their web of deception." She balled her fist and Emma braced for its impact. Leader did not hit her. She clenched her hand for a moment before grabbing the gearshift and changing gears abruptly. "I am restraining myself from violence. You should know that."

"I know," Emma answered, looking up at Leader in surprise and fear. "I don't know *why*. I expected you to kill me. Or are you waiting until you find a place to dump a body?" They were driving toward Branson, and there was little in the way of cities once Ozark was behind them. She could be buried and never found in these rolling wooded hills.

Leader laughed. It was neither warm nor friendly. "I don't kill the people in my Guild, Emmalyn Stone, not even when they do something utterly stupid." She pulled her glasses down and looked at Emma over the rims. "And this isn't even the stupidest thing that's happened in the Guild this week."

Emma did not feel any relief to learn Leader did not intend to kill her. She expected to feel something—relief or gratitude that her life was spared—but the realization only made her colder. Nothing Emma did made an impact or influenced anything. She went to the CIA, and Leader laughed it off as if it was all in a day's work. It was almost as painful as realizing the photo she cherished was nothing but a deception.

"What was the *stupidest* thing?" Emma wanted to know. She earnestly wanted to know. She had betrayed this Guild and not even managed to win the title of stupidest act of the week.

Leader scoffed again, and her disdain coated every word. "Piper spoke to an Air Force recruiter. Wait until you've walked through the Loyalty curtain and then betray me and see how I handle it." She must have seen or sensed Emma's numbness, because she went on. "Oh, don't worry, Emma, yours is definitely top-five material betrayal, but I deal with this kind of garbage on a regular basis, so don't be offended if I handle it in stride." She sounded furious, though. She swore out loud and accelerated to well above safe speed. Emma clutched at the edges of her seat, hoping Leader slowed soon, or was seen by a cop. Leader drove until she sailed onto the Jackson Street exit ramp. She managed to brake in time to avoid a collision with the cars stopped at the light.

"I don't know what to even say to you anymore," Leader announced when the slow car in front of them managed to hold them up at the light for a second round. She jerked her glasses off her face and turned an enraged expression on Emma. "You are completely self-involved."

Emma felt a wave of emotional pain at that pronouncement. "Me?" she demanded. "Everything I ever do is for you!"

"By all means, explain how hacking my system—yeah, I know about that. I require a retinal scan for a reason!—Explain how that in *any way* serves me? What were you after? I assumed it was for your personal file, but if you were embezzling my information for outside sources, they must have wanted something very specific."

Emma let out a short breath, furious with herself for being tricked into revealing this information. She should have just kept her silence and Leader might never have known. "They wanted Atlantis."

Leader glanced at her. Then she laughed. "Fools," she said in the same tone she might have called them a dirty word. "Utter fools. I got Atlantis secured before the New Year. They could never have gotten close to it." She laughed again, and when she saw Emma did not share in her mirth, she said, "You take things too seriously."

"Leader, someone was killed!"

"Yeah . . ." Leader agreed and her laughter died. "That's not funny." She hit the gas as soon as the light turned. "If it makes you feel better, he had it coming."

"It does not."

They drove onto West Jackson Street away from Ozark City, into the hills. Emma furiously thought about Leader's words. She was disgusted by the callousness with which Peterson's death was treated. She wondered if anyone would give him a funeral and who might attend.

"Did Leader get a funeral? Or did you laugh it up when he died, too, like you are over Agent Peterson?"

Leader dismissed her first question with a simple, "The Guild always cares well for their dead." But it was her second statement that drew Emma's gaze back to her. "And that man was not an agent. His name is not Peterson. I don't know under what pretense he approached you, but he lied."

That was entirely possible. It was more possible that Peterson was a liar than that Leader fabricated this story to justify a murder.

"Who was he? Arrow Guild?"

Leader's snort was expressive and hateful. "No, not them. They won't be back up to running capacity for a long time, if ever. They'll think twice before they cross us again." Emma could not be certain, but she suspected Amos severely damaged the rival guild after their attack in Salt Lake City.

"He's what we refer to as a PIC, Personal Interest Case. Everyone has personal interests, of course, but some people have malicious private interests. As soon as Waylon identified the man as a PIC, I gave a kill order. Waylon Obeyed me. And do you know why?" Emma looked away, refusing to guess why Waylon would ever be tempted to Obey a kill order. "He Obeyed me because he learned Obedience properly when he was a Twelve."

Emma let out a disgusted breath. "Is that what you want? You want drones who will kill when you point and say 'kill?' Hire hitmen!"

Leader pulled down a country lane moments before, but she now jerked the wheel, pulling over to the side of the road, although there was little in the way of space.

"I don't need to hire hitmen when I can raise and train them." She jerked the keys out of the ignition and snapped, "I'm going for a walk. I can't sit here with you without resorting to violence." She got out of the car and slammed the door. Emma watched her cross the road, jump the little ditch that served as the opposite shoulder, and stalk away through the woods.

Chapter Thirty-Nine

Emma sat alone in the car, feeling painful emptiness. She felt like in a matter of hours that all of her hopes came crashing down around her. There was no mother, no family, no normal life to escape into. There were no agents, no safety to be gained. Emma's eyes filled with tears when she realized that Leader wasn't even impressed with Emma's attempt to betray the Guild. She was only frustrated and disappointed.

Waiting in the silence made Emma's mind wander to ridiculous places. She considered how simple it would be for a truck to come through and rear-end the Volvo while Emma sat in it. Her death could look like an accident, even to the people within the Guild. No one would know she had been murdered for a failed attempt at betraying Leader.

Scott. Emma's mind seized on him hopefully. He saw Leader in the school. He knew she was pissed.

On the other hand, if Leader could convincingly show devastation over Emma's death, maybe even Scott wouldn't think twice. They could grieve her—or not grieve, since that seemed the Guild way—and move on. She could be replaced in the blink of an eye.

A flash of scarlet on a white shirt made Emma's breathing shallow. Her head started pounding.

Anxiety, she knew. But she did not know how to stop it. Breathing exercises didn't work when her mind kept finding a thousand ways for Leader to kill her on the roadside and be done once and for all.

With a shuddering sigh, Emma unlocked her door. The soft ground met her feet as she jumped down. She considered heading the opposite way from where she saw Leader go, but there was nowhere to run. Even if

Emma could manage to get away from the Guild, she did not have a family waiting. That was a lie. Emma felt the photo in her pocket like it was on fire, taunting her. It had been the beacon of all her dreams for days! It had kept her awake at night and daydreaming in class.

Emma let out a disgusted breath, but she did not rip the photo out of her pocket like she wanted. Scott told her to keep it. Maybe he thought it would bring her some comfort. It didn't. It couldn't. All it was now was a reminder of how foolish it was to ever think about escaping from the Guild.

Running away was not a realistic option without somewhere to run to. Emma did not have a job, or a vehicle, or any acceptable social skills. There was no way she could obtain emancipation without a birth record or social security number. She did not even know if she had a social security number.

She couldn't very well take a stroll through the woods without Leader thinking she was trying to run away. Shivering at the thought of what Leader would do if—after everything Emma had already done—she made her chase Emma down, too. Leader was very unforgiving last time when Emma had only run ten yards.

Standing outside the car did not make Emma feel safer, though. A truck could still kill her if it came up from behind. Her vision darkened on the edges once more. She folded herself in half and forced herself to breathe slow and steady, so she could trick her amygdala into thinking she was safe—when she wasn't safe at all.

Emma crossed the street in the direction Leader disappeared. If Emma followed Leader's tracks, she could not be accused of trying to run away.

Leader walked lightly, but the ridiculous boots left small impressions in the ground that Emma followed easily. As she tromped through the woods, she had a spark of memory come to help calm her. She remembered walking through the woods with Leader when she was only a little girl. The woman hadn't been Leader then, of course, and Emma still thought she was the most beautiful, frightening woman in the world.

Monique walked beside Emma, showing her how to track prey and recognize disturbances in the underbrush. She focused explicitly on human tracking, although at the time Emma did not recognize it as such.

They came across a flower trying to grow under the roots of a massive tree, and Monique squatted down beside it. "This is true Diligence," she said, smiling warmly at Emma. "One day, when you learn to be quickly and completely Obedient, you will get to study the art of Diligence, and you will look like this flower."

Emma reached out a tiny hand and plucked the flower from the ground, tossing it away. "It's only a wildflower," she said dismissively.

The woman gave a soft laugh. "You say that as if being wild were some kind of flaw. Well, I'll tell you a secret, Little Girl: the wild ones are the strongest. It grows in the shadow of this giant oak even though everything else cannot live without the sunlight." She took Emma by the shoulders, shaking her gently. "It's like you. You're going to grow up strong and beautiful, but your only light will be hard to find. You'll have to stretch for it. Can you stretch for the sunlight?"

The five-year-old Emma smiled at the question and stretched up onto her tiptoes.

"I can't reach the sun," she pronounced after a moment. And, laughing, Monique grabbed Emma at the waist, hoisted her in the air, and held her high.

"You don't have to do it alone!" Monique pronounced. Their loud laughter frightened a flock of birds out of a nearby tree.

Emma walked now in woods similar to the ones she saw that day more than ten years ago. Her perspective of growing up without light was different now. Light was trust, family, and affection. Light was compassion and empathy. The light she wanted most was information, and she certainly *had* stretched for that on her own.

She nearly stumbled into the clearing where Leader stood before she realized she caught up to her prey. Leader was posed with her back to Emma, on the ball of one stocking foot, clearly in mid-form. Form twenty-three, Emma thought it was. A relaxation form. Emma stepped backward silently and watched from the edge of the clearing. It was impossible to look away from Leader when she did forms. Her movements were flawless and her method exquisite.

Leader turned with an arched block and a succession of three strikes. Usually when doing forms, there were required shouts given on the strikes and blocks, but not in forms twenty-two through thirty-seven. They were meant to be calming even though the moves were as deadly as any other form strikes. When she spun to face her direction, Emma felt a shock that redefined the word for her forever. Until this moment, she never felt real shock.

Leader had tears on her face.

Emma's world shook. Leader was the strongest of them all. She was the boldest. Leader was not human. She was not fragile and feeling. Shout, yes. Scold, yes! But Leader did not cry! Yet . . . Emma watched in growing alarm as the woman, eyes closed, completed the form in utter silence, but the tears sliding down her cheeks were unmistakable.

Emma was an intruder, walking in on Leader in this moment of absolute privacy. She wanted to walk away but she could not as much as avert her eyes from the cascade of tears leaking down Leader's cheeks.

Leader continued to the end of the form, spinning again to face the other way, striking and blocking, kicking higher than Emma's head. She landed in the alternative ending Emma had not yet mastered for this form. It was an awkward half-split, with one knee beneath her, toes against the ground to make rising quick and easy. The other leg was stretched in front of her, fists down near the ground but not touching as if they held weapons. She drew deep breaths from that position, faced away from Emma.

"I thought I told you to stay in the car," she said. Tears did not affect the authority in her voice.

"You didn't," Emma contradicted softly.

"It was implied." Leader rose from her crouch, sheathing imaginary blades in perfect formation, but remained with her back to Emma.

She let out a short breath of alarm and quietly said, "I'll go." She turned to walk away.

"No," Leader answered sharply. "Stay. Come here." Emma's Obedience was instantaneous, but her heart wished she dared to hesitate. Weeping and out of sorts was a side of Leader Emma feared to see. When Leader turned to face her, though, she was much more composed. All traces of tears were gone except a lingering glassy look to her eyes. She even cried beautiful! Emma had not thought that was possible.

Leader stood proud and silent, beckoning Emma closer when she halted several feet short. Emma took the last few painful steps until she stood directly in front of her superior. She expected anything from a slap across the face to the appearance of a weapon, but Leader only looked down at her, eyes narrowed in consideration.

"They must have had something really important if you were willing to risk my disappointment again." The words were ice. They made Emma's stomach drop, but she sensed the urgency behind the tone. Leader needed to know what the agents had offered her.

"It was all lies," Emma whispered in reply. "I should have known."

One thin brow rose. "You *did* know. You didn't want to believe they were lying."

Emma allowed that was probably true. She gave a single nod. "They promised to reunite me with my mother." She retrieved the crumpled photograph that was in her pocket. In her fingers, it felt warm like embarrassment and foolishness. Emma couldn't look at the image again. She handed the photo to Leader. "They said this is her."

Leader took the picture, smoothed it against her leg as Scott had, and studied it with a surprised smile. "Amelia," she whispered. "She looks young here." Leader looked up into Emma's face thoughtfully. "You do resemble her a little. I can see why the PICs thought to use her photo. I'm surprised they got a smile from her. She was kind of . . . well, never mind. She's gone."

Emma let out another breath, this one was pained. She imagined a lot of things about the woman in the photo but none of them included words that had to be edited from Leader's vocabulary. It was just one more agonizing detail that brought reality crashing through her dream.

"Scott told me he knew her as Leader. How did she die?"

Leader tucked the photo in the back pocket of her jeans and said, "She didn't. Her time in the Guild came to an end and she moved on."

Once more, Emma had a jolt of shock that could only be considered small in comparison with her most previous experience. The world seemed to tilt for a moment, and she reached out for Leader's arm in an effort to be grounded. Her voice was strained with shock, but she choked out, "She moved *on*? What does that mean?"

Leader made a sound that was half-sigh, half-groan. "Did you think *death* was the only way we moved up in the Guild?" She captured Emma's chin in a gentle hand. Her sigh was an apology. "Of course, you did, Little Girl!" She squeezed her chin gently before pulling away. She explained, "When Eric died," she swallowed and said, "*Leader*, you called him. When he died, the Guild Ascended. We all moved up to the next position. You were in Obedience, Number Twelve. Once he died, you became Eleven. Diligence.

"I know he told you about Lela-Cate, who died before you came on. How could you have had any idea that Ascension could be gained in a way other than death?" She sighed again and shook her head. "Death is the most infrequent reason we Ascend, Emma. When Eric was killed, that bumped us unexpectedly forward. He was Leader almost eleven years because every time he attempted to move on, the world around us began to fall apart and he couldn't bear to leave me with all those problems." She gave a snort that sounded almost amused and murmured, "That or he was ultimately too controlling to relinquish his hold."

Emma remembered that about him. He watched surveillance like their lives depended on it, which they actually did. She wondered if he hadn't died, would he still be with them or would he somehow have moved on as Amelia did?

"Where did Amelia go?"

Leader shook her head. "The Ascended Guild is above your Disclosure Level." As was everything Emma ever wanted to know.

"Amelia was Scott's first Leader?"

Leader nodded. "Yes. He was so tiny then. He probably doesn't remember much about her. He was only in kindergarten when she left. I remember, because I had to pick him up from school that day and try to explain to a six-year-old why his mommy was going away forever."

Emma's eyes narrowed slightly in thought, trying to imagine what that must have been like for Scott, barely getting to know his strange family, and losing a key player when he was so young. Emma did not remember much beyond her first day in kindergarten, but she remembered how tall Leader seemed when he waved to her from the front door of the house on the first day of school. She beamed at him proudly and he smiled at her—a smile Emma forgot about until this moment. She did not remember many smiles after that one. Emma couldn't imagine what she would have felt to lose him back then. However, being the cause of his death ten years later was perhaps more scarring.

Staring into the middle distance, Emma said, "I guess there's no chance she really is my mother."

"No," Leader answered with a slight shake of her head.

Emma's eyes slid shut and she gave a pained laugh, almost more of a scoff at her own foolishness. "I was so hopeful. So stupid."

Leader cupped her chin again and said, "How many times do I have to ask you trust me?" Her grip was almost painful, but her words were passionate. The passion in Leader's voice reminded Emma of that day in the woods, years ago, when they reached for the sunlight together.

"I don't know what to do, Leader!" Emma complained. "You promised me I wouldn't have to do this alone, but I feel like I reach and reach, and all you ever do is shoot me down. I just want a place where I really belong, with people who want me to be there." She pulled herself from Leader's grip, turning away to control her emotions, regulate her breathing. "I'm tired of being confused and scared. I just want to be normal."

"Hey," Leader said with soft insistence. She grabbed Emma's face again, turning her to look at her again. "You're *not* normal, Little Girl. You are complex and determined, and fascinating, and damned frustrating. You do not know what you're capable of, and I would never risk loosing you on the world until you do." Leader leaned until her forehead touched Emma's. "I know you must feel stymied every day when I hold you in this gilded cage, but I'm doing it for your protection and, furthermore, for the protection of the world. Whether or not you choose to believe that is figurative or literal, you're going to have to trust me."

"Why won't you just tell me what I want to know? Just tell me who I am and where I came from!"

Leader's fingers linked behind Emma's neck, holding her there in place, staring into her eyes from mere centimeters away. "You need to trust me," Leader insisted. They stood locked in that bizarre embrace for several moments while Emma felt anger give way to stubbornness and finally grudging acceptance. She did not want to, but she did trust Leader. And even if she chose not to, where would she go? What could she do about it? She had trusted outside the Guild twice and twice been in serious danger.

Leader stepped back and lowered her hands to her own hips. She studied Emma and sighed. "As for being alone, I don't know if you fully understand the definition of 'alone.' There are eleven other people in this Guild. If you're feeling alone, get outside of your head, out here into the world with the rest of us."

Emma heard the order, considered it, but rejected it. "Leader, I don't belong with the rest of you. Your dedication to the Guild baffles me. Scott's insistence on following the letter of the law infuriates me. Even Victoria, with all her sweetness, is so serious about everything that I can't relate with her about anything except schoolwork. I've tried to build a relationship with her, so she knows she belongs, but I honestly think she's better suited to all this than I am."

Leader smiled a slow smile and shook her head. "Oh, you are *so* sixteen," she murmured. The smile fell away and she pointed a finger at herself. "Listen to me, Emmalyn Stone. You belong to *me*. You belong with me. You may not have a traditional family with a soccer mom and parenting-magazine dad, but you have a family that suits you better than anything else ever could. You would not be here if it did not." Emma opened her mouth to speak. Leader held up a hand. "You belong to the Guild! You were made for the Guild."

Emma bit back her arguments and questions. Leader's pervasive passion insisted Emma shut up and process the words. When Leader saw that Emma was willing to be teachable, she went on in a milder voice.

"Let's talk about what this is really about: the day Eric died."

Emma shook her head, shutting down immediately. "I don't want to talk about that." She turned away.

"I'm sorry, but did I say, 'if it please your Highness?'" Leader demanded. "Get back here!" She pointed a rigid finger to the forest floor beneath her feet.

The dangerous tone called her back. The insistence. The predictable ferocity. Emma trudged back to face the older woman. Once she was in place, Leader spoke quietly, "You clearly decided from what you saw that day that I have no respect for life. It must have been extremely disturbing for you to witness a shoot-out. But then to see *me* completely unaffected by it must have devastated you." Leader pressed her lips together for a moment of contemplation. "You don't know what I know. You were innocent. I did not want to upset or frighten you more by making a scene, especially not when your boyfriend was lying on the pavement with a bullet in his head. On top of that, there were crowds of witnesses, emergency vehicles approaching, and Amos was in shock."

The memory swirled up in Emma's mind. Benjamin's snarl as his cover was blown. The appearance of a gun in his hand. He aimed as he backed away. And there was no time. No heartbeats. There was nothing except his fury.

The sound of two gunshots, within heart beats of one another, reverberated forever in Emma's mind. And she was tackled to the ground, shoved out of the path of a bullet meant to take her life. Pinned beneath the man who saved her by sacrificing himself. She never saw him alive in that moment. She did not see him rescue her or take the bullet. Everything was a blur of sound and pain and screaming as two people shot and two people died. Emma's eyes burned with the memory.

"I could not take my time mourning. The next and perhaps most important reason for haste and cool distance was Arrow Guild surely witnessed the shoot-out and was on its way. I was not about to further endanger your life or Amos' or my own, for that matter, simply because social protocol insists we mourn.

"This may not bring you any comfort or understanding, but there is a Guild Book edict that insists on swift succession in a violent Ascension. I'm sure you remember that I had Victoria enfolded inside Guild walls before we even crossed the state line."

Emma did remember that. The shock was crippling when Leader showed up with Victoria at the hotel where they were hiding overnight. She did not even know Leader left the hotel until she walked in holding the hand of a beautiful five-year-old girl sucking her thumb. Leader did not even introduce her before announcing, "We're moving out of state. Let's go." The devastation of all of Emma's pains and losses stood reincarnated in a little girl with spritely curls and a somber expression.

"You did not mourn him at all," Emma accused Leader. Words she never got the chance to say burst out of her now. They were like flames whose kindling had been piling up for more than two years. "You did not let any of us grieve. You said, 'Emma, you're in Diligence. I expect you to live up to that value!' as if that was all the acknowledgement Leader deserved after eleven years!" The flames licked higher as she recalled the horror of the weeks following his death. "Ilene was physically ill from the loss. And Lara, Adam, and Scott cried nonstop. But you, who spent years—*decades*—with him . . . You didn't bat an eye."

Leader gave a low snort and shook her head. "You know me so little."

From her pocket, she removed her keys. She held up the miniature barrel that served as her keychain for several years. "Eric was cremated. Most of his ashes are in an urn in the Guild Catacomb, but I couldn't bear to imagine my life without him every day. And so—against regulation—I kept this little bit of his ashes, and I carry it with me all the time." Emma stared in shock at the tiny urn. She never gave it any thought before. "You may not think I'm sentimental or that I have feelings, but I am as real as you." She tucked the keys back into her pocket. When she met Emma's eye again, her gaze was sharp. "I just *know more*, Emma. That knowledge is demanding. I don't have the luxury of pretending it's not, like the rest of you do."

Emma tried to imagine what it would be like to lose Scott. He was her senior in the Guild, as Eric was to Monique. If current processes resembled past, they grew up together. If Scott died tomorrow, Emma could not imagine how devastated she would be. And she and Scott had only known each other twelve years. How much more difficult must it be for Leader who probably knew Eric for decades?

Emma felt shame crawl up her spine for ever assuming Leader had no heart. "I'm sorry. I did not know you were even upset."

"I didn't want you to know," Leader insisted. "No one could know. Well, Amos knew because he's worked with me a very long time. And Julianne because she had to medicate me so I could function." Leader sighed at Emma's start of surprise. "I had to mourn in secret because someone had to be there to comfort the rest of you. Ilene, bless her heart, was barely more than a child. Way too disturbingly young for Eric, as I told him multiple—" She bit off her words and shook her head, letting her eyes slide shut for a moment as she tamped down whatever she intended to say. Instead, she said, "The point is, Eric was a part of the Guild and a part of me. I know it must have looked cold from your perspective, but if I let everyone see me cry, we would never have been able to carry on and do what needed to be done. I had to be stoic."

It made so much sense. Emma felt like an idiot for not seeing it earlier.

"Eric died for what he believed in, and as hard as it was on me, he made that choice with his eyes wide open." She stroked Emma's face gently. "He knew that you were of utmost importance. And he loved you dearly." Emma was stunned by the words and could not make herself believe them. Leader didn't pause to be argued with. "He sacrificed his life to defend yours. And I am grateful for that every single day."

Tears burned in Emma's eyes but she held them at bay. Leader shook her gently.

"If I let you disappear into idleness and doubt, Eric's sacrifice will have been for nothing. I cannot let that happen. The Guild has an important role in this world and you're part of it, Little Girl, for better or for worse."

Emma covered her face with her hands, shaking her head in denial of the ominous words. She tried to back away from the guilt, the shame, the overwhelming doubt that her life was worth the loss of his.

Leader grabbed Emma's hands and jerked them away from her face. "Say the things."

Emma Obeyed. "I'm a menace and you just keep insisting I stay on and be good. I can't even self-destruct like other kids because Scott throws away the cigarettes and if I punch kids at school, I get suspended." She knew she was rambling, but the words were as jumbled as her emotions. She had to get them out before they consumed her! "And now the cycle repeats! It's all happening again. My lack of Obedience killed Leader. My lack of Diligence killed Peterson."

"Emma, you are not to blame for Eric's death," Leader declared in a voice of insistent persuasion. "He made a choice. It was not your fault!"

"You said—" Emma began, remembering for the millionth time the words *"The Price of Disobedience . . ."*

"I was angry!" Leader snapped back. "I was irrational. I just watched the most important person in my life get shot in the streets. It made me furious, and hurt, and dangerous. I lashed out." She grabbed Emma's face again, drawing her near. Her voice dropped to a whisper as she admitted, "And I am so, so sorry."

Emma crumpled. Leader caught her and held her on her feet, against her shoulder. "Why did Waylon kill him? Why? I just lost sight of my responsibilities for one moment and . . ." She cut off, sobbing against Leader who, for a wonder, said nothing at all. She held Emma against her like she would never let go.

"All I ever feel is anger and devastation," she admitted on a wail.

Leader stroked her hair. "Well, you've had a hard life."

The admission of that truth made Emma's tears fall harder. She clutched at Leader for several long minutes. The woman did not let her go until Emma's tears subsided and she pulled away on her own.

Leader walked over to where her boots waited and pulled on first one and then the other. When she stood up straight, she said, "'Agent Peterson's' death had nothing to do with *your* behavior. I told Waylon to kill him quick and complete. I'm sure he came to you under false pretenses. Probably CIA; that's his routine." Emma blinked in surprise and Leader snorted. "He's so annoyingly predictable. He's one of the guys who attacked me in Beijing and managed to take me as a hostage."

Emma recoiled. They had *tortured* Leader! And Emma stood alone in a room with the guys. They could have done anything they wanted to her.

"Who was Agent Caldwell?" she asked but was afraid to find out.

Leader rolled her eyes. "Caldwell," she said in a scoffing tone. "Oh, very funny, Christopher." When she made eye contact with Emma again, she looked more serious than Emma had ever seen. "Caldwell was the name of the Atlantis file before I renamed it. He thinks he's so clever." She scoffed again. "He's Rogue. That's a PIC of the highest order. The Rogue Movement is organized, it's ugly and destructive. He wanted Atlantis because he thought he could do something with it he would never be able to do." Emma wanted to ask what but Leader's expression warned her off. "Christopher is the most dangerous man I could think of off the top of my head, and that's an impressive achievement if you think about how many dangerous men I know."

Emma swallowed. "I'll take your word for it."

"I hope so!" Leader barked in response to Emma's dry humor. "If he gets you alone after he knows I tampered with his influence over you, he'll destroy you long and slow as a message to me."

Chills climbed Emma's spine and she whispered, "He'll try to get his hands on me, Leader. I got the access codes to your satellite . . ." She avoided the arched look Leader shot her. ". . . but I refused to give them to him without payment first. He was a little put out."

"A little?"

"I didn't give them anything," Emma insisted.

Leader's expression became more arched than before. "You gave them hope." That was true. Emma did not try to argue but neither was she willing to look at Leader's face and see condemnation.

Leader reached over and grabbed Emma by the arm above the elbow. She propelled her in front of her. "Come on," she ordered. "Let's get to the safe house and see what damage has been done. I wasn't picking you up early so we could have a heart-to-heart. The Guild status just went to three, but I think with your information, I can safely say we're at two and we might need to go to one if I can't catch Christopher soon."

Emma went willingly enough. "Since we already had a heart-to-heart, does that mean we don't ever have to talk about my failed betrayal again?"

Leader snorted. "Oh, Emma, I think we'll probably talk about it frequently and with much spirit. It will be like: 'remember that time Emma went crazy and decided that she needed an extra-special lesson in the importance of Diligence?' 'Oh, yeah! Good times!'" She dropped her sarcastic cheerfulness. "Repeat after me, 'Diligence keeps me focused on my mission and saves me from murderous super criminals.'"

Emma did not repeat the words aloud, but she heard them reverberate in her skull.

When they broke from the woods, Leader released Emma's arm and clicked the unlock button on her keys. "Get in."

Once they were seated in the car again, ready to drive away, Leader looked at Emma and said, "You're under lockdown." She started the car.

Emma had no idea what she meant. For several minutes, while they drove down the winding country road, Emma thought about what it could mean. When her infinite number of guesses began to circle around again, she said, "Leader, what is lockdown?"

Leader shot her a stern look. "You wanted to be normal, Em. Lockdown is the Guild version of 'you're grounded.' And it won't be anything like the enjoyable good times of suspension."

Emma sighed and looked away. She couldn't really protest, considering she entered this vehicle today thinking she would emerge in a body bag. No punishment seemed too severe.

Chapter Forty

Leader's presence in the safe house ensured Emma toed the line. It was so much harder to misbehave when Leader might pop up anywhere. The safe house had been a large, two-story house from the outside, but inside it was similar to the farm, with its bizarre undefined rooms and scattered high-tech equipment. Emma got to know the place well as she scrubbed every corner and cranny. If her hand even strayed toward the equipment, Leader or Amos appeared to firmly return her to her work.

Leader did not let her anywhere near Stone University, but her studies were not allowed to wane. She was given a course load from Leader that, while not difficult, was exhausting. It was different exhaustion than Stone U, which actually challenged her intellect. Leader's academic workload was tedious and unending, but not very difficult.

For days in the safe house, Emma did not see Piper or Waylon. Waylon came down from upstairs on their third day, disheveled as Emma had never seen before, and clearly distraught. Leader met him at the stairs and led him into the office. They were in there several hours before he returned and went back upstairs. Emma wondered if his current state was a result of killing Peterson, but she did not dare ask.

Piper was an even more disturbing sight. She came inside from the back door five days after Emma arrived. She was so transformed that Emma recoiled in surprise. Her beautiful red hair was shaved off completely, and one side of her face was swollen from a serious impact. She had chapped lips and hands that were cracked and bleeding. The most startling thing about her though were the tears glistening in her eyes.

"Leader!" she called, ignoring Emma and Adam completely though the two of them stood transfixed by the horrifying sight of her.

Leader emerged, took one look at Piper, and said, "Come in here." She held open the office door.

Piper approached Obediently, but she snarled, "I hate you," in a bitter tone as she passed Leader. It did not seem to affect the dark-eyed woman. In fact, she shot Emma and Adam each an arched look to hurry them back to their work.

Adam shot Emma a concerned look. "Sometimes I have no fucking idea what's going on." It was possibly the mildest thing he ever said to her. Afraid to jinx it by speaking, Emma only nodded her agreement. Then Amos descended on them to put them both back to their respective chores.

Emma was exhausted and immensely relieved when they finally loaded into cars two weeks later and headed back to the Guild House.

"It's the only way to smoke him out," Leader told Amos within Emma's hearing.

Emma rode home with Amos, who spoke cheerfully, as usual, though Emma could see his mind was preoccupied. Piper rode with Leader, a position Emma did not envy. Adam and Waylon followed them in the Charger. For a wonder, Waylon allowed Adam to drive. It was a solemn group that parked at home that morning and tumbled into the house.

Leader snapped her fingers at the floor and said, "Emma, vacuum these carpets." The mother of all groundings was not meant to end just because they were home. When Adam smirked at Emma's misfortune, Amos sent him to scrub the Mats downstairs.

By evening, the house was back to its former state of cleanliness, devoid of the dust it had accumulated in their two-week absence. Leader used the house-wide intercom to inform everyone they would eat dinner together. "Get cleaned up and get here on time."

After a shower, Emma set the table in an informal family setting with only one plate and set of silverware per place. Amos brought the serving containers to the table instead of serving the plates as he often did. This was going to be family-style, evidently on Leader's order, because Amos was not pleased to displace the centerpiece in favor of the platter of stuffed peppers. He fussed over the bowl of mixed steamed vegetables until Leader came in and declared, "It looks good, Amos. Leave it alone."

He glanced at Emma quickly, obviously swallowing his arguments due to her presence, and said, "Yes, Leader." Emma carefully hid her smirk behind the water pitcher as she placed it on the table.

Waylon arrived, cleaned up as Emma was accustomed to seeing him. He still had a haunted look in his brown eyes. He took his place, unfolded his napkin to place it on his lap, and then he sat in silence. Emma took her place at the end of table, far away but across from Leader. When Adam came next, he sat near Emma and next to Amos. That left the seat across from Amos, next to Leader, for Piper. When she didn't come, Leader got up and went upstairs to collect her. Emma strained to hear, but a murmur of low voices was all she could make out. Then Leader walked down the stairs with Piper on her heels. Piper looked better than before. She had a scarf tied around her head, and all traces of bruising were gone from her face. She wore her customary cargo pants and rock t-shirt, clothing Emma had pilfered from the laundry more than once this school year.

When they were all seated, Leader nodded at Amos, "Let's eat," she prompted and broke a cracker on her plate in standard Guild ritual. The dishes were passed around the table and everyone served themselves in silence. They ate in silence. Emma was slightly amused that Leader insisted on family dinner when there was so much tension in the House. Everyone came because they had to be Obedient, but they refused to interact as a rebellion against the order.

"I made a choice," Leader declared. Amos was the only person who did not look up in surprise. "We'll stay here until my Leadership term ends."

Adam let out a defeated breath. "Split like this? This year has been hell! I want to get back with Lara." When Piper smirked, he added, "And Scott." He, like Emma, was isolated from the two people closest to him in the Guild.

Leader nodded. "This has been a difficult year. I am tired with the split, as well. It's no longer necessary since our missions here are mostly complete. I purchased a big house in Stone Meadow Community. When Amos is done getting it ready, we'll move back in together."

Emma felt a surge of excitement over that pronouncement. Having everyone all together made the house seem crowded, and tempers spiked easily, but it was home. The only home she ever knew. Emma would be relieved to see Scott on a regular basis and be able to talk with him.

"What will that do to school?" Emma asked, realizing that she had been "Chandler" and Scott had been "Jameson" and they were considered enemies. If they suddenly moved in together, that would look suspicious.

Leader arched brows. "You're done with school this year. After an entire year wasted in idleness, Amos and I both feel that you could benefit from some time in the Guild House. If, at the end of the summer, we feel you are ready, we'll enroll you in a private school somewhere. Until then, I would like you to meet your professors." She jerked her thumb and her own chest. "How do you do?"

Emma exhaled slowly but didn't argue. She had not truly expected Leader to send her back to Slope Oak. The election happened when they were still in the safe house. Emma did not know the results, but she suspected that she won. If she returned now, there would be an entire student body furious with her for abandoning them at the polls.

She ate her food. Leader was an unbearable taskmistress, but Emma was not really in any position to argue about academics. Amos and Leader both clearly expected her to. They watched her with stern expressions, ready to pounce. She said nothing. She took a bite of her food and nodded at each of them in acceptance.

Piper glanced aside at Leader. "Do we get to go to Scott's graduation?"

"*You* don't," Leader replied crisply. Emma forgot Scott was graduating this year. That was over a month away still.

Piper's breath escaped in an exasperated sigh, but she too said nothing.

"Can I go?" Adam asked, as usual not worrying about breaking the tension in the room.

Leader considered him and nodded. "Yes, I think so. He'll like to have as many people there as possible. His mission this year was difficult, and he did not have as much support as he wanted. I don't want him to think graduating, which took thirteen years, was a waste of his time."

"Can I go?" Emma dared. It was a risky question, but it was worth it to her. She and Scott teased about graduation before, and she expected he would probably do something showy—like streak under his robe and flash the audience. She would not miss his prank for anything. He did so few.

Amos answered, "We'll see," but his tone suggested he doubted it.

Their meal was interrupted by a knock on the door. Leader held up a firm hand and rose silently to her feet. She removed the knife she carried on her person, tucking it against her wrist in a concealed hold. She placed a finger to her lips to indicate quiet as she moved toward the front door. Amos followed her, also on light feet, but he unsheathed his pistol. Waylon paled visibly, and Piper looked as if she could spit nails, but Emma and Adam just watched with disturbed interest as Leader approached the door and looked through the peephole.

"What the . . . ?" She sheathed her blade and wrenched the door open. Amos did not lower his gun, but he stepped to one side to have better aim and be concealed from view. Standing on the doorstep in his preppy clothes, carrying his car keys and a single rose, stood Scott. He only recoiled slightly at the sight of Leader's fury. He did not know there was a gun trained on him, but Amos lowered the weapon at a small gesture from Leader.

"What are you doing here?" Leader demanded.

Scott smiled like a door-to-door salesman and proffered the flower. "Good evening."

Leader took the rose and tossed it over her shoulder. "What are you doing here, Scott?!" Then she snapped at Amos, "Get Julianne on the phone!"

Scott held up a stalling hand. "I have my mother's permission to be here, I assure you, Mrs. Chandler."

At his use of Leader's alias, Adam and Emma rose with intrigued curiosity, coming closer to see Scott more clearly. What was he doing?

Leader crossed her arms on her chest and said, "Really? What is it exactly you have permission to do, 'Mr. Jameson?'"

Scott's grin was asking for trouble. "I would like to speak with Emma Chandler, if I may."

"No," Leader snapped. "What do you want?"

Scott's smile faded a little and he shrugged uncomfortably under Leader's glare. "I did not know Emma's mother to be so unpleasant," he informed them. Then he smirked. "But I can see now where she gets her temper." Amos snorted from behind them and even Piper chuckled.

Leader was not amused and her smile was not kind. "I'm losing my patience."

Scott lifted his hands in surrender. "Very well." He tossed his head slightly to get his hair out of his face and stood to his full height. "I am here to ask Emma to prom."

Adam busted out laughing, a sentiment in which he was joined quickly by Piper and Waylon. Amos stepped from the darkness with a smile and a murmured, "He has balls." He moved to the background, unconcernedly leaving this for Leader to manage. Not pleased with his lack of support, she shot him a furious glare, but it was Scott who received the full brunt of her fury.

"No! Go home!"

Scott stepped inside, placing a firm hand on the door to keep her from shutting him out. "Mrs. Chandler, I know you are probably extremely protective of your daughter, and I understand that sentiment completely. I am prepared to offer you an itinerary of the evening's events as I have them planned out, and I will have Emma home by midnight. I am a fairly respectable fellow, as well, and if your husband actually does call my mother, she will attest to my Obedient and well-behaved nature."

"Are you crazy?" Leader put a hand on him to push him outside, but Emma stepped up.

"You have a girlfriend," she snapped, at least as annoyed as Leader. "I wouldn't go to your prom with you if you paid me."

That seemed to amuse Leader. She stepped aside to allow Emma to eviscerate Scott with her words. But Scott, since he knew Emma's ability with words, had by necessity learned to be faster.

"I broke up with Chastity today. I was only dating her for my mission, and it's done, so I'm done. *You're* the person I'm taking to prom."

Emma felt a surge of anger at his presumption, but what she said was, "You broke up with that poor girl when her father was arrested, and her mother is abusing her? You're a horrible boyfriend!"

Scott rolled his eyes dismissively. "Come on, Emma! Chastity gets to be president by default since you unenrolled. That's all she ever wanted!"

Leader pointed to the car in the driveway. "Go home, Scott. You are not supposed to be here, and you know that."

Scott held up a finger at Leader, asking her to be patient. "You said I could take anyone I want to prom, Leader. You told Julianne to tell me I did not have to go with Chastity if I didn't want to. You said I can ask anyone. I want to ask Emma."

"You can't ask Emma! You're not supposed to be associating with her."

Scott looked discouraged, but he still tried to argue. "The mission is over. We're moving back into the same house. This is the only chance I will ever get to ask Emma out without people being like 'Ew, he's dating his sister.' The only redeeming quality of the Guild split is that we can go to prom together. It's making the best of a horrible situation. Leader, please!" His eyes were pleading and his hands clenched around his keys. He expected to be rejected, but he was hopeful.

Adam leaned down and retrieved the flower that Leader had thrown. He handed it to Emma. "I think this was meant for you," he said with a grin. Emma took it from him with a soft smile. Adam returned to the dinner table across the room.

"This was how you planned to do this?" Leader finally asked. "You planned to show up here and say 'Leader, may I please take Emma to prom even though I know I am not supposed to be associating with her, and against your orders I sat in the ladies' room with her for an entire class period?'"

Scott pulled a face. "Not at all. I planned to say, 'Good evening, Mrs. Chandler. May I please speak to your daughter Emma?' And then when you graciously agreed, since you're not really supposed to know me, I would say . . ." He looked past Leader at Emma. "Emma, I know we have had our differences this year, but I really like you. Would you like to go to prom with me?"

Emma did not know if she was supposed to answer but she certainly felt her objections had been satisfied. It was kind of funny, she thought, that he just showed up here hoping to be treated as an unrelated schoolboy looking for a date to prom. And she thought it would be kind of funny to come to the event with Chastity's Monez's ex-boyfriend.

Leader stepped into Scott's line of sight. "Emma is on lockdown."

Scott responded firmly, "That's not my fault. And I deserve this."

When Leader started to argue, Amos made an objecting sound in his throat. Leader turned furious, wide eyes on him. They said nothing, but they managed to communicate a lot to one another without using words. When Leader finally stepped back, scoffing under her breath and tossing her arms in the air, Amos stepped forward and took her place at the door.

"Young man, you can take my daughter to prom if she consents to go, but only to prom at the school and back here right after. No drives, detours, restaurants, movies, or anything else. Is that clear?"

Scott's bright smile returned. "Yes, Mr. Chandler."

Leader looked at Emma. "This doesn't change anything. You're still on lockdown and I will expect you to breathe, sleep, and eat Diligence."

Emma nodded. "I will." She looked at Scott and nodded. "When is it?"

He smiled. "For someone who won Student Council President, you sure are out of touch with school activities." Amos cleared his throat and Scott hurried on. "Prom is next weekend. I'll be here at seven." He took a step back as if to leave, but then halted and added, "Thomas told me to let you know I will be wearing a black tux with an ice-blue vest and tie."

Emma nodded. "Okay." She was excited, suddenly. There was something to look forward to in her life other than the end of summer and the possibility of private school.

"Young man!" Amos called after Scott turned and whistled his way back to his car.

"Sir?" Scott said, spinning to look at him.

Amos flipped the porch light on then pointed at his eyes with two fingers. "I'll be watching you," he promised.

Scott stifled a chuckle. "I have no doubt about it, sir."

Amos stood on the porch until Scott was safely in his car and on his way down the road. Then he stepped in and pointed a firm finger at Emma. "That goes for you, too."

She nodded. "Yes, Amos."

Then Amos smiled. "We need to get you a dress."

Leader stepped in then. "No! She is under lockdown and for no silliness will I allow her to leave to pick out a dress and shoes. I'll go shopping in a couple of days and I will pick something." She pointed back to the table. "Go eat!"

Emma immediately Obeyed. Amos scowled but also returned to the table. Leader grabbed her phone from her back pocket, clicked one button, and walked away up the stairs. Once she was safely gone, Emma smiled to herself. Prom with Scott would be fun. There was no other circumstance in which she would have wanted to attend a prom.

Chapter Forty-One

The dress Leader delivered to her room the night before prom had tags in French and was clearly marked from a little shop in Paris. One tag indicated that it was made to order and rushed. It was a light-blue chiffon, floor-length strapless dress with black beadwork across the fitted bodice. It included black heeled designer shoes with similar beadwork. Emma looked the outfit over with amusement as she thought about Scott's assertion that they flaunted their wealth. This dress could not have been cheap.

The evening of the prom, Leader came into Emma's room carrying a black box from which she drew a diamond necklace. "If you're going to do this, you may as well do it right," she said, clasping the necklace around Emma's neck. She also slipped a bracelet and earrings into her hands and said, "I'll do your hair."

Emma, wrapped in a towel from the shower, sat in front of the vanity in her room, holding the jewelry in her hand while Leader carefully and deftly arranged her hair in an up-do.

"Are you nervous?" Leader asked.

Emma thought about it. "No, I don't think so. Should I be?"

"No. You know your forms. If Scott tries to get fresh, you can smash him up, so he never forgets."

Emma pulled a face. "Ew. I think that's enough friendly chit-chat for the night."

Leader smiled at her discomfort. "You realize you're showing up to a school of kids who voted for you and now hate you because you inflicted them with Chastity for another year."

Emma considered that. "It's *senior* prom, so most of these kids won't even be here next year. They don't care about Student Council."

"You tell yourself that, if it comforts you," Leader teased.

Emma lifted one innocent shoulder. "Well, if there are problems, I do know my forms and I can smash people up, so they never forget."

Leader's expression was doubtful. "I'll be watching on surveillance, Emma, so I don't suggest doing anything to get you into more trouble with me."

"I won't," Emma promised. "What could I possibly get away with when Scott's standing over my shoulder?"

"I don't know . . . Smoking, lying, idleness, bullying, going to outside sources for information . . . Shall I go on?"

"No, ma'am," Emma pouted back. "I will be good."

"And Obedient," Leader prompted. She tapped the bracelet. "I had Amos trick this out to send or receive messages so you don't have to carry your phone. He'll show you how to use it." Emma picked up the bracelet and studied it closely, seeing in the silver a place where she would see messages when they were sent. While she was looking, it flashed **Chin Up** in tiny script that appeared like an inscription but disappeared right away. Emma shot her head up to look at Leader in the mirror. Leader waved her phone. "See?" she said. "I only have twelve characters max, and your responses are even fewer, but it will do for tonight."

"Are we expecting trouble?" Emma was concerned.

"No more than ever," Leader said, pinning Emma's hair into place. "So, yes." She grinned. Emma rolled her eyes, an act that earned her a light smack on the head with the brush. "Hold still."

Leader finished her hair, painted her nails, and zipped Emma into her dress. Standing in front of the mirror, Emma hardly recognized the reflection as herself.

"You look beautiful," Leader said softly. Emma smiled up at her.

"Thank you, Leader. I love the dress."

"Paris does evening gowns right," Leader shrugged and walked to answer the tap at the bedroom door. It was Adam. He wolf-whistled when he saw Emma, earning him a clout to the ear.

"Scott's here," he announced, rubbing his ear with a glare for Leader.

"Good," Leader said as she stepped past him. "I'm going to give him his orders." She pointed back at Emma. "Don't leave here without Amos showing you how to work that bracelet."

"Yes, Leader," Emma acquiesced. When Leader walked off, she beamed at Adam. "I look pretty," she bragged at him, presenting herself with the flourish of a hand.

He pulled a face. "Less ugly," he countered and then grinned as he walked away. Emma glared at him, but she suspected he was only teasing.

Emma got to the stairs before Amos caught her. He started his explanation, then halted when he noticed her.

"Don't you look beautiful?" he said sweetly and kissed her on the head. Then, abruptly, he returned to his explanation of the bracelet. It only had a couple of quick responses; yes, no, and the like. There was a laborious process for forming words, but she was also restricted to twelve characters. She did not think she had needs outside of yes and no.

Amos informed her that Leader would be the one on the receiving end of the bracelet communication all night. "Just, whatever you do, don't ruin this night by defying even Leader's most benign orders. She did not want you to go in the first place and I put my neck out to allow for it."

"I'll behave as if you were watching my every move," she answered sweetly. He scowled at her.

Scott was in the parlor with Leader, nodding along with her brusque instructions. When Emma descended, his attention was diverted, and he smiled brilliantly. Leader hit him in the ear.

"Pay attention to me when I am talking to you!"

Scott sighed. "Leader, I know what you're worried about. This PIC character could be anywhere and if I spot him at any time, I am to immediately notify you via . . ." he removed his phone from his pocket. ". . . phone and get Emma to safety. I will maintain my cover and be good all night. And I will have Emma home by midnight."

"Eleven," Leader countered.

Scott sighed. "Eleven it is. Can we please go now?"

Leader let out a frustrated breath, but she leaned forward and pinned a boutonnière to his jacket. "Be careful." Amos grabbed Leader's shoulder and pulled her away from Scott. Leader went willingly, making it seem almost as though it had been her idea to recede.

Emma retrieved her shawl from where it was draped over the back of one of the parlor chairs, slipped it over her shoulders, and walked to the door.

"Home by eleven," Amos repeated firmly.

"Yes, sir," Emma agreed. Scott opened the door and held it for her. Emma nodded back at Amos and Leader and walked out.

Once they were in the relative privacy of the front yard, Scott said, "You look hot."

Emma laughed. In her best mockup of a southern accent, she said "Oh my, Scott Jameson, you do have a way with words."

He shrugged unconcernedly and opened the passenger door for her. She climbed in, arranged her skirts carefully, and he shut the door. She had never ridden in the Audi before. It was Thomas' baby, and he was very possessive of it. When Scott got in, Emma said, "How'd you swing Thomas' car?"

His eyes gave her a mischievous twinkle. "I went over his head and asked Julianne. It went like this: 'People will be expecting me to show up in a limo, but there's not enough time for Amos to get one or to look one over. But I can't show up in my regular car! That would be pitiful, and Emma's already gotten enough crap this year from these Bible thumpers.' And then I put on my best charming smile. 'You know who has a perfectly respectable car? Thomas. Since it's a one-of-a-kind, I don't think it would be looked down on.'"

Emma looked at him doubtfully. "And that worked on Julianne?"

Scott shook his head. "Not at all. But I begged her, and then I begged Thomas, and after a *lot* of talking, he said I could drive it under some conditions. I am not to let a valet driver within even ten feet of the car, and neither of us are allowed to have liquids or food of any kind. He gave me an exact number of miles that I am permitted to go, which he clocked earlier today. I'm pretty sure if I go even a tenth of a mile over, he'll skin me alive. And God Forbid we get rear-ended or someone in the parking lot puts a ding in the door."

Emma laughed. "It's going to happen now, because your life is on the line."

"Pessimist."

Emma was pleased when the car did make people turn heads. Even though they had to park it in the lot themselves, as far from other cars as possible, and walk the long way to the school doors, Emma was glad he managed to get Thomas' car.

Emma expected not to have to see Chastity at prom, since she was not a senior until next year, but she was at the entrance taking tickets with several other committee members. When she saw Scott and Emma approach together, wearing similar colors, she glared spitefully.

"What are you doing back here?" one of her committee cronies asked.

Emma gave him a quizzical look. "What does it look like? I'm coming to prom."

Scott withdrew two tickets from his pocket and handed them to the boy. "Here you go," he said cheerfully, evidently oblivious to the hatred with which he received by his ex-girlfriend and former friends.

The young man took his tickets and waved him through the doors with a disgusted scoff.

Behind them, Emma heard Chastity say, "He gets what he deserves, showing up with that hussy." Before Emma could turn back to confront her, Scott grabbed Emma's hand, smiled at her pointedly, and jerked his head in the direction they were to go.

"It's not worth it," he prompted. Emma nodded once and walked beside him. He did not relinquish her hand until they walked through the doors to the main party. The decoration job had Chastity written all over it. It was exquisite and precise. There were lots of twinkling lights and balloons everywhere. The photograph corner had white benches and an array of flowers that could have served a wedding. Emma could not help chuckling when she saw the room so decorated brilliantly.

"What's funny?" Scott asked, leaning to be heard over the loud music. They had a live band playing on the stage at the back of the room.

Emma shook her head. "It's just . . ." She motioned around the room. "Election processes are clearly not about who is right for the job. I could never have done this."

Scott looked around and smiled at the thought of Emma trying to pull this off. "Well, her world is very small."

Emma looked up into Scott's eyes. She had missed him! He was the same annoying boy she always knew with his utter loyalty to the Guild and dark secrets in his eyes he was unwilling to reveal. He was her very best friend.

"What was your mission?"

Her words caught his attention. He turned his soft blue eyes on her.

"Want to dance?" He changed the subject gracelessly and led her onto the dance floor.

"You can't even tell me a little bit?" she begged. He turned to face her, hand at her waist and the other open to receive hers. She reluctantly gave him her hand and allowed him to pull her into the dance. They danced well together, but then they had always fought well together, and it was much the same thing, in Emma's opinion. The difference was that she had to submit to him while dancing since he was in the lead. While fighting she would never, ever submit.

After some time enjoying the dance and thinking about the simple steps required for school dances, Emma looked up at Scott again. "Can you at least tell me why you dated her?"

Scott raised one brow at her, but he sighed and finally admitted, "I had to get close to her father. I worked it from the Chastity angle and Waylon from his job side. Waylon actually made the most progress, but I managed to be in the right place at the right time to catch what I needed. Thomas called in the police and the guy was jailed the next day during Bible Study. It was simpler than I expected it to be, but it took a lot longer than any of us planned."

"Who is he?" Emma asked. "Arrow Guild?"

Scott shook his head. "No. No Guild. Just a regular bad man. I don't know much else. It's not like Julianne sat me down and explained the whole thing to me. She just said, 'Do this' and I did it."

"Well, that's the nature of Obedience," Emma replied. "You don't have any idea why the Guild would concern themselves with a regular bad man?"

"No," Scott replied. "But that doesn't even matter to me. What does matter is how your opinion of me was so low that you thought I was doing everything just to be a jerk. If you hadn't turned Chastity against you on your first day here, we might have friends this year instead of pretending to be enemies. Did you think of that?"

"All the time. There were even a couple times I considered making nice just in the hope that I would be invited to eat lunch with you. But I really did start to wish bad things on her, and all that energy would have been wasted if I simply made up with her."

Scott gave a snort. "Yeah, it would be a shame to waste that energy!"

The music changed, and Scott slowed their speed, moving both hands to her waist. Her hands went to his shoulders. A buzzing on her wrist announced a message: **Sct kp Dstnc.**

"What is it?" he asked.

"Leader wants you to keep your distance. Evidently, your change in hand position alarmed her."

Scott smiled and softly said, "I am being extremely respectful, Leader." He did not change hand positions. Then, he looked into Emma's eyes and asked, "Did you two make up?"

Emma lifted a shoulder. "I don't know. Maybe. I told her everything, and she didn't kill me. Apparently, she does not kill the people in her Guild."

"Seems like a sensible provision."

Emma rolled her eyes. "She also told me I'm selfish and to get out of my head."

"I second that motion."

"I don't really *like* anyone out here," Emma replied with a shrug. "I guess that's the trouble. You are almost the only person I tolerate. And I do only *just* tolerate you."

"Oh!" Scott crowed. "Let's play 'Who does Emma hate?' I'll go first! Amos?"

Emma shook her head and gave a tiny smile. "No. Amos I like."

Scott lowered his voice to a conspiratorial whisper. "Are you only saying that because he's watching?"

"No," she replied in mock anger. "Me and Amos go way back. I had a relationship with him before I even stopped wishing you would get hit by a bus."

Scott laughed. "All right, so Amos you like. You *tolerate* me. Leader?"

Emma made a thoughtful sound. "Leader and I have a love-hate relationship. I do think she cares about me, and I would certainly be upset if she died, but most of the time she scares me half to death."

"I think that's part of her job description," Scott agreed. "Okay, let's do the good ones. Julianne?"

Emma scowled. "I like Julianne. She's not completely detestable like a lot of you."

"Okay, then it must be Adam!" Scott pounced. "You hate Adam!"

Emma refused to answer. Scott pulled back from her slightly. "Really? I *love* Adam! He's the bomb!"

"Yeah," Emma agreed doubtfully. "The bomb that knocks down a building!"

Scott laughed and shook his head. "He grows on you."

"Like cancer," Emma agreed.

Scott's laughter slowly died. "Okay, so you hate Adam. Thomas?"

Emma shrugged. "I don't know. He's pretty distant from the rest of us."

Scott scoffed, "'Pretty distant.' This from the girl who tried to run away from us."

Emma seized on something else, "Also, he's gay."

Scott's mouth dropped open. He lowered his voice, no more amusement in him. "You did not just say that, Emma! First of all, I don't think Thomas *is* gay, and also, you can't predicate your dislike due to sexual orientations. That's homophobic and gross. Veto!"

Emma smirked at his scandalized tone, but her stomach squirmed at his disapproval. Still, she pressed on, "You can't just veto my feelings because you don't like my answers. "

"I can veto because you're being a bigot." Then his voice dropped to deeper seriousness. "It's not really because he's gay, right? Because we can't be friends if that's your reason."

Emma looked at him, doing her best to appear serious although she felt lighthearted. "Are you coming out of the closet to me right now?"

"No!" he snapped, backing away to look at her seriously.

She smirked at his discomfort. "That's a pretty violent reaction from an advocate," she scolded him. When he was back into dancing position, she smiled and said, "I guess Thomas is all right. And, no, of course I would not base my decisions about people on their sexual preferences."

He pulled her close and insisted, "Emma, sexual orientation is something too big to joke about. Really. You might be straight as an arrow, but you need to be understanding of others' experiences. I really *can* only be friends with advocates."

She swallowed and nodded at him. "I shouldn't have joked about it." But more than that, Emma needed to think about this because she didn't understand sexual orientations except her own—if she even understood her own—and it had always made her a little uncomfortable.

"No," Scott agreed. "You can't be homophobic, Em. Leader will beat that shit right out of you." Emma nodded solemnly.

Her bracelet flashed, *Truth.*

"Sorry," she told him and Leader both. "I'll work on it."

"So, what is it really about Thomas that's off-putting?"

She shrugged. "I don't really have a relationship with him."

Scott leaned toward her. "Because you're in your head."

"Probably."

They danced in the quiet and Emma thought about it. The only person in the Guild she truly despised was Ilene. Even Adam had his moments of okay-ness. Ilene clearly hated Emma for no reason Emma could understand. And Emma did not think it was a mistake that Scott skipped over her in his rundown.

"What about Piper?" he wanted to know.

"She's all right."

"Waylon?"

"Growing on me."

"Lara? Please tell me you like Lara. She's super sweet."

Emma nodded. "Lara I like, and before you say anything about Victoria, I like her, too. In fact, besides Amos, I like her best. She's not jaded yet like the rest of you obnoxious asses."

Scott nodded in satisfaction. "All right, so, basically, you're saying you like more people than you hate. You may actually be human, after all!"

Emma jerked away to look into his eyes. "Was there a debate going on about that?"

Scott glanced toward the back wall where someone had tried unsuccessfully to cover the graffiti that declared **Emma Chandler is a snake!** She rolled her eyes.

Scott led her to get some punch. After one swallow of his own drink, he confiscated hers and dumped them in the trash. "Spiked," he said by way of explanation.

"Way too sweet," she replied.

Chastity approached Scott and demanded, "I need to talk to you."

Scott presented Emma and said, "I'm on a date."

The Student Council President leaned in closer and hissed, "That's what I need to talk to you about."

Scott looked askance at Emma. "I can't talk right now." He reached out a hand for Emma's in a peremptory order to come to him. She Obeyed, taking his hand and stepping up beside him to face her former rival. Chastity was not at prom as an attendee, but as a representative of the Student Council. Still, she looked plenty beautiful in her simple purple floor-length gown with wide straps. Her hair was only half up, held in a feathered clip. Next to Emma in her diamonds and designer dress, Chastity looked like a servant.

The girl ignored Emma, keeping her glare on Scott. "I need to talk to you."

"I can't talk to you right now, Chastity, and honestly, I have nothing else to say," Scott answered and pulled Emma behind him as he turned to walk away.

"I don't understand what's wrong with you, Scott!" Chastity cried after them, turning several heads. "How can you bring *her* back into this school? She's a bully and a hateful, horrible person. She should never be allowed to walk into this school again."

Scott released Emma's hand and walked back to Chastity with an angry stride. "You don't know anything about Emma. You built a prejudice based on *one* conversation with her. Even though Emma has stayed away from you, dropped out of school to allow you to win the election, and even gone out of her way to be kind to you, you have continued to be nasty to her."

Scott held up a hand at the approaching boys who were formerly his friends. "You all call her a bully and talk about her behind her back. I know she started this fight, but *you* turned it into a vendetta. You are not willing to let go of your prejudice and snap judgments."

One of the boys muttered a phrase. The only word Emma picked out was the word "Whore." Scott punched him without the slightest hesitation. Emma tried to intervene, but it was over before she could move.

"I'll get you thrown out!" Chastity screamed as she went to the aid of her fallen friend.

"You are a very little person, Chastity," was Scott's scathing response. "You are a sad little queen on your pitiful little hill. I told you when I broke up with you that I did not want to continue this charade as your boyfriend when the only feelings I have left for you are disgust and pity." He shook his hand, the one he had punched the other kid with, and backed away. Emma examined his hand as he went on, "Emma may be mean but as far as I'm concerned, she's honest. And that's damn attractive." He pointed at the kid who was trying to sit up, and he cowered back against the ground. "And she's *not a whore*!" He grabbed Emma's hand and stalked away.

Emma stared up at him in surprise. "You really think I'm honest?"

He scowled. "Where it counts. You just spent the year learning to be honest with yourself. I mean, you're never honest with the world. None of us are, but you backed out of that race when you knew you were the wrong person for the job. And you admitted everything to Leader that you intended to keep to yourself. And you're coming to terms with the fact that you're a bit selfish." She glared at that. He shrugged. "Don't worry. We all have that tendency." He smiled. "Admitting is the first step to changing."

Emma almost rolled her eyes. "I'll remember you said that."

Scott led her to the cloakroom to retrieve her shawl, but once they were in the hall, she spun to face him. "You defended me," she said exultantly. "They attacked me like they always do, and you did not just stand there and let them do it."

He gave her a pained look. "I had to abide by my mission. Until I had the information I needed, I had to stay in her camp, Emma."

"I don't care," Emma replied. "I mean, I did care, but I don't anymore." She turned back to walk beside him and she squeezed his arm. "You defended me."

He stopped beside the lockers and looked down at her. "I always will," he replied. "Missions are part of life, but I wasn't about to stand by and let her continue to attack you when you didn't deserve it. It killed me to stand by before."

It was quiet in the hall after he finished speaking. Emma looked up at him, studying him, thinking about how it must have been to stand by and watch her get attacked and not do anything about it. Sure, the first couple days had all been fun and games between them, but after that, Emma soured to the mistreatment, and Scott backed off. He stood by and watched every time the Student Council launched an attack her way. That must have been extremely difficult, especially during the race when no one he spent time with had good opinions of Emma.

"Where are you?" he asked quietly, staring into her eyes intently. "What are you thinking about?"

"You," she answered, studying his eyes. "I guess I more-than-tolerate you."

He slid his arm around her onto her back. "I more-than-tolerate you, too," he said with a smile. Then his smile faded and he stared seriously at her. She returned his look of concentration. He leaned and kissed her. For a moment, she was surprised by the act, but immediately after, her arms slipped around his neck, and she returned his kiss with passionate fervor. This was a moment she could live in forever.

Chapter Forty-Two

Emma's bracelet gave a slight vibration. She would have ignored it, but since it was on his neck, Scott backed up and looked at it with an annoyed expression.

"What does it say?"

She looked at it and saw the words **thats enuf**. She glared at it, hoping Amos put a surveillance camera in it so her displeasure would be known.

"Leader says 'that's enough,'" Emma informed him.

He nodded, but he was clearly as disappointed by the order as she was. "She's probably afraid of having another Adam and Lara on her hands when we get to the Guild House altogether again."

Emma pulled a face and backed away from him. "Yeah, they're annoying. Well, moment's over now for sure, especially once you start comparing me to Adam and Lara." She walked toward the cloakroom. He pursued her.

"I wasn't comparing you to anyone!" She shrugged and he growled, "I was just analyzing how Leader would react if this became a regular occurrence."

Emma looked up at him in mild annoyance. "You're analyzing *Leader's* reaction? Romantic," she said sarcastically.

Scott groaned. "That's not what I mean."

Emma arched a brow and slipped a hand onto her waist. "What makes you think this is going to become a regular occurrence? Do you think I am so easy to woo that the first time you kiss me I fall head over heels?"

He could read her expression now she was facing him. He saw she was teasing him, and he said, "Stop it." She felt a little thrill that she had gotten to him.

He shook his head and backed away. "Get your shawl. I'll go get the car and drive it up front and meet you like a real, proper valet."

She laughed at his back then drew a heavy breath when he was gone. Her heart was still beating at a rapid pace and her lips had the ghost impression of his. She could easily fall for Scott as she had for Benjamin so long ago. Benjamin had been a disaster. Scott was her best friend! Couldn't that also become a disaster?

Emma walked to the cloakroom, retrieved her shawl from the glaring Student Council representative, and walked toward the front doors to meet Scott.

The world is full of crazies, she thought. Everywhere she went there were people like Chastity who was desperate for affection to the point of dangerous reliance on other's opinions. There were people like Josie, who had no niche in the world, so she created her own. There were people like Peterson and Caldwell, who lied and went to deadly lengths to get what they wanted. And Emma understood all their reasons perfectly. But then there were people like Scott and Leader, Amos, and Waylon, who were all crazy in a way that baffled Emma. *How am I crazy?* She wondered if she was like Chastity and Josie or Caldwell and Peterson. Or was she, as Leader seemed to believe, crazy like the Guild?

She smiled to herself. It did not much matter. If she defied the disaster possibility between her and Scott, she could have a stronger reason to stay with the Guild. She could have more to look forward to than endless training and schoolwork. If she opened herself to him, really tried to be a part of his world, would the Guild still be the ominous, mysterious, hateful thing it sometimes was in her mind? If death was not the only escape, could Emma bear to follow the Guild trail to its top?

The car pulled into the drive-thru and she moved to the building door so she could meet it. Out there was her future and it might not be all bad.

But the door did not open. Confused, Emma tried again. When she turned to try and find a someone to help her, she saw Caldwell walking toward her, eyes trained and dangerous. Emma panicked. She remained still, but in her head, she screamed for Leader. She looked around and for the first time realized that the hall was empty. She ought to have noticed right away. He must have been planning this since she arrived. But then, how could he have known they would be leaving early?

"You okay, Einstein?" he asked as he approached. His voice was the same as it ever was, grating and sardonic. "I couldn't get to you any sooner. After they killed Peterson, your Guild buddies went into hiding and I couldn't track you until you returned to school. I have been waiting."

Emma was thinking faster than she ever had before. "I'm okay," she told him, making her voice cool and detached. "It took you long enough. Why didn't you come get me at my house?"

Caldwell shot her a dry look. "Peterson was killed on your street, Einstein. You think I was going to risk millions of lives by risking myself and your codes. You do still have the access codes?"

Emma would remember them forever, but surely Leader had changed them by now. "Yes. They changed but I got the new ones, too," she lied. She had to lie. She had just realized he would probably not kill her if she had something he wanted. He would wait until he got the codes.

Emma wished Scott would come in. She wished he would wonder why she had not met him yet. If he came in, she would not have to face this man alone.

"Well, let's go," Caldwell said, jerking his thumb toward the darkened hall off to one side. "I have a van waiting around back. We can be to a helicopter pad and out of the city in twenty minutes if we move fast. I have no doubt Monique is monitoring your position. If we don't move now, we won't get far and we'll both be killed."

Emma nodded in agreement, but she fidgeted with her bracelet, attempting to send a sequence of yes and no repeatedly so Leader, if she did not happen to be watching, would be alerted. Emma followed the PIC into the dark hall. The only light came from the doors at the very end of the hall that led outside to the lighted sidewalk. In the dark, she was afraid she would not be able to see the bracelet if Leader sent her a message, like **run**. But Emma could not run well in these shoes, certainly not to outrun someone with a gun.

Her bracelet flashed a single blue, fluorescent number: **29**. Caldwell saw it and snatched the bracelet from her wrist. The number had disappeared by then.

"What is this?" he demanded.

Emma thought hard. "I couldn't bring my phone to prom. They gave me a bracelet so I could receive messages. Leader just sent me the number of minutes I have until I am supposed to be home."

But the message was actually a covert reference to a relaxation form. Leader was telling her to relax. It was hard to relax when Caldwell was staring doubtfully at her and leading her away to a van where Amos had no surveillance. But she placed herself into training mind where complete concentration and a calm self were required.

Caldwell held the bracelet and walked on. "Let's go," he said urgently.

Emma forced herself to trust Leader. She wanted Emma to relax. Calm down. Did that mean she was on her way? Emma would bide her time.

The bracelet lit up again and Caldwell said, "203?" He looked at her pointedly with a questioning expression.

Emma calmed herself down completely, focusing on form two hundred three. She had learned it only this year. It was one of the hardest forms she had ever done because Leader was relentless that she do it in exactly the right way.

"It's a killing form," Leader had told her. "You will need it one day, so learn it well."

At the time, Emma never imagined a scenario in which she would ever kill another person. Right now, she did not think. She focused, she calmed, and she Obeyed.

Her first strike was to his throat. He wasn't expecting it, so it hit true. But Caldwell was not like other people; he did not go down after one hit from a little girl in a prom dress. He was trained, and he was powerful. Fortunately, her forms taught her to move quickly and automatically.

He dodged her second hit, knocking her to her back as he went, and she sprang up again. She ripped her dress to free her movements and was fast enough to kick the gun from his hand. It skidded across the hall, banging into the wall as it went. She dodged his strike and the hands he tried to hold her with. She became liquid death, sliding through his grip. Her force was then used to off-balance him. He caught his balance again and managed to shove her away from him. She hit the lockers and bounced back to him immediately. High kick to the head from form seventy-three missed but she spun into the cruise-dodge from form one hundred ten, spinning low on the ball of her foot. She swept his feet out from under him, and he fell heavily.

Emma stomped on his chest in the hope of doing serious damage with her shoes, but he turned enough that the heel grazed his side. By then, he pulled out another gun. She dove for the weapon, managing to throw his attack off just enough that when the gun discharged, the bullet flew beyond her and embedded into the wall above the lockers.

Caldwell swore at her, losing his concentration. But he was also stronger. He tilted the weapon toward her. Emma moved faster than she ever had and bit his hand until she drew blood. He loosened his grip. She tossed his second gun away.

He heaved her over but managed to hold her so she was beneath his weight. He punched her once, jarring her, but she had been taught to take a hit without losing her focus. Using her legs as leverage, she freed herself from his grip with a few deft twists and turns. She kicked him in the head when she managed to get to her feet before him. He grabbed hold of the remains of her dress, trying to drag her back down. She stomped on his groin when for a moment he failed to protect it. Fool.

He rolled onto his side, trying to get a breath to continue his defense, but Emma brought her knee down into his back, a move she had never paid much attention to from form eighty-seven. Without thought, without hesitation, she stomped on his neck in a maneuver from form ninety-four. It was not nearly as easy as Emma remembered from training exercises, but it worked. His neck broke under the force of her foot. He whimpered once—a sound Emma was certain she would hear in her head forever—and convulsed beneath her.

Emma backed away quickly to the resting place of one of his guns. She had only ever shot twice in her life, but she remembered the lesson. *"If you have a gun available, don't be over-confident and expect that it's all you need to kill an opponent. Too many people shoot first, hoping it will save their lives."* That was Caldwell's problem today: he expected his gun to save him. He should have known Emma would be trained to disarm her opponents. *"But don't be a hero. If you have a gun, use it. And don't shoot once, shoot twice. When we shoot, it's to kill. One shot is always for the head."* Eric—Leader—had given her those instructions the year before he died.

Emma approached her opponent, still expecting by some miracle for him to get up and attack her. She trained the gun on him, closed her eyes, and fired. Once. Twice. He was dead. *We shoot to kill.*

Thought returned slowly, but it came. She squatted and dropped the gun from trembling hands. Fortunately, the darkness concealed her victim, but Emma screamed. The logical part of mind knew that screaming would only result in campus cops or prom students rushing onto the scene, but her emotions could not be restrained. She screamed again, shrieking until she ran out of breath and her throat ached. She backed away from the man she killed, backed until she hit the lockers. She screamed again.

Then Scott was there. She did not hear him, but his hands were on her face, and he was speaking. She had never seen him so distraught. *He hates me!* How could he not, if he knew what she had done? He shook her once, trying to get her to hear him, but all Emma could see was the dark silhouette of the body in the hall. The body of the first man she had ever killed. All she could hear was the sound of the gun she had shot to make sure he was dead.

Light flooded the scene as suddenly the school police decided to do their job. Scott shielded Emma from the sight of the dead man on the ground, but she could still see him in her mind's eye. She saw his face contorted with rage as he had grappled with her for the gun. She saw his body rolling over in pain. She saw her foot on his neck. Emma screamed again.

The school police and several faculty members were there. Emma was vaguely aware of Principal Morley speaking to her and Scott. She was aware that she was being held in Scott's embrace as he moved her away from the body, away from the place where she had committed murder. She was only slightly aware of the fact that students were being physically held back from the scene by adults. One of the police officers was on a radio calling for the local police backup. This would be a day this school would never forget. And unfortunately, Emma never would, either. She screamed again, but her voice was hoarse, and it came out more as a desperate whine.

Leader stepped through the crowd like she owned them. The awe factor made people move out of her way, even the adults. She did have to pass over a badge of some sort when the police refused to let her near Emma and Scott. As she approached, she became all Emma could see. Leader was the reason Emma killed that man. What if she had meant something different? What if this had not been an Obedient act at all and Leader handed her over to the authorities? She started the fight with the intention of killing Caldwell. They would try her as an adult and send her to prison forever.

Leader pulled Emma from Scott's arms and encompassed her into her own. "It's all right, Emma."

"I killed him," Emma croaked out, fortunately in a voice too broken to be overheard.

"Shh," Leader prompted softly. "*I* killed him. It was my order. You were doing what you were told." Emma clutched at Leader, holding to her as tightly as she would a rope thrown over a cliff ledge. "Give it all to me, Emma. He would have killed you if you had not been Obedient. Give it all to me. All the fear, the pain, the regret, the shame, and the horror. Let me hold it. I'm really good at holding it."

Emma's grip tightened further, if that was possible. She buried her face in Leader's chest. "I don't know how," she panted. "I want to give it to you, but I don't know how."

"Do you trust me?" Leader whispered gently at her.

Yes, she did trust Leader. She made the commitment to herself to trust Leader when she had Obeyed the order to kill Caldwell.

"Yes."

Leader pressed something onto her tongue and held Emma's mouth closed when the bitter herb began to dissolve and demanded to be spat out. "Swallow it," Leader ordered in her authoritative tone. Emma forced the root down her aching throat. Almost immediately, her knees gave out and her eyes tried to close. Leader picked her up easily as if she was tiny child.

Emma's head began to clear, but she had to struggle to keep her eyes open.

"Get my badge, Scott," Leader ordered. "Let's go." She started toward the crowd, carrying Emma in her arms. Emma's eyes slid closed, but she forced them open again.

"You can't take her!" one of the officers declared. "We need a statement!"

"You can have my statement," Leader replied coldly, but only quietly enough to be heard by the officer and by Emma whom she was carrying. "Don't mess with my Guild."

That was all the statement they were going to get. And it was the last words Emma was conscious enough to hear. Words she would never forget, because she was a part of them. She was a part of Leader's Guild. If she hadn't been before today, she definitely was now. *Don't mess with my Guild.*

EPILOGUE

Emma awoke from her nightmare to find Leader sitting beside her bed in the desk chair. Emma sat up and let out a cleansing breath as Leader had taught her to do months before. She stretched her arms up above her head and took another deep breath into her lungs. After months of conversations and training sessions with Leader, thousands of exercises to combat trauma, and several very firm, very direct orders to release the guilt to Leader, the dreams seemed to be the only thing Emma held on to about the horrifying incident at the school.

"You okay?" Leader asked, studying her face with worried eyes.

Emma nodded. "I'm fine. Just another dream. I can't quite shake them."

Leader nodded. "I still occasionally dream of my first kill. Of course, I was several years older than you are, and better prepared." This was a comment Leader had made before and would probably make again next time Emma awoke to find her there. Somehow Leader always knew when Emma's dreams were of Caldwell.

"I'm fine," Emma repeated as she reclined once again on her pillows. And she was. Leader had told her about some of Caldwell's crimes, heinous acts that did not bear thinking of, and it softened Emma's pain over killing him. Her last bitter complaint against the kill order had been that killing was a crime, but to that Leader had said, "Not for me." Emma had been under orders. She was not responsible. Emma was never questioned by the police or brought in to make a statement. Except for the occasional dream, it was as if the horrible event never happened.

Leader rose from the chair. "Good. It's time for breakfast."

Emma shot up once more and demanded, "You let me sleep through training? I can't miss training!" Training was the only thing that had kept her alive.

Leader's arched brow was a warning against her tone and attitude. "We got in from the amusement park late last night. Everyone slept in, Emma. We will train after breakfast." She moved toward the door but then stopped and looked back. "If I wanted to skip training, it's my prerogative, you know. I am the Leader of this Guild and that means I can pretty much do whatever I want."

Emma smiled and even gave a laugh. "Yes, Leader, I know you are all powerful and all important. Would you like me to call you 'the big cheese?'"

Leader seemed to be considering. "Yes, I would," she finally declared, and turned and walked out with a very straight face.

Emma laughed again.

She jumped out of bed to dress for breakfast. Normally, the requirement was showers before breakfast, but since training was postponed, Emma only washed her face, brushed her teeth, and put on her training clothes before going downstairs. The tantalizing scents wafting from the kitchen sped her along. The table was already set by Victoria, who was present now filling water glasses. Emma squeezed her shoulder as she stepped up beside the child.

"Morning."

Victoria smiled. She was also dressed in her training clothes of purple stretchy pants and a white shirt. Emma wore black on black every morning now, but she remembered the days when colors had been as important to her as they were to Victoria now. Amos gave Emma her first training clothes when she was younger even than Victoria was now. They had been blue with butterflies embroidered up the sides. The first time she walked onto the mats, Eric—Leader—rolled his eyes at Amos and said, *"Really? Butterflies? Why not stamp a couple rainbows on there while we're at it?"* To which Amos smiled, ruffled Emma's hair, and said unconcernedly, *"Why not, indeed?"* That was Emma's third day in the Guild House.

"Good morning," Victoria said with a smile. "We go back to school next week."

Emma almost groaned but Amos shot her a warning look through the kitchen window, so she stifled the emotion.

"Yeah," she answered instead. "Are you excited?"

"Very," Victoria replied. "I'll be in second grade this year. I hope I get Mr. Dasher. He's the best teacher in the school!"

Emma strolled over to the window and leaned on it. "Can't you arrange for her to get the teacher she wants?" There were a lot of things outside of their control in the Junior Guild, and that made life difficult. Something as simple as a nice teacher could make their lives so much more bearable.

"Yes," Amos answered, passing a bowl of grapefruits through to her. "But Leader wants to let it happen naturally." Leader walked into the kitchen behind him as he spoke. He pretended not to notice her. "And since this is Leader's Guild, and she's feeling very powerful today, I guess we should let her stomp around and pass out orders like a tyrant."

"Ha ha," Leader said dryly. "Is breakfast ready?"

Amos turned and pointed a wooden spoon at her. "Not if you pester me. Blend those vitamins." He pointed the wooden spoon toward the three industrial blenders attached to the counter filled with daily vitamins and proteins. Leader agreed and did his bidding as if she had thought of it herself. Emma wished she could pull off following orders that way, but she suspected it came with the territory of being on top. Amos pointed the spoon at Emma. "Make a call: The last one to get down here is on cleanup for the rest of the week."

Emma smiled, mostly because she was already eliminated from the possibility. She crossed the room to the intercom and pressed the house button. "Amos says get down to breakfast now. The last one to arrive is on cleanup for the rest of the week. Over and out."

Adam was on the stairs almost before Emma finished speaking. He pulled a funny face at Victoria as he sat down, indicating relief that he would not be on cleanup. She giggled and, not for the first time, Emma wondered why he was always hostile to her when he seemed to be perfectly sweet to Victoria.

Thomas came from downstairs wearing full dress and clearly recently showered. He must have been up for training despite the "sleep-in" order. He glanced around the table but did not sit. After a moment, he joined Amos and Leader in the kitchen.

Piper and Lara arrived together. Lara was dressed in her black training clothes and her hair was already up. She squeezed Victoria's shoulders as she stepped past her to her seat at the table. As soon as she was seated, she spoke to Adam and the two of them began a quiet argument about something Emma tried not to hear.

Piper was subdued, as she always was these days. Her hair had grown in some, but she still wore a scarf most of the time, and she watched Leader and Amos warily. Unlike Emma, Piper had been shown no mercy. Emma could not understand what was so bad about speaking to an Air Force recruiter that it caused Piper to fall from Leader's good graces. Clearly, the rest of the Senior Guild understood, though, because even Julianne, as she arrived, shot Piper a sizing glance before joining the others in the kitchen. Piper did not go into the kitchen.

Ilene arrived next, and Emma was disappointed. She hoped Ilene would be last and be placed on cleanup duty. It would have been interesting to see someone in the Senior Guild scrubbing dishes as a punishment. Ilene also sized Piper up and then went into the kitchen to speak to the Senior Guild. Piper pretended not to notice, but she sighed.

The Senior Guild emerged from the kitchen together, carrying plates to place on the chargers at every seat. Amos went back for the last two and the entire Senior Guild was seated before Waylon dashed down the stairs. Leader glanced significantly at the clock on the wall and Waylon shrugged apologetically. He wore his workout clothes, too, but he was showered and styled—as always.

Scott came in no apparent hurry, earning him an arched look from both Leader and Amos. He ignored them. His appearance was the opposite of Waylon. He looked as if he had rolled out of bed to come to breakfast. His hair was a disaster and he wore plaid pajama bottoms and pulled on a white shirt before he approached the table.

"Good morning," he said cheerfully. He leaned over Emma's chair and kissed her softly upside down. "Morning," he murmured.

She could not help but feel a fluttering excitement when he spoke words for her ears only. He smelled very strongly of his own deep scent. It was the most attractive scent in the world.

"You look hot," she teased as she touched his uncombed hair.

He backed away and lifted his hands. "It's what I do," he said, pretending not to hear the mockery in her tone.

"Sit down!" Leader barked at him.

Amos pointed a stern finger his way and said, "Cleanup duty." Scott did not seem concerned.

The bread on Leader's plate this morning remained where it was for a moment while she looked around at her Guild. Amos reached over and squeezed her hand once to show his support, and suddenly Emma became alarmed. This was not just a regular breakfast or a regular day. She was not the only person who noticed it, either. The supportive gesture at the head of the table had drawn every eye. Even Victoria looked around with a puzzled expression, sensing the change in mood.

Leader was not a person to beat around the bush. "I gave Amos access to the Guild Books today." That meant nothing to Emma, but it caused a huge reaction from almost everyone else. Julianne drew a sharp breath and looked at her hands. Thomas turned his face toward the ceiling and closed his eyes. Ilene reached a shaking hand toward her water glass and drew it to her lips. Adam and Lara reached across the table to clasp one another's hands, although their eyes never left Leader. Waylon let out a long breath and shook his head several times. Scott nudged Emma with his foot under the table and widened his eyes questioningly at her. She shrugged. Victoria also looked confused. She turned to Emma as if hoping for answers, but Emma had none to give.

The most alarming reaction came from Piper. She had been holding herself erect as if the words meant nothing to her, but she suddenly folded herself over on her knees and wept. It was like watching a rock cry, and it shook Emma to her core.

Leader rose and placed her napkin on her chair. She went around to Piper, squatted in front of her, and took her hands in her own. She whispered words Emma could not hear, but it apparently brought no comfort to Piper, who was inconsolable.

"Amos," Leader prompted aloud, looking up at him. "Sleep tincture." Amos removed the herbs from his pocket and Emma stared at him. Realization began to settle. Amos had told her he did not have clearance to touch the stuff. He was holding it now as if he had every right. That meant...

"Ascension?" Emma looked pained at Scott. He nodded. He had seen the sleep root, too.

Piper pulled back from Leader, waved off the need for sleep tincture, and walked away from the table to pull herself together. Leader and Amos both followed her.

"God help us," Thomas whispered at Julianne. She glared sternly at him since his voice was clearly audible in the now dominant silence at the table. She rose from the table, reached over for the bread on Leader's plate and tore it into two pieces.

"Eat," she ordered the table. She walked away after making a jerking motion at Thomas to follow. After a moment, Ilene also went. That left the Junior Guild to themselves.

"What does it mean?" Scott demanded of Adam as soon as they were left alone at the table.

Waylon answered. "It means Leader is preparing Amos to take over. She's moving on."

Victoria grabbed Emma's arm. "Moving without us? Why?"

Emma patted her hand gently, and said, "No. Her time with the Guild is coming to an end and she's going to leave it to Amos. He'll be the new Leader. Leader never leaves the Guild." She tried to sound confident, but she felt boiling fear and sadness.

"Where will she go?" Victoria asked, tiny voice full of fearful misery.

"I don't know," Emma answered honestly. Where did an ex-Leader go to live out the rest of her life? Emma tried to smile at the little girl. "I hope you are extremely Obedient, because when Amos becomes Leader, the rest of us will ascend. You'll be in Diligence."

Lara sat up straight and whispered, "I'll be in Loyalty."

Waylon muttered, "Good freaking luck." That was not comforting at all. Lara paled slightly.

Emma shook her head. "We've misunderstood," she declared, her thoughts turning to Eric, her first Leader. "It's too soon. *He* was Leader since I was four. We must have misunderstood."

Waylon shook his head in denial of that. "*He* served for a dynasty. That's very unusual."

"A dynasty?" Scott asked.

"Anything longer than five years," Adam explained.

"Two to five years is fairly normal," Waylon went on. "Leader always goes when it's time to go, and only Leader knows when."

"I remember a couple of one-year Leaders," Lara countered.

Waylon nodded. "There have been several, but Leader assured me that's been a new fad because the work is getting more challenging." He did not seem even a little concerned. Emma felt sickened by the thought of losing Leader. She could not imagine the Guild without her.

"How can you not be more distressed?" Emma demanded of Waylon. "You're going into Senior Guild this Ascension."

Waylon rose and grabbed the water pitcher to refill his glass. "Are you kidding? I'm ready for some Disclosure! I've been waiting twenty years for some answers!"

Emma could not feel so nonchalant about Leader leaving the Guild.

Adam felt similarly. His eyes were clouded and he stared into the distance as if trying to imagine the next stage of his life.

"I'm scared," Victoria suddenly declared. Emma reached to comfort her.

"There's no reason to be scared," Scott answered a little more sharply than Emma liked. "This is the way the Guild is designed. Leader can't stay on forever. She's served us for as long as she can. And you'll be fine! You're a good, good girl, so I'm sure you'll find Diligence no harder than Obedience."

Victoria muttered, "Obedience isn't easy." Scott would have snapped a response, but Leader returned and the Junior Guild fell silent. She saw the broken bread and nodded, but then she noticed no one had touched their food.

"Eat," she ordered. She leaned through the door to the living room where Thomas, Julianne, and Ilene had gone. "Get in here and eat!" She returned to her seat.

Adam took a mouthful of food, but he watched Leader while he chewed, studying her. When he swallowed, he said, "What's wrong with Piper?" in a tone that sounded as if he was asking about the weather.

Leader shook her head as if she was not going to answer, but she looked around into the faces of the Junior Guild, and the now approaching Senior Guild, and said, "She's stacking up."

Adam nodded as if that made sense, but Emma pulled a face. "What does *that* mean?"

Ilene snorted. "I'm sure you'll get to know the sensation pretty well, Emmalyn Stone. Stacking up is when Ascension happens before you perfect your skill. When you move on, you have to learn and abide by both. It's what's going to happen to you if you don't learn very quickly how to demonstrate Diligence."

Emma bit back a retort even though she had several nasty ones in mind. Leader came to her aid. "I think Emma has demonstrated admirable Diligence this summer." Emma was pleased by the praise until Leader followed up with, "The real test will be when she's back in school." Emma scowled, but it was a fair analysis. Emma did have a tendency to slough off at school.

Amos returned then and communicated silently with Leader for a moment as he took his place. He seemed oblivious to the silence that descended at his approach. Emma was certain everyone was thinking the same thing she was: What would Amos be like as Leader of the Guild? Emma might have enjoyed thinking about it if it meant she would not have to lose the current Leader.

"Is there a timetable on this?" Thomas asked suddenly, looking up from stirring his food around.

Leader arched a brow. "If there is, it's none of your business." She pointed at his plate. "Eat your food." He sighed, but he ate. They all ate.

Although the food smelled divine, Emma did not taste it. She ate because Leader commanded her to, but her mind was on the possibility of living life without her in the Guild. She could not wrap her mind around it without feeling like she needed to cry the way Piper did. Emma stared at Leader, afraid her heart might break.

Three days later, on the first day of school, when Emma went downstairs to train, Leader stood on the mats in her business suit holding a briefcase. In all the years Emma knew her, Leader had never been on the mats in street clothes. There was no one else there, either, and the room was lit only by the few wall sconces. Normally, the Senior Guild was all on the mats by the time Emma got down there. The change alarmed her.

After Leader announced the Ascension, apparently nothing in the Guild House changed. Amos still jumped at Leader's commands, as always. The Senior Guild still met each morning for Summit before the Junior Guild was even awake. Nothing had changed until today.

"No," Emma said, dropping the short sticks she had carried in from the weapon room next door. "Not today. Not yet, Leader!" Emma wasn't ready to live without her.

"Come here," Leader commanded, placing her briefcase on the floor. Emma came, giving Leader her hands when the woman opened hers to receive them. "Emma, there are things for me to do. The Guild is like . . ." she floundered for a metaphor. ". . . an incubator. Once you're fully developed, it's redundant to stay. I'm developed. I have to go."

Emma shook her head. "But not today."

"Today," Leader replied firmly.

Emma felt tears coming, and she hated them. She jerked back from Leader's grip. Anger was so much easier than grief. "You're just a coward. You're just leaving because things were hard this year, and you don't want to have to deal with it anymore." Emma felt anger building. "Or maybe

I'm too hard for you to handle and so you're just going to pawn me off on someone else! 'It's too hard to deal with Emma, so I'm just going to leave!'" She shoved Leader with all her might, hoping to push her down, push her away, prove to herself that Leader was weak and insignificant, and she could live without her.

Even in six-inch heels and a business suit, Leader was superior to Emma's skill. When Emma moved toward her, she grasped her and twisted Emma around until she was pinned tightly against her chest. She had Emma in a headlock before she could make another move. Emma was like a toy to Leader. She could do whatever she wanted with her.

Emma cried when she realized that all her fighting would not make Leader stay. She sagged against Leader's hold, allowing the superior woman to hold her up. "Don't go, Leader," she begged, even knowing as she said it that it would be denied.

Leader held Emma tightly and rested her cheek on top of her head. She said nothing. They both knew how this was going to end. Leader would leave and Emma would Ascend. But Emma had to plead for her to stay because she did not know how to live without her. This woman had been in her life since the very first day in the Guild. She had been her parent, her disciplinarian, and the scale against which Emma had always measured herself.

When Emma regained her composure somewhat, she pulled out of Leader's loosened grip and stepped away. She folded her arms and drew long breaths to calm herself down, but she kept her back to Leader.

"Take care of Victoria and the new Number Twelve," Leader instructed. "He's cute. You'll like him."

Emma turned her head and peered back at her. "You know who he is?"

Leader's face did not change, but her eyes twinkled. She gave no answer. "Show real Diligence in school this year and maybe Amos will let you graduate so you don't have to return for your last year. I know you hate high school." That was true. This year would be even harder, she thought, since Scott had graduated and would be going on to college. Emma would be alone.

"Promise me you will trust Amos and you will stay inside the Guild," Leader ordered, her voice becoming stern and very serious.

Emma spun and gave her a haughty look. "What point is a promise to you when you're getting ready to leave forever?"

Leader cocked her head to one side, peering at Emma. "Oh, I'll be watching you. Don't think I won't."

That brought Emma comfort and unease at the same time. She glared at the woman but knew better than to ask any questions. Leader raised a stern brow and Emma relented.

"I promise. I will trust Amos and stay in the Guild. I already promised Scott I would turn to him before I try to go outside the Guild again."

Leader nodded in acceptance of her word. She collected her briefcase and stepped toward Emma. She touched her face with a gentle hand.

"I can't imagine life in the Guild without you," Emma whispered. "I keep trying, but I can't. The idea that I will never see you again sickens me."

Leader cupped her face, staring hard into her eyes. She smiled and winked. "Be good," she told Emma with so much affection that she felt desperate to keep her there.

Leader raised her voice slightly. "She's all yours." Emma turned to see that Amos joined them in the doorway of the room. "Don't take your eyes off this one for a moment."

Amos gave Leader a sad smile, but the look he shot Emma was a challenge. "I won't."

Leader stepped back. Emma reached for her. "No," she said urgently. This could not be all. This could not be the end. Emma couldn't bear it.

The woman studied Emma with beautiful dark eyes and looked deeply into her face as if memorizing her. Then she leaned and kissed her. There was real emotion in her voice when she said, "I love you, Little Girl." And with that, she turned and strode away, heels clacking on the tile at the edge of the mats. Emma's heart was full near to bursting because she truly believed her.

Leader paused beside Amos to hand him her keys and phone. She kissed his cheek but did not meet his eyes.

"Good luck, Leader," she said and walked out the door. Emma slid down onto her knees, hands over her eyes, and wept.

The End of Book Two

Coming Soon!
Confidence: The Guild Book Three

Thank you for reading *Diligence*! If you're left wondering what's next for Emma, you won't have to wait long. *Confidence,* the third book in The Guild series, is releasing soon!

Sign up for the newsletter at linktr.ee/nicholemwillden to be among the first to know all the details.

Enjoy the Guild? You can make a BIG Difference!

Reviews are the fastest and best way to get attention for my books. Let's face it, reviews and stars matter, and most people (me included) make choices based on feedback. I may not have the force and flex of a major advertising agency, but I do have something valuable:

A loyal bunch of readers!

Your honest review of my book will help bring it to the attention of other readers.
If you enjoyed this book, I would appreciate the gift of your review.
Please spend a couple minutes leaving a review on the book's Amazon or Goodreads page.
Thank you so much for helping me spread the word of The Guild. (Please disregard the culty feeling of that last sentence.)

Acknowledgements

Thank you, Readers! I know Emma is a lot, especially in this book. *Come on, Emma! Seriously, expelled a hundred million times in one book?* She's exhausting. But thank you for your Diligence in reading all the way to the end. You're a rock star!

Next, I must again acknowledge that I in no way condone or support child abuse. Nor do I think Leader, or any other person, has the right to verbally, physically or emotionally abuse any other person. That being said, Leader does a lot of things that are not okay. It would be unwise to follow her shitty example in real life.

Thank you, Amber! You are my rock and my reason! This year has been hell for us both, but it's also been magical. Without you, I know this book would never have made it to publication. (Trust me: you were literally the reason I finished revisions!) I love you More.

Thank you to my amazing, patient, and encouraging editor, Samantha. You help make my words more powerful, more beautiful, and much more readable.

Thank you to my family. You're the reason I am broken, angry, and artistic. I could never have created the Guild without you. Take that as you will.

Thank you McCall, Julie, Elaine, Mae, TJ, Sandi, Debb, DJ, Kami-and-Sam-Team, Shubach Jewelers, P!nk, Christina Perri, and my amazing students. A BIG thank you to Mrs. Erickson for encouraging me to write all the way back in fourth Grade. Thank you also to the Constellation 16. I needed you and there you were! Like magic. Or insanity.

Thank you, Haley and Emma—an Alpha Team any girl would be lucky to have.

Thank you, thank you, thank you, Hilary!

And last, but not least in my head or my heart: Thank you, Et Al.

About Author

Nichole M. Willden is a poet, writer, and author of The Guild series. A survivor of indoctrination and abuse, Nichole has spent decades writing fiction that sizzles with themes of enslavement, hope, and resilience. Nichole lives and writes in the Rocky Mountains with her wife, who is helpful to the writing process, and their puppy, Potion, who is delightfully unhelpful. She works a stellar day job, reads everything she can get her hands on, and watches too much TV. If she was queen of the world, there would be no slavery, no child abuse, no loneliness, and no PowerPoint.

Find Nichole M. Willden at www.nicholemwillden.com, on Instagram www.instagram.com/nicholemwillden, on Facebook www.facebook.com/nicholemwillden, on TikTok www.tiktok.com/@nicholemwillden